What Edward Heard

Megan Easley-Walsh

What Edward Heard

Megan Easley-Walsh

WHAT EDWARD HEARD

Dedicated to

Those who listen for the voice of truth
and for Stephen, with love

CHAPTER ONE
The Republic of Venice
1566

The bells of the Campanile sang their morning song to those rushing along Saint Mark's Square. Glistening in the early sun, the mosaics on the facade of the Basilica smiled at Francesco. With a canvas tucked beneath his arm, he scurried past those gathered. His heart beat as swiftly as his feet moved, quickening at the thought of Elena. The docks of the Arsenal had been busy this morning when he procured the canvas and packet of aromatic pepper from the merchant. Each day a new culinary delight, presented as an exotic spice, seemed to debut on the shores of the canals. Now that the Ottoman Empire traded with the Venetian Republic these past six years, a whole new market opened to those such as Francesco who had set their dreams among the scintillating delights of the east. When Marco Polo journeyed to China two centuries prior, the seduction of the west by the enticing Orient had begun.

The intricacies of the architecture surrounding him attested to this subsequent mingling of all that lay familiar in the west and all that stretched provocatively to the east. Bronze horses captured in Constantinople proudly adorned the high walls of the Basilica. Its alabaster beauty perfectly offset the pale pink of the Doge's Palace that stood adjacent to it, the way that Elena's cheeks and lips were drawn out by the creaminess of her skin. From the blue above, wispy clouds caressed the scene, the way that Elena's hair fell across her body.

As he rounded the corner a woman, dressed in the most fashionable silks with her hair piled high in thick tresses, perched atop a gondola. A man who exuded luxury and whose clothes were arranged so perfectly that the elbows of the jacket did not even show a crease from bending over a table, the way a merchant's did when he settled his accounts, sat beside her. He mentally mixed the pigment that would best depict their finery of dress. Francesco became so mesmerized in watching them that he missed seeing the gap in the pavement and tripped. The canvas dislodged from under his arm and flew to the ground. Embarrassed, he stooped down to retrieve it and glanced at the couple to see if they had noticed. Already they were sailing away from him though, as the gondolier struck his long pole into the lagoon and pushed off from the mud flats below, propelling the black-painted gondola on its way. Flecks of dirt marred one corner of the roll of canvas from where he had dropped it. Blowing it off, he chided himself for being so careless. If he had been a step closer to the edge, the costly material could have been lost entirely. Having tarried too long already, he continued on his way to the workshop.

All day as he worked over the vats of color, dying materials for the citizens and for export, his mind wandered to Elena. Knowing that any piece he labored over might soon drape her body as a stylish new dress focused his hand on the perfect distribution of pigment on material. Elena had first entered his life when her father came to him one day, saying he had heard that Francesco charged a fair price and had excellent craftsmanship. A quick perusal of the tiny shop tucked behind the baker's convinced him that what others said was true.

"I won't buy anything today. Elena will come with me to pick out what she wants tomorrow."

Francesco had nodded, bidding the gentleman adieu. He thought nothing of it at the time. Men had returned with women before, to have their opinion included in what materials would be sewn into the family's fashion or what silks would line the walls. Francesco's silks were renowned for gleaming beautifully in the candlelight of the chandeliers crafted of the delicately fashioned colored glass made on the nearby island of Murano. The following day the man had returned as he said he would, but the woman he brought with him came as an unexpected delight for Francesco. This Elena, whom he had assumed would be the man's wife, was his daughter. As daughters went, Francesco decided she was the loveliest of the species.

"Here Elena, you will find something to your liking, I am sure, and if not then I'm sure that—"

He was looking at Francesco, waiting for his name to be supplied.

"Francesco," he said quickly, glancing up at Elena as he did.

"I'm sure that Francesco will be happy to dye something to your liking."

"Oh yes, sir," he answered, hoping he did not sound overly eager.

"I am Ludveccio," the man said to Francesco, as he bent over the table to thumb through some of his samples.

"It is very nice to become acquainted with you, sir," Francesco had said over his back. And then, it happened. Behind her father's back, Elena smiled at him. Whether out of politeness or if she had been stirred by him as well he could not know, but her smile gave him hope. He lived on that hope each day after, praying that Ludveccio's pretty daughter might be in need of something new from his shop.

His workday was drawing to an end and, though his ledgers recorded considerable business for today, the balance of his heart had not been settled and he felt a decidedly poorer man than he was as he closed shop that evening. To cheer himself, he walked beside the newly built *Scula di San Rocco*. The door was open as he passed and he tried desperately to get close enough to peer inside. He knew that Tintoretto and his students had been busy painting within these walls the past two years. If only he could catch a glimpse inside!

The door, though open, did not allow significant light inside for him to see. Maybe, if he were very quiet, he might be able to slip inside and just catch a glance at what was being done.

Francesco looked both ways and tentatively stepped inside with one foot.

"You there!"

Francesco froze, startled at being addressed. He slowly turned.

"Yes?" he asked the man who stood before him, splattered in paint.

"We don't want any trouble. We're doing serious work and can't have people standing about causing mischief."

"Me?" he asked, confused.

The man stared at him, as if he were crazy.

"What's wrong with you? Don't you understand me? Are you not from here or something? Are you a spy?"

"A spy? No! I understand you and I am a proud citizen of Venice. I only wanted to catch a glimpse at the work inside." He smiled slowly, hoping the other man might oblige him. Instead, he shook his head.

"That's not possible. Only painters are allowed inside."

"But, I *am* a painter," Francesco said, suddenly.

"You're a painter?" The man eyed him suspiciously, his glance lingering on the color that had seeped into Francesco's hands from the vat of dye.

"You look more like a dyer."

"I am. That is to say, I am a dyer but I want to be a painter. I paint now sometimes. I'm really rather good."

"Oh you are, are you?" The tone of the man had grown condescending, obviously believing himself far superior to a lowly dyer.

"We paint with brushes, not our hands," he said in one final jab, before beginning to shut the door on Francesco.

"But, I really can paint. If only your master could see."

"Sure, you do that. Paint something and bring it for my master to see. Maybe we'll work on the next series together," he said, laughing sarcastically as he shut the door, leaving Francesco alone.

He clenched his fist, breathed in, then out, and opened it again.

"I'll do it. I'll bring Tintoretto my painting," he said, through gritted teeth and then he turned and hurried home.

"Hello, Francesco," Ludveccio greeted him warmly the next morning. Hearing his voice Francesco looked up expectantly, hoping to see Elena beside him. His eyes were disappointed though, as only Ludveccio, slightly stout of belly but plumper still of heart, stood before him. He summoned a smile to his face, dutifully playing the part of cheery merchant.

"Next week is Elena's birthday."

His interest piqued, Francesco no longer had to pretend to smile.

"I would like something special for her. She's a dear girl. Her mother has been departed from us for many years now, but I know she would be proud of her little Elena and pleased at how beautiful and kind she has become. Oh excuse me, I do love to talk on her and can become carried away in all my prattle."

"Oh really, it's quite all right," Francesco replied.

"You see Francesco, that is why I like you. You sell superior merchandise and afford a man his stories."

"Well, thank you, sir," Francesco said and then continued, "Am I right to think that you would like my help in deciding on the gift?"

"Yes. What is your suggestion?"

Francesco's mind flew to the blue silks and red velvets, any of which would perfectly frame Elena's beauty, but what he said came as a surprise even to himself.

"I have many fine materials that would be most becoming on her, but might I suggest something different. What about a portrait?"

"A portrait?"

"Yes, something to commemorate her as she is now, that she will be able to keep for years to come."

"A portrait," Ludveccio repeated again, this time warming to the suggestion.

"Francesco, my boy, I think that is an excellent idea. And would you happen to know of an artist who would be willing to do such a thing?"

"Me, sir."

"You paint?" Ludveccio asked, a look of amusement passing over his face. For a moment Francesco feared that Ludveccio would laugh away his aspirations, as the painter had last night and the chance would disintegrate. Instead, though, he looked Francesco in the eye and said,

"Can you start tomorrow?"

He arrived at Elena's house early. Unsure of whether to go inside now or wait until the appointed time, when the bells had chimed, he looked up at the palatial grandeur. The evening sun bathed the *loggio* in its glow, transforming the stone walls into a dazzling encrusted jewel case. Angular windows boasted the Venetian style that so seamlessly incorporated not only east and west, but also the more ancient with all that was new. The saltiness of the sea gathered at his nose, as he gazed at the beauty. He knew they were moneyed, but until he stood there before their home he did not realize just how rich they were. The well-dressed man and woman in the gondola yesterday morning could easily feel like paupers in such grandness as this.

His knees wobbled beneath him and he began to wonder if his ideas had been ill-founded. What was he doing here, painting the portrait of a beautiful woman in attempts of swaying her heart toward the successful but far poorer dye merchant, while capturing the perfect painting to show to Tintoretto? It all seemed ludicrous, when he thought of it now. Perhaps, he better just go. The door swung open and Ludveccio stood there.

"Oh Francesco, hello! Good, good, come in."
It was too late for second thoughts or to turn and leave. Ludveccio opened the door wide and Francesco had no choice

but to follow him inside. Elena was waiting for him, seated on a chair in front of a window that was dressed in velvet curtains. They were drawn to one side and the early evening light streamed in across the room.

"Hello," she greeted him, with a shy smile, "Will the light be all right here?"

"Oh yes, it will work just fine. Have you ever had your portrait painted?"

"Yes, when I was young, but never by someone so— " She paused and he clung to the silence, wondering at what she would say. She seemed to change her mind and concluded,

"Such as yourself."

He looked at her, puzzled.

"I mean, I was very young."

Elena seemed uncomfortable with the words and he desired to put her at ease, first because it is difficult to paint someone who is not but more importantly, because he yearned for her to relax in his company. As he began to paint her, pushing the pigment gingerly onto the canvas, swirling the strokes, she seemed to grant his wish. Painting her gave him open license to stare at her and he felt slightly guilty at what he had arranged. The larger part of him, though, congratulated himself on the master plan he had concocted. When the light began to fade too much to accurately capture her likeness, he packed away the supplies and walked home, fancying himself the cleverest man in all of Venice.

Each day, Francesco hurried his hands in the dying and nearly skipped toward Elena's home at the close of the business day. He found himself slowing in his work, as he reached completion of her portrait to prolong his daily visits to her any way that he could. He purposefully did not bring enough umber one day, so that he would be forced to complete that section on the next day. As the painting developed, so did their friendship. Long gone was Elena's uneasiness of that first afternoon. Freely, she discussed her life with him and even spoke of her dreams of journeying east, to see for herself the lands where the spices she relished abound in their natural habitats. His paintbrush caressed her delicate neck and angelic face as she spoke, acting as some substitute for his hands that desperately wanted to linger on her cheek with their warmth and flesh instead of the bristles of the brush. Try as he might to lengthen their time together, a small portrait could not be the work of endless days. He allowed himself to trace her portrait with a dry brush, the paint already applied in all of its needed places, one last time as she spoke. Her voice sounded like a tinkling bell in the evening's breeze. He knew it was her birthday, on this evening that he finished, and he had brought a present of his own for her. Francesco reached into his pocket for the small wrapped package. Elena's eyes grew wide at the sight of the gift and she looked at him eagerly, as if to ask if it were for her.

"Yes, the gift is for you," he said, with that smile she had lit his face with on the first day that he had seen her. He handed it to her and she unwrapped the silken ribbon, delighted at the present.

"Your father's present is also finished."

"The painting is finished?" she said, looking up excitedly from the ribbon.

"Yes, but I have to set it in a frame still."

"Oh, let me see it," she said pleadingly, her eyes fawning at him. It took all of his resolve to turn down her request, but he wanted her to see the work completed.

For one last evening, Francesco packed away his paints and brushes and prepared to walk home. He would be kept company by the luminescence of moonlight dancing on the canal. Even the heavens would celebrate Elena's birthday. Though he had been delaying this occasion as long as possible, he now felt a surge of hope. Long into the hours of last night, he had gone through his account records. He had been so distracted since meeting Elena two months prior that the steady stream of accumulating business, and its lining of his coffers, had slipped past him largely unnoticed. Could it be true? Had he really amassed so much? He did not trust the good fortune of his figures and reworked them again and again, until he had no choice but to accept this news of his burgeoning wealth.

His stomach tangled in anticipation. Before walking home, he would speak with Ludveccio and put forth his case. He had ingratiated himself to father and daughter. Both had warmed to him and invited him openly into their home and lives. He was certain now that Elena felt as he did for her and Ludvecio, who cared so deeply for his daughter, surely would wish to see her blissful in marriage. Though he could not provide every luxury that her father could, he would offer her a good life, a happy life, and a wealth that was sure to accumulate through his business and painting.

Ludveccio sat behind his desk, rifling through a stack of papers. Francesco still did not know exactly what he had made his fortune in or if his wealth were inherited. He waited until Ludveccio was finished and then spoke to him,

"I have finished the painting."

A smile burst forth over Ludveccio's face, the way that the waters rushed over the squares during the flooding.

"Oh, that's marvelous! What did Elena think of it?"

"I've not yet shown her. I'm going to frame it this evening and bring it back tomorrow, if that is all right?"

"Oh yes, of course. Splendid! Splendid! Now, about the matter of payment—"

He paused mid-sentence, to rummage in the drawer of his desk and produced a hefty bag of coins. Francesco waited for him to retrieve a coin or, if he were feeling especially generous, two. Ludveccio took nothing from the bag, though, and instead offered it entirely to Francesco, who was so taken aback that he nearly forgot what he had intended to say.

"Thank you very much, but I do not wish to take the payment. I hoped instead that I might discuss something with you."

Ludveccio's face showed his surprise, but his words remained level, as he said,

"Yes, of course, what is it?"

"I have come to ask for Elena's hand in marriage. My business is thriving and I have every confidence that time will only serve as a catalyst to greater wealth. I believe that I can make her happy and give her a good life."

Ludveccio studied the man before him, so young but so infused with passion. He was brimming now from the curve of the smile on his face, which Francesco was obviously trying to suppress, as he awaited the answer.

"Francesco," he said, with a patient smile, "I've no doubt that you have honorable intentions toward Elena, that your business is in good order, and you are talented, that is sure. But my boy, Elena is to be betrothed."

"She—I—I didn't know," Francesco stammered.

"Rodrigo comes from a strong family with important connections to the doge. It is an honor that he has sought out Elena. I'm sure you will find someone else. Venice is full of beautiful women; they're good inspiration for a painter, no?"

"Yes, of course," he said quietly, realizing that Ludveccio had not merely told him of Elena's unavailability, but had also informed him that he was good enough to paint his daughter, but not to marry her.

"I will bring the painting back tomorrow," he said, turning to leave.

"Here Francesco, take this," Ludveccio said, pushing the money into his hand.

"Really, you don't have to," Francesco protested.

"Your request has not been granted. It is the least I can do."

With no other choice, Francesco took the money and departed with a heart heavier than the bells of the Campanile.

⟡

Francesco unwrapped the painting, not wishing to prolong the moment. He knew it would be difficult to gaze upon the likeness of the woman, who had transformed him into a spurned lover. He lifted the frame, which he had lovingly carved and secured the portrait within it. Through his open window, he heard the gentle sloshing of the moorings. The moon, which he was sure would be in celebration tonight, shone with a melancholy hue. Feeling dejected and more alone than ever, he took one final look at the love that was not to be. As he reached for the cloth to wrap the painting again, a solitary hot tear slipped down his cheek and stung his wind-blown skin with its saltiness. Annoyed, he lifted his hand to brush it aside, but it was too late and it landed on the canvas, right on Elena's cheek.

"How very sympathetic of you. You are the one crying for me," he said in a whisper and then hastily covered the painting, unable to face it any longer.

⟡

Ten Years Later
1576, Venice

Ludveccio sat at the desk, his head in his hands in grief.

"How could you take her from me?" he hurled into the emptiness of his house, which now seemed far too large for comfort.

"My beautiful Elena, my Elena." He choked on the words, collapsing into sobs.

Her portrait, returned to this house by Rodrigo as an offering of solace, taunted him now. How could she be gone?

"How can you be gone?" he roared at the painting.

If only things had been different. If he had accepted—oh what was his name?— Francesco's proposition, then perhaps none of this would have happened. He had heard that Francesco left Venice not long after that night ten years ago. Rumor held that he had sailed east to broaden his business ventures. He could have taken her away with him and she could still be alive today. Ludveccio knew that this latest terrible plague cursed the lands beyond Venice, but it was the only thought he could cling to. It was good for that merchant and painter, Francesco, that he left, Ludveccio decided. Francesco was the lucky one. Had he stayed, he would have faced the sorrow of losing Elena. The sickness that claimed his Elena had taken that painter whom Ludveccio thought Francesco's work vaguely resembled, Titian, as well. Mustering all the bravery he could, he looked to Elena's portrait. Her beauty was perfectly captured. Francesco really had loved her; it was evident in every shadow and swirl. She looked at him now, smiling, happy, and he knew that his own heart would never know joy again.

"Nicholi," he called to his servant.

"Yes, sir?"

"Take the painting from here."

"You wish for me to move it, sir?"

"I wish for you to get rid of it."

"Sir?"

"Sell it or something. Give it away. I don't care. Just be gone with it. I never want to see it again!"

CHAPTER TWO

340 Years Later
The Western Front, France
Autumn 1916

In a turret of autumn leaves, Edward fell to his knees. The harsh ground pressed back against him through a layer of mud. The presence of autumnal glory—the scarlet, gold, and whispering orange—so ubiquitous at home were a scarcity here, like some long-forgot jewel unearthed by khaki-clad explorers. Home, the word hung heavy in his thoughts. The leaf beside him could just have easily fluttered south from the arching maple trees beside his house so far away. His finger reached for its crisp cloak now and traced the raised vein of his foliage companion. He tried to feel its coursing heartbeat and a small assurance that life, threatened constantly around him, continued in some normalcy here. The leaf did not oblige and instead the jarring of the machine guns thundered in his ears.

He lifted his eyes to the cacophonous horizon. Shells lobbed at each side from across the sparse border of No Man's Land. Earthy embankments stretched across the fields. Trenches, rather than wheat, were this year's crops. The wounded, dying, and departed were this season's harvest. Fields, which dotted the landscape of his childhood, would soon abound in fragrant masses on the plates of Thanksgiving tables. Across the country hands would join and heads would bow in gratitude thankful for the harvest, for those gathered, that sons and husbands were not absent from these chairs, that this war was not their own. Was it wrong to say so? But, what business did America have in becoming embroiled in this war? That had been the sentiment at the beginning anyway, when he had stood in line beside the others. When asked his name, the recruitment officer had looked up in surprise at hearing his accent. "What are you doing here? This isn't even your war," his look had seemed to say.

"Not my war," he whispered against the soil of France, as he pushed himself up and stood facing the bombast of battle. The burlap sack hoisted over his shoulder weighed heavily on his back. Its muskiness, from the damp of the days and from sitting in the puddles at the bottom of the trenches, assaulted his nose as he traversed the field to return the acquired provisions from the small farm to his comrades.

"Edward, find us some food?" the thin solider on his left asked, as he returned to the trench. The solider, whose name Edward seemed never able to remember, looked at him expectantly, the hunger growing steadily in his eyes. He reached into the bag and presented a piece of bread for the soldier.

"Oh thank you, Edward. Bless you," he said and scampered away, like a mouse escaping with a crumb of cheese to its home.

Bless you, Edward. Oh bless you. His cousin Agnes's voice echoed from the recesses of his mind. Considerably shorter than him, she had stood on tiptoe and still struggled to be tall enough to brush her lips across his cheek in appreciation. In substitution for her brother John, who was only sixteen, and her fiancé, George, he had stepped in to take their places.

"They will leave you alone now," he had said to Agnes. Her eyebrows sloped in the center, collapsing into a question, unsure of what he could mean.

"They don't want John or George. They just want a man. I'm a man. I will go."

The look of relief, which bathed her face and washed the sorrow away, affirmed that he had made the right decision. Already a feeling of uncertainty had begun to gnaw at his stomach, but he pushed it aside as he accepted her kisses and blessings. Agnes existed in flesh and blood to him barely a hundred days when he risked his life for her happiness. What had begun as a simple visit to his cousins resulted in volunteering to fight on their behalf.

The fire crackled, setting adrift a woodsy intoxication that caressed his nose, drawing him with its seductive spell into the present. Over his shoulder he looked down the row of men shivering against the cold and damp, gritting their teeth in determination at the maelstrom of fiery rain. Though he suffered no illusions of grandeur that others had, when they had eagerly enlisted two years ago, he too had thought he would not be gone for long. By Christmas, the war would be over and the battles would only be of snowballs between the neighborhood children waged in laughter. But Christmas of 1914 came and passed and then two more years as well. There was no going home. Not yet.

Having already shared much of the returned food with the men around him, he began to eat some of the bread now. It was crustier than what he was accustomed to the maid making at home. They were not on par with the Astor or Rockefeller families, but fortune had been good to them and Edward knew the opulence of luxury. His wealth was not the endowment of the gentry, though, but the self-made eked out riches championed by Andrew Carnegie and embedded in the youthful American spirit. He had no qualms with being among the farmers and fishermen gathered around him, because though he had not known the oppressive yoke of the plow on his own back, he was not so far removed from such a life as to find no kinship with these men. He did not consider himself better than those here, just more privileged and perhaps a bit luckier.

Luck had not landed him here. Though he had asked himself a thousand times in the past two years why he had done it, why he was here, he still did not know entirely. Why had he traded his safety, his freedom, his very life for two people to remain together? No, he knew there was more to it. In the summer of 1914, it may have been easy to swallow that one man could take another's place; but in the late autumn of 1916, no one could pretend such simplicity of number substitution. The equations were no longer balanced. Men were shipped out and were supposed to return, but this war was leaving far too great of a remainder in its division of lives. Tucked into shallow dirt-clad beds, they slipped into an eternal slumber from this life, departed for that great, and to Edward near impossible to fathom, utopia of perpetual peace. If Edward of California, who had survived the San Francisco earthquake of 1906, and more recently Edward of England, could believe that George's freedom had been purchased with his own enlistment, Edward of France knew that no such bargain could be struck. War had unclenched its bony fingers, beckoning for the nations to come, unwavering in what it demanded, insatiable in the lust of torment and blood. The faces of the men immediately surrounding him were familiar, but those farther down the line were hidden beneath helmets. Any one of the anonymous tin-covered heads could easily have been George. And John, he must be eighteen now. His young cousin could be armed with bayonet and gun, if he were not already buried in some untraceable grave. Edward shuddered.

The clouds gave a mighty shake in companionship, unleashing their tears. The men below had no time to contemplate those fallen; their business focused on the living. It was too easy to slip into the canyon of death. With no human mourning present, the weather filled the void. In vain, the rains attempted to remove the latest shame of humanity. The waters only muddied the grounds and mixed with the debris and blood to carry it farther down the trenches. Edward sloshed through the murkiness.

"I'll watch for a while," he said, to the bleary-eyed soldier standing guard from the top of a turret.

The solider nodded wearily and let Edward replace him. He leaned against the sandbags lining the trench. Holes, patched by the men, threatened to burst open once again. Rain pelted against Edward's helmet, magnifying the thunderous booms in his ears. Tempted as he was to remove the helmet, there were far worse fates than clanging water. He busied himself constantly, unwilling to face the torture of befriending one only to lose him.

He had made that mistake before, in the beginning. It was easier to stay occupied in tasks and uninvolved in people. A movement caught his eye through the barbed wire. He lifted his gun, prepared to fire should he need to. His heart quickened. Another movement came, followed by a clatter.

"Hold your fire," he whispered to himself, to ease his fingers into retreat as they hastened toward the trigger. He swallowed, to force himself to breathe again. His eyes remained fixed on the strip of land so important to their livelihood. No Man's Land stood as these warriors' outer gate of defense. Wisps of smoke floated toward the heavens from behind the German lines. No gunfire roared. For the moment, only the rain could be heard against the low din of the men's chatter. Perhaps, it had only been the wind. His shoulders slumped, easing out of the tense position he had unknowingly bent himself into. He breathed in and then, choking on the mix of wood and cigarette smoke that the wind had suddenly affronted him with, turned his mouth to the inner elbow of his sleeve to muffle the rising cough. From above the crook of his elbow, he spotted another movement. He straightened himself and prepared to fire. Just as he was about to pull the trigger, he saw the flash of the tail.

"Rats," he whispered, relaxing his hold once again. The furry body darted into a discarded tin of food, to scrounge what remaining morsels it could.

"How is it looking tonight?" the voice of his superior officer asked from behind him.

"Quiet, sir. Just rats."

"They're a nuisance. All of them! Horrible creatures. What they do to our boys, I'll never forgive them."

"Yes, sir," Edward returned, involuntarily conjuring a sickening memory of the rats feasting not only on the remains of the rations, but on the bodies of the fallen.

"I'd kill every one of them, if we could spare the ammunition. And I will, after the war. Any rat that crosses my path will have to make amends for its vermin brethren." Only the volume, not the anger, of his voice dissipated as he moved farther down the line.

Edward shifted from one foot to the other, his body stiffening in the cold. His mother would be furious with him for not living up to his birthright. He was not a common man and could easily have been exempt from such menial service. He should have been an officer, not a lowly soldier, standing guard like the others. But, Edward had felt no entitlement. His own clothes, tailored and laundered to the highest standards, he had left for John when he enlisted, exchanging a set of his cousin's considerably less fine but more practical clothes for his own. The pants had been too short but they were quickly replaced with the garb of uniform, as he knew they would be.

Now, his pants were the right length, though they were soaked through and had loosened on his already trim build with time. The jacket was far too thin to offer any true warmth or protection, but such things did not concern Edward. Here, on the Western Front, already a veteran of so many battles and wrapped within this most recent battle of the Somme that had begun in July and still waged on, he devoted himself only to survival, not in a desperate attempt of a scared man his junior but in a steady, deliberate, planned existence. He sank deeper into the cover of his helmet, which served as shelter from the bullets and bombs, but not the nightmares that had trespassed against the fibers of his mind. For now, there was only the rhythmic patter of the rain.

"If I can stay awake, I am free," he told himself.
The sky had darkened to the blackest form of a rain-drenched night. He cloaked himself in its solitude, finding some quiet in the bleakness. His eyes became heavier and he knew he should find a replacement soon. Falling asleep at his post would be disastrous for all of them.

"Just a minute more," he told himself. He opened his eyes

abruptly, realizing they had momentarily closed.

"Here to replace you," a voice spoke from behind him, as if his internal alarm had sounded a summoning bell for the next man. Edward climbed down the short distance, until he stood once more in the river at the trench's floor.

"Quiet tonight. Just rats," he told the man, already climbing to the turret to replace him.

"Good," the man said over his shoulder. Edward turned his back to walk to the dugout where his mattress was.

The chatter of gunfire sparked somewhere in the distance, igniting the hostilities once again. The sound of the bullets magnified, casting a reverberating echo across the expanse of land. Shells joined the brassy orchestration of the night's strained tunes. Edward prepared to crawl into bed to at least rest his tired limbs encumbered by the cold and rain, if the noise prevented sleep. With a touch of irony he marveled over his last thought; his sleeping being inconvenienced by the fighting had, somewhere along the way, replaced the paralysis of fear that gripped him in those early days.

Suddenly, lights streaked the sky and the eerie whine of the gunfire splintered the darkness closing in on his own trench. A monstrous roar ripped open the sky above and then an explosion, brighter than the San Francisco fire, louder than anything he'd heard before, tore him from his bunk and flung him against the crumbling wall of the trench. Screaming bullets and shells rained down continuously, but Edward, ground into the mud, saw and heard none of it. The war, which was not his own, had tracked him down and claimed him as its prey. The war was not his, but he was now the war's.

CHAPTER THREE

"Edward? Edward, can you hear me?"

Harry bent beside Edward and turned him over, to prevent the mud and water from entering into his nose or mouth. Edward didn't respond. Harry pulled him into a sitting position and leaned him against the sandbags and then scampered up the wall, firing with the other men as the incoming bullets rained down over them. Harry didn't know much about Edward, who kept to himself, but he knew that Edward had given him bread this evening when his stomach felt at the verge of that extreme pain of a gnawing growl and so he felt a sort of loyalty to him. As concerned as he was for him, the man had to be ignored for the moment or Harry would end up wounded as well. Turning his back on Edward, he stood at attention, his helmet jammed down as far as it would go to protect him as much as possible.

"Fix bayonets!" the order sounded from down the line. A thousand flashing blades clicked into place. Hearts thundered, as perspiration rolled like raindrops down the men's bodies.

"Charge!"

A mighty roar lifted from the men as they prepared to go over the wall, but Edward heard none of it.

"Help me!"

"Help!"

The cries of the wounded mixed with the moaning from the pain of their injuries and suffering.

"This one here needs some help too," the medic said, as he leaned over Edward. There was still a pulse and he was breathing, but was completely unresponsive. Seeing no visible sign of trauma, he shook Edward gently in an attempt to rouse him. He was just about to turn his back on Edward to continue helping the others and check on him later, when he felt a hand reach out and grab his arm. Edward's eyes were open, but he stared straight ahead.

"You're going to be all right after all," the medic said, with a smile. Still, Edward did not respond. For the first time, the medic now noticed that Edward was cradling the left side of his face in his hand.

"Something wrong with your head?" he asked, but still Edward did not reply. Gently, the medic pried Edward's fingers loose. As they pulled away, much to Edward's horror, they were covered in blood. Seeing the terror in his face, the medic tried to reassure him.

"It will be all right. It's really not so bad." He slipped a hand into his pocket and found a roll of gauze, which he wrapped as a bandage around Edward's head.

"We need to move him out," the medic said to another.

"Right, I'll take care of it." Then, he turned to Edward saying,

"We're going to get you out of here now."

Edward still made no reply, but his hand had returned to the side of his face, covering the bandage with his blood-soaked hand.

"Poor chap, probably too scared to talk," he thought, as he helped Edward stand and leave the trenches and two years of his life behind.

The doctor at the field hospital stood over Edward, examining his wound now.

"How are you feeling today?" he asked, but still Edward made no reply.

"He doesn't talk," a nurse said and then continued, thinking of that newly discovered malady that affected the minds of some of the men who fought and paralyzed them with fear,

"Do you think it's shell shock?"

"Maybe," the doctor said, "but, I think perhaps—" He paused and snapped his fingers in Edward's left ear. There was no response.

"I think he's gone deaf. Get me a piece of paper, please and a pen." The nurse gathered the requested materials and then handed them to the doctor.

Can you hear me? He wrote on the paper and then held it up for Edward to see. Edward tried to move his lips, but nothing came out. Seeing his attempt, the doctor placed the pen in his hand.

No he wrote.

"But, doctor," the nurse said, who had been watching the events, "he is only injured in his left ear, shouldn't he be able to hear in the right?"

"It's probably just the trauma of it all. I think that with time, his hearing will return in his right ear."

"Now, where are you from?" he said to Edward, as he quickly wrote it on the paper and slid it to him.

Edward took the pen and wrote his answer.

"California!" the doctor said, in surprise. Edward realized then that, without his accent and in the uniform of an English solider, no one would have had any reason to suspect he was not English.

"I'm afraid that is a bit too far," the doctor said, to the nurse. Seeing the doctor's surprise, he took the paper back and wrote,

I have cousins in England.

"Oh, wonderful! Yes, that will be much better." Edward couldn't make out the words, but he understood the general meaning and was too tired to carry on the written correspondence, so he settled back into the hospital bed and slept.

Slumber accompanied Edward for the majority of his journey back to England. In the trenches Edward had busied himself with the necessity of survival. Sleep had often been the casualty, sacrificed by so many thousand on the Western Front. Now, for the first time in the many rain and blood-soaked months of the past two years, Edward had a bed at his disposal and used it to its full advantage. How wonderful it was, first in the hospital and then on the ship, to be a stranger to the hostile rains and cold he had become so familiar with!

And sleep also offered sweet escape from the reality of a too quiet world. He had sought solace and a peaceful corner away from the bloodcurdling, fear-inducing, terror-stricken noise of war. The shell lobbed at him from across the wall, exploding in a truly deafening blast, was the last thing that he had heard. His ears were silent—at least for the moment—but his mind was not and his mind insisted on playing the sound over and over, like some spinning phonograph. Only sleep could silence the sound of memory, so long as the nightmares did not invade stretching their torturous, snarling fingers over him in entrapment.

Terrified as he had been at times while on the front, he had not had time to really dwell on the danger. But now it confronted him daily, building in strength, growing in strife. He shut his eyes to it quickly, to squeeze out the images, but they were emblazoned too deeply like scorched earth after a fire and the ash and soot could not be easily swept away. Seared into his mind, like the cattle that were branded on the ranches of his native state, was the suffering of men who were strangers and yet a part of him. He had distanced himself, unwilling—or unable—to lift their burdens as his own, but now they stalked him unrelentingly.

He had made that mistake once—with James in the beginning. They had talked freely under the wide-open star-strewn skies, like two boys on the grand adventure of a camping trip. James had said it reminded him of that, because he had been a part of that group called the Scouts that was started just a few years before. He had been one of the older members, acting primarily as an older brother to the younger ones. It gave him a sense of purpose, he had said. But, war with its own purposes—too cruel and unimaginable—had taken James and would not release him from its icy grip. His mangled body, lying somewhere in the now frozen grounds of France, was too hard to bear thinking about, and so Edward closed his mind to that part of his life and made a vow of silence about his friend to command some dignity to the event.

Agnes hugged Edward tightly to her, when he returned and he wondered if she would ever let go. She eventually did though she insisted on helping him with every task and Edward, accustomed to doing so much for himself, soon felt suffocated. He knew she was well-intentioned, but he often felt the need for sanctuary away from her. The afternoon walks, which he took through the meadows alone, caused her great worry. Slowly his hearing, just as the doctor predicted, was returning to his right ear but still Agnes felt it was unsafe for Edward to be by himself without full usage of his ears. Though he felt a quarter of his age when doing so, he had (at her insistence) promised to remain away from the road, so as not to unknowingly wander into the oncoming path of a horse and cart or, even worse, a horseless carriage. He knew that her protectiveness stemmed not only from her concern for him but also because, much as he had presumed, John and George were now on the Western Front as well. Unable to ensure their safety, she channeled her protection and love for all three men into Edward.

On one particularly cold day, near the approach of Christmas, Edward set out at a brisk pace across the expanse of undulating countryside. Wisps of smoke ascended from stone chimneys, as if they were people sending out puffs of steam as they breathed into the frosty air. With a pang of sadness, he realized that the sounds he associated so closely with the season—the chiming bells, carol singing, chestnuts popping on a fire—would be muffled whispers this year.

He could picture his parents gathered by the fireplace with wreaths and garlands hanging festively around them. All the accompaniments of the holiday would dress the table and Father would give a toast saying—

Edward froze, not only in his thoughts but, in his steps. From the inescapable cold rose a large manor house that beckoned to him. Much like Edward, it stood proud, solid, with an obvious history of grandeur but showing signs of harder days more recently, with its cracked windows and crumbling porch. Edward instantly felt a kinship with it and, for the first time since he could remember, a true sense of belonging. With a sizable fortune already, at the age of twenty-five, he knew at once that he would find whoever was responsible for it and buy it. There was an inexplicable need in him to become a part of the history of the house. It was almost as if someone were calling to him from inside of it. But that, of course, was crazy.

"Agnes, who owns the house in the field past the lake?" he asked upon his return. His volume varied in an unnatural way, since it was still difficult to judge exactly how loudly he was speaking. She looked up from her knitting. She seemed always to be knitting these days. Not only did she mend her own mittens or Edward's socks, but also mounds of scarves, mittens, and socks for the transport ships to carry to the men on the front.

"The house past the lake—the old deserted manor?" She spoke louder than usual and slower, enunciating each word clearly, to help Edward hear her better.

"That's the one."

"I don't know to be honest. It's been abandoned as long as I can remember. Why do you ask?"

"I'm going to buy it."

She felt compelled to question his decision, wondering if his nightmares—which he never spoke of but that she knew he suffered from because of his moaning that she awoke to in the middle of the night—were depriving him of sleep and wreaking havoc with his mind. When she looked at him now though, eyes full of life and clear with jaw resolutely set, she knew there would be no persuading him otherwise.

"All right," she said, "I'll help you find out."

"Thank you, Agnes," he said and, for just a moment, she thought a hint of a smile— unseen since his return—had lit the corner of his eyes.

CHAPTER FOUR

A man on a mission, Edward sought out anyone who could have any possible connections to the house. His parents, relieved to hear he was returned to England, urged him to come home. Not only the war, with its hold on the Atlantic, prevented his crossing though. Each day he felt greater certainty that the house was meant for him. Abandoned, it needed him.

Agnes worried for him and pleaded with him not to overexert himself. She supported his mission, but a week had now passed and still no one knew anything of the house. Yet, Edward insisted on leaving just after breakfast and remaining out for most of the day. She decided it was a good thing that he had returned in the winter with shorter days, so that his hours wandering were at least somewhat reduced. When she had heard that he had broken his promise and wandered into town, with its dangerous roads, she became cross.

"Please Edward, let me go with you into town. Can you ask in the houses along the edge of the forest?"

"The edge of the what?"

"The forest," she repeated, louder.

"I've already asked everyone there," he said, sounding annoyed, though she knew it was not annoyance at her.

"Well, can't we go together Edward?"

"But, I'll lose so much time that way. You are not returned from school until the afternoon."

Agnes taught the young pupils of the town, imparting math and history while helping them in their reading and writing and encouraging them to do their part to cheer the spirits of the soldiers. How many bright-eyed faces had rushed at her, holding up slightly uneven mittens or a lopsided hat, anxiously awaiting her praise?

Edward knew she was admired, and rightly so he thought. In some ways, she reminded him of his mother. Orphaned now, she had reportedly looked very much like her mother and Edward had often noted the similarity between the two sisters in the photograph his mother kept on her dressing table. And the cousins bore likenesses as well, if not so much in appearance then certainly in mannerism. Edward really couldn't fault Agnes for her stubborn insistence that she accompany him, because the same streak of determination ran through him. In some, stubbornness may illustrate a propensity toward closed-mindedness or an unwillingness or inability to be flexible in the mind or persuasion. But in some persons, such as Edward and Agnes, stubbornness is really a positive attribute that adds strength to one's character and provides a glimpse of the resolute determination that churns the mechanism of the soul, much like the internal workings of a clock.

Deciding that perhaps Agnes really could be helpful, when he spoke with little old ladies— who are renowned for their knowledge of a town's most pertinent information, fortunately for Edward, but are also, unfortunately for him, equally known for their softness of voice as if they are perpetually afraid of waking a sleeping cat so apt to curl into a bundle of coiling warmth on their laps—he consented to her.

"All right, I will wait until we can go together."

⟿

Sitting beside the fire, with book in hand, Edward awaited Agnes's return. He found his head swelling with too many thoughts lately. After James's death, Edward had distanced himself as best as he could from the hold of the war, but now it hounded him as a hunting dog pursues its prey. As he read Mr. Dickens's *A Christmas Carol*, he empathized with Scrooge's fear of Marley. Everywhere he turned, he was accosted by the ghosts of war. He knew that he was not alone in what ailed him and that it was a malady suffered by all who had returned. One day, he had seen a returned solider on a crutch to compensate for his amputated leg and the poor man had nearly jumped out of his skin when a box fell behind him. For the first time, Edward felt thankful for his dulled hearing. He began to find the little things and be grateful for them; he did not have a visible injury that provoked looks of pity or have to make small talk over eggs with people he had known all his life but who could never understand the horror he had not only witnessed, but lived.

The things he could not transform into something beneficial, he simply shut out. All that tormented him the most, he locked away in a dungeon of his mind. Perhaps, that was why he now felt the need for the monstrous house. A body can only contain so much, but a house with a sole occupant can lighten the burden and share the load. No longer must everything be carried by the person, but the house too can begin to accommodate what must be locked tightly behind its doors. A house opens its sheltering arms, as a friend does, but without supplying the accompanying questions that are meant as support but that so often pry the wound open more deeply.

⟡

On a Wednesday afternoon, while buying food from the town's grocer's—which seemed less stocked as of late—an elderly man said to Edward,

"Did I hear you're asking about the manor house past the lake?"

Edward, whose back was to the man, did not hear him and made no reply. Agnes had stepped next door to check if there were any letters—or heaven forbid, telegrams from the War Department—for them and so she was not there to be his ears.

"I say, were you asking about the house?" the man repeated.

Annoyed at being ignored, he gave Edward a swift rap on the shoulder. Edward was caught off guard and spun abruptly, to see a graying man balanced on a cane and staring up at him as if he had offended him.

"Yes?" Edward asked.

"What do you mean 'yes'? Didn't you hear me asking you about the house?"

"I'm sorry sir, you'll have to speak a little slower. I lost most of my hearing in the trenches."

Ordinarily, Edward did not like to share this information. But the man seemed determined to speak to him, even if he were now annoyed for some reason, and if Edward were not mistaken it seemed as if the man had said the word "house". Upon hearing Edward's explanation, the man's face immediately transformed and a look of regret at how he had spoken to Edward passed over it.

"I'm sorry. I didn't know," he said, placing his hand on the younger man's arm.

"That's all right. Now, what is it that you were saying? Did you mention a house?"

"Yes, I was asking if you were the one looking for information about the manor house, past the lake."

"I am, yes," Edward said enthusiastically, hoping he had at last found a lead, "Do you know who owns it?"

"I own it."

Agnes returned to the grocer's to meet Edward and continue on their way. As she entered the shop, though, he was nowhere to be found.

"Excuse me, have you seen a man, tall, blond hair?"

"Hmm?" the shop owner said, as he looked up from his account book.

Seeing her distress, he asked,

"Did you say you're looking for a blond child?"

"No, a man, my cousin."

"Well, I'm sure he's fine, Miss, especially if he's an adult."

He felt bad for Agnes. He knew that her brother and fiancé were on the front and no doubt her nerves were on edge, adding to the concern in her face now. The owner's wife overheard the conversation, as she emerged from the storeroom.

"I saw him, Miss. He left with an older man. They said something about a house."

"Thank you," she said over her shoulder, in a rush to leave the store. It was surprising how quickly she had to walk just to keep them within sight, when she had thought she would easily catch up to them. By the time she reached the bend, the two figures of the men disappeared into the house. Agnes had intended to accompany them, but now she felt it would be trespassing to barge in on the men in the middle of their mission. She leaned against the arching willow that she had loved so much as a young girl. Frost coated every blade of grass, crackling under her feet as she shifted from one side to the other to warm herself. She stuffed her hands in her pockets, waiting for the two to reemerge.

She stood watching the house, wondering at what gripped Edward so about this place. She was certain that it wasn't just its size because of what he was accustomed to, because it would have been far easier for Edward to hold off until returning home rather than transforming the house from the foundation up. Besides, the man that Agnes knew him to be was not wrapped up in the trivial nature of the size of a house. As she waited, her mind drifted to a thousand beautiful dreams of the home she would build with George. Shutting her eyes tightly, she tried to block out the thoughts. It was too painful to think of what might be—when it was no longer the promised certainty that she once thought it was. Her deepest fear was that she would be a widow before a bride.

"Please God, protect them," she prayed simply, afraid to say more lest tears should slip from her eyes and become icicles on her cheeks. The sky was beginning to gray with the approach of night, when Edward and the other man stepped from the house. For a moment, Agnes wondered if Edward's search would be fruitless. Perhaps, the man did not wish to sell, assuming that it was his house. No, it seemed that some sort of deal was being struck in the chilling December air. Edward shook the man's hand heartily—and surely her eyes must be deceiving her—was that a smile? She squinted, concentrating on the figures in the distance, feeling like a spy on some important mission as she watched them from behind the concealing boughs of the tree. She thought perhaps she would get to speak with the man, whom she did not recognize, but he turned and walked away in the other direction.

Agnes took a step forward to join Edward and congratulate him on whatever had transpired. She stopped though when she saw Edward fall to his knees. At first she worried that he had hurt himself, but his arms soon stretched forth toward the sky. He threw his head back, looking at the heavens as the first stars of the night began to twinkle in their natural procession. The breeze, gusting through the trees and threatening to invade her skirt, tousled his hair. Facing the house, on his knees with head thrown back and arms spread wide, Agnes watched as Edward welcomed his future.

⁂

If Agnes had any hopes that Edward's determination would be quieted now that an agreement had been made on the house, they quickly dwindled. She found herself digging out buckets and brooms from the attic to satisfy his need for cleaning equipment. The house was in too great a state of disrepair for him to move-in, but just after breakfast until the sun set he diligently worked, transforming bricks and wood into walls and support. There seemed always to be something more that needed to be done. There were crumbling walls to be repaired, broken windows to replace, floors to be scrubbed, windows to clean, corners to sweep, and cobwebs to clear.

The house had offered its consent to its new caretaker. Showing its gratitude, it strengthened Edward from his fatigue and suffering as well. It was a rare occasion now when he did not ask Agnes for a second helping of stew or soup, which helped his waistline, and he began to look like Edward again. Of course, the war had changed more than his appearance and some alterations were not so easily remedied. His hearing had been gradually improving, though Edward suspected there would still be quite a while of his time spent in this subdued state. His thoughts by day were busied with the work in the house. He was relieved to be able to distract himself by throwing himself into a task once again and committing so fully to it.

By night, the battles still raged in his nightmares. The most frequent one attached James's face to the bodies of hundreds maimed and mangled. Looks of agony, chiseled by such twisted cruelty, consumed each of the many faces of James. By day, he hammered nail spikes into those tormenting anguishes to lock them behind the steel bars of his own mental Alcatraz. As the house began to right itself into a suitable dwelling, he felt its work within him as well. Some things the house could not fix, but some things, such as his appetite, it already had. Although he had spent much time rooting through Agnes's attic, he had not yet entered the attic of the house. Behind its locked door stood something that would be far greater and more profoundly powerful over his life than the sum of the entire rest of the house combined.

CHAPTER FIVE

It was a few days past Christmas, which had been a quiet but still nice affair for the two cousins. They spent the day praying side-by-side in the pew of the church, for protection of all who fought and a resolution to bring about peace soon, and there had been a meager Christmas dinner. Food shortages were becoming more real with the naval blockades in the ports. Agnes had been particularly nostalgic, regaling him with stories of Christmas past. Just like Scrooge, she revisited these memories fondly but they were coated in the bitter reminder of what was now missing this year. Her reminiscing stirred up so many memories he had suppressed. The faces in the trench had spoken as she did and, though he knew she was oblivious to the pain she was inflicting on him, he felt suffocated. At the first chance he had, he burst free from his cousin's home and slipped into the welcoming sanctuary of his house. It was the first time he thought of it as his house, because it was not his place of dwelling but it was, in its own drafty way, comforting. Cold air whistled down the chimney.

What was that? Edward thought he had heard a small chirp, but he must have imagined it. His ears lacked the clarity to distinguish so small a sound. He turned back to laying a fire in the stone hearth. He struck the match to set the spark and bent in to catch the wood with the flame, when he paused, hearing the noise again. Extinguishing the match by shaking it out, he heard it once more. Thinking perhaps that the chimney was carrying the sound, he half-climbed into it to investigate. Cold air from the howling wind slapped his face, stinging his cheeks. There. He heard it again and it did seem louder from inside the chimney.

Hastily, he scrambled to his feet and rushed up the stairs. On the second floor he examined the fireplace, which was directly above where he had just been. The noise grew louder, but it was coming from higher up still. Edward raced from room to room, searching the ceiling to find the entrance to the attic. He found it at last, in what certainly must have been the servants' quarters with windows and room area both much smaller than in other parts of the house. Pushing a chair into the center of the room to pull down the hatch to the attic, he wobbled slightly on his feet. He soon recovered his balance and, with a clap, the door was released, sending forth an enormous cloud of dust as it swung open. Edward coughed on the particles choking him, but wasted no time in pulling down the ladder. He tested its sturdiness and then climbed up quickly.

Tight and cramped, the space in the attic wrapped around him, enfolding him in darkness. Lack of light complicated his difficulty in seeing in the small area and he felt momentarily overwhelmed. Ordinarily, compromised sight was easily compensated for by careful listening, but Edward did not yet enjoy this privilege.

As a young boy, he had become lost amidst the black expanse of night and found his way home through the winking glow of the North Star. How many thousands of times had he looked to it when on the front? Now, he must find the aural beacon pulsating with its chirp to gain his bearings. He stood very still and concentrated all of his effort into his ears, encouraging the sound to travel forth again. He waited, willing his ear to cooperate. Nothing. Perhaps, he was too far away. Tentatively, he stepped forward. Not yet. Once more, he took a step. Stumbling onto a box, a loud crash resulted. *That* he had heard.

He jumped back, more so from the pain of hitting his shin than from the noise that he was sure was magnified many times in actuality from what he heard. The ruckus also alerted whatever was near the chimney and a chorus of chirps rang out. Light from below, on the ladder, floated skyward as the clouds cleared from in front of the sun and he saw a flutter of activity. He crossed the rest of the way to the chimney and found a tiny robin redbreast tucked into a corner of it. He wanted to tell it hello, but feared frightening it if his voice came out louder than intended. The bird had calmed after the disturbance and tucked herself in beneath her wings.

His eyes were adjusting to the dim light of the room and the freshly unveiled sun greatly aided his ability to discern objects in the attic. Boxes were strewn haphazardly beneath the creaking rafters. Mounds of silver, carpets, and furnishings cluttered the small space. When he bought the house from Henry, he had been told that whatever he found was his. Henry had never lived in the house, but had been bequeathed it by a friend who had no heir. The friend had already allowed the house to deteriorate as he aged. It was simply too large and too much work to keep up. The house had passed from generation to generation for a good many years before Henry's friend was ever born. By that time, the grandeur and riches that had built the house had long since dried up, leaving him with a lavish house but no means for upkeep. When Henry inherited the house he was already far along in years himself and his body no longer enjoyed the agility it once had, which would have been mandatory to make anything of the sickened house. And so these past five years it had sat, proud but alone, until Edward entered its life. Henry had been flabbergasted when Edward inquired about buying it. Like his friend, Henry lived alone and there was no one to entrust the care of the home into until Edward came along.

Edward dusted off an old leather armchair and sat down in it, as he rifled through a nearby box brimming to the top with fine silks and velvets. Buried at the bottom was a set of tarnished silver cutlery. He picked up a spoon, seeing his blurred reflection in its surface. His features stared back at him, offering the familiar view that he had faced for so many years. Something in his eyes had changed; there was age beyond his years. Staring into the spoon, he became acutely aware that the span of his life when it had run its course was minuscule compared to the age of the objects stored in this room. People perished, but now he was confronted with the heavy realization of the permanence of objects. They exist for centuries, witnessing the rise and fall of houses, families, or countries. They exist as the most tangible link to the past.

The sleuth in him wanted to uncover the many treasures buried in piles here. Buried in piles, the phrase repeated in his head. Images of young men, who didn't belong in graves laid there prematurely, paraded in an endless stream in his mind now. His hands cradled his temples, attempting to push out the horror.

In a moment of perfect clarity, he opened his eyes and knew what he would do. Having witnessed youth massacred in the form of countless men, Edward felt the insatiable urge to preserve what was aged. In a celebration of all that had survived from the past, he would set up an antique shop. The house with its many rooms and ample space would be the perfect location. His mind raced forward in excitement to a time when customers would flock to see the young American selling the priceless heirlooms. At home he had studied history and art and from a very young age, finery surrounded him and so he felt well-equipped to discern an item's story and offer an accurate appraisal.

He pulled out the box nearest him and began unpacking china figurines, a silver tea service, and a stack of old letters. In another box he found maps, a coin collection, and books, so well-read that the pages lacked all crispness of a new volume. The binding too had loosened and the adhesive had long since lost its stick. Edward had made considerable progress in his discoveries, when he slumped back in the chair to rest for a minute. His findings had distracted him from the harshness and he realized now that, for the first time in a very long while, the afternoon had passed in happiness.

The already dim light of the attic was waning quickly.

Agnes would be worried, if he did not return soon for dinner. A chilly gust greeted him now, sending him into a cough as he shivered. The unexpected shiver caused him to drop the book he was holding. With a thud, it fell to the ground emitting a cloud of disturbed dust in its wake. He stooped to pick up the book and his eye caught the corner of something protruding from a rich material wrapped around it.

Intrigued, he reached for the object, forgetting for the time being the dropped book he had bent to retrieve. He lifted the object and sat down again in the leather chair before he began to unwrap it. The fabric covering in itself would have been a wonderful find with its ornate detail and luxurious texture. Edward could have been unwrapping the object from a paper coat though and it would have had the same effect on him. The fabric was merely a covering to move aside, much as the husk is discarded to reveal the golden glow of the kernels of corn. When it was completely unwrapped he looked it over, marveling at the age of what he held. The reverse of what he thought would be a painting faced him now. Making a game of it, he paused and imagined for a moment what might be depicted when he turned it over. Perhaps, it would be a still life painted in the Netherlands a couple hundred of years before. Maybe, it was a painting of the house in its younger years when it must have been glorious to behold. With a tingle of excitement, which had rested dormant in him since before the war until finding this house, he turned the painting over.

"Why, hello," he said to the woman who greeted him. Her dark eyes met his and in that one look all the centuries were bridged. She looked so vital that he couldn't help but speak to her, as if failing to acknowledge her would be tantamount to being rude and not greeting a stranger who had just entered the room. Her lips, painted in rosy pink, looked as if they would part and speak to him at any moment. Her eyes, which had instantly locked with his, held the duality of shy admiration and reserved flirtation. Youthful, glistening skin peeked from the lavish silks robing her body. Brown barrel curls cascaded down her back like the rippling waves rolling peacefully off the ocean. Some artists adhere pigment to page out of necessity of paycheck or familial obligation, but whoever painted this portrait did so out of compulsion of heart. Edward, fashioned out of the hard, embittered, rough edges of a war veteran, became mesmerized by the soft and almost heavenly benevolence captured in the delicate lines and perfect portrayal of love embodied.

Moved by the painting, the art critic in him began its examination now. Her complexion looked Mediterranean, but much fairer than Spanish. Perhaps she was Italian, probably from the north. Her fashions spoke of the aristocratic Renaissance. The colors lacked the vibrancy of some of the great masters but if that were because of the effects of age or if they had originally lacked the luster of brilliance, perhaps from a poorer artist who could not pay for such costly pigment in too great of quantity, he could not be sure. Whoever she was, she made an agreeable subject for someone's sitting room and she would be able to undoubtedly garner an attractive price when he was able to set up shop.

CHAPTER SIX

Silvertown, West Ham, Essex, England
January 19, 1917

Clara awoke to the biting cold of the January morning. Frost laced her window in a delicate pattern, like those of the cloths that had dressed the tables of the best houses in London she had worked in before the war. If she were willing to forget the frigid fingers that had embroidered the frost on the pane and that encircled her hands and feet now, it would have been pretty. She yawned and her breath exhaled into puffs of smoke like those in the factory. The basin of water beside her bed had frozen during the night. She considered breaking the surface to wash. No, her face would just have to present itself to the world unwashed today. The shock of the icy water would be too much to bear.

Clara's room in the building she shared with the other workers was small, but spacious enough for the few possessions she had. A knock at the door interrupted her thoughts. She crossed the freezing floor that seeped in through her thin socks to answer it.

"Good morning, Clara," a girl slightly shorter than her, with rose-tinted cheeks from the cold, greeted her.

"Good morning, Abigail."

"Clara, would you mind terribly if we switched shifts today? You see, Tommy is leaving soon and I would like to spend the evening with him since he's training during the day. I know it's asking a lot for you to work the night shift," her voice trailed off, as her yellowed fingers, from the sulfur at the factory, reached up to replace a strayed hair behind her ear. Clara didn't enjoy the night shift. The already unbearable cold was only made more acute with the black of night around her. Walking beside the Thames at night, when drinking escalated the unease of an already jittery splice of society, only made it worse. Seeing

Abigail's innocence before her and knowing that thousands of Tommys would not return decided for her, though.

"Of course, Abigail."

"Oh thank you, Clara! If I find any good bread, you can have my share."

Clara nodded with a smile and climbed back into bed, puling the covers over her head and curling up to try to stay warm. Quickly she began to doze, dreaming of white bread, instead of the awful black mess that could only be found now.

It was late in the afternoon when Clara awoke. Long slanted rays of sunlight striped across the floor, making the most of its final moments before slumbering for the night. Dressing quickly and hastily eating, for sustenance—not enjoyment because food lacked all essence of flavor in this utilitarian form, she readied herself for the shift. She bundled warmly and set off in the east London evening on her way to the factory. Clara had worked here since its conversion in 1915 to a TNT producing facility. The heavy stench of chemicals, which had first appeared here in the end of last century, assaulted her nose now. It was difficult to think of a time when this had been marshland—which she knew had been only a couple of generations ago—before the docks were opened, bringing the new industrialized way of life with them. How wonderful it would be to walk among the reeds, hearing the birds above now! With each step toward the factory, the rising tide of nausea strengthened in anticipation of the chemicals' hold. Other girls she worked with suffered from chest pains and, given the choice, Clara was glad to only suffer with an upset stomach.

The factory, nestled among housing and other factories producing all manner of goods, came into sight. As she saw the flour factory now, she was reminded of Abigail's promise of bread. Her stomach lurched forward, up-churning bile in protest at her thought of food. She swallowed and diverted her mind to other things. Some of the girls greeted her as she entered the factory and took her place among the hundreds who worked here. Despite the many difficulties, it was comforting to know she was helping her country and doing her part in bringing men like Tommy home.

Her back ached from bending over her work, as if the elephant she had seen at London zoo when she was young were sitting on her. Already her fingers were cramping in the cold air. She paused momentarily and stretched them. Glancing up at the clock, she was surprised that the hands seemed to be moving so slow.

"Only ten to seven," she whispered in disbelief.

"Did you say something, Clara?" the girl beside her asked.

"Just surprised at the time."

The girl looked up now and said,

"Yes, only nine to seven. I'd have sworn I'd been here longer."

Clara nodded wearily and the girls returned to their work. To help pass the time, Clara conjured memories of her childhood. She was seven, no eight, and she was at Grandfather's house in the country. It was the most beautiful day of spring and the flowers peeked their yellow bonnets and blue hats out among the field of luscious green onlookers, jealous of the flowers' splendor. Grandmother served tea cakes in the garden that tasted of sugar and rosewater. Her stomach lurched forward again. Perhaps, she had better leave the garden behind for now. In her memory, she stepped through their doorway and was met by a thousand delights to discover. Sparkling silver and finely carved wood presented themselves in pristine form, bristling in pride for the young Clara to inspect them. Her eyes traveled over the walls, amazed at—KABOOM!

Roaring thunder, empowered with the machinery of hell's fury unleashed its anger. Ashen soot and burning cinders charred the ground around her. Gripped by panic, Clara had no chance to plan what to do or to figure out what had happened. Only a second had passed since the explosive noise, but already it was too late. Knocked to the ground, Clara watched as the factory rained down around her. On the floor of Silvertown's ammunition factory, Clara felt the world fall on her, until everything was swallowed in black.

Edward paused in his dusting. What was that? His ears must be playing tricks on him again. It sounded like the earth had shook, but earthquakes didn't occur here in England. Besides, he felt sturdy on his feet. He brushed it aside, thinking nothing of it, and continued dusting off the objects on the shelf. He stood back to admire his work. It was shaping up nicely and beginning to look like a real home or, much to Edward's delight, a successful antique business.

Of course, he couldn't open shop yet. There was a war going on and everyone's mind was far removed from adding to their collections of attractive curios. Edward, for his own salvation and peace of mind, had to dwell beyond the war. Sequestered from the winter's harsh extremes and even bleaker reality that lay across the sea to the east, Edward thrived in his muffled world. Much as his hearing was muted, his acceptance of all that had happened was as well. Ignoring the pain of the horror, he sought solace in the comfort of the old.

Agnes, haunted by her own ghosts of war, born of her suppositions and worries rather than experience as Edward's were, attempted to draw him from his solitude whenever possible.

"Let's go to the pictures," she had suggested one recent Saturday afternoon. The suggestion caught Edward off guard and no reason to decline was readily forthcoming, so he had no choice but to oblige her. As they sat there side-by-side, newsreels began to flash onto the screen. Music played somberly in accompaniment from the young girl seated at the piano, as Edward sat transfixed by the sterile black and white of war. Many in the audience gasped in horror, but for Edward it was merely a shadow of truth like Plato's in the allegorical cave. The public had first been exposed to such images this past summer during the earliest weeks of Edward's own Battle of the Somme.

Agnes reached across to slip her small ivory hand into his larger calloused hand.

"Is that how it is?" she whispered, not wanting to arouse pain but unable to silence her internal screams and pleadings for information on George and John.

No, it's a hundred thousand times worse. Everything is in color—vital red turned to deathly crimson, blue skies turned to impending gray. No melodic notes accompany the scene, only the piercing cries, agonizing screams, and thunderous explosions. The air does not smell of the delicate rosewater worn by the women around you. It reeks of mud, mold, and putrid flesh. And it's personal, so painfully heart-wrenchingly personal. They are not strangers; they are the men you eat with, sleep with, fight with. They are James.

The thoughts erupted in his head like molten lava, which had bubbled uneasily to the top, but Edward, stoic and steady, swallowed them all, dismissing them from duty and from reality.

"Yes, it's like that," he said, simply.

Agnes's fingers clenched around his own, as she squeezed his hand, half to comfort him and half to console herself. She reached into her pocket and retrieved a lace-edged handkerchief to dab at her moistening eyes. For her, this version of reality, diluted and cheapened, was difficult enough to bear.

Broken from the memory, he was returned to his house and the rumble through the room. Under the weight of too high a stack of books, the shelf he had just dusted gave way and tottered uneasily. He reached out quickly to steady it. When he had returned it to its rightful place, his hand lingered there for a moment. He felt strangely off-balance himself. Maybe something wild was happening and there really was an earthquake. No, the ground was steady. It was Edward who was off-balance. He knew that balance was affected by the inner ear. Perhaps, his was simply readjusting with his changing levels of hearing.

Regaining his balance, he looked up, spying the girl's portrait in the mirror. He had hung her above the fireplace, because she seemed to demand attention. There was something pleasantly bossy in her demeanor that commanded respect and recognition.

"Why did you lie?"

Edward's brow furrowed. Who was talking to him? He turned, expecting to find Agnes. No one was there.

"I must have imagined it," he muttered into the empty room. He had just been thinking about Agnes and her voice resonated within his head. His ears had only been confused. It was really in his mind. Yes, that had to be it. Speaking of Agnes, the hour was getting quite late and it was high time to return to her home for dinner. No doubt she'd call out a search party, if he did not soon return. He locked up his house for the night, leaving it and all its secrets unturned and in the dark.

⟜•⟞

A throbbing, like someone had jammed a metal helmet down too tightly on her head, confronted Clara now.

"Ohh," she moaned, not at all sure what had happened. Her eyes opened slowly. It was dark, but a huge glare flooded the darkness in a burning glow. Cold air nipped at her now. "What am I doing outside?" she thought. She really wasn't sure what was going on, but whatever it was she had an acute awareness that being outside now was something out of the ordinary. As her eyes opened more, people materialized before her. They darted about, most looking shocked or greatly distressed. Red dripped from some of them. They had certainly made a mess of rolling around in the cherries. No. That wasn't cherries. That was blood. Suddenly, a great unease filled Clara. She lifted her eyes and saw a huge fire with leaping flames off to the side in the distance. Buildings around this central furnace shot into flames, as char and embers sparked and threw their fiery tongues to all within reach. Voices cried frantically in pain and desperation to locate others.

"Jane?"

"Sarah?"

"Elizabeth?"

"Where are you?"

"Can someone help?" Clara shook her head to try to loosen the iron fingers causing the aching in her head, but to no avail. From a few feet away, a woman met Clara's eyes and approached her now. Her hair, graying but full, was drawn back in a tight bun. Little wisps of stubborn hair jetted out, unwilling to remain captive. There was a sturdiness in her build and a determination in her cornflower blue eyes.

"Hello, dearie."

It took Clara a minute to realize she was the one being addressed. Clara attempted to stand, but a rush of dizziness overcame her.

"Perhaps, you best not rush it," the woman said.

Clara had no idea who she was or if she were supposed to know her. She took a paper and pen from her pocket now.

"Well, dearie, why don't you tell me your name and then I'll get you a nice cuppa."

Clara thought tea a funny suggestion with such chaos around her, but decided that the woman must just be trying to put her at ease. At least, she knew that she wasn't supposed to know who the other woman was, but—she was supposed to know who she was. Clara opened her mouth to speak.

"I...I..."

"Yes, dearie, what's your name, love?" she coaxed gently.

"I... I don't know."

CHAPTER SEVEN

The sky was as gray as the murky water from a painter cleaning the brushes, as Edward began his morning. He had already eaten breakfast with Agnes, but a second cup of tea was required by this morning. He felt like a pioneer at home on the wide-sweeping plains that stretch endlessly for miles, as he built a fire in the downstairs hearth and hung a copper kettle filled with water over it. He sat down in the high-backed chair that had been made during Queen Victoria's reign. Some might say that it was beginning to look outdated and out of touch with modernity, but Edward the antiquarian thought it might someday be just as sought after as Georgian furniture now was.

Walking to the house this morning, Edward had been struck by the immensity of the grounds that he owned as part of the surrounds of the house. German blockades were hampering the import of much needed food. Some of the other returned soldiers and locals could surely help him in turning the land and raising crops. It would be hard labor since many of the farm horses were away with the cavalry, but it could be done. He dug into his pocket and his finger slipped through a hole that had formed where the seams had pulled apart from each other, much as the fabric of Edward's own life had. Bypassing the coin and handkerchief, he took out the piece of paper he recorded notes on about the pieces as he unwrapped them. Unfolding the paper from around his pen, he began drafting a potential plotting plan for the garden. He had some knowledge of which plants grew when and how long they needed, but he would have to consult some of the farmers to broaden his understanding. It was easier, somehow, to consider becoming a part of life here. After losing James, he had avoided all in the trenches. But, here farmers were not likely to slip into their muddied fields and be plowed under, as so many were on the front.

The water began to bubble as it grew from a soft simmer,

too faint for Edward's ears, into a babbling boil. He paused in his writing and took out a teapot from the kitchen.

"Hello," he said to the woman in the painting, as he bent to take the kettle off the fire. In a very sane way she had become his companion and, from time-to-time, he spoke to her.

He looked into her dark eyes again now. There was something concealed behind them and her enigma had become his own Mona Lisa. As Edward completed the very ordinary act of inspecting a painting and reading into its meaning, something done the world over by students of art history everywhere, something extraordinary and quite unexpected happened. The painting began to read him.

"Why do you hide?" Edward jumped back at the question, which had not been spoken aloud but had risen in decibel level within him. He shook his head to clear the meddlesome voice away.

"What are you trying to prove?"

Again, the question rose from within him.

"I... am not going crazy," he said aloud, to overpower the rising voice within.

"Why do you hide?" the voice said inside of him again.

"Why was it James and not you?" the voice confronted him now. His hand shook as he was overcome by the emotions that were forced forward, which he always fought so strongly against.

"Why?" the voice said, as Edward's hand continued to shake. In a crash, the teapot fell to the floor, shattering its porcelain sides.

"James, hide, why?" The voice had become distorted and fragmented, awkwardly assembling the pieces together. Edward left to retrieve a broom and swept up the broken pieces, discarding them in a box he gathered trash into. He returned to the painting and looked at the lady framed therein.

"What's happening to me?" he asked her aloud, as if she

could part those painted lips and offer comfort to him. There was, of course, no reply though and the internal bombardment that had risen from within him now lay silent as well.

The house, which usually offered such sanctuary, lacked what he needed for the moment and so he departed, while it was still early in the morning. It was Saturday and Agnes would be suspicious if he returned after being gone so shortly, especially because she usually had to delay supper because he became so involved in the house that he forgot all sense of time. No, he could not return there, which was probably for the better. What he needed was a distraction.

⁂

"Are you cold, love?" Clara looked up, her shoulders convulsing in a shiver in reply. The nurse looked sympathetically at the frightened girl before her and handed her a blanket.

"Thank you," Clara said, "you're very kind."

"Poor girl," the nurse whispered under her breath to another nurse that appeared at her side.

"The girl there, you mean?" her companion asked. The first nurse nodded, her cheeks rosy from the cold bobbing from the motion.

"She's been here three days, she has. But every time she looks at me, it's like she's never seen me before."

With the added warmth around her, Clara sank into the woolen layers and, overcome with the burden of amnesia, soon fell asleep. Slumber, with all its deceptive tendencies, allows one to easily feel that all time has passed when only a few seconds have or that the eyes have just shut when in fact they have been closed for hours. The latter was true of Clara now as she awoke, not refreshed and alert, but into another kind of tiredness—dulled but still as real as the acute sleep that had demanded her obedience.

"Here, I've brought you some soup, Clara," the nurse

said, as she approached. Clara did not look up and at first the nurse wondered if perhaps she were still asleep. But as she turned to walk away, Clara called after her,

"I'm frightfully hungry. If I could have something to eat?"

The nurse looked at her sadly. Although losing the use of a limb or partial hearing or sight could be severely limiting, losing one's memory was a sadness she could not get used to and reconcile.

"What is it?" Clara asked, seeing her reaction.

"You... well, it's really rather early still after what you suffered but you..."

"I forgot who I was again and didn't recognize my name," Clara finished for her, so she would not have to say it. Though Clara was the one to have suffered so deeply, she acted now to protect this stranger from the pain. Besides, the nurse would remember this incident and there was a good chance that she would not.

The days, in their winter haziness, took on a similar guise to each other and smeared into one foggy stream. Clara gradually began to remember daily life in the hospital, but the sum of the years before was blank. She perfectly embodied Rousseau's *tabula rasa*. One of the other girls in the factory had identified her as Clara Banks to the nurse that first evening, but the girl knew nothing more of her. Clara sat staring out the window.

"Clara?" At times she still forgot her name, but if caught on a good day she would turn with a pensive smile when hearing it.

"What are you thinking of?" the nurse would ask, when seeing the concentration firmly set on her face. Most often she answered that she was trying to remember—where she lived, about her family, her life, her dreams, anything really. Though the nurses were sympathetic and offered what consolation they could, she was just as much a stranger to them as to herself and thus there was no one to help her remember.

She turned from the window now, as a russet squirrel scampered up a tree, at hearing her name. Today was a good day and though she remembered nothing else, she knew she was Clara Banks.

"Yes?"

A gentleman stood beside the nurse, looking at her cheerfully through his small spectacles resting on his rather large nose. Clara looked from the man to the nurse and back again, wondering who he might be.

"I'm sorry, but I don't know who you are—if I am supposed to."

She hoped that a frown would not crease his friendly face. Instead, a wrinkle of a smile danced around his blue eyes, which still held the joviality of youth that his creaking joints no longer did.

"No, my dear, we've not met before. Allow me to introduce myself. My name is Harold Emerson and I was a friend of your grandfather's." Clara nodded politely, but his explanation had not cleared anything for her. The person they were meant to have in common she could not remember either. Acting in kindness at the realization that she might not remember her grandfather, he did not prattle on about his friend but instead steered the conversation, as stealthily as a ship's captain through murky waters, toward how he came to be here now.

"I saw a list in London of people involved in the accident that the hospital was trying to contact the families of. I saw your name there and stopped right in my tracks. 'Why that must be William Banks's granddaughter,' I said to myself. He always was so proud of you, talking to me about his little Clara," he said, lapsing temporarily from his silent pledge to not bring up too much of the past. Realizing what he had done, he brushed the thoughts aside and continued,

"The point is, your grandfather was like a brother to me and I wanted to come to see you, to see if I might be of some help."

"Thank you," Clara said, not sure what else to say.
He allowed her time to process what had been said and the nurse slipped away to help someone else as they spoke. With practiced patience from the accumulation of years, he waited to speak again until she did first. Faced with the first true link to anyone from her life since the accident, a wealth of questions presented themselves suddenly.

"So, you know my family then? You could help me find them?" The frown, she had hoped would not line his face, now glimmered at the corner of his eyes.

"Clara," he said gently, and then paused, unsure if he should proceed. The nurse, who had left to attend to a burn victim from the explosion, looked up at Harold now having heard the conversation. She nodded at him, to confirm that he should tell Clara and then she continued changing the bandages on the girl's arms.

"My dear, your grandfather was the last of your family on this earth and he went to join the rest of them a few years ago. You must have moved to London to find some work after that. After all, your grandfather was a man of immense heart but limited wealth. All of his possessions were sold to pay the debts. I'm afraid we had that in common—the money part I mean." He felt foolish for having digressed to talk of currency, when he had just delivered such heavy news of her family.

She looked away from Harold, out the window again. The squirrel had drawn his tail around him in a bushy blanket to fend off the chill. Harold was concerned that he had burdened her with too great a quantity of sadness too suddenly, but the truth was Clara felt as if the words did not apply to her. In a way, they did not because she was not the girl who lost her family; she was the girl who lost her memory and any recollection of her family as a result of it.

"I see," she said, not turning from watching the squirrel.

"I know this must be very difficult, but I will help you however I can," he said, patting her hand reassuringly.

She turned away from the window to face him now and those kind eyes met hers, sealing a bond of friendship between the two.

CHAPTER EIGHT

Edward wandered through the fields, intently studying the composition of the ground, the proximity of the river, the height of trees, the indigenous shrubbery that hedged in the garden, the darting animals and flickering birds with their long melodious high-pitched calls. All of them added color to the strong gray canvas of the backdrop Edward lived among. He walked until there were no steps left within him. His delicate ears burned in the piercing cold. Turning toward Agnes's home, he hastened his steps. Consigned to the knowledge that he would be required to answer her questions of his early return, his cold hands welcomed the thought of the promised cup of tea that would soon fill them.

When he entered the house it was eerily quiet, as if all livelihood had disappeared down some dark hole. It was more than that the house was quiet in Edward's dulled ears. There was a palpable difference in how it felt.

"Agnes?"

No reply. He moved into the kitchen, where he so often found her soaking up the warmth of the fire as a cat basks in the sun's glow.

"Agnes?" he said, again.

She came to the doorway now and stopped before entering the room. The frame hugged her, as if upon seeing her tense expression even the house sought to comfort her. She said nothing, but stood fixed with a somber look on her face. His eyes questioned her.

"What is it?" he started to ask, but the words stopped in his throat in an impassable lump, when he saw what was in her hand. No, this is not what he had meant. This was not the distraction he had wished for.

He crossed to her now and waited for her to speak when she was ready. He waited to see if his cousin had not lived to be a man or if the love he had tried to protect had been cut short. No doubt, George or John had been killed in the terrible fight and the news arrived in the telegram Agnes clutched in her long pale fingers. Still, she did not speak and so he gently reached for her hand to pry her fingers loose from the page. He lifted it and read, rushing his eyes over the words to get to the name.

"Martin Henderson," he read aloud, looking up at Agnes with a question in his eyes.

"I thought— " he began.

"You thought what I thought—that John or George— "

"Did you know him?" he asked now.

"No," she said, quietly.

"Agnes, I don't understand."

"When the telegram was delivered, I felt depths of sadness I have never known, all my very worst fears were realized. With shaking hands, I opened it—both wanting to postpone the moment and desperately needing to know," she paused.

"And then?" he prompted.

"And then, I read Martin Henderson and I felt such relief. It wasn't John! It wasn't George! And then, I felt so overwhelmingly sick." She looked as though she were on a boat and would lose her footing momentarily. He put his hand out on her arm to steady her.

"Because?" he coaxed.

"Because, he wasn't *my* John or *my* George but he was *someone's* Martin. And so I felt immense guilt and—I also began to worry if someone else had received a telegram intended for us." Her voice quivered, as she spoke these last words. He held his arms out to her and she melted into her cousin's sheltering embrace.

"Edward?"

Her voice was muffled against his coat and so he did not hear her. She took a step back to help him hear her better.

"Edward, we have to find them."

"Them?"

"Martin's family. We have to deliver it to them."

He nodded, accepting a new mission of search and recovery.

Though Edward and Agnes had committed to a mission that neither had any way of knowing how long would last, it proved far easier than either could have imagined. Their first stop had been the post office. Yes, the clerk had indeed heard of Martin Henderson. He slipped the address into Agnes's hand and bid the two farewell.

"Is it far?" Edward asked Agnes as he read the address, still unsure of the intricacies of English geography. So many of these small towns had similar names and it was easy to mix them up.

"Not far at all, really. We could walk there in half an hour."

"Oh my, that is close then. Shall we go now?"

Her eyes hesitated just a moment, unprepared to face the difficult circumstances ahead. An altruistic streak, so alive and widening daily, within Agnes won out though.

"Yes, let's go."

They walked in almost complete silence, both preparing themselves for what lay ahead, until they had walked a good twenty minutes already.

"Tell me about the house," Agnes said suddenly.

"My house?"

"Yes. I have been replaying too many difficult scenarios in my mind about what will happen when we reach the address. We are about to break someone's heart—at least someone, perhaps several hearts—and I need an encouraging word."

"I suppose the very reason you gave is why I want to open my house as an antique shop. There are so many beautiful things that have survived. It seems we should celebrate what has lasted, not only mourn what has been lost."

"Tell me what you've found."

"There are several dozen teacups, piles of embroidered linens, books of postcards, yards of the finest fabrics, enough furniture to outfit two or three houses of similar size."

"And are there paintings? I always love paintings—a pristine landscape, a carefully arranged still life, or best yet a portrait that can see into you."

He looked at her, surprised at the words. Could she know? Could she know that the painted girl had looked into his heart and read him? No, of course not. It was too crazy even to think. Agnes misinterpreted his surprise for confusion or perhaps she had not spoken loud enough for him.

"Did you hear me all right? Do you know what I mean?"

He nodded slowly.

"Yes, I have such a painting. I've hung her above the sitting room's mantel."

"Oh, you must let me come see her sometime," she said. Though he thought perhaps he better not consent, seeing the momentary distraction of happiness it caused made up his mind for him.

"All right," he said, "I'll show you. Just let me fix the room better for you to visit first."

"You really don't— " she began but then, deciding to allow Edward the courtesy of showing his house to her in the condition he chose, stopped herself.

"Thank you. I will look forward to it."

"Ready?" Edward said, as they stood on the doorstep. Agnes, still clutching the telegram in his hand, reached for Edward's hand with her other. She took a deep breath in, scattering the cold air around her in wispy clouds.

"Ready."

Edward raised his hand to knock. When there was no

reply, he wondered if his touch had been too light. Perhaps, the soft rap he had heard was not as amplified as he assumed it would be.

"Did I knock loud enough?"

"You did. I don't think anyone is home."

The two turned away to return another day. Agnes paused in her footsteps and turned abruptly.

"What is it?" Edward asked, and then turning, saw the man at the door.

"Did someone knock?" he asked, but across the expanse Edward only heard the word "knock".

"Yes, we did," Agnes said, quickly crossing back to the house and pulling Edward along with her.

"Who is *we*?" the man asked and it was then that Agnes saw the bandages over his eyes.

"Agnes Walters," she introduced herself, "and my cousin, Edward Jamison."

"Hello," Edward said, when he had been introduced.

"Well, if my ears don't deceive me, I believe you must be an American."

"That's right. My mother married an American," he explained.

"I see," he said, "Well, I don't see, but I understand."

His said the words, not in bitterness, but with a sense of humor.

"Please, come in," he said to the two, opening his front door wide to welcome their entrance. Agnes looked at Edward, not quite sure what to make of this man in front of them. His shoulders drooped in a half shrug and he held out his arm to indicate that he thought they should oblige this stranger. The two entered the house that was very dim since its occupant seemed to have no need for light.

"You are probably wondering if I live alone," he said to Edward and Agnes, who were indeed wondering such a thing.

"And if I do, then how am I able to manage?" he said with a knowing smile, as if performing a magic act as part of a parlor trick. Without waiting for either to reply, he continued,

"Well, the answer is that yes, since returning from battle, I live alone. I will be joined soon though by my brother, I'm sure when he returns. The neighbors come to check on me and so I manage."

Edward stared at the man, who employed so opposite a coping strategy to himself.

"Your brother," Agnes said slowly, turning the attention to why they had come. Edward had momentarily forgot, as he marveled at this man.

"Yes?" the man asked.

"Well—I'm not sure how to put this, but I'm afraid we are the bringers of unhappy news."

"Oh?" he said and for the first time in their knowing him the smile had been dismissed from his face. Agnes looked at Edward, imploring him to say something as a fellow soldier.

"You see, we received a telegram today, by accident. We think it was intended— unfortunately—for you."

"A telegram, well, please, read it to me," he said.

"Perhaps, we better just tell you," Agnes said.

"Yes?" his voice now bore the extreme curiosity so apt to grip a person's mind, when confronted with such a situation.

"Sadly, your brother has—in a valiant effort—died in France. I am so very sorry." Agnes said and then reached her hand out to reassuringly touch his arm.

"My brother? But, how can this be?"

Edward, so familiar with the feelings of detachment when faced with such news, spoke now.

"I know, as a soldier myself, that these things can be difficult to believe."

"Yes, that's true, but you seem to misunderstand. It is impossible."

"Sometimes war causes that which should be impossible and so we think it is," Edward said, risking his own vulnerability he felt in saying it.

"Would you tell me the name it gave on the telegram please?" The man asked.

"Martin Henderson," Agnes said. The two watched the man in front of them digest the information. Agnes leaned in, lest he should suddenly collapse in tears and need her comforting arms. Perhaps, it was the teacher in her that always believed a troubled soul could be consoled with a welcoming hug. She was quite progressive in that respect and employed mutual affection rather than harsh punishment in dealing with her students.

The man began to shake and Edward thought his tears must be too quiet to hear. He looked up at them though and, rather than tear-strewn cheeks in long tracks, he was smiling again. And now, he began to laugh!

"Martin Henderson isn't my brother."

"Oh?" Agnes said, thinking that the telegram had mistakenly been delivered again and dreading the thought of having to live the whole ordeal again—same heartbreak, different stranger.

"You see my brother is not away at war. He has simply gone to London to oversee the work in his factory."

"Oh!" Agnes said now, quite surprised, "Sorry, to have bothered you. I suppose we'll be on our way to find Martin Henderson's real family."

"But, you've found something better. You've found Martin Henderson. I am him."

CHAPTER NINE

After their strange, unorthodox meeting, Edward found himself returning often to Martin, if not literally, then mentally. Martin had an infectious love of life, despite the cruel hand he had been dealt. Edward decided a few days later that he had avoided his house for quite long enough. Edward, who had faced the fighting so willingly, was ashamed to admit that a painting had got the best of him.

Having decided to accept the inevitable and realizing that it would not only be wasteful but also completely crazy to never return to the house, Edward unlocked the door now with trepidation knocking on the chambers of his heart. When he had made up his mind to confront his fear, he wasted no time in seeing it through. Edward the soldier marched straight to the painting and stared it down, waiting for the attack, believing he had the resolve within him to not only stand and fight but to win.

She looked so pristine from the painting, not at all exhibiting the smugness that now accompanied her in his mind. He felt suddenly foolish, as one does when wrongfully accusing a friend or becoming cross with one who merits only respect. He stood eye-to-eye with her now, waiting to see if anything would happen. No questions came. There was no taunting or torment or internal whirl of oppressive protest and interrogation. There was only the ticking of the clock and a veteran standing before a very old painting. Having made his peace, he turned away to resume his work.

Edward reached for the box propped against the wall that he had left off at. It was about half unpacked and papers torn open peeked their heads out of the top of the box. The paper fell away from the opalescent gown surrounding a slender vase, the way a dancer's costume flows with her body with each step on the dance floor. He turned the vase to see if there were any visible markings to indicate its maker, origin, or age. Something was etched into its base, but time had dulled its appearance presenting Edward with the challenge of discerning what it said. To aid his reading, he crossed to the fire and held the vase nearer to it. The flames crackled softly in the hearth and he coaxed greater light from them.

"You know why you do it," a voice spoke. Edward's head spun, dizzied by the rising voice that he assumed was departed from his house.

"You're beginning to understand," it said again. Edward looked to the painting. Surely, surely those lips had parted! But, he knew that they had not. When he raised his eyes to the painted lady, she had not opened her mouth to speak. But, her appearance was changed. A mirage of kaleidoscope colors splashed from the vase and flames onto her ordinarily solid-colored dress, the way a prism scatters light.

Edward placed his hand over the vase and stared intently at her. No sound, no words, and no message were forthcoming. Removing his hand, he waited,

"Ah, you're getting it now."

"Good heavens," Edward exclaimed, suddenly realizing what was—or at least seemed to be if it could be believed—unfolding before him.

Edward set down the vase and gathered all the glass around him that he could find. One by one he held each piece: saucers, teacups, vases, spectacles, pocket watch, and hand-held mirror up to the painting. Sure enough, the voice spoke each time a piece reflected against the painting and silence filled the gap when there was no reflection.

Edward picked up a fluted bowl and held it up for the lady's inspection now.

"What are you hoping to learn?" the voice asked, pitching awkwardly high and low with the undulating glass.

"Amazing," Edward said aloud, "absolutely amazing."

Gone was the fear that had previously gripped him, when the painting had first read him. In its place was the excitement encountered when one has discovered something that no one else knows. Only, what if others did know? The thought struck him now that the painted lady was three or perhaps even four hundred years old or more. Surely, in that time someone else must have encountered this fascinating secret. He pressed his palm to his temple, in hopes that applying pressure would force a solution more readily to the surface.

"I have to investigate. I have to know more about the painting!"

His declaration spoken aloud, he tore up the stairs and searched through the papers he had found in the accompanying boxes near where he had first discovered the painting. Suddenly, he wondered if there were perhaps more paintings endowed with the ability and if he had been too limiting in assuming this gift, or whatever it was, lay only in the one painting. In a bevy of excitement, he peered into every portrait he had uncovered. To an onlooker he would have appeared daft. None of the portraits, nice as they were, returned the same reading of him as the woman's portrait did. What was it about her? It was not that her painting differed in size from the others. It was neither larger nor smaller. Indeed, all the paintings varied. It was not that she was older than the others, because there was a religious icon that he was certain predated her by at least two centuries. As nice as she was painted, if one were objective, she was not especially grander than any of the others.

"Animals," he said aloud, thinking that perhaps his focus had been too limited when considering only portraits of people. Ordinarily, animals could not hold a conversation with someone as another person could, but then ordinarily neither could a painting.

Edward spent the better part of an hour peering into the painted faces of dogs and cats, horses and fowl. He even looked at a rabbit—fat and slain—on the board of a Dutch still life warning against the unnecessary excesses of life. In all of the paintings, Edward found himself reading the story of the piece before him. It was natural and involuntary for him to do so, but none of the pictures returned his reading with an evaluation of him as the painted lady did.

Returning to the piles of paper, he scanned them quickly, separating the stacks of what might be of use and what was not. He had no idea what he was searching for and when he had completed dividing the first stack, only two papers lay in the discarded pile—one a receipt for paint and the other a diagram of the roof. Glancing down at these two stragglers, his mind changed altogether and he hastily shoved them back into the middle of the pile. Realizing he was accomplishing little but undoing his weeks' work of tidying the house, he decided his frenzy had to be channeled. Working in a feverish frantic was getting him nowhere.

"Edward?" a voice said behind him and he jumped in his surprise, sending a stack of piled papers balanced on the arm of a chair cascading to the floor.

"Oh, I'm sorry. I didn't mean to frighten you."

Edward turned and saw Agnes standing there. From the movement of her face, she seemed to be talking very loudly.

"Is something the matter?" he said, coming to his feet now and dusting off the seat of his pants.

"Oh no, I just thought I would come by. I know I said I would wait—"

"But, you don't like to wait," he finished for her.

A hint of a smile slipped through her lips.

"Oh Edward, don't be cross with me. I wanted to see what occupies you so." Bathed in the streams of the setting sun, she looked half her age. Her impish grin only added to the appearance. Since their days of meeting Martin, she seemed lighter. She smiled more easily and did not seem as sad. Hope had been injected into both of them that expected negativity could vanish in a moment and that this war could mean more than mounds of horror. She still worried, of course, for George and John but her burden had lightened.

"I'm not cross with you," he said and her smile forced his own curvature of the mouth.

"Come on, fix me a cuppa," she said, still with the aura of a young girl delighted at the thought of a tea party.

"A cup of tea," he repeated.

She nodded with a smile, thinking he was merely ensuring he had heard her correctly. Edward, though, was not repeating for clarity and was suddenly faced with the uncertainty of how he would be able to honor her request. The only chimney and hearth that had been safely cleared for a fire rested just beneath the portrait. Serving his cousin a cup of tea unquestionably demanded the use of glass. Agnes, in her way, would undoubtedly insist on helping him and that would place her in exactly the same position he had been in when first discovering the secret of the painting. He was not prepared to tell Agnes of his discovery. She would worry that he had been gassed in the trenches and it was only now showing its effects. He was also unwilling to allow her to discover the secret for herself.

"We could do that, but actually I have something I want to show you."

"Oh?"

"Yes, I have an idea for a project but it requires your help."

"Oh good!" she said and clapped her hands together in delight.

He led her down the stairs and crossed the foyer to the coat rack. Agnes looked confused.

"The project requires coats? I thought you had decided to catalog the antiques and wanted my help."

"Actually, the project doesn't have anything to do with

the house."

"Oh?" she said, following him outside now, after he had bundled up to fend off the cold.

"What do you see?" he asked, as they stood just outside the door.

"What do I see," she repeated, scanning the horizon to see if she had missed something.

He lifted his arm now, passing it horizontally through the air, mapping out some grand design.

"Land," he said.

"Land," she repeated.

"Yes, land, for farming, for gardening. We can help feed England! We can assist like the Army Agriculture Labor Corps. Other veterans, like Martin I am sure, would want to help and you could organize a brigade for the women's land army—if you wanted that is."

Agnes slipped her arm through Edward's.

"Land," she said, smiling.

Clara's heart thudded nervously against her ribs, as she bounced along in the carriage beside Harold. The doctors and nurses had declared her fit enough to be released and travel. Her memories did not accompany her on the journey but she could not be kept in the hospital until they all returned, especially because no one knew if they ever would return. Clara peered out the window of the carriage, swept away in a sea of green grass, watered generously by the overflowing clouds so apt to unleash their showers like a stream of life from a watering can's spout.

"Just there is the Smithersons' cottage. He's a blacksmith and she makes the finest apple tarts for miles."

Clara nodded politely, wondering if she had ever met a blacksmith or if she liked apple tarts. From the way that Harold spoke, he seemed to accept it as fact that everyone did.

"And here are the Smiths, a rather plain name but a quite interesting family. There are seven sons and each brother is taller than the one before him, so as their ages increase their heights decrease if you stood them in a line."

Harold had a story for every cottage and Clara was convinced he knew the whole of England. The cottages began to congregate more closely now, like friends gathering to speak when church has let out. A meandering stream wove through the countryside, like a perfectly placed silver ribbon. Below the raised seat of the carriage lay a land foreign but pleasant. Despite being foreign, there was a friendliness in the unfamiliarity.

"Have I been here before?" she asked Harold now, feeling especially brave. It was difficult to admit that she could not remember.

"Yes," he said, with that smile of his that was filled to the brim with joy. Her curiosity was piqued and she turned to him, wondering when she had visited such enamoring countryside.

"Actually—you used to come here often. Your grandparents lived not twenty minutes from here."

"Really?" she said.

He nodded with that slow and steady smile of his.

"Whoa," the carriage driver said, as they pulled up in front of a house.

"We're here," Harold said. For the moment, Clara's questions of her grandparents' home were quieted by the tide of nervousness swelling in her stomach. The house before her was larger than she imagined it would be. It lacked the quaint nature and the pretty thatch of so many houses and cottages that they had passed. Still though, there was a definite charm. It was not the charm of petite hidden treasures, but the grandiose delight of a manor house. Clara stepped from the carriage with Harold's assistance and stood staring, wide-eyed at the palatial home that seemed to deepen and grow the nearer they approached.

"Hello, Harold!" a stout woman of similar age with the

same warm and easy smile greeted him, as she clamored down the front steps.

"And you must be Clara," she said, before allowing either the chance to say anything first.

"Yes," Clara said.

"Now, Emma is a fine sister and an even better friend. Don't you worry, Clara. Everything is going to work out just fine."

Clara bid farewell to Harold and turned to enter the house with Emma, where Harold had generously arranged for her to become a housekeeper. He also hoped, though he had not told Clara, that living so near where she had spent so many happy moments of her childhood would help her remember. Besides, Clara was sure to like it here. There was the fresh air instead of the stuffiness of the city, beautiful countryside, his sister Emma to watch over her and kind neighbors. Harold thought that Miss Emily, cheerful despite the war, would be especially helpful to Clara. He supposed that the benefit of eighty-three years, come June as she always reminded everyone, allowed her the experience of knowing that though trouble and hardship came there was always the promise of all that truly mattered providing a stronger permanence. The seeds of hate and suffering though planted deep, were always capable of being uprooted by love, joy, hope, peace and faith. Miss Emily was always reminding Harold of that message. There was that veteran who lived nearby as well, the blind one. Yes, young Martin Henderson was sure to provide a little sunshine for Clara.

CHAPTER TEN

Edward interested Agnes in the garden plan to such an extent that, he spent the rest of the day discussing it with her. Though he was glad to see her spirits raised and took pride in the enthusiasm his idea caused, the revelation of the painting kindled a fire in him that hungrily consumed all the greater part of his attention. In its wake stood the arid landscape of a despondent mind. By the time Agnes busied herself with correcting her students' papers, it was far too late for him to leave for the house.

Early the next morning, he tore from the house. Like a wind gusting through a grove of pines, he hurried his steps and nearly galloped toward the house. His mind was agitated, driven to uncover the answers of the painting. Burrowing his nose in a stack of papers, his heart raced as he scanned the documents searching for any clue he could find.

"Aha!" he said suddenly, clapping his hand against the stack of papers and sending forth a cloud of dust.

"Invoice for three chairs, one bookcase, an eight piece serving set of silver, and a portrait of a young woman," he read, aloud. He raced to the painting now and addressed her,

"Young lady, I have found your travel papers and now you too will divulge your secrets to me!"

"1909," he read in surprise, when seeing the date of the bill of sale. He had assumed her history extended longer with the house, but it seemed as if they both were newcomers.

Edward read the documents, attempting to garner any additional information. Whoever had sold the purchase had signed his or her name illegibly and it was written nowhere else. Feeling like he had progressed much less than he originally thought, he turned his attention back to the stacks of paper in the other room. Behind her smile, the painting challenged him to solve her mystery and he provided every reassurance that her story would unfold for him in completion.

Edward huddled against the wooden floor, hunkered down in the fortress of his new campaign. Gone were the sandbags and the walls of earth. Now, there were only cushions stacked in towering piles on armchairs and boxes and tattered crates for walls. With the same immediacy and resolve for success, which he had approached the trenches with, he faced this problem now. The enemy no longer lurked just beyond that wall or over that hill, but Edward's motivation sprang from the same desperation of survival. Tightly entangled within the web of mystery surrounding the painted lady, Edward had no choice but to press on. He would gain whatever ground he could, no matter how small or impractical it might be.

Coming to the bottom of yet another box with no new information, he sat back with his leg extended in front of him and pushed aside the box with his foot.

"What's this?" he said, jumping forward to lift a thin paper notebook that had become dislodged from between two boxes as he moved the one aside. He lifted it tentatively, as if it might crumble and turn whatever secrets it held to dust. Edward ran his finger between the stiff outer cover and the more delicate pages inside to open it.

"The collected drawings of Mr. Lefront," he read, from the top of the first page. He turned the page.

"Normandie, 1884." He read aloud the writing that differed from the first page and was in French.

The drawings had presumably been done in Normandy, France and in the latter part of last century. This person may have known the Impressionists! It was an exciting thought for Edward and he quickly became emerged in admiring the soft pastel lines and dots that seemed committed in areas and more experimental in others. He was drawn into another version of France entirely, from the one he had experienced. Traces were the same: the way the trees gathered in lines or the way the houses were constructed, though they were built from a different material than the ones he had seen. They stood with the same stature and he was quite certain that they would have walked with the same gait, had they been persons and not buildings. Here was a France of sun-streamed beaches, of majestic sea swelling with lazy boats perched atop its crestfallen waves formed at the caprice of the gentle winds. Flowers danced merrily within the fields of this France. The images of bodies littering the fields in place of flowers flashed before him now. He shut his eyes tight to dismiss them. Swallowing hard, he forced his eyes open again and returned his attention to the brightly-colored petals, captured—if not perfectly accurate—at least very lovingly, here. Flowers would return to the fields where Edward fought, tokens left on the stone monuments erected above shallow graves, but also—he now realized—as annual occurrences as well. The flowers had marked the seasons for eons before Edward lived among their roots and they would return, silent, oblivious observers of all that had transpired. And beauty, newness of life, would grow in Edward's own soil of existence. Already, new shoots were emerging in his scarred heart.

France and he had both seen storms before, he was reminded as he turned the page and saw the little boat tossed in the currents of a gruff sea that pages before lay so pristine and slept in such serenity. And just as assuredly as the next page depicted the same boat, tied peacefully at dock on a still sea, the storms of his own reality would quiet and one day, perhaps, abate completely. The waves that swirled so mightily, sending torrential rains onto his weary body would fade into ripples one day. It had been that way after the earthquake. Young Edward was certain that life would be altogether different from then on, but it really wasn't. Years passed and the thundering waters of turmoil quieted into gentle rushes, calm pools, and at last dewy drops that watered the memories of his youth. Their potential for harm long gone, now they merely offered sustenance to his personality, aiding his strength.

He was nearing the end of the notebook now and had begun to feel privy to the private thoughts of a stranger, as if he were eavesdropping not only on someone's conversation but upon the longings and stirrings of this Mr. Lefront's heart. Turning the page, he wondered what the last image would be.

Edward's heart seized momentarily in surprise, as if he just sneezed.

"You," he said softly, as the likeness of the painted lady stared up at him.

The same hand that had drawn the flowers and boats, which he had sailed away with in his thoughts, now abruptly brought him back to reality. Her portrait lacked the precision of the original, assuming his painting was the original. To his trained eye, it was clear that this sketch was later than the painting but, what if—

His thought trailed off, as he leaned forward to inspect her closer. At first, he had believed it was an exact copy and that the small differences could be attributed to the inferior mastery by this copy artist. Now though, Edward noted that there were small markings around her basic structure that placed her in the 1870s or 1880s. It was as if the artist had felt some need to make her his own contemporary and companion. One would almost think that Mr. Lefront was not copying a portrait, but attempting to capture some living person. Edward's breath drew in rapidly, the way a quick moving tide swallows an expanse of sand as it retreats to the sea. Could it be? Had Mr. Lefront looked into the painted lady and been met with the same surprise that Edward had been? Had the painting read Mr. Lefront as well?

Edward sat back, leaning against the box on the ground nearest him. It was almost too much to comprehend. He had every intention of discovering the painting's story, but now suddenly he had been made part of some secret gathering of those who gazed into a portrait and were read by the painting! Or at least, maybe he was now part of such a society.

He picked up the notebook again. This time, he doubted whether the same hand had drawn this as the rest of the work. She was at the end and could easily have been added later. It was not as if she were found in the middle of the pages between outings in Normandy. Someone could have just drawn her in later, when seeing the painting. But, he argued with himself, the flowers at the edges were so similar to those on the previous pages. Those could have merely been copies too though. His head spun in exhaustion. Maybe he was losing his mind and had been averse to telling Agnes because she would have confirmed it.

Shutting his eyes to the noise of his mind and reopening them again, he picked up the drawing and stared hard at her. He set down the notebook and stood to find the nearest piece of glass. Feeling like a scientist conducting an experiment, he held up the vase and peered at the drawing through the glass. He waited, thinking he would appear mad to anyone who saw him, but this did not discourage him from doing what he felt he must. When she made no utterance, if it could be called that, to him he set down the vase. He was not yet determined that his temptress was silent and fetched a large magnifying glass to hold to the drawing, the way a doctor would magnify one's heartbeat through a stethoscope for better detection. She was, after all, just a copy and perhaps needed more assistance in being coaxed from her less grand shell of graphite, rather than glorious oils. Holding the magnifying glass to her, he succeeded in noticing where a very faint sketch lay beneath and in determining that her eyes were composed of more lines than on first inspection but, that was all. She remained silent and if her voice could not be summoned through amplifying it, he decided that she did not hold the same gift that her sister portrait did.

Edward had hitherto determined that it was not the oil that provided her voice, because no other painting caused the same result. Furthermore, the image itself did not seem to hold the ability. Could it possibly be the materials she rested upon, rather than the girl herself? The canvas seemed ordinary enough to Edward, with nothing unusual about its composition, but then the painted lady had also aroused no suspicion and so looking ordinary was no true indicator of undercover secrets. Edward was well aware that many, especially in the Medieval era, believed that miracles were capable of being produced from touching sacred objects, especially those related to the Passion. Perhaps, in a similar vein, the painted lady's canvas was derived of some substance endowed with charitable and special qualities. It was not that Edward thought she might be imbued with a holy past, but rather that he entertained the idea of something grand and noble giving rise to her being. Rise to her being?

Landsakes. If his mother heard him now she'd send her adult son off to bed like a small child, thoroughly convinced that he had succumbed to delirium.

"Edward, you've been out too long in the sun," she always told him, when she decided an idea of his had crossed the border of peculiar and entered the territory of outlandish.

"Think Edward, think," he said aloud, to channel all ideas and willpower into the solution. No explanations were forthcoming to offer any insight on why the painting possessed such a unique power. Unable to further deduce anything from the materials at hand, Edward decided that his only course of action could be to seek out Mr. Lefront or whatever remained of him. It would be no easy feat considering that war raged in his home country. Instead, Edward had to hope that Lefront, and not just his notebook, had journeyed to England. Like Hansel and Gretel's trail of breadcrumbs, Edward would search for whatever clues Lefront or the smiling lady had left for him.

CHAPTER ELEVEN
French-speaking Switzerland
1577

"Fire! Fire!" The calls filled the street in a haze of frenzied confusion. Thick smoke wrapped around Jean like a blanket of the roughest material, assembled from long coiled ropes rather than threads. Jean sputtered on the smoke. Her eyes burned and the heat of the flames lapped against her face, like tongues of hellfire.

"You feel that? You will soon feel it for eternity!" an angry voice shouted.

"Burn them, burn them all!" another voice said now, adding to the mayhem.

"Please sir, spare my child!" a voice cried in desperation. Jean could not see the woman who spoke the words, but from her crouched position behind the crates in the streets she could hear the agonized screams that came mere seconds later. As response to her pleadings, the man had killed both her and her child.

"We can't have anyone growing up outside of the true faith," he said, to no one in particular, when the act was completed. Jean's stomach lurched forward violently, as the bile rose and mixed with the remains of her morning meal. Too afraid to move for fear of detection, she struggled to not faint as the smoke pushed in around her.

Shaking like a tattered leaf in a gale Jean sat and waited, forced to witness the terrible slaughter around her. Footsteps pounded loudly against the street now, as a long shadow fell over her hiding place.

"You! Come out here and face God's judgment!" a voice roared, angrily. Was he talking to her? She had seen no one else but others could be cloistered in the shadows, seeking sanctuary as well.

"Jean! I said come out!" Her heart became a leaden weight, as a cold dread crawled over her skin and seeped into her bones. Panicked, she looked for a way to escape, but there was none. She was trapped. Mercilessly, there was not even any stick within close enough reach to wield in defense as a club. Jean had no other choice. She swallowed hard and prayed that God might be merciful and the horror short. Broad shoulders towered above her now, as the man ripped aside the crates she crouched behind.

"Time to meet your maker," he said, as he lifted her from her position by pulling harshly on her arm. His fingers gripped her neck. Jean's air supply dithered beneath the firm grip of his strangulation. His fleshy fingers pressed in stronger against her jugular. The man's eyes burned in conviction and seared his fingers to her neck. Jean struggled to break free.

"No, no, no," she woke up saying, as she gasped for air through her heavy panting. Her heart beat ferociously within her chest, as if it had decided that it would be the means of escape through its quickened paces and racing. Jean sat up. Her hair clung to her, plastering itself to the back of her neck. As she sat up, the blanket pulled from the sleeping form next to her. Sleepy eyes opened. Seeing the terror in Jean's face, she gently said,

"Another nightmare?"

Jean nodded. Anne sat up and hoisted her legs over the bed to cross to the water bucket.

"Here," she said softly to the younger woman.

Jean drank the water appreciatively, feeling it cleanse the fire of the man's grip and the weighty smoke that inhabited her lungs, though this reality had cleared five years before and not five minutes as it had in the dream.

When Jean set down the cup, her aunt opened her arms in a welcoming embrace to her. Ordinarily, those days were further removed from Jean. Painfully, their memory still could grip her in paralysis. At least, the everyday tasks of assisting a silk merchant, her uncle, usually kept her happily occupied to distract her from such thoughts. Nightmares could attack still though, unprovoked and unwelcome but still crippling, heartbreaking, and panic-inducing.

Certain that she would be unable to find peace if she tried to return to sleep now, Jean stood to pull her skirts and shawl over her shift. Anne was busy dressing as well, as she pulled up her long stockings. Jean shivered, more so from the chill that gripped her heart than from the gust of air that whispered through the crack at the bottom of the door.

The two ate breakfast mostly in silence. Anne knew that Jean would speak if she wanted to, but that sometimes the solitude was needed to restore a stillness to her heart. Five years ago, Jean had appeared at their doorstep in Paris, dripping wet from the rain and frozen in expression.

"What is it? What's happened?" Anne had asked her. Jean had been unable to speak.

"Come and sit beside the fire," Anne had offered to her niece, in an attempt to learn what horror had transpired.

"No! No! There mustn't be a fire! Put it out! Quickly!" Jean said, her eyes grown wide in terror at the sight of the flames.

Anne looked at her husband, who shrugged as if to ask if he should put it out. Anne nodded to Matthieu above Jean's head.

"It's all out, Jean. See?" Matthieu said in comfort to his niece a moment later, when he had doused the flames. Her eyes leaped up to him, as if surprised that there were others present than just her aunt.

"Who else is here?" Jean said, her eyes wide.

"Just Matthieu and me, Jean. You know that we live alone."

Jean nodded, but scanned the room to convince herself that they were really alone. Matthieu took a blanket from the bed and offered it to Jean.

"No! Don't choke me! Don't smother me!" she said, in

near hysterics. Though she addressed her uncle, she looked through him and seemed to speak to someone else.

"Jean," Anne said, "You are safe. You are with your Aunt Anne and your Uncle Matthieu. See?"

Jean's eyes focused on her aunt and then moved to her uncle and back again.

"Yes," she said at last. Anne reached for her hand and squeezed it gently.

"Now, suppose you tell us what happened." Matthieu stood behind his wife with his hand on her shoulder, so that Jean would feel their support but not be crowded.

"They're gone," Jean said, in barely a whisper.

"Who's gone, Jean?"

"They're gone, all gone," she repeated.

"Your mother, has something happened to your mother or to your father?"

Jean nodded.

"Which, Jean?"

"They're all gone," she repeated, "Mother and Father and little Louis."

Exhausted from the untold ordeal and having delivered so somber and heavy a burden, her head drooped and she fell asleep.

Early the next morning, before even the sun awoke, a knock pounded at their door. Matthieu stumbled from bed, having scarcely fallen back asleep after his niece's arrival.

"Matthieu, take Anne and leave. It isn't safe. It isn't safe for any of us!" their neighbor said, without first offering any greeting.

"What is this, Alain? What do you mean? What has happened? My niece arrived terrified in the middle of the night and now you say none of us is safe."

"Your niece is here? Then, your family must already be affected. They are coming to kill us all!"

"Who is, Alain? The English? Have the English returned?"

"No, Matthieu. It is our own countrymen. It is the Catholics."

Having learned of the imminent danger and of this horrible massacre of St. Bartholomew's Day, Matthieu had quickly packed what little belongings they could carry and fled Paris with his wife and their niece. They journeyed south, banding with other Huguenots along the way and eventually settling here in the French-speaking region of Switzerland.

Jean had grown from the young teenage girl, who lost her parents and brother and nearly her own life, into this sturdy and bright woman of twenty. Life with her aunt and uncle came easily, despite its difficult beginning. They had no children of their own and thus were able to devote their time to Jean. Pitying her loss and wanting to draw her from her darkness into the cheerful gilt of youth, Anne and Matthieu taught her their craft of selling silks. She learned to discern poorly made pieces from those that warranted a higher price tag. She became a valuable companion and source of help to them. With pride, Matthieu would remark that Jean could pick the best pieces and bargain for them better than any young apprentice. He observed her accomplishments with satisfaction, but he did not notice that one of these apprentices had set his sights on something else in the marketplace.

Paul had heard rumors of the terrible past that Jean had lived. Neighbors became concerned when a young girl awoke screaming, as she had so often in those earliest days. Questions had been asked and, when Jean was not present to hear, answers had been whispered. After all, they were among friends, many of whom had suffered similar fates of losing loved ones. Paul knew that if these rumors were correct, he would have to tread lightly lest he frighten Jean like a spooked horse and send her running. With a slow but steady persistence, he flitted around her that spring. Within a month, he was rewarded with a smile at their meetings. Within two months, there were discrete kisses at their partings. Matthieu had seemed surprised when Anne told him.

"But, I was right there. How could I have missed it all?"

She smiled patiently at her husband of fifteen years and kissed his confused face. By that autumn there were talks that when Paul accumulated enough money, arrangements would be made for their marriage. Anne would miss her constant companionship but Jean, who had endured so much, deserved this happiness.

Matthieu was away, helping a friend in a neighboring town repair his roof and so the two women were alone for now. The cold of night settled around them and it was warmer to share the one bed. It had been at least a month since the last dream and Anne wondered what had caused this one.

As their breakfast ended, she broke the silence to speak to her niece now.

"When Matthieu comes back, why don't you go to the market with him? There should be some lovely new pieces." Jean nodded, though she looked distracted.

"Perhaps, you will see Paul," Anne said, with a smile. Jean did not return her smile, but at least a look of focus appeared in her eyes.

Matthieu returned two days later and was delighted to have Jean accompany him. In the marketplace, Jean became lost in a world of textured fabrics from embossed brocades to the decadent creamy silks that were her family's specialty. Aromatic spices, newly popular from the east, greeted her nose as she strolled through the stalls with her uncle. They both knew where they were headed—to the little stall wedged between the tanners and the dyers that was near the back of the market. Despite being small, the most sumptuous fabrics flowed from these boards like the cascading waterfalls of the towering Alps around them. The merchant drove a hard bargain; Matthieu and he often squabbled over a matter of difference in price barely weightier than the air. But, he sold the fabrics that were of the highest quality and always the most in demand. Whatever expense Matthieu incurred here, he was certain to make double the amount in his own sale.

"Hello, ah, I see you have brought your niece. Hello to you too, Jean," he greeted them. Having returned the greeting, Jean asked,

"Anything new today?"

"So, it is straight to business young lady," he said, with a chuckle, "Yes, as a matter of fact, I have some new fineries from Venice. There are some beautiful pieces, dyed by a man named Francesco. A servant of a man was selling these pieces, told by his master to get rid of them. His wife or daughter or someone died and he wanted to be rid of everything associated with her. I am sorry for him, but it's good anyway for me and for you, my friends. I am sure you will agree." He pulled out a piece of the most beautiful silk that Jean had ever seen, as he said this. She could not help but reach out and touch its beauty, as if it were calling to her.

"Oh my," she said, softly.

"The lady likes!" the merchant said, clapping his hands together in delight.

Matthieu reached out his hand for his own inspection. Soon the deal was completed. The merchant smiled with the weight of the coins in his pocket from the agreed upon sum and Jean and Matthieu walked away with the box, well pleased with themselves at the purchase they made.

Later that evening, Jean unpacked the materials from the box. She held each up to admire its sheen in the soft flickering light of the fire. She no longer feared the flames and loved to watch them illuminate the silks, much as the moon sparkles on the sea.

"Oh that's beautiful!" Anne said in delight, at the deep blue that Jean held up for her to see.

"We certainly found treasures today, didn't we Jean?" Matthieu said, with a smile.
Jean dove into the chest of jewels to retrieve the next piece, a scarlet that seemed to burn with the intensity of the fire in the hearth.

"Oh, this is my favorite," she said, happily.

"I thought the green was your favorite," Anne said.

"Ah, but each piece is grander than the last, don't you think?" Her face shone as she spoke and Anne squeezed her husband's hand, both thankful for the upturn in Jean's demeanor.

"Well, you enjoy looking at the purchases, my girl. I must get some sleep," Matthieu said now.

"Yes, goodnight, Jean," her aunt said to her.

Jean sat closer to the fire, when the two had left for bed. The presence of another in a room has the ability to warm it, in a manner that is soon missed when one is left alone. The beautiful fabrics filled her lap. A handsome price would surely be gained for each piece, but it would be difficult to part with such objects of beauty. As the pile on her lap grew, she came to the bottom of the box more quickly than she would have wished. She began to refold the pieces to put back into the box.

"What's this?" she said, noticing something at the bottom. She set the silks onto the table and bent to loosen the piece from the box. She pried what seemed to be canvas free from the base. Lifting it out and turning it over, she momentarily forgot her silence to not awaken Anne and Matthieu.

"Oh!" she said, upon seeing the woman before her. She looked at this girl hidden beneath silks. From the painting, it looked as if she were dressed in some of these very materials or at least material similar. The silk mercantile industry captured her first observations, but her second thoughts were of the exotic nature of the painting. She had never seen a painting from so far south, assuming it was of Venice. Surely, it must be.

Jean tilted the painting in the light to better investigate

this new style. A piece of silk at the top of the pile tumbled loose and fell against the painting, catching the light of the fire as it did in a sort of prism.

"Why did you leave me?" Jean jumped at the words. She looked over her shoulders quickly, but no one was there.

"You left me. Why was it me?"

Gripped with fear, she pushed the painting back into the box and piled the fabrics over it. She dove into bed, burying herself beneath the blankets. Her heart thudded uncontrollably. For a long time she lay awake, too frightened to sleep. If the nightmares had new power to be this strong in the day, what would become of them with all the advantages of sleep? It was not something she wished to face.

When at last she did sleep, she was plagued by violent nightmares, not the one that repeated itself, but a nightmare of what had truly happened. She watched in horror as the baby that was killed was her own brother, Louis. Fear shattered her heart, as the man killed her mother moments later. From behind the box, she watched as her father was strangled. And then, most painfully of all, she watched herself run from them and abandon them.

She awoke with the belief that she was a traitor and the fear that she would not be forgiven and cast aside, if she were found out. The painting had to disappear, before it told her terrible secret to Anne or Matthieu or Paul. She couldn't bear the thought of any of them turning on her, if they knew the truth.

When Matthieu awoke, she was already dressed and offered to sell the fabrics. Having noticed the night before what delight she took in them, he consented that she should be allowed to complete the sale. The silks were divided among three patrons and by the end of the day, she walked home with coins jangling in her pockets and freedom from the painted lady.

CHAPTER TWELVE

Edward sat alone and stared at the painting. There had to be some simple explanation. Paintings could not read people. It was impossible. Wasn't it? Disbelief and then excitement comprised his first reactions. By now, his investigation getting him nowhere but deeper into confusion, he began to approach the problem with frustration. He began to convince himself that the painting had conspired with reality to play some elaborate prank on him.

"What do you want from me?" he thundered at it. But, of course, it made no reply. He hadn't bothered to give her mocking smile any reflection to cast her voice into. He knew that there would only be more questions. She was so apt to interrogate, but unwilling to answer any of his.

Edward paced from one side of the room to the other and wracked his brain. Was it the canvas? Was it the paint? The more he tried to unravel the answers, the more tangled they became like a ball of yarn a kitten clumsily dug its claws into until nothing but a chain of knots remained. Feeling claustrophobic from the questions, he needed to break free. The house, which opened its rooms to him to help shoulder the pain, no longer had enough space to hold his plague of questions. Grabbing his coat, he swung it over his shoulders and his arms jetted into the sleeves with the haste that he had once slammed down his helmet over his wearied head. He locked the door behind him and stepped onto the grounds. The first shoots of greenery reared their tiny heads above the soil. Tentatively they crept up, as if testing whether they preferred life in the cool early spring air or the dark but warm earthiness of the ground.

Agnes and the women of the town had been joined by the few men available to aid Edward in his garden plans. He was drawn, for some reason unknown to him, to the renewal of all that had been abused. Just as value and life had shattered before his eyes and inspired him to so carefully guard the fragile beauty unwrapped from the paper sheets of his home, having witnessed the marred and distressed ground diseased by battle found him needing to transform his own plot of frozen tundra into the hope and life of food to feed these people he now dwelt among. Long lines of seeds had been planted but, for now, only traces of these dormant possibilities appeared. Still, it was enough. Results had been produced and crops would yield their bounty. Edward's bitterness toward the painting defrosted some in the morning sun. Seed turned to shoots and would turn to food. Battle would turn to victory; for didn't every seed struggle for its survival from the earthen tomb that bound it? As unaware as it was and lacking all cognizance, still it succeeded. Surely the God who allowed such small seedlings to flourish would water the greenery of Edward's own struggles.

"Remember Edward, the birds are fed and the lilies clothed. God will always bring you what you need or help you get to where you need to go," his mother used to say.

He was not sure why her words came to him now. He had not thought of them for a long time, but upon remembering them his burden seemed a little less heavy.

"I remember," he said to the fields.

In reply, a gentle breeze blew across the land, sending a robin from its nest to the muddied ground below. Edward watched, as the robin fished for a long worm that he pulled loose from the ground and proceeded to gobble it. Another bird soon joined the first.

"You're right," he said to them, "I must go and speak to someone."

As he walked, thoughts of the painting leaped at him. The woman of paint had become the jealous female of his life who demanded all attention and became cross with him when she was too long neglected. Like the dutiful suitor, her beauty still captured him and he remained devoted and loyal even if he did find her methods taxing. Besides, it really was rather ridiculous to become upset with her. Real as she seemed to him, she was not. She had no feelings for him, so why should she rustle him? Having recommitted himself to the discovery of her secret and exhibiting only traces of residual agitation, his destination came into view.

"Edward! Is that you, Edward?" a voice called to him from the front porch.

"Yes, it's me, Martin," he said, in surprise.

"Well, go on," Martin said.

"Go on?"

"Aren't you going to ask me how I knew it was you?"

Edward still had not acclimated himself to the sense of playfulness that so enveloped his blind friend. Asking Martin how he knew it was him had not even crossed his mind. It seemed rude to ask him, but now it seemed that he would disappoint Martin if he did not ask.

"So, how did you know it was me?" he said, giving in to Martin's game.

He now stood before Martin and could see the smile plastered across his friend's face at the chance to provide the answer.

"Firstly, it is Tuesday morning." He looked pleased with himself as he said it, but Edward lacked the clarity to understand his deduction.

"Three people come regularly to visit me," he continued, "Mrs. Samuels brings me a bit of soup or bread every Saturday evening. Agnes does not have a regular day of visitation, but she is the second most frequent—lovely girl your cousin is and such a nice singing voice. And, then of course, there is you. Seeing as how this is a Tuesday morning and we are not at a time of school holidays, since it is early March, then my visitor must be you."

"But, what if I were not myself and someone outside of the three regular visitors?" Edward had forgot his earlier concern of seeming rude and was now drawn into the reasoning powers of Martin's mind.

"Well, in that case, I still knew it was you because you walk briskly, approaching quickly, as if you are escaping something, and then you shuffle as you draw nearer, perhaps because you do not wish to intrude."

Edward wasn't sure he liked this sudden ability that all around him seemed to have to read into his private stirrings and movements—first the painting and now Martin. He knew that Martin had not meant his observation as intrusion, though, and that he was forced to more keenly observe these nuances to adapt to his surroundings. Edward too had employed coping mechanisms.

"Well, you would make an excellent detective. You remind me of Sherlock Holmes," he said in reply.

"Oh have you read him? He really is fascinating, isn't he?" Martin said now, obviously elated at the praise.

"Well, come inside," he invited, as he stood from the chair and opened the door.

Edward followed Martin inside, noticing the impeccable nature of his house. On the few occasions that he had visited, he always marveled at the perfection of the upkeep. His own house burst with the contents of so many previous owners and eras. Edward knew, though, that if abrupt sounds and heavy silence could cause one to stumble, everything acoustic would be perfectly arranged in his domain as well.

"So what brings you here today, business or pleasure?" Martin asked.

"Both," Edward said. Just as Edward predicted, Martin had become invaluable to the garden plans. He knew the mechanics of the land and made several solid recommendations to Edward on how best to till the land and maximize the potential of the grounds. They discussed the optimal watering for the new sprigs, which Edward had noticed on his way out this morning. Perhaps, it had been a bit deceptive to allow Martin to believe that he had come to consult him on matters of the earth, when really he had come to seek sanctuary from the tempestuous relationship he shared with the lady of his house.

"Care for some tea?" Martin asked him now.

"Tea, yes. I'll get it for us."

Edward darted into the kitchen to prepare the tea and Martin continued to speak to him as he did.

"What do you make of this Zimmerman affair?"

"How's that?" Edward asked, unable to hear his muffled voice with the clatter of teacups.

"The Zimmerman affair," Martin repeated louder for him.

"It will certainly get the government's attention. And to think that Mexico would pull a stunt like that!" Edward said.

"I'm more surprised at the gall of the Huns!" Martin said.

Edward nodded and then realized what he had done and that Martin could not see his response.

"Yes," he said and then continued, "It worried Agnes. She started to wonder if California would be included in annexing the south."

"Is that where you're from? I never can seem to keep all your states straight past those original thirteen you stole from us," Martin said, with a teasing smile.

"I am, yes. San Francisco to be specific."

"Well, I'll tell you something Edward. If I were American and my country weren't part of this, I wouldn't have signed up to join." It was one of the few things that Martin had spoken without any hint of a joke. The moment of sobriety quickly passed, though, as the winsome smile reappeared and he said,

"What are you trying to do, become a hero before the others join so you have something to brag about? It might become your war soon enough. You didn't have to get a head start."

"It's been my war for a long time," Edward said. It was

the first time he staked a claim on it, the way the gold miners had in '49, when someone suggested it wasn't yet his war.

Martin nodded, that somber look crossing his face once again.

"Do you ever—" Edward began. They had come to new ground that required careful treading lest any ice remain from winter to slip through. Though joviality was more their style, they shared the common language of a battle-wearied veteran and thus their conversation on the matter required few words.

"Think about it all, you mean?"

"The fighting, the men," Edward said.

Martin looked thoughtful, an expression he wore rarely. That is not to say that he was immune to melancholia.

"I think we all do. How could we not?" Martin said at last.

"Then how do you face everything in jest? I suppose it must just be your character."

"Oh, I've not always been this way. I live in humor more than I ever did—before."

"How do you do it?" Edward asked now, in an earnest need to know.

"Because," he said, all traces of the smallest hint of a smile now in retreat, "if I do not live in humor, I will break."

Edward said nothing for a moment, suddenly feeling he had trespassed too far. He had pressed Martin, but would not have answered himself.

Deciding their chatter had become too cumbersome, Martin turned the conversation with the swiftness that a summer rain can be swept from a brilliant blue sky.

"I have a tart on the counter. Well, I say it's a tart but, Mrs. Samuels tells me only half the ingredients are present. Anyway, I think it smells divine. Would you care to join me?"

"A tart," Edward said, trying to keep up with the rapid change in topic, "Yes, that sounds nice."

Already, he was standing to fetch the tart for them.

"Oh and Edward," Martin called to him.

"Yes?"

"Put it on the blue plate, would you? I always eat tarts on the blue plates." To others, this request may have seemed eccentric. But, Edward reasoned that a blind man had the right to decide what color plate he wanted to eat from. After all, there were others with oddities even stranger than this. Some people talked to paintings and expected them to reply and, what was more, they actually did! It had seemed unwise to breach the subject with Agnes, but perhaps Martin could offer some insight. He had been able to speak to him today about things he had not even thought to bring up with others. Still, though, warfare was a commonality. They had both experienced the reality of it. Though at times it was insane, no one would debate its authenticity of existence. Edward, motivated by the quest for answers, pressed on in his decision.

"Martin, I—"

"Yes?" he said, as he busied himself with the tart before him, obviously taking no note of the missing ingredients.

"I want, no, I need to find out about—"

Martin continued eating either not noticing, or else ignoring, the seriousness in his voice.

A painting who is talking to me.

"The way the other houses are managing their lands," he said, instead.

"There's a few large houses around here that I'm sure you could find your information out from. To tell you the truth, I wouldn't mind walking there with you now when we finish. A nice spring walk may just be the perfect follow-up to this tart."

When Edward had cleared away the dishes, they embarked upon their journey in the crisp breeze of spring. Despite now being delayed from his true intention and being forced to walk with Martin, since he had seemingly suggested it, he didn't mind the walk. He had wanted to immerse himself in the subtle approach of the warming days, but his thoughts piled themselves too heavily when he was alone. With Martin's stream of verbosity, like the steady chirping of a bird, his thoughts could mingle softly with Martin's words but there was not the space for them to assert their oppression. Edward still had to concentrate in order to catch the words, like drops of rain in a bucket. Too heavy a rain could cause drops to miss their mark and too many stray thoughts could distract Edward from collecting the words.

"Now, we should be, I believe, approaching a rather large estate. You will, no doubt, wish to observe it for your research."

They had indeed stopped in front of a far-stretching piece of land with a house, both larger and grander than Edward's own that he had purchased.

"Aren't you going to ask me how I knew where we are?" Martin asked, in much the same manner that he had earlier.

"Was it based on the amount of time we had been walking?"

"By George, the Yank's got it," he said, with a chuckle. The house stood proudly among several acres.

"They've planted a garden, too," Edward said now, noticing faint traces of greenery that looked much the same as his own sprigs at home did.

"Good, good—what was that? I hear a female voice. She sounds pretty. Oh Edward, is she?"

Edward had not heard the voice. They were separated by a fence and she was a fair distance from them, but sure enough there was a girl there and yes, she was pretty.

"She's pretty," Edward said, "but, not alone. A man's with her."

"Shame."

CHAPTER THIRTEEN

"Lovely day," Clara said to Frederick.

"It is, but not as lovely as you," he replied.

Clara felt an inner blush at the stable boy's words. She hoisted the basket from one arm to the other. The wet clothes inside of it, freshly wrung and ready to be hung on the line, weighed heavily on her small frame. Her shoulders ached from the cumbersome load.

In her time here, she had taken on more than her share of work. Perhaps, she could have got away with completing half of it, but she knew that she had been taken in out of mercy and she wanted to convince everyone that her arrival had been a good idea.

Frederick certainly thought highly of her arrival. He had made it his personal mission to acquaint her with life in Rosebrim Manor. Often when Emma was showing her where next to go, Frederick would appear as if her very presence had summoned his coming. He was dark and swaggering in appearance and Emma had, on more than one occasion, remarked that he reminded her of a drawing of a pirate she had seen.

Emma herself embodied the quintessential English housekeeper to the point of reliability, but not to the point of tedium. Place settings always sparkled their best when she laid them out. Food, although limited with the blockades, managed to turn out that extra bit tastier when she touched it, even if she had only strained a soup or sliced the bread. Emma was both ubiquitous, overseeing and tending to all areas of life within the house, but also strangely absent whenever Clara needed to consult only her on a matter, when no other face—no matter how cheery or helpful—could provide the needed assistance. Though never married and without children, Emma instantly fell into the role of grandmother to Clara as if such a bond had always existed between the two. She wore a welcoming smile and provided a reassuring word when Clara's memory slipped, as it was still prone to do.

Emma, for all her normality, had eccentricities of her own. Clara soon learned, and then relearned on a few occasions when having forgot, that Emma took her tea always with the tiniest pinch of pepper. Why she did such a thing, Clara could hardly guess and Emma herself could not even explain. It was something that she had started many years before Clara was born and it had become a habit that she had been unable to abandon. And then, there was the humming. Emma would hum a different tune depending on what activity occupied her. When asked what song she was humming while folding the linens one day, Emma replied that she hadn't even realized that she was. With the back of her hand, she had secured a stray graying hair behind her ear and continued humming as she returned to the folding. Clara smiled, realizing that Emma was most likely oblivious to her melodic song.

Rosebrim Manor provided many occasions for a smile to leak from Clara's mouth. With a feather duster in her hand, she became acquainted with the leather clad volumes of gold-edged pages of the books on the library's shelves. With a polishing cloth, she admired the delicately etched flowers and birds on the silver. When she folded the tablecloths, her fingers were caressed by fine linens, silks and damasks. In the kitchen, Emma would often ask her opinion on a sauce or dish. Clara suspected this was more so that she would be subjected to the tasting of delicious food, than that someone with Emma's years of experience really needed Clara's culinary advice. In the garden, she watched with delight as the first shoots from the seeds they had sown began to appear. Overhead, birds gathered twigs to build their nests for spring. It was a gentle life that Clara found herself embarked upon, full of the demureness of the country and the benefit of cheerful friends.

The sea is not without ripple, though, and neither was life at Rosebrim Manor without event. At night, a cold wind blew through the cracks beneath the doors and sent an eerie wail racing down the corridors. Lady Pemblebrooke would often awake, shrieking in a haunting duet with the wind, and waking all others in the house. Clara had shot up in bed, her heart racing like a thousand horses, when she had first heard the noise.

"Clara," Emma called to her now, as she spoke to Frederick under the decidedly more pleasant, pale sun than the unsettling cries of night.

"Yes?" she said, turning so quickly that the basket tottered and Frederick put out a hand to disrupt its fall.

"Lady Pemblebrooke wishes to see us when her tea is served at four. Come to me when you're finished with that, would you?"

"Yes, Emma," Clara said.

Though Emma spoke in her usual tone, her face slightly betrayed her calm demeanor and, in that moment, Clara knew that she was not the only one who had come to feel uneasy toward the lady of the house. As if reading her thoughts, Frederick said now,

"I think I have the better deal, on my way to visit the animals rather than Lady Pemblebrooke."

"Is she really so bad?" Clara said.

Frederick stopped abruptly in his walking and turned to her,

"You mean you have not even met her?"

"I— " Clara's head began to whirl. She had no recollection of having spoken with Lady Pemblebrooke before, but now she realized that surely she must have spoken to her at some point during the month, two months, oh how long had it been? As her nerves heightened, her memory's reliability deserted her. A great unsteadiness swooped down upon her, like a hawk circling it prey. Frederick took note of her paling complexion and panic-stricken face.

"What is it, Clara? Are you unwell?"

"I—I can't remember," she said, quietly.

"You can't remember what?"

She swallowed. Her stomach hung heavy within her, from the tangled mess of knots it had succeeded in tying itself into. Feeling very ashamed and exposed, she said,

"I can't remember, if I have met her before."

Frederick blinked and she could not tell if it were in disbelief or if the sun had irritated his eyes.

"Frederick?" Emma reappeared, calling to him this time.

"Yes?"

"Come and help me move this chest, will you?"

He disappeared to help Emma, leaving Clara holding the laundry and their conversation unfinished.

"Have I met her before? I've been here awhile. Surely, I must have met her," she said to the sheets and towels, as she hung them on the line. The stark white fluttered easily in the breeze, billowing out like sails of a boat. The beauty and purity of white disappeared in the emptiness Clara saw there. The vast whiteness mirrored her mind- one blank and open abyss. Others may have seen such a situation as an opportunity for possibility, but for Clara it was a desperate reality of isolation and separation. A bird broke into her thoughts with a cheerful song as if he had taken it upon himself to bolster her spirits.

Clara's hands trembled, as she draped a tablecloth over the line. Her conversation with Frederick had rattled her nerves and unseated her confidence. She finished the task and hurried back inside to help Emma with the tea. Glancing at the carriage clock on the mantel, as she entered the foyer, she saw that it was only half past three. Perhaps, she could find Frederick and finish their talk. Just then, though, Emma hurried down the stairs.

"Oh good, you're here. Lady Pemblebrooke has requested that we serve her tea now. She says she does not wish to wait until four and that we are to bring it to her presently."

Emma's face reddened in her haste of movement and a handful of curls had come unpinned and bounced rambunctiously around her ears. Clara had never seen so much of Emma's hair before and hadn't realized it was curly. If Lady Pemblebrooke could send Emma, so calm and steady, into a fluster then she must be a very stern woman indeed. Clara opened her mouth to ask if she had met Lady Pemblebrooke before, but Emma was already rushing from the room toward the kitchen. Feeling like a duckling running after its mother, when a seagull is in pursuit of the two, Clara followed Emma who promptly pushed a tray into her arms. Clara held the tray as Emma bristled about, filling it with teacups and saucers and then changing her mind and switching the teacups with those locked in the china cabinet.

An uneasiness spread through Clara, as she watched Emma turn to the table and cut sandwiches she had prepared earlier into quarters. Emma, who was never without a song for a chore, was silent. No humming slipped from her lips. Clara stood silently as well, unsure of what to say or how to say it. The tray, weighted down by the teacups, saucers, teapot, creamer, sugar bowl and now sandwiches, pulled on Clara's already strained arms. When she had just begun to warm to the idea of leaving the kitchen to go to Lady Pemblebrooke, so that she could at least put down the tray, Emma took the teacups off once again and replaced them with those originally present. For a moment, Clara wondered if she weren't the only one with a faulty memory. The thought, however, was dismissed when Emma said,

"She likes those cups better."

Clara nodded not so much in agreement, for she had no idea which tea service Lady Pemblebrooke preferred, but out of acknowledgment. Somehow, she felt that this woman who had been her anchor of memory so often now needed the same steadiness of companionship from her.

"Right, we'll go now then," Emma said and turned to leave.

"Emma?"

"Yes? What have I forgot? The milk?"

"No, you've not forgot anything. It's just that your hair slipped free."

Emma's hands hurried to her hair, lifting the pins and tucking the curls back into place.

"My heavens! So it has," she said, as she did.

When complete, Emma turned to leave the kitchen once again with Clara at her heels. They were halfway up the stairs, when Emma turned abruptly. Clara steadied herself against the sudden halt, so as not to drop the tray.

"When we get inside, I'll serve. I know how everyone takes their tea."

"Everyone?" Clara asked, weakly. She had thought she would soon be face-to-face with the formidable Lady Pemblebrooke, but she had not envisioned others present with her.

"Albert, she always was a devoted servant of Queen Victoria, and Mary, named for our present queen."

"And they are—friends?"

"Oh no, they are Lady Pemblebrooke's children."

"Oh—yes, of course," Clara said. The uneasiness, which had begun to abate, returned with a new vigor. She had never seen children here and why should they be hidden? Or, if they were not, then she perhaps had not only forgot Lady Pemblebrooke but two other persons as well. Either predicament was chilling, but there was no time to think about it any longer. They had reached the top of the stairs and Emma's hand stood poised to open the door. Before doing so, she turned her head over her shoulder to ensure that Clara was ready. Clara nodded and Emma opened the door more slowly and tentatively than

Clara had seen her open other doors.

Clara followed Emma inside and was surprised to be met by so dreary an interior. The plush curtains were drawn closed, though the sunlight still filtered through the windows in the rest of the house. The colors of the furnishings were darker here than in other rooms and more muted, as if even pigment feared seeming too ostentatious in front of Lady Pemblebrooke. The oaks and maples Clara polished in the other furniture of the house were absent here and instead the darker and more somber mahogany almost entirely outfitted the room.

Emma rushed forward to prepare the tea and from the shadow Clara saw the prim and diminutive Lady Pemblebrooke. She lacked all the harshness that Clara thought she would embody and seemed more like a frightened child than the beneficiary of so grand a manor. And as for the children, Albert and Mary lacked all the regalia of their names and instead flitted like nervous birds around their mother's skirts. Lady Pemblebrooke spoke hardly a word but looked up, startled at Clara's presence as if she had suddenly appeared having materialized from the dust beneath the floorboards. Quickly, the event was completed and Clara's anxiety had been supplanted by confusion.

"Let's have our tea now, Clara," Emma suggested. As they descended the stairs, a song once again whispered from her lips in that pleasant hum that Clara had missed earlier. When they'd entered the kitchen, the humming changed and yet another tune issued forth as they sat to tea. Emma's humming was really rather comical to watch, because as soon as her hands switched to a new task the notes followed. On many occasions Clara had found herself humming along in her head, only to have the next note lurch horribly off key because Emma had drifted into another song entirely.

The steam rose tantalizingly from Clara's cup, bathing her face in its warmth. Emma dropped the habitual pinch of pepper into her cup and sat back against the chair. For awhile they enjoyed the break in their routine without words, but a question pressed against Clara's mind and had its way at last, as she said,

"Who is Lady Pemblebrooke in mourning for?"

"England," Emma said, without further explanation and then continued in her humming.

CHAPTER FOURTEEN
London
1686

Jacqueline slipped her hand into Richard's, as they stood side-by-side at the ship's rail. He squeezed it slightly, but said nothing as he watched the shore come into view. Wisps of smoke rose from the timbered houses of the crowded banks of the Thames. Jacqueline hoped that their dreams would not dissipate into the smoke, carried away by a fire like the one that had swept the city twenty years before. So much could change in an instant, without any need of intervention from fire. Hostile tempers could erupt in dangerous flames that were not content, until every life was charred and all hope was snuffed out. Jacqueline shut her eyes momentarily, to block these thoughts. They were here to begin a new life and she would not allow Louis XIV, who had outlawed their religion yet again when he reversed Henri IV's Edict of Nantes from 1598 and enacted his own Edict of Fontainbleu just months before, to take this moment from her.

"There she is," a voice beside her said. It was not Richard who had spoken, but a voice that sounded very like his. In fact, Jacques was growing more like his father in voice and mannerism every day it seemed. And though Jacqueline took pride in the man her son was becoming, she sometimes found herself longing for the days when he had climbed onto her lap. Now was not the time to dwell upon the past though. The sun in the sky above spoke of bright hope for the future. With decrees issued that all Huguenot churches must be destroyed and with the practice of their religion outlawed, one could easily fear that those horrible days of the War of Religion at the end of last century would return. They would not wait for the murderers to hunt them down and kill them in cold blood, as they had in generations before. Louis and his queen were sending a clear message that no Protestants were welcome in France. When he announced on

January 17th of this year that only about a thousand of the original 800,000 to 900,000 Huguenots were still present in France, Jacqueline, Richard, and Jacques were not among them.

Not all the royalty of Europe was so opposed to the Huguenots, though. Charles II of England offered his country as refuge for the discarded French. Their friends had journeyed to other nations, as well, including Denmark, Brandenburg-Prussia, Hapsburg, South Africa and Switzerland. Jacqueline had been tempted at the thought of Switzerland. Her family had sought sanctuary among the Alps a hundred years before, but had returned to France when it was safe enough to do so. Part of her felt that such a move would send her family backward, though, and the prospect of England seemed like the way forward. More than this, her brother Michel had settled in London already when tensions had begun to tighten at Richelieu's bidding.

"I don't want to find that these ropes of curtailment have been pulled so taut they've formed a noose around my neck," he had told Jacqueline, when announcing his departure. She had dreamed of this day since Richard and she had decided to relocate to London. A hundred questions had encircled her mind: what would it look like? What would it smell like? Would the people accept them? Would Charles change his mind and force them to once again leave, to become vagrants? She hoped that they might stay, if her first glimpses as they walked through the street now were any indication of what the city could provide. Yes, it was crowded but, she found the masses of people invigorating. Yes, it was dirty but, at least food scraps lined the streets and not blood. As for the smell, the horses mingled with the sewage, but every once in a while someone's bread baking would waft before her and she would be reminded of the gnawing hunger in her stomach and that it had been a considerable amount of time since she had eaten.

Her hunger was soon satisfied at her brother's table and, what was more, her heart was filled with delight.

"Jacqueline! You are here," Michel had said, overjoyed at the sight of his sister and throwing his arms around her in a warm embrace. They sat together now, filled with the satisfaction of food and the promise of a new life.

"You will like it here," Veronique, Michel's wife said, as she cut another slice of bread and offered it to the others.

"Here in Spitalfields, our lodgings are cheaper than in other parts of the city," Michel said.

"And the food too," Veronique added.

"And what is best," Michel said, the others pausing in their eating to look at him as he spoke and he prompting them to continue, "we have more control over our rights, including in our guilds."

Richard nodded, pleased at the thought of freedom in his silver working. Jacqueline's family had a long history in the silk industry and Michel carried on the craft here.

"Come on, Jacques I will show you where the work takes place," he said to his nephew, when the boy of sixteen seemed at last to have reached his full, after three heaped plates of food. Jacqueline and Richard, curious themselves, followed the two for the tour of the house. It was larger than any of them had expected and filled with the finery not only produced within this house, but of neighbors as well. Silver glittered with decorative motifs that Richard paused to admire. Jacqueline found herself in a dream of curtains and carpets and she was transported to the years now long past when she had watched in wonder as her father unpacked new silks he brought home.

"And now, the best part," Michel said, as they stopped in front of a small door several flights up from where they had eaten. He opened the door and the four gathered inside a room, which much like the house itself, was larger and grander than anyone expected.

"Look at the windows!" Jacqueline said.

"Such light!" Richard marveled. The room shone with

benefit of greater sunlight than one would expect in an attic. Windows, much larger than ordinarily bedecked such dwellings, stationed themselves around the walls and cast a warm glow on several looms. They were abandoned now, their workers scheduled to return the following day.

As he gazed out the window onto the rooftops of London, Jacques noticed that many of the other houses close by also had these same large uncharacteristic windows.

"Are there many weavers here, Uncle?" Jacques said.

"Ah, you are very observant. You have surmised this from the other windows," he said, smiling, "Yes, indeed, there are many weavers. In fact they now call Spitalfields, 'Weaver town'."

Jacques looked thoughtful and continued to observe his new home from above.

"Perhaps, you would like to study with me? I can teach you all about the family industry," Michel said. And then, looking quickly toward Richard to ensure he had not caused offense said,

"If your father does not mind that is. Of course, the silversmiths are a fine guild to study in as well." With a shrug of his shoulders to convey that no harm was committed, Richard said,

"Jacques is free to choose what he would like to study. This is a new land for us after all."

Jacques made no reply as the two men discussed his future, but as he stared out the window Jacqueline watched the smile play across his face. Yes, England would provide all they hoped for.

⁂

Life in England agreed with Jacqueline and Richard. At Michel's and Veronique's invitation, they took up residence within the house while Richard established his silversmith business. With Richard's skill and Jacqueline's support, a viable business grew in the heart of Spitalfields and soon enough money was accumulated to move into a home of their own. Though she loved her brother and sister-in-law dearly, Jacqueline relaxed into life in London within her own home. A steady community of other Huguenots built around them, complete with industry and churches. In freedom, the Huguenot community flourished. If one could forgive France for its grave injustice, Louis almost had to be pitied for allowing so much talent to leave its shores.

Jacques, ambitious to a fault, was not content to choose only one trade and studied to be a silversmith under his father and learned the intricacies of the looms and silks with his uncle's guidance. Craftsmanship was not the only thing that Jacques learned in his new home. Having spoken French all his life, he found himself immersed in a land of English. Within Spitalfields French often surrounded him. When he ventured farther into the city, to sell his wares with his father or uncle, the business necessitated English. What began as strange sounds that clashed harshly in his ears soon rested easier, until one day he found those same combinations of letters—which had been such horrible foreign utterances—escape from his own lips as intelligible snippets of communication. With time the words found themselves strung together as sentences that conveyed their meaning, if somewhat awkwardly on occasion. Just as those sounds warmed to his hearing, the sentences began to smooth themselves into straightened lines that no longer wobbled in uncertainty.

In his adopted country, with benefit of the language and with his parents' business now thriving, Jacques learned what it feels like for the wind to tug at one's heart and urge one onto the next adventure that can be claimed as one's own. His parents' dream, born of necessity, fashioned Jacques into the man he was. Now, a man well into his twenties, he felt the need to eke out his own life. It was not that Jacques felt any need or desire to distance himself from his family, but rather that he was pulled toward the horizon. Since the first day in his uncle's attic, when he had smiled at the prospects of his future, the idea of something bigger ingrained itself within his life. Each boat that sailed into England brought stories of the New World. As he began to understand what was being said by the sailors, he found himself swept away in a sea of longing.

His parents, especially his mother, had claimed England proudly as their new home. Jacques's life offered satisfaction, but he was imbued with the restless spirit of one who has not yet entirely settled.

"What is it, Jacques?" Jacqueline said now, as she rested her hand on her son's shoulder.

"Just thinking," he said. She sat down in the chair across from him and looked into his eyes from across the table.

"Tell me," she said and the look in her eyes, that she already suspected the stirrings of his heart, compelled him to speak. He was not fully decided on the matter, until he spoke the words to her now,

"I have decided to go to the New World."

She said nothing and sat perfectly still, letting a smile wash over her as his words sank into her, like a boot in the soft sand of the shoreline. She reached for his hand and clasped it in hers.

"Do you remember what you said to me, when we first sailed into London?"

"No, I don't remember," he said, wondering at what his words had been.

"You said 'there she is' but I think I always knew, at least relatively soon anyway, that London would not to be all there was for you. You were always a little boy of dreams and some lose these dreams as they age but the lucky ones, the special ones, their dreams grow bigger as they become older. Your dreams have grown with you and heaven knows I will miss you my boy, but I know this is a journey you must take. God bless you on it."

He swallowed, digesting his mother's words that had taken him off-guard.

"Thank you," he said at last.

"Now, I have something I want you to take with you." She stood to retrieve whatever it was. Jacques said, with a laugh,

"I am not leaving tonight."

"I know," she said, "but, I want you to have this. The time is right."

From the bottom of a cabinet, made by one of the local merchants, she pulled out a beautiful blue silk that shimmered with the luminescence of the moon's glow on the water. She passed the silk to Jacques and he could tell that something was wrapped inside of it.

"Go ahead," she said, with a nod of affirmation. His hands deftly unwrapped what he could now see to be a canvas from the silks.

"This has been in my family since the days we were in exile in Switzerland."

Jacques looked down at the portrait his mother spoke so fondly of now and took in the young lady smiling up at him that was to be his companion.

"Thank you," he said.

"The painting has traveled to France and then with us to England. Now that you are journeying to the New World, take her along. She's always been special."

CHAPTER FIFTEEN

Somewhere in the Atlantic

1700

A path of silver satin emanated from the aura, surrounding the blazing moon, across the sea toward Jacques. The saltiness of the water clustered in his nose, seasoning the journey as the vessel rocked slowly from side to side in the lull of the waves tonight. He leaned back against the mast, watching the horizon for the approach of his future with each passing moment. The excited titter of French, which danced through his ears from the other passengers by daylight, was absent now. Only the lapping of the waves against the hull and the creaking of the wood, giving in to the power of the sea, offered their gentle serenade.

His mother would appreciate such beauty, though when the weather hissed about the stern throwing up the sea and wrapping it in a prison of tempestuous winds she would pray for land. No, she would not endure a passage with the ease that he did and ease was a relative term, for even Jacques had suffered the nauseating powers of a lurching boat and feared that it would snap in two under the mighty and merciless winds.

No, it was better that he was alone. His parents he feared, though not feeble, were too fragile for the crossing. His mother's eyes were framed by creases and his father's shoulders seemed thinner, when he had told them goodbye at the docks. When had they aged? For a moment he had doubted his decision to leave, but a look in his mother's eyes soon convinced him to carry through his plans. He had not noticed the effects of the years' advance in his daily life with them. When he had taken in each detail of their faces to carry with him, the images merged to produce a portrait in his mind that had been unnoticed before.

Of course, he was not alone. The painted lady smiled at him often on his voyage, as he unwrapped her to peer into her loveliness. His mother had said she had been a part of the family for many years and he wondered if the woman depicted were some distant relative. His family had handled silks for many generations and his uncle's establishment, already successful, was sure to strengthen with silk dresses becoming the fashion for far greater numbers than before. The women in his family, he presumed, had always worn silks. Perhaps, he looked into the eyes of some great-grandmother now.

He took a biscuit from his pocket and gnawed at it. His appetite, difficult to satisfy on land, had become unquenchable at sea. The biscuit was hard and hurt his teeth as he bit into it and, what was worse, it tasted of sawdust. No doubt the rats, which he had seen aboard, would enjoy the food more but he did not have the luxury of being picky with his rations. Reaching into his pocket he pulled a similar shape out. It was equally as hard, but far superior. The moon's glow caught the gleam of the silver in his hand and magnified its brilliance. His father had placed a bag of silver on the table in front of him in those days shortly after he announced his decision to leave.

"What is this?" Jacques had asked Richard.

"You will need it. Silver has provided our livelihood and silver will give you a new life."

"But, it's too much. I can't take this," Jacques had countered.

"Consider it your salary for all your years of work," his father said, knowing that he had raised a man who was content only in having what he had earned. And so, with the gift of silver from his father, silks from his uncle, clothing, supplies, and the portrait from his mother, Jacques ventured to the other side of the world and the very reaches of the fringe of civilization.

He spun the silver coin through his fingers now, the cold metal contrasting with the warmth of his hand. With his legs stretched before him and the painting resting against them he looked again into her face, drawn to her likeness with an inexplicable need to commune with her.

"Remember," a voice said. Jacques jumped. The voice had sounded like his mother's but was stronger, more vibrant, and more urgent than a memory. He looked at the painting hard, confused at what had happened.

"Remember that," the voice said again. In his surprise, the silver coin dropped from his hand and landed with a thud on the deck. Without moving his eyes from the painting he felt around for the silver. His fingers crawled across the deck like a spider. For awhile he felt only wood, but at last the metal pressed into his flesh and he scooped it up and pocketed the coin.

"Remember what?" he whispered, now focusing solely on the portrait and without distraction.

Jacques sat in captivated silence, waiting for the completion of his message but the words did not come. Sleep remained absent for the rest of the night and Jacques continued to stare at the painting. As the first whispers of dawn danced across the horizon, he breathed in the new day. With the comfort of light, he began to doubt that he had heard anything at all the night before. Tiredness crowded his senses, confusing his faculties. Sailing had numbed his perception and he had been thinking of his parents and so it was natural that he would hear his mother's voice. How many times had she told him to remember something before? Hundreds. Thousands.

"Remember to say your prayers."

"Remember to stop by the workshop after lunch."

"Remember to deliver this order."

"Remember where you have come from."

With the constancy of the new day breaking over him and dissolving the bewitching magic of the night, he wrapped the portrait and laid her aside.

⟶•⟵

"Look!" an excited young voice called out, with finger

fixed firmly on the horizon. A bevy of movement coursed through the ship, as the Huguenots aboard raced forward to see their first glimpses of the New World. Jacques's mind was drawn to a memory he had stored in the annals of adventure. He could almost smell the streets of London; he could fairly taste the bread of Veronique's and Michel's table from that first morning in England. His hand settled on the rail of the ship now, as his memory transformed the rail to his mother's shoulder. He had rested his hand on her when entering London harbor.

"Remember," he heard a voice within him say, much as it had last night. It was muffled now, though, like an echo of the past recalled rather than the clarity of a conversation as it is spoken.

"What do you think?" a sailor, who had spoken with him throughout the journey, asked now throwing his thumb toward the land to gesture to it. Jacques's eyes traveled the length of the land. Thick gatherings of conifers crowded the shores much as the buildings of London had. In contrast there were no signs of life here, though he knew that settlers had lived in Virginia for almost a hundred years now.

"Plenty of land," Jacques said, in reply. The sailor chuckled and slapped him on the back.

"Well, you can keep your land. Too wild for me. No, give me the sea and a real town to come home to."

Jacques nodded in politeness, hoping his own sentiments would not soon echo those of the sailor. What exactly was he doing anyway? He had a strong future of lavish luxury built on the sturdy foundation of dedicated hard work and he had turned his back on it, exchanging it for a life of wilderness. Perhaps, he had been too hasty in his decision. Only a crazy man would chose the barren and dangerous over the established and secure, wouldn't he? For all these doubts that gathered at the corners of his mind, as he stepped from the ship, his footing fell firmly onto the Virginia soil as if it had drawn him to its shores.

As he walked his first steps, his feet wobbled under him confused by the sudden levelness of the ground beneath them. The sun, though shining brightly, seemed smaller when he looked to it and higher in the sky than he was used to. Instead of the competing smells of the city, a slight muskiness mingled with pine clung to his nose. His journey was not yet complete, though, or his destination reached. Governor Nicholson had determined the arriving Huguenots were to settle up the James River farther inland, rather than remaining in the Hampton area where they had docked. Not all the settlers were planning to remain together. Jacques was to travel onto Manakin Town, while many of the others stayed in Jamestown, their first stop up the James River.

Stone buildings dotted the landscape, as Jacques saw his first settlement in Virginia. A fortress, unlike the sturdy walls of the Tower of London, encompassed the settlement with its walls of wood. Jacques knew it had been built as protection against the native tribes and that unfavorable interactions had sometimes taken place. Some of the stories told could turn a grown man's blood to a river of ice, but Jacques paid little attention to the tales. Where he would settle in Manakin Town was on the remains of an old Manacan tribal village and now served as a sector of frontier intended to provide a buffer between the native tribes and the English settlers.

Just how remote the town was became clear as Jacques departed the first capital of Virginia, which had proceeded the current capital of Williamsburg, to press deep into the untamed lands. He carried few belongings and did not have to pay for the transport of his goods since they fit tidily into his bag slung across his broad back, which had bent over the silver that he hammered in his father's shop so many times. Though he had contributed to the pooled funds of the settlers and received a portion of his allotment to buy food and supplies in Jamestown, a considerable number of coins were still tucked safely into the pouch his father had given him and—if he momentarily lost his footing—he would both hear and feel their reassuring jangle.

Life in Virginia was difficult, but steady. Cold winters exasperated illness among many of his fellow settlers and threatened their depleting food supplies. By the first spring, Jacques found his pouch of coins considerably lighter than when he had first arrived. The spring brought with it the first signs of his planting. He nearly jumped for joy at the sight of them, after what had seemed to be a never-ending winter. His house was a skeleton of starved bones compared to the homes he had lived in all his life. The James River parceled the land into desolate outposts of civilization scattered among a savage boundary of life in this New World.

The Old World had sprung from the hands of the farmers and so it seemed life would here as well. The years of training as one of the finest craftsmen of Europe were set aside, temporarily hibernating as the wild beasts and snakes of this land did in the winter, until a time when life dictated that enough was established for them to find a place again.

Symbolically, the portrait did not yet have a place either, because Jacques had decided that it would remain packed until he brought in the first harvest. Dreaming about the portrait of the painted lady, and when he would again gaze on her, had motivated him through some of the coldest and darkest days of winter. As he watched the corn plants begin to grow now, he said aloud,

"I shall see my friend soon!" His voice thundered through the lands surrounding his with only the squirrels and deer frolicking through the countryside to hear. Jacques was the only man for miles around in this secluded pocket of land. At least that is what he thought, but as a bush rustled now and he raised his rifle toward it if he should need to fire in defense or to provide meat if it were a juicy piece of venison or hare, his breath drew in quickly. It was not an animal that had stepped from the foliage, but a man. He was dressed in animal skins and his hair was as black as the ravens in London. He stood in the clearing, his tanned sun glistening in the sun. Jacques's rifle remained trained on the man, but the man showed no sign of fear. Why should a man look so confident when standing unarmed before the threat of bullets? Unless—a chill descended over Jacques. Unless, he was not alone and others waited to emerge from the trees as he had. He took a step forward and Jacques's grip tightened.

The man gestured toward the rifle and moved his hand to one side to illustrate that Jacques should discard of the weapon. Jacques, who had never trained as a fighting man, had common sense enough not to throw aside his only hopes of survival should a war party suddenly descend on him. Perhaps, these tribes were in league with the Catholics and would not be satisfied until every Huguenot was butchered. The other man did not easily give up his request though and when Jacques would not relinquish control of his weapon, he changed tactics and threw aside his own spear so that Jacques would be clear of his intention. Jacques, still skeptical, waited to be certain it was not a trick and then he laid down his own rifle.

"Friend," the man said, in shaky English.

Jacques's head cocked to the side in surprise.

"You speak English?" Jacques asked, himself now fluent in that which had once been foreign.

"Friend," the man repeated. Jacques remembered that he had just declared aloud that he would have a friend, moments before the man appeared. Perhaps, he was only repeating what he had heard. If that were true, though, then it seemed very coincidental that he was acting in a manner synonymous with the word he was using.

"Friend," Jacques said now.

As if some treaty had been signed the man stepped forward and shook his hand, obviously acquainted with the ways of the white men.

"I am Jacques," he introduced himself.

"Jack, yes, friend," he said, without offering his own name. Jacques was about to ask him for it but the man had already turned away, busying himself in the inspection of Jacques's crops. He crouched low to the ground and whispered something in an ancient language to the tiny sprouts. Turning back to Jacques, he said,

"Good. Use fish."

"Fish?" he said, as he bent to more closely see what the other man had.

"Fish helps grow," he explained, picking up a handful of soil and showing with his hands how to mix the two together.

"Thank you," Jacques said.

He nodded.

"It makes good. My fathers do this for many moons."

"What is your name?" Jacques asked now, thinking it was only fair to know who had delivered such sage advice.

"Too hard for you. You say John for me."

Jacques laughed and John's smile spread steadily as well. Though never asked or arranged, John visited Jacques and the corn daily after the first meeting. When John saw the silver and silks and Jacques told him it was the work of his fathers for many moons John wanted to set up trade. Jacques agreed that after the corn was complete, he would trade with John and his tribe. The day of the harvest brought an extended visit from John. The yellow kernels glowed more beautifully than any gold he had seen and the corn's silk felt more luxurious than any fabric he had dealt with. Jacques bent to retrieve the bag with the painting inside, when the two men had eaten the evening meal together. John watched expectantly for what Jacques would unveil.

"My mother gave me this."

"Very beautiful," John said, bending in for a closer look.

Brightly colored beads, traded by the whites with the tribes since the last century, adorned his shirt. As he bent in to look, Jacques noticed the painting reflected in one of the beads. John jumped back, as if he had been stung by a bee.

"What is it?"

"It talks."

"What did it say?" Jacques asked, sitting forward.

"I go now," John said and stood to leave.

Jacques sat there with the painting before him, unsure of what had happened. He hadn't imagined it after all! The night on the boat the painting had spoken to him. But, what had it said to John? He had left abruptly and so must have received a more coherent message than that which Jacques received. He stared at the painted lady, but her lips were tightly sealed and she was unwilling to divulge any further secrets to him.

Jacques waited all the next day for John to arrive, but he did not come. The following day passed without any sign of him either. Perhaps he had never intended to come after the harvest, but Jacques felt that the painting must have something to do with it. Seven days passed without a visit from John. Having had a friend and fearing him lost now was more painful and lonely than being isolated in a foreign land. When the eighth day came, he was convinced that he would not see John again. Silently, though, he appeared in the clearing the way that he had on the first day of spring in those months before.

"John!" Jacques said, in delight.

"Jack," he said, but looked serious as he continued, "I must go."

"Where?"

"My people must go south to the place you call North Carolina."

"Will you return?" He felt foolish for asking, but he felt he had to. John shook his head.

"Come and eat with me before you go," Jacques offered.

John consented and they sat together, as they had so many times before, for one last time. As John prepared to leave, Jacques glanced up at the painted lady reminded of his last painful parting. He noticed how once again the bead captured the reflection of the painting.

"I will remember you. Remember me," a voice said and this time Jacques did not doubt its origin.

CHAPTER SIXTEEN

"Clara, hello!" Frederick said, as he came into the kitchen now.

"Hello, Frederick," she said, still unsure of what to make of Lady Pemblebrooke. He sat beside her, inviting himself to some of the soup that she was eating. He ladled a bowlful of the thick broth punctuated by dollops of vegetables. Clara's own bowl laid half uneaten in front of her and she couldn't help, but feel the murkiness of the soup crowd in among her own thoughts.

"Some hidden message in your soup?" he asked, a smile on the verge of escaping from his lips but not quite breaking through.

"Hmm?" she said, looking up now.

"You were staring at your soup," he explained.

"I was just trying to figure something out."

"Well, maybe I can help," he said, as he shoveled in mouthfuls of soup. Frederick seemed never able to have his fill, despite the amount he ate.

"Bit bland," he said, when he had devoured the bowl in a span of a few moments.

"You don't like it?" she said. Despite eating hers at a fraction of the pace, she always found Emma's food to be remarkable. She didn't think it was solely because Emma's food was all she could remember.

"I like more spice, but I guess we must wait for that. Now what is it that's on your mind, Clara?" Her eyes moved from the soup to his expectant face now.

"I am confused about Lady Pemblebrooke," she said.

He leaned in, resting his strong angular face against the palm of his hand as he balanced on the table with his elbow.

"What about her?"

"Her mourning."

A look of surprise crossed his face.

"What is so confusing about her mourning her husband?"

"Her husband?" Clara said quickly, her eyes gone wide.

"Yes, who did you think she was mourning?"

"England."

"England? But, England is not dead. We are here, are we not?"

"We are, but Emma said she was mourning for England."

"Emma, no doubt, said that in deference to Lady Pemblebrooke's assertion that her husband embodied all that England is. She felt she was losing her country."

"I see," she said, though really she did not understand at all but Frederick spoke as if all of this were common knowledge. What he said next sent her frayed nerves into a disturbed state.

"You were here when it happened. Do you not remember?"

"When—it happened?" she stammered.

"Yes, when Lady Pemblebrooke received the telegram that he had died. No doubt, you remember the nightmares that set in—how she calls to him in the night?"

"So, it is not just the wind?" she said, quickly.

"Oh dear," Frederick said, his eyes growing darker.

"What is it?" she said, her fingers tensing in her fear at discovering what next he would say.

"You don't remember, then?"

A new look spread across his features, replacing his surprise, but Clara's memory could find no label for it. She sat nearly at the edge of the chair.

"Tell me," she said, in near desperation.

"We had this conversation before."

"This very one?" she asked, her voice now trembling.

"We did."

"When?" she asked, reaching out to grip his arm in earnest.

"Oh Clara," he said, softly.

"What is it?" she said, now frantic.

"We've had this conversation so many times before, each day when you visit Lady Pemblebrooke."

"Each day?" Dread clawed at her skin, sending a wave of panic over her. She struggled for the surface, to break free of its grip. As if someone had just thrown her a rope, she remembered something from their conversation earlier.

"Then, why did you ask me if I had met her before?"

"Because, each day I hope that today you will remember."

The rope slipped from her grasp, burning her hands as it tore her skin raw. A wave, larger than the last, erupted over her and dragged her down in its current. She struggled to break free, fighting desperately to breathe. Perhaps, she was going about it wrong. Struggling against the oppressive weight was only burying her more deeply. If she gave in, instead of fighting, she could find out what had happened. She could vow that this time she would remember.

"Today I will remember," she said, with all the courage she could muster and all the resolve of a general at war. A peculiar look played around the corner of his eyes.

"Tell me," she urged.

"You have said that before." A new wave threatened to tow her under, but she dug her feet firmly into the shore.

"Help me remember," she said. He sat back against the chair, settling in to tell her what she perceived would be a long story.

"You are sure? It won't be too painful?"

"Please, I need to know." He studied her carefully, weighing her fragility against her request. Having decided to do as she implored, he nodded his head slightly in affirmation. His eyes moved from side to side, recalling everything that had happened.

"I suppose I should start at the beginning."

"Yes," she said, hoping her shaking nerves that rattled her stomach ajar would not betray her and make themselves known to him.

"You were in an accident in Silvertown and the factory —"

"That part I remember," she interrupted. She did not wish to curtail his story, but she feared that in order to remain calm she would be unable to hear the terrible beginnings.

"Well then, Harold, Emma's brother, brought you here in hopes that you might recover your memory. Also, he knew it to be a hospitable place and that we would look after you. Well, I say we, but I was not yet here."

"Oh?" she said, sitting forward.

"I thought— "

"Yes?"

"I thought that you had grown up here." He said nothing, shifting his thoughts from one side to the other until they had arranged themselves properly at last.

"Then, you don't remember that part either?"

She had no idea what he was going to say and so shook her head no. Frederick sat back and shut his eyes briefly before reopening them. Their brown held the depths of what he was about to divulge to her. Frederick said nothing and she felt like a cat waiting for the string to be dangled before her nose, so that she might leap at it and having caught it bask in all the satisfaction it warranted.

"Go on, please," she urged, feeling the anticipation growing steadily. Frederick's eyes narrowed in concentration and he looked at her so hard she felt he must be drilling a hole through her.

"Perhaps, it is too much," he said.

"What is too much?"

"To tell you all of it now."

"Is there a lot, then?"

"There is," he said. He nodded, as Clara's heart beat swifter.

"You must tell me!" she said now. Her desperation having got the better of her, she was unable to contain this last plea for information. The back legs of the chair lifted from the floor now, propelling her forward and closing the gap between them.

"I am concerned for you, Clara."

"Whatever for?" she asked, becoming aware that her anxiety had perhaps marked itself upon her face and aimed to betray her now. She steadied herself on the chair and made a conscious effort to place her shoulders back now, realizing that they had raced forward to hear the news. A burden of tension eased, as she moved them and she felt herself breathe more naturally. Surely, such acts would aid her cause and present a better portrayal of herself. Though her stomach churned tempestuously, her mind acted as arbiter and declared that Clara would be calm. She knew that she must be, if she were to regain any iota of her memory and her person in so doing.

She was content in her life at Rosebrim Manor with Emma and the others. She was content, but not happy. For happiness rests in identity, in security of self. How could she feel that serenity of joy, when memory failed her and she was unable to conjure the images of the faces of loved ones? And while it was exciting to discover anew the scents of flowers, the sound of the rain on the windowpane, and the taste of each dish, there was also a feeling of loss stemming from the inability to remember her favorite flavor of tart or her most cherished childhood dream. There was a perpetual process of reinvention of self at all times and, while there are certain nice components involved in such an experience, it was also more taxing. No matter the burden now, though, Clara had decided that she must have the truth.

"I fear there may be too much for you to hear and that you will be unprepared for it."

"Have I done something horrible?" she asked suddenly, clutching the table. And then realizing that she was being counterproductive in her attempt to convince him of her hardiness, she forced herself to relax and relinquish her hold on the table. He shook his head no.

"I should say not. At least, not that I am aware of. And, I should know."

"Oh?"

He looked at her again, judging how much to reveal.

"We were close?" she asked, when he had not yet answered. He nodded slowly.

"We were."

"Then," she cocked her head to one side, trying to remember what he had told her earlier in the conversation. A light flickered in Frederick's eyes at the observation that she was remembering something or forming a hypothesis from the pieces. He couldn't yet be sure which it was. Clara's eyes shifted from one side to the other, as she attempted to reconcile what she knew.

"You and I knew each other before you came here?"

Now, it was Frederick's turn to sit forward.

"Then, you do remember?"

Clara pressed her palms to her temples, attempting to dislodge any stray and useful information. When she said nothing after a few moments, he fell back in his chair, exhibiting all the despondency of one who has had his dreams dashed. Not wanting to disappoint her friend and feeling she had, she shut her eyes as she continued to search for answers.

"Perhaps, that should be all for tonight," he said.

"Oh please, don't give up on me," she pleaded in earnest. Frederick shifted in his chair.

"It's not that I wish to give up on you, only that I fear it is too strenuous."

"Is it tiring you terribly?" she asked, feeling the heavy

burden of disappointing another, especially one endeavoring to assist.

"It's not for myself I worry, but for you."

"Oh really, I'm fine. I feel we are on the verge of discovering my memory. We can't stop now. It may be in a treasure box just below the surface and if we give in with only a few inches of topsoil covering the lid it would be such a pity, such a disastrous tragedy." She had committed herself fully and spoke with all the conviction and passion that those true treasure hunters must have exercised in front of the royal courts in the times of the great explorers when the world was still divided into the hemispheres of "old" and "new".

"All right," he said at last, consenting to her determination, "but perhaps, a cup of tea will help."

"Oh yes, of course," she said, nearly bolting from the chair to prepare the tea. Time seemed an especially scarce commodity to Clara.

"Emma always says tea can help solve all problems," she called over her shoulder to him. Then, excitedly, she turned to him and said,

"I guess my memory is improving. I've remembered what she says!" He smiled at her, pleased that she was progressing, though with that look of wariness around the eyes most frequently worn by skeptics.

"You think a lot of her, don't you?" he asked now, as she sat to join him with the tea.

"Who? Emma? Why certainly. Why shouldn't I?"

"No reason," he said, but he would not meet her eyes as he answered.

"You take issue with her?" she asked, not realizing that any animosity existed between members of the staff.

"We have our differences," he said simply, dismissing her statements and sweeping them away into oblivion. She sensed that he did not wish to speak further on the issue and so she turned the conversation back to where they were.

"Where did we know each other?"

"London."

"We are both from there?"

He nodded.

"And, you said we were close. Did we know each other long?"

"We did."

Clara's eyes lit up and she took hold of his arm abruptly.

"I know what it must be!"

"Yes?" he said, sitting forward and prompting her to continue.

"You are my brother!"

The happiness that descended over her nearly broke his heart.

"No, Clara, I'm not," he said, gently.

"Oh—I had hoped you were."

"You see me as such?"

"Oh yes," she said, strengthening her grip on his arm.

"I see," he said, sadly.

"What is it, Frederick? Tell me. How do we know each other?"

He took in a deep breath and looked into her eyes.

"Clara, we're engaged."

CHAPTER SEVENTEEN

The winds whispered their chorus of change over Edward's land. The tiny sprouts of spring, which had brought him hope, transformed into the hearty plants of early summer. No longer was imagination required to look toward their fruitful promise. Now, mere observation was the only necessity to comprehend their abundant harvest. Already, the drab sparsely-filled plates of winter were becoming populated with the leafy vibrant greens of the lettuces. Bright stocks of orange dressed as carrots and later earthy clumps of culinary gold, in the form of potatoes, would grace the plates as well.

Edward bent to affectionately pat the potato plant now in a reassuring gesture. The soft dense mounds of fluffy potatoes beaten with milk and butter danced in his memory, so tantalizingly close to his taste buds but just far enough removed to provide no pleasure. How many times had he left spoonfuls of the potatoes laced in undulating meaty gravy on his plate, as he stood to leave the table at home in California? If only he had been able to devise some sort of storage system, to borrow from the excesses of the past for the wants of today!

He was, by no means, starving though Germany's submarine warfare had sunk thousands of tons of food and supplies since those cold months of February and they aimed to starve the whole of Britain. Edward knew that others were starving, though, their pride prevented them from asking neighbors for help. The embers of aggression, which had been stoked to a massive roar as his comrades and friends were towed down around him by the never ending barrage of bullets, kindled hot again at the thought of their starvation. His grip tightened into a fist of defiance to smash through the enemy line.

Under his too firm grasp, the tender leaves of the potato plant snapped and spewed its watery lifeblood onto his arm. He stared at his arm, seeing not the dirt and remnants of a broken plant but the spattered blood and mud of the trench. The muskiness of the dampened ground and soaked canvas choked his nostrils.

"Edward, help!"

"Edward, help me!"

Agonizing cries tore into him with more ferocity than the metal of bullets could muster.

"Stop! Stop!" he said aloud, dissolving the memories into the early morning light of an English June day. Seeing the potato plant still in his grasp, he tossed it aside and pushed away the memories.

The terror by day and the nightmares by night, though never absolved of, hounded him more often lately. He felt as if he were retreating in his progress to return to normalcy. In fact, the nightmares had become so frequent that he hastened along the completion of preparing the house to a livable standard so that Agnes, whom he was certain was aware of their frequency but was too polite to say anything, would no longer be witness to them.

And so he settled not peaceably, but uneasily, into the house that had summoned him into its story. He had committed himself to the house as he had volunteered for the war, not because he desired to but because he felt he must. In both cases, Edward saw no decision.

As Martin predicted, the war had officially become his when the United States declared war two months ago in April. Already thousands of men were training to march into France, the way that he had two years before. In the trenches he feared for the men he lived with there, but this was secondary to his own survival. For the first time now, though, he began to feel as Agnes surely must. No man he grew-up with was guaranteed to be unharmed by the war. No one in Edward's life was any longer immune to the savage beast of struggle and destruction. This realization could account for the recent terror attacks his memories waged against him. Yes, that must be it. He took satisfaction in attributing a logical reason to his difficulties. But, even if they were explained, that did not change the pain.

And so the seasons changed, the plants grew, and the war broadened. Information was coming from the east that Russia seemed to be in the midst of revolution, much as Ireland fought for its own government in the west. The world spun in a tumultuous loop and Edward wondered if it would go asunder. Yet, for all the change that did occur, that which he desired most to alter remained the same.

George and John still fought on the frontiers of France. Their letters arrived only intermittently. On more than one occasion, Agnes had been certain something horrible had happened only to be relieved at the delivery of a letter the next day. She would quickly remember that considerable time had passed since the letter had been written and something terrible could indeed have happened, which would renew the whole process, sending her into a dither. The wounds of battle remained as well. Martin's laughter intensified during his especially bitter periods, Edward had come to notice. His own hearing, which had been steadily improving, began to stagnate around mid-May and he began to fear his ear had reached its full healing potential.

Leaving the garden behind now and entering his home, he wiped the mud of the garden against the coarse mat at the front door. He sank into the leather chair he had moved beside the fireplace and looked to the painting.

"And you," he said aloud to the painted lady now, "you remain unchanged, as well." Behind her enigmatic face, he had been unable to find out anything further. He had spent hours scouring through piles of papers desperately seeking the elusive Mr. Lefront but he, like the painting, was unrelenting in helping frayed Edward.

He had been avoiding his more intimate discussions with her, since the nightmares flared back up again. He felt ridiculous at the realization but he was terrified at what she would speak to him, as if she had the power to condemn his soul for what she revealed in her reflection of it.

Feeling suddenly claustrophobic in her presence, he exited the room nearly as quickly as he had entered. Back on went the mud-caked boots. Out the door he burst and hurried down the lane. He was undecided on whether he would visit Martin or Agnes and allowed his feet to carry him to the doorstep of the school building. His boots thudded noisily against the steps at his ascent. As he stepped through the door, he saw Agnes with her back to him as she cleared the blackboard from the day's lesson. Hearing him, she turned,

"Oh Edward, hello. I thought one of the children had left something."

"Hello," he said. Hearing so short a greeting troubled her and her worry set in almost instantly.

"There's not been news has there? Something's happened?"

"Oh no, everything is fine," he said, realizing that she had misinterpreted his preoccupation.

"Well, do you need anything?" she asked, trying to determine the purpose of his visit.

"No, I don't think so," he said.

At least, nothing you can give me.

"Well, please, sit down. I'll just be a few minutes. Then, perhaps, we can walk beside the ducks. Their nests, my students tell me, are brimming with eggs."

"Fine, fine," he said, still distracted. He sat in one of the desks, feeling like he had walked into a world that had shrunk. His knees bent awkwardly and pushed against the wood. Agnes seemed always to be attempting to fit Edward into a world he'd outgrown. In her pity for him, she sought ways of simplifying life. He supposed it was the teacher in her, searching for ways to make the world accessible for those that grasped at it.

"Nice of you to stop by," she said, as she continued clearing the board. "I would have been gone already, but the students insisted upon showing me their pictures."

"Their pictures?" he asked, intrigued at the word.

"Well, I use the word rather loosely. I am sure that they would pale in comparison to the many great works that you have studied." She had turned to him, to ensure that the conversation was not made more difficult for him. As she looked at him now, she seemed on the verge of discovering the truth about the portrait. But no, how could she? His nerves were shaken by sustained nights of poor quality of sleep and paranoia had set in.

He nodded politely, not trusting himself to speak on the subject lest he should give something away. His silence was soon broken, though, in response to what she said now.

"There was one particular painting that used to capture me. I felt as though I had a connection with the painting, but I'm sure that must sound silly."

"A connection?" he asked, sitting straighter and in so doing, bumping his knee against the child-sized desk.

"Yes, well a kinship or something. It's difficult to describe."

"Where did you see this painting?" he asked, feeling like a dog begging for a treat.

"Oh, in one of the surrounding houses. Mother had a friend that had married well, like your mother I suppose. Not that Mother married poorly! She chose love over riches. Not that your mother does not love your father!" She added these last points in quickly to avoid offense but Edward, concentrating only on details of the painting and feeling he might at last have discovered his trail of breadcrumbs, urged her on.

"Of course, of course. Tell me more, though."

Agnes misinterpreted his request and supplied him with a complete tale of visiting the woman's house, of the food she had served, and the many details of her furnishings. Edward chided himself for asking so broad a question. In his earnest for information without rousing suspicion, he had allowed himself to fall victim to Agnes's loneliness and penchant for long conversations. They seemed longer as of late, since he was no longer living with her and she attempted to fit every piece of information since last they'd seen each other into each visit. Edward wondered if, perhaps, it would have been better just to move back in with her. These long conversations caused his ear to ache by the end of them. But no, he had moved out with her best interest at heart so that the horrid hands of the nightmares would not dig their claws into her as well. He felt a twinge of guilt, as he realized now that he had not been concentrating on all she was saying. She really was amiable company, but he wanted information and after months of getting nowhere he could nearly smell the clues at the end of the speech. The end seemed triumphantly in sight, as she said,

"But, those days were long ago. Everything has been sold since then."

"Do you know to whom?"

She looked at him queerly, a tiny frown creasing the area between her eyebrows.

"I suppose it could be in the houses all over the country now, the contents I mean. But, why do you ask? You have the most peculiar look that has come over you."

"Oh, I was only thinking that if the painting meant so much to you, perhaps, I could find it and you could be reunited."

Agnes let out a little drop of laughter, like a teapot that has been poured too quickly and missed its mark of the teacup.

"Reunion? You speak as though the painting were a person. You Americans really can be rather funny," she said and slapped him playfully on the back.

"Yes, I suppose so," he said calmly though the hairs at the back of his neck had not sat back down since he realized the painting could have been sold to his house. 1909 was not so far removed and yet it was far enough away that Agnes would have been a young girl. But, she said her mother had been there and hadn't his aunt died when they were younger? He really should have listened better. But wait, no, that didn't matter. The painting was sold sometime after Agnes visited and there was no reason at all that it had to occur in the same year. In fact, it made more sense that she had visited before 1909.

"Agnes?" he said.

"Yes, Edward?" The traces of her laughter disappeared from the corners of her lips, as she noticed how serious his expression had become.

"As you said, it was very long ago but do you by chance remember the name of your mother's friend?"

"Remember her name? Oh, so that you can trace her for the painting?"

He nodded and her face lit-up at the idea of a treasure hunt.

"Oh, what was it? What was it? Brown, no, that was the name of our neighbors before John was born."

Her voice quivered ever so slightly, as she mentioned her brother's name. They had not heard from him for nearly two months now.

"No, wait, I know what it was. It was foreign, French I think."

Edward's neck tingled in anticipation.

"La, Lu, Le, Le—Lefront!" she said, looking delighted with herself and sending a cold chill of excitement rushing over Edward.

CHAPTER EIGHTEEN

His hand poised above the teacup, Edward stared at the painted lady. He felt like he was playing chess and each move must be carefully considered to outwit his framed opponent. He realized he couldn't avoid her any longer and that he would have to face her in order to progress. Sensible or not, Edward had engaged in the battle to determine her story and still felt an urgency in doing so. His very survival, he feared, was invested in his ability to unravel her mystery. He had no explanation for why he was convinced of her importance. Perhaps, it was the forthright manner that she confronted him in, forcing him to expose what he attempted to bury so deeply.

In the trenches the men hunkered against the walls, nearly clinging to them the way that spiders do to a web. If a man burrowed too deeply against the wall though, he could be plowed under in a sudden avalanche of falling mud and dirt. Lately, he had begun to wonder if he were harming himself by escaping from the problems that haunted him rather than protecting himself as he intended to do.

Agnes, at his request, had agreed to search through her correspondence to find any mention of her mother's friend, Mrs. Lefront. She had been so young and only had a vague remembrance of the visit. Unable to remember the location of the house, they relied solely on the hope of finding some postcard or letter with a traceable address. Though Agnes seemed keen to rediscover a treasure of her past, she could not know the significance of her task. He could not press her on the matter, because it would force him to admit that a painting held the ability to read him and that in seeking out its history, he was attempting to restore his soul.

He looked at the painting now with an odd coupling of malice, at the torture she subjected him to, and dependency at the hope of a future she could provide. With his hand still hovering just above the teacup, which had forged the bond between them, he changed his mind. Perhaps, he did not have to lay bare his soul in entirety. He looked over the room. Wood, metal, no, no. Even if they were polished enough to catch the painting, it would be too distorted with its texture. No, that wouldn't do. There had to be something else. His eyes continued to move around the room. Lace, no. Pillows, no. More wood. He needed something that would provide a clear reflection. Yes, of course. A mirror. There would be the shield of the double reflection to act as a barrier. He would be entering a sort of No Man's Land.

He had been there once, to the real No Man's Land. There was an eeriness that wrapped itself around the land and claimed whoever entered as its own. In a perpetual purgatory it opened its arms to those who dared to enter, offering proximity to hell if one should be cut down in a fiery blaze of gunfire and bombast, while tottering uneasily at the edge of grounded earth. Heaven was absent from this reality where man was held in the balance of bad and worse. The only reprise from such horror was to seek sanctuary beneath the ground in the tunneled trenches of uncertainty. And so they became the buried living, entering the depths. Some remained there as corpses.

The loss of one of these departed souls was the reason Edward entered No Man's Land and the alter world of densely-packed peril.

"*Poor boy. He was looking for food,*" James said to him, as they stood above the lifeless form.

"*Must be only sixteen or so, wouldn't you say?*" Edward replied in a whisper, as they retrieved the paper from his pocket.

"*I'd say even younger, lied about his age no doubt,*" James said, softly. They had ventured into purgatory to return the lad safely to earth, but their mission was interrupted by those vipers of hell: machine guns. Their fire lobbed toward Edward and James from the enemy's burrows, sending them scampering back into their hole like rabbits hounded by famished foxes.

Edward had been unsuccessful in his first foray into No Man's Land and had been forced to leave without that which he had set out to bring back. This time, he would not settle for defeat. In the battle for his livelihood, he would emerge with what he sought.

He held the mirror to the painted lady now.

"Why, why, why," the words bounced at him in a constant spray, as the machine gun bullets had. Planting his feet firmly on the ground, he braced for the impact of her words.

"Why? You left me. Why?" Edward's stomach seized in protest at the confrontation that seemed to pound at him from the inside out. Perhaps, he was not yet ready to face her and had rushed too quickly, ill-prepared, into battle.

"Why? Too afraid. You left too soon. Why? Why?"

A rush of dizziness welled inside him, as he struggled to maintain his footing in the attack. It was too much. He reached to turn the mirror away.

"Coward," she flung at him, in one final insult.

He sank into the chair, ensuring that the mirror was turned away from him.

"So much for that," he thought grimly as he sat forward, his head in his hands. He felt nauseated by his churning stomach that seemed to have gained a centrifuge under the painting's direction and order. If anyone else were saying this to him, he would think they were quite possibly insane. With each dealing with the painting, it seemed increasingly like she was purposefully retaliating against him. Her words seemed more powerful with each meeting, as if her ability to read him were growing stronger. But, why would that be?

"Make a study of it, Edward." His father's voice sounded in his memory now. He was transported to his bedroom when he was eight or nine years old. His father, having completed another successful business dealing, brought him home a miniature train

locomotive model.

"How does it work?" he asked, intrigued at its spinning wheels and tiny smokestack.

"Make a study of it, my boy."

"How, Father? What do you mean?"

"When I am trying to figure something out, I make a drawing of it. It always seems to help."

Edward had immediately begun copying the details to the page, causing his father to chuckle as he bent to tousle his son's hair on the way out of the room. His father had thought the project would keep him busy for a few minutes, maybe an hour at most. He hadn't been prepared for the dedication his son poured into the drawing. Edward could still remember the look of amazement that crossed his father's face as he showed him his findings, adding plenty of accompanying commentary. As he aged, his determination matured into that sturdy streak of stubbornness he had recognized in Agnes as well. Some pigment and canvas was not going to foil his plans for answers!

He would make a drawing of her the way that Mr. Lefront had. Yes, that must be why Lefront seemed to hold a relationship with her that was marked with the amiable addition of flowers and foliage. Mr. Lefront must have uncovered some valuable knowledge about the painting in the depiction of her.

Edward took the ever-present pen and paper from his pocket, but he had crowded the page with facts and figures about the collections and columns of sums worked out about the vegetables and growing times. Momentarily delayed, he rooted for a piece of paper and having found one, returned to his place before the queen of torment. With long-sweeping strokes, he sketched her outline. He noted the youth in her frame, the suppleness at the bend of her neck, the texture of her hair, and the furrow of her brow though her cheeks were marked with the slightest hint of dimpled laughter as if amused by something the painter had said to her. Her lips curved graciously in polite surrender of her defiant affections. He saw defiance because her eyes, though shining with the light of intelligence and the warmth of compassion, displayed an ardent shyness. His stomach relaxed as his hand tightened, cramping at the array of details he included in her likeness. No longer did she threaten him from her tower of superiority. As he looked at her now, she seemed incapable to even have an aggressive thought or one not rooted in the epitome of goodness. This was not the austere witch who had cast an intoxicating spell over his unexpected mind. This was someone meek, altruistic, even vulnerable before him. He felt a protectiveness for her build within him. It felt odd and out of place, but still it came as naturally as his commitment to Agnes had come in the summer months two years before when he had gallantly offered to take George's or John's place.

"Who was she?" he began to wonder anew as he sketched her. He was so captivated by the mystery that, he forgot she was once a person—real or imagined. Using only the medium of drawing, his experience with her was limited. Still, he appreciated the gentile beauty she graciously displayed. He had not painted in many years, but was suddenly overcome with a longing for the feel of a brush in his hand. His perception of her had shifted so entirely that he wondered what new dimension paint would have added to their interaction. As he added the last crease to her neck, where she bent it in a soft angular line, he paused to admire his work. So accustomed to only seeing the results of his draftsman's hand, he congratulated himself with a measure of surprise at the progress his drawing had made since last he tried these more artistic creations. With his pen resting beneath his thumb and his index finger balanced atop it, he was intrigued by a sudden change in thought.

"Look at me, again," she seemed to say from her sketched identity and, rather than scorn the suggestion, he wondered if he might be met with something other than her brash criticism. He set down the pen, laying aside his anxieties and fears with it.

"Shall we have a cup of tea?" he asked her, this time looking to her original portrait rather than the sketched image he had just drawn. As he saw her canvas form, his stomach dipped in momentary uncertainty.

"Look for the lines," he said, aloud to himself in reassurance. As he looked to her, his eyes peeled away the thick layers of pigment to reveal the lines that he had copied. Seeing her in simplified form provided a diagram for him to outline those qualities he had observed. There was the curve of compassion. And there lay the arc of humor. Her shyness rested beneath the paint, but yes, there he could see it.

He took his time, waiting until the tea was prepared to lift a cup to her. He convinced himself that she was a guest and with diplomacy he would be a gentleman, despite their past grievances. Tentatively he raised a cup to her, but he set it down again too quickly for a message to be delivered. He had not given her time to speak in the brief flash. He took a sip of his own tea. "The fuel of fortification" his friends in the trenches had called it. He purposefully did not look to her as he did so. Now though, with his full cup firmly on the table again, he raised the empty cup to capture her voice in it. He would have to hope that what he caught would not sting him, as a bee caught beneath a cup is so apt to do if it should escape. Perhaps, he was playing with fire. Either way though, he had committed himself and had to follow through in the conversation.

"Courage, Edward, courage," he said, to the empty space between himself and her. He lifted her teacup now, letting it remain long enough to catch her reflection this time.

"Why?"

His hand shook in a slight tremor. Was it to be this again? He hoped they had progressed beyond her irksome ways. Steadying his hand, he left the teacup raised before her.

"You seek," the voice said now.

"I seek," Edward repeated aloud, wondering at her

meaning and pleased that the usual disturbances were absent.

What was that? A strange noise filled his ears now or was it his mind? He didn't think it was coming from the painting, because she spoke in words and this sounded like a door or creaking wood.

"Agnes!" he said suddenly, setting down the cup and bolting from the chair. She must be on the stair now and entering the house. In a leaping dash, he sprung from the room to intercept her before she could enter. He had thus far remained successful in keeping her away from the painting. If she were to enter now though and see the very painting he suspected had captured her when young, she would surely give it more than a cursory glance. He couldn't risk her discovering the secret, not yet anyway. Feeling like a scientist forced to abandon his laboratory mid- experiment, he shut the door behind him just in time to see her at his door.

"Edward! I'm sorry not to knock, but I wasn't sure if you would hear."

He had known she would think this and enter without knocking. That is how he had known it would be her.

"Is anything the matter?" he asked now, putting away his thoughts of the painting long enough to notice the ruddiness in her cheeks and the winded nature in her breathing as she spoke.

"Oh no!" she said, her eyes sparkling joyfully. She dug into her pocket and smiled triumphantly at what she pulled from it.

"Your grading scale?" Edward said, confused at the excitement elicited from the sturdy paper in her hand. She looked down quickly, and seeing her mistake, let out a laugh.

"No, here look!" she said, pulling an envelope from her pocket. Edward's heart quickened. Could it be?

"A letter from a certain Lefront," she said, smiling.

CHAPTER NINETEEN

Virginia

April 1775

"Have you heard?"

"What's happening?"

"The Governor's gone too far."

The rumblings of revolution reverberated through the marketplace, biting at the ears of all assembled. As swift as a plague, talk of freedom and changing relations with England swept through the colony.

"Did you hear the news, Jeremiah?" Jacob, his older brother, asked him now as they hammered the smoldering metal in the blacksmith's shop. Their father had set up this shop before either of them was born. He had poured his life into forging the fledgling business, before the brothers had inherited it three years before.

"The news of Dunmore?"

"Aye."

"How could I not? It is all anyone is speaking of," Jeremiah said, in a low voice as the hot rod he was twisting into shape hissed under the heat and a cloud of steam, fed by the bellows, encircled his work.

"Jeremiah," Jacob said, looking serious and turning his gunmetal gray eyes from the furnace fully to his brother now. Jeremiah resisted hammering the rod into shape, so as not to interrupt his brother's words.

"I agree with Henry," he said.

"You agree with the tavern owner?" Jeremiah said, not at all sure what Jacob was talking about. It poured over him steadily now, though, as heat continues to pour from coals raked over hours after the fire has gone out. His eyes, deep brown like their mother's, grew in shock as he realized what Jacob must mean.

"You're talking about the speech, last month—in Richmond, aren't you?"

He nodded, with the somberness that such admittance to his statement required. Addressing the House of Burgesses, the red-headed Patrick Henry had declared, "Give me liberty or give me death!" His declaration, the two had heard, was met with rousing cheers to take up arms against England and the King.

"I am going with Henry and his men to the capital."

"Shh!" Jeremiah cautioned, feeling his brother—who had always been slightly more reckless—was committing himself hastily to the sure danger that would follow. Ignoring his brother or not having heard him, though he did speak more quietly now so perhaps he was paying some measure of heed to Jeremiah, he continued,

"We must march to Williamsburg."

"But, the shop—we cannot abandon it," Jeremiah said.

"What difference does it make to have a shop, if there is no freedom to conduct business in?" Jacob said, his face growing animated with that strange sense of enthusiasm and overconfidence Jeremiah had observed in it so many times before.

"And when Ma has no food to eat, because her sons have abandoned their livelihoods and source of income, then what?"

A steeliness flashed in Jacob's eyes for a moment, not at his brother but at the unfairness of the situation. With two competing ideals vying for his attention, both gravely important, there was only one solution.

"I will go to Williamsburg with the militia. We will demand that Dunmore return the powder he has stolen from the magazine! We will not allow them to take our defense from us. We must not! And you can stay here, with the foundry and Mother until I can return." Jeremiah knew Jacob was trying to sound wiser and older than his years through the proposal of the solution and in calling her *Mother*. He only ever called her that when trying to convince her that he was old enough to complete some feat she questioned. Jeremiah, younger in years but older in action and mind, had to accept his brother's proposal. Even if it were delivered with a measure of showmanship, there was no other viable solution.

At daybreak Jacob left with the men of Virginia, gathered in the militias to march toward Williamsburg. Life continued for Jeremiah in the forge much the same as it had before Jacob departed. By early May, rumors spread that negotiations had been reached and without Dunmore carrying out his threats of ordering the navy to attack Yorktown. Jeremiah and his mother watched each day for Jacob's arrival.

Covered in dust, Jacob's tall lank frame filled the doorway one early evening. His shadow spread across the floor and consumed the room, as the setting sun shone on his back. Soon more than the shadow filled their home, as he regaled tales of his own campaign to his mother and brother and brought news from further afield. He shoveled mouthfuls of his mother's rich pork and vegetable stew in, almost as quickly as the words poured out. He'd pause only briefly when absolutely necessary; chewing and swallowing were luxuries he could hardly afford on this night.

"And it's not just here in Virginia," Jacob said, gobbling down thick slices of bread in accompaniment to his stew, between words.

"Oh?" his mother asked, as she ladled more stew into his bowl. Jeremiah and she had eaten only one bowl each and were trailing considerably behind Jacob's four bowls. It seemed he had been gone for a year instead of a couple of weeks the way he ate, ravenously and without fill.

"There have been shots fired in Massachusetts," he said, slapping the wood of the table for emphasis. Drawn into the conversation and concerned at this newest information, she tolerated her son's rambunctious show of enthusiasm for the cause he spoke of. Jeremiah, who had been largely silent, spoke now,

"Then it's true what I heard—about Lexington and Concord."

"Aye. We can't let them take our land and our rights from us. We must fight for it!" His face took on the glow of determination, while his cheeks reddened in the bombast of the rhetoric.

Jacob, who counted patience as a vice rather than virtue because it dictated delay and tedium, gave Jeremiah and their mother hardly any time to welcome him home before leaving once again at daybreak. As he ate his fifth bowl of stew, his mother came to realize that he was not merely making up for lost sustenance from the proceeding weeks; he was fortifying himself for the work ahead. Recapturing gunpowder had taken less than a month, but how long was needed to recapture a country? When Jacob left, he would journey north this time. His uncle lived in Rhode Island during part of the year and was funded by his rice fields in South Carolina that grew the remainder of the year. Jacob had every intention of joining the fight once there. Many men were joining the militias in Virginia now, but Jacob was not content to wait for the fighting to arrive.

As the year progressed, Jacob's restlessness spread like wildfire. By the following July, a little over a year since Jacob had departed, all eyes turned to Philadelphia as the representatives of the Second Continental Congress transformed rebellious colonists into citizens of a new nation in signing the Declaration of Independence. By August, all thirteen of the colonies had pledged devotion to the United States of America, as the declaration was now determining them to be. Of course support was not unanimous and Loyalists fought alongside the red-coated British, rather than joining the new colonial army led by the newly-promoted General George Washington. Others, like Jacob, joined the newly-created navy. His uncle had ties with some of the men at the American naval station in Rhode Island and Jacob earnestly delved into the work as a seaman. Running blockades to relinquish the enemy's control of vital supplies provided the adventure he so craved.

As for Jeremiah, he remained in the more subdued work of the blacksmith shop. His work, which had greatly increased without his brother to take his share, only grew. Weapons, in place of the kitchen and farm tools his father founded the business upon, were needed in increasing numbers.

Early in the new year, a letter arrived in Jeremiah's shop.

"Letter for you, Jeremiah."

His hammer rang against the metal and sweat glistened on his brow from the heat of the fire.

"Thank you," he said over his shoulder, "just leave it on the table." He finished the task, wondering how large of an order was requested in the new letter. When finished he set aside the metal, wiped his brow with the back of his hand and opened the letter.

"Dear Sarah and Jeremiah," he read and then paused. This was not an order; it was personal correspondence. His eyes ran to the end of the page.

"Thomas," he said aloud. A cloud of fear descended over Jeremiah now. Quickly he read his uncle's letter, his heart nearly stopping as he read those words.

The naval base, where Jacob was, has been taken over by the British. On the day after Christmas, they captured it and I fear Jacob may already be on his way toward England to be held as a prisoner of war.

Jeremiah's stomach churned with the intensity of the glowing embers in the fire. Not wanting to face his mother, but knowing he must, he shut the shop early and hurried home, encumbered by the weights that lay heavily upon his back.

"Oh Jeremiah, hello! You are home early," Sarah greeted her son, when he came home. And then, realizing what she had said, she repeated,

"You are home early. Has something happened?" He pulled the letter from his pocket, charring the envelope slightly with the black on his hands he had not taken the time to wash off. Sarah noticed this oversight, which she would have readily expected from carefree Jacob but not from meticulous Jeremiah.

"News from Uncle Thomas, I'm afraid."

"Oh?" she said, rushing forward without wiping her hands of the dusty flour that covered them now.

"Jacob's been captured," he said. Sarah swayed in her step and Jeremiah reached out to steady her. She didn't say much for the rest of the evening. Jeremiah was consumed by his own thoughts. From time to time, he would look up at her and see her lips moving silently in prayer.

Jeremiah lay awake, tired beyond exhaustion, but resistant to the sway of slumber. When morning came, no answers had yet arrived but, Jeremiah rose to face the day.

"You have been kept awake, as well," Sarah said, when seeing her son.

"Aye, Ma. I have been trying to figure out what to do."

"I too have been searching for the answers," she said.

"And have you come to any conclusions?" he asked her.

"Aye. It is time for me to show you something."

He thought perhaps she would give him something of his father's, preparing him for the inevitable battles ahead. Instead, she reached deep into the pine cabinet and drew out a heavy blanket.

"Sit here," she instructed, patting the bed beside her. He did as she requested and watched her small hands unfold the woolen covering. He waited for the gleam of a knife or some tool to catch his eye. Instead, he was faced with a portrait of a young woman. Seeing his confusion, she began her explanation.

"I suspect that you are feeling the pull to go away, now that Jacob is missing."

He nodded.

"I also suspect that you may be questioning if you should go, because of me."

"Aye, Ma. First Pa left a few years ago and now Jacob is missing. I can hardly abandon you."

"Jeremiah," she said gently, but with authority, as she reached out to cover his hand with her own,

"My great-grandmother survived her son fleeing to the New World. I would be a hypocrite, if I did not allow my son to fight for the freedom of that country my grandfather helped found in his settlement. And Jeremiah, I am not the feeble older woman that you see me as."

"Then, you think that I should fight," he said, surmising her opinion from what she said. She shook her head no.

"Then, you wish for me to stay?" Again, Sarah shook her head.

"What is it that you want, then?" he said, feeling he was missing his mother's point entirely.

"What I want is for you to follow your heart and she will help you do it," she said, gesturing toward the painting.

"I don't understand."

"When I was a very young girl, my grandfather would set me on his lap and tell me stories about his life. He would tell me about life in France when he was young, though he spared me the horrible details of the persecution. Happily he would talk about London, where he moved next with his parents. He would tell me that I was a part of a special family of skilled craftspeople. Jeremiah, I am certain he would greatly admire your work that you do with the metal. You have such a way with it." She paused only for a moment, taking in the man before her that so shortly before had been the age she was when hearing her grandfather's tales. Not allowing herself to be distracted any longer, she continued,

"I loved his stories about coming to America and about

his Indian friend that he called John. He would tell me about meeting my grandmother and how their farm spread and even allowed for him to set up a silversmith shop, like his father had in London. But, of all of his stories, my favorite was always about the painting."

"Oh! Then she must be very old," he said, surprised at the lady's age because she bore such youth and grace.

"Oh, yes. She must be around two hundred years old now."

His eyebrows dashed up in surprise, but he said nothing to allow her to continue.

"My grandfather told me that the painting was very special and that she was a gift from his mother. What he said next surprised me but, in the delighted innocence of childhood, I accepted fully what he had to say. 'Sarah, my love, this painting is very special. She can talk.'" Sarah paused, gauging her son's reaction and seeing the skepticism she expected to find written on his face.

"I accepted what my grandfather said. After all, I loved him dearly and why should my grandfather tell me a lie? As I became older, I packed the story away with my toys and fairy tales."

Jeremiah shifted on the bed, more from confusion than anything else. He was certainly not bored by his mother's story, but he failed to see how a magical painting would bring back Jacob or give him the answers he needed to decide what to do.

"You are probably wondering why I am telling you this."

"Aye."

"I am telling you, because your grandfather was right. The painting can talk. It once helped me decide the most important decision I ever made—whether to marry your Pa or the rich farmer my father wanted me to."

"And the painting told you to marry Pa?" he asked, incredulously.

"Aye, but not in the way that you and I are having this conversation. You see Jeremiah, the painting speaks to you what is in your heart. It is like a mirror and reflects that which is deepest inside of you."

"How?" Jeremiah said, intrigued at the possibility. It seemed beyond belief, but just as his mother had no reason not to trust her grandfather, he had no reason not to trust her.

"I do not know how the painting does it, to be truthful. But I know that to hear it, you must hold something in front of her that can reflect your heart."

"A mirror, you said?"

"Aye, you could use a mirror or something shiny like metal or transparent like glass. I discovered it quite by accident when dusting off the portrait. She must have caught the gleam of the silver medallion on the necklace my grandfather made for me."

He looked at his mother, who spoke in such honesty that he wondered if somehow the impossible might be true. His eyes moved to the painting who, other than her age and beauty, seemed like such an ordinary portrait.

"You think the painting will give me my answers?"

"Aye. Look into your heart, Jeremiah. You will know what to do. Sometimes, you just need a little help in being able to see what is there. Sometimes, there are too many thoughts in our heads to quiet to get to an answer. Sometimes, we are afraid of what we will find. The answer is there, though. You will find it." She gestured toward the painting,

"With her help."

CHAPTER TWENTY

"There's a carriage arriving," Emma said, as she drew back the upstairs' landing curtains to bathe the pale walls in the sun's warm glow.

"Are we expecting company?" Clara asked, as she polished the wooden windowsill until it shone with the radiance of the solar blush kissing it now.

"Not that I know of." She continued tidying the area and commenced her humming, glancing out the window occasionally as she did.

"Oh dear, don't tell me we will have to draw all of the curtains shut again," Emma said, observing the shifting light in the room as a cloud passed before the sun, shutting out its light. Clara moved to look out of the window now.

"They do seem to be building," she said of the accumulating clouds blowing toward them.

"Perhaps, it will just be a quick shower, if there is one at all," Emma said.

"Perhaps, yes." Clara's eyes fell to the scene below them, as she spoke. The carriage was indeed pulling up to the house. From the front door, Frederick rushed across the grounds to it. They had not spoken, since last night's encounter.

In the weeks since Clara learned of their engagement, she had watched him at every opportunity hoping to observe some mannerism of the man she was betrothed to. She had discovered he had many amiable traits. He could whistle a pleasant tune, he was of strong stature and he had quick wit bringing laughter to Clara when he would transform an everyday task, such as the dusting, into a hilarious tale. But for all his good points, she had also noted characteristics that she was not as fond of. She still did not know the source of his dislike of Emma. When she had questioned Emma about her opinion of Frederick, she had merely remarked,

"I don't make it a habit of discussing others when they are not present." For this reason, Clara had decided against asking her for any information about Lord Pemblebrooke and Lady Pemblebrooke's mourning of him.

"I think it's disgraceful the way she keeps those poor children locked up with her," Clara had remarked to Frederick recently.

"What would you do?"

"I would tell her that grief is a terrible thing, but one must live."

"Maybe, you should write her a letter," he had said. She looked for the wry smile that slipped from the left corner of his mouth when he spoke in jest. Seeing no trace of it she said,

"I cannot write her a letter! She would throw me out."

"Dear Clara, you do not have to give her the letter but perhaps it will help you merely to write it. Besides, your memory seems to be doing better. You are not forgetting nearly half as much as before. You have not forgot that we are engaged. Perhaps writing your thoughts will help you remember."

Actually, she thought she was now remembering a good deal *more* than half of everything. Emma seldom had to repeat a request to her any longer, as she had to so many times in the beginning. Her life before the accident was still blank, though, and it would be wonderful to remember. Taking a chance that her memory might be helped, she did write the letter and tucked it away. The entire episode was forgot, not in the sense of a memory lapse but simply that it was put out of Clara's mind, until last night.

Frederick had appeared at her bedside, holding a candle before him that flickered against his dark eyes.

"Frederick! What are you doing here?" she had whispered in surprise.

"I wanted to see you," he said, reaching for her face with his free hand. He cupped her cheek beneath his fingers, which she noticed felt velvety soft for one who had worked with horses and in fields all of his life. He set the candle down on the side table by her bed.

"What if Emma awakens?" she said, in a worried whisper.

"Emma is snoring. I heard her as I came into your room."

Something about the way he said "into your room" made her tremble slightly inside, not from fear, but from the nuance of the situation. Unless, this wasn't so new for her.

"What is it?" he whispered, noticing the change in her eyes.

"I was just wondering if you had ever seen me in my nightdress before."

"Clara, my sweet, you are buried beneath blankets. I am not seeing you in your nightdress now. But yes, we would walk through the gardens at night. I would knock upon your window."

"But, why did you not visit me in the day?" she said.

His eyes flashed with something that she couldn't quite name, a painful memory no doubt, but the look quickly dissolved as he said,

"Because, it was the only time I could do this. Your father never left us alone for a moment."

He leaned into her, pressing his lips against hers. She had lately been wondering why he had not kissed her, if they were engaged. Of course, it would seem unladylike and forward to suggest so tender a touch. And now that she had felt his lips upon her she was not sorry, but she was not moved in the way she expected she would be. It felt as if it were an awkward first kiss, rather than the natural embrace of two who had kissed so many times before. Perhaps, it was simply because she did not remember their life together before. Perhaps, memory was required to add warmth to such an embrace. Frederick had not felt as she had though, for as their lips parted he said,

"Ah, I have missed that. Clara, come away with me."

"What?" she said, her eyes growing wide in surprise.

"I have found you. You remember we are engaged. You are not happy with your life here. You dislike the way that Lady Pemblebrooke acts toward her children. Come away with me. We can be married at once."

"But—how will we live?"

"What is more important to you, being with me or being here? I thought you wanted to be with me. You promised after all."

"Yes, Frederick. I suppose I did," Clara said, surprised at what he proposed and grappling for some sturdy ground to stand on. His look of hurt morphed into elation.

"Wonderful! Then, I will help you pack and we will leave at once."

He opened the drawer and began lifting items, stuffing bits of clothing into his coat pockets and a burlap sack he pulled from his trouser pocket.

"Frederick, don't you think this is a bit sudden? Why must we leave right now?"

He stopped abruptly and spun to face her.

"Then, you don't want to be with me."

"I just want some time. Let us save a little money first."

"Fine, yes, that makes sense," he said. She looked to his face for signs of what he was feeling. She didn't know whether he was upset or had really consented to her wish so easily. His back was turned to her, marring her view, as he emptied his pockets just as quickly as he had filled them. Without a word, he turned and left her alone in the room, not bothering to take the candle with him. For the better part of an hour, Clara sat up in bed too stunned to sleep. She pressed herself to remember something, anything, but only worked her stomach into knots without producing any answers. Well past one in the morning, she blew out the candle and laid down to sleep.

As she looked at Frederick out the window now, she

could still feel the pressure of his lips against hers. Confusion weighed heavily in her tired mind.

"Oh! It's Harold!" Emma said now, as she watched him step from the carriage. Clara watched as Frederick shook hands with this man who had brought her here, after rescuing her from the hospital. He moved through her memory as a vague shadow of kindness. He stepped into the sunlight, which had reappeared as the clouds passed harmlessly overhead. His profile looked familiar to her, but his appearance was dulled as if she had only seen him by dim light before. She realized how similar his features, at least from afar, seemed to Emma's. She had been euphoric and encouraged when his appearance seemed familiar to her, but her heart sank now as she began to think that the familiarity could perhaps be attributed to the resemblance between him with a person Clara spent so much of her time with.

She watched to see if Frederick knew Harold. The older man laughed at something the younger said, but whether this was a positive first impression or a joke shared between friends she could not determine. Emma raced downstairs to visit with her brother. Though he did not live so far away, it was too far for a man of his stature and age to walk and with the shortage of horses because of the war, visits were more infrequent than either would have liked. Clara dawdled upstairs, knowing that Harold would surely want to see her and yet allowing the siblings a chance to speak together first. At least, that is the reason she told herself that she did not rush downstairs with Emma. A gnawing feeling in her stomach, as she watched Frederick cross the yard now, convinced her that apprehension over seeing her fiancé also slowed her descent. She prolonged her absence as much as she could, but even very large houses can run out of windowsills to dust. Besides, Emma was calling for her now.

"Clara, come and see Harold." They were in the wing

opposite of Lady Pemblebrooke and so voices carried here without a second thought, in contrast to the austere quiet that they surrounded Lady Pemblebrooke with. Clara had begun to feel as though it was really their house and Lady Pemblebrooke, Albert, and Mary were merely shy lodgers who quarantined themselves to their room.

Clara's stomach protested, as she descended the staircase. At least Emma and Harold would be present, so she would not have to face Frederick alone. She heard Emma's shrill laughter, which made her think of a bird crying for his supper, accompanied by hearty guffaws that she presumed to be Harold's.

Frederick must be keeping them in good spirits.
She took in a deep breath and pushed open the door.

"Oh Clara, hello my dear. You look absolutely lovely. This fresh air seems to be agreeing with you, just as I predicted it would," Harold greeted her, pleasantly. She really had no reason to worry about facing Frederick, because he was nowhere to be seen.

"Introduce yourself," Emma said in a whisper to Harold, which was not quite as low as she had intended. A look of confusion filled his eyes at his sister's comments, but he quickly realized that Clara's memory problems must have continued past the time he had met her. A look of sadness for her, which he tried to mask with a wider grin, came across him at the realization.

"My name is Harold. Your grandfather was my best friend and that makes us friends, young lady." He held out his hand to her and mock-bowed to coax a smile. His strategy worked and Clara's worries melted, as she was drawn into a world of stories and laughter and occasionally a somber piece of news about the war. Harold was quick to veer from too heavy a subject, though, and did not wish to burden "dear Clara" as he continually referred to her as. By the time he left he had completely ingratiated himself to her and promised her and

Emma another visit, just as soon as he was able to find a carriage again.

"The war will be over soon, dear Clara, and everything will be made right. Then you shall not be able to rid yourself of me, though I suppose your fiancé might like you for himself. Fine chap you have there," he said and, with a nod of his cap, the carriage rushed away taking the kind gentleman with it.

Harold's words replayed in her mind, as she lay awake in bed that night. He knew then that they were engaged so perhaps he had known Frederick before and furthermore he seemed quite agreeable to the man whom his sister reserved judgment for. Clara lay awake, listening to the ticking clock on the wall, certain that any moment her door would burst open and Frederick would be standing there illuminated by the candle to continue the conversation. She glanced to her side table and noticed the candle holder was still present.

Oh no, I'll have to return that in the morning.

She knew that it belonged upstairs and Lady Pemblebrooke preferred its design to the others. If there were anything that Emma had taught her, it was that Lady Pemblebrooke's preferences must always be observed to ensure a happy house. Out of the near silence of the night, Clara leaped forward at a shriek of sheer terror. It resonated through the house, lodging itself in her blood and coursing through her. Lady Pemblebrooke's cries in the night had been less frequent lately. Now though the screams reverberated through the halls, sending a gripping chill over Clara as if she were being consumed by a thousand carnivorous spiders.

"Good Heavens! Good Heavens!" a new voice screeched in horror.

"Emma?" Clara said, aloud. She lit the candle and raced into the hall.

"Emma? Emma!" she called before her, as she raced up the stairs. Frederick burst from the room now.

"I'm afraid she's dead," he said.

"Oh my! Oh my!" Emma said, rocking in a state of despair.

"What is it? What has happened?" Clara asked, fright holding her closely.

"Lady Pemblebrooke is gone."

"What?" Clara said, horrified.

"What of the children? What of the children?" Emma asked, frantically.

"They too are gone, I am afraid."

"But, I don't understand—" Clara stammered.

"Clara, where have you been tonight?" Emma said, eying the candle in her hand.

"What? I have been in my bed."

"Asleep?"

"No, no, I couldn't sleep."

"Emma, I'm sure she didn't mean to," Frederick said, softly.

"Wh—what are you talking about?" Clara stuttered.

"Clara, why did you kill her?"

Clara wavered and fell to the ground with a thud.

CHAPTER TWENTY-ONE

Agnes stood triumphantly before Edward, ready at once to chase after the address on Lefront's letter.

"Do you know where this is?" he asked her.

"Not far," she said, with a smile.

Edward should have known by now that Agnes's idea of "not far" often stretched the definition of standard measurements. For an hour, they trudged through the early summer mud that testified to the healthy crops in the field.

"Here it is," she said, as the house came into view.

"Smaller than I expected," he said.

"Ready?" she said and Edward felt a twinge of déjà vu from the day they had stood on Martin's doorstep. Neither knew what to expect but they were both ready to find out what the house, which was really more on the large side of a cottage than the estate house that Edward had imagined, held. Somehow, because he believed it to be pivotal in his quest, he had decided that the house must be grand. When Agnes spoke of her mother's friend having married well, his mind had filled in the blanks with luxurious excess and riches. He realized now that his own affluent past had colored his assumption and also that everything appears larger when one is small and Agnes had been quite young when she was last here.

He raised his hand to the knocker now, hoping to be met with answers on the other side. The door cracked open.

"Yes?" a voice said, which sounded youthful but had the crackle of age in it.

Agnes looked at Edward and shrugged her shoulders.

"Hello, my name is Agnes. I'm a teacher in Meadowsbrooke and this is my cousin Edward."

When he did not say anything, she elbowed him to get him to speak.

"Yes, I'm Edward, hello."

"I don't know you," the voice, which began to sound more female, said now.

"We were hoping to talk to you about a letter."

"A letter? What kind of a letter?"

"My mother used to write to a Mrs. Lefront at this address. We were hoping she might live here still," Agnes said.

"Or that you might know of her at least?" Edward said.

"There's no Lefront here. This here is an English cottage, I tell you."

"Yes, thank you," Agnes said, "but, can you tell me if anyone used to live here?"

"I used to live here," the voice said again.

Edward looked at Agnes, imploring his cousin to call upon some streak of sudden genius.

"Does anyone else live here?" Agnes said.

"Why? Are you trying to rob me?"

"No, no! We're sorry to have bothered you. We must have the wrong address," Edward said and put his arm around Agnes to guide her away. He knew that if it were up to her, they would have pushed their way in and gotten their answers. Clearly, their politeness was getting them nowhere and so any attempt would be useless.

They had walked a hundred yards from the cottage, before Edward stopped walking so quickly.

"Well!" Agnes said, in disbelief, "Accusing us of robbery! It's a good thing that we didn't mention the painting. She really would have thought we were after her belongings!" An idea began to form in Edward's mind. Perhaps, she did have information about the painting and had taken over the position of guardian of it. He had chased his own cousin away from his home; was it really so strange that someone else would turn away strangers to prevent them from finding out about the painting? On the other hand, she could merely have been skittish.

"We must not have honest faces," he said, trying to smooth away her unsettled disposition.

"Well, really. It's quite shocking that anyone would treat us like that," she said, missing his attempt at making her smile.

"Maybe, she's just frightened with the war."

"Maybe," she said, softening, though only slightly.

They had stopped walking, as they spoke and now Edward began to lead them on the journey back. Birds sang overhead, keeping rhythmic time with their steps. The flowers were dressed in bright yellow frocks and crimson coated poppies smiled at them from the grassy knolls that lined the dirt strewn path.

"Funny," he said, not realizing he had spoken his thought aloud.

"Did you say something?" she asked, turning to him now.

"Oh, I just was noticing how nature keeps the season and is steady and dependable, when we have turned the world on edge."

"Yes, I know what you mean. There is peace in this meadow, despite our destructive ways."

They continued walking, both in silence for awhile. The breeze rustled softly through the trees, as if dancing around them in celebration.

"Do you think—no, I don't suppose it could be," Agnes said.

"Hm? Do I think what?" he asked, "and what did you say after that? You said it lower and I couldn't quite hear."

"Oh, I was just wondering—" she paused to face him now, to ensure that he heard what she said.

"Do you think things will ever be the same again? That they'll go back?" It was an odd sort of question for Edward to hear. The painted lady had made him decidedly contemplative. The trenches had changed everything for Edward but now, as a piece of a much larger story surrounding the painting, he had begun to ponder if normalcy could return. Perhaps, normal was not the word he was looking for. Normal implied ordinary and commonplace and neither one of those adjectives would have been sufficient or remotely descriptive of the adventure he had embarked upon.

"What's that?" Agnes said, stopping abruptly and pointing through the clearing.

"We didn't come this way," Edward said, suddenly realizing they were walking home on a road different from that they had come on. He had been swept into an all-encompassing whirl of thought and had not noticed they'd turned left instead of right.

"No, I wanted to come this way past that grand house. I wasn't sure if you'd seen it before. Had you?"

Through the clearing, Edward spied the very large house that he had admired once before.

"I have, yes. I was here with Martin before."

And then, realizing what Agnes was pointing at, he said, "Is that—is it what I think it is?"

"Appears so."

"Well, is it the son, perhaps? Was he away?"

"Oh, no. There is a son but he's very young. His father, the Lord, is at war. Well, maybe something has happened to him, but it seems we'd have heard something. I'm really not sure."

Edward probably would have continued walking, thinking nothing of the June burial if he hadn't suddenly recognized the undertaker. A man who appeared about his age and with dark features was digging a hole, piling the dirt high against the emerald grass.

"Pack it in good, Edward. Pack it in," he heard James say now, as he was transported to those first days when tools had rested firmly in his hand as he also sculpted the land with shovel and pick. Edward had felt like a mole immersed in a world of mud floors and dirt ceilings. But for all the aches that racked his

body from a greater quantity of manual labor than he had ever done before, he soon found himself longing for the days of a builder when bullets transformed him into a soldier.

Through the gates the man came into view more clearly now. Yes, he was definitely the man whom he had seen speaking to the girl the day that he had passed this house with Martin.

"I know him," he said to Agnes.

"You do?" she said, surprise clustering around her eyes.

"Well, I mean I've seen him before. Martin and I walked this way once to observe their garden."

"Pardon me," Agnes said, clearly louder than for just Edward to hear. The man paused in his digging, surprised by the voice, not having realized someone was watching him.

"Yes?" he said, across the expanse.

"Might we speak with you for a moment?" Agnes said.

"Oh Agnes, what have you done now? We already made ourselves unwanted to one stranger today," Edward said, softly.

"I just want to find out what's happened. Besides, he seems more cooperative."

Edward looked up and the man was nearing them.

"We were wondering what misfortune had befallen the house. Is it bad news from the front of Lord Pemblebrooke?"

"I understand there has been no news from the front," he said, leaning heavily on the shovel as he spoke.

"No, I don't suppose you would be digging a grave if the news were from the trenches," Agnes mused, trying to pry him for information. So many families received the terrible news of their loved one's death, but had no body to bury. What would have seemed impossible to accept became all the more incomprehensible, with no means of closure provided. The man had not yet replied to Agnes.

"Or, perhaps, you're digging for something else? A new well, maybe?"

Agnes, as a teacher, knew all the backgrounds of her

students and her intellect predisposed her toward natural curiosity. Edward often felt she would seem nosy to someone who did not understand her good intentions and feared the man before them would consider her intrusive. Those fears were quelled, though, and his own interest was piqued as he said,

"No well, I'm afraid. It's graves I'm digging."

"Graves?" Edward said, speaking for the first time.

"Three of them, I'm afraid," he said.

"Oh my, oh my," Agnes said, reaching out and holding Edward's arm to steady herself against the sudden dizziness that whirled around her. A shiver of dread pulsated across Edward. His nightmares were coming to life. This was too close to him. Graves were dug in France, not England. He had left all that behind. Death's dark dominion was constrained to across the sea —to the Somme, to Flanders, to Verdun. Wasn't it? Wasn't it? He swallowed hard, to suppress the rising tide of tumultuous waves. And then, suppressing his fear enough to see reality at least for a moment, an equally frightening thought gripped him.

"Who?"

"Pardon?"

"I think my cousin is wondering to whom these unfortunate circumstances have happened?"

"Oh, do you know the family then? I didn't recognize you and so I thought you did not."

"No, no, I don't know them. I just admired their garden. I too have a plot of vegetables," Edward said.

And the girl who stood beside you in the sunlight.
He did not even know her name, but the thought of misfortune touching her seemed suddenly unbearable.

"Well, it was the lady of the house and her two children, I'm afraid," the man said.

"Oh goodness!" Agnes said, her face taking on an ashen pallor.

"Then the girl who works here, who is similar in age to all

of us, she is all right?" He studied Edward, challenging him for knowing so much about the people he claimed to not know, but maintaining a politeness as he did.

"Clara you mean. She needs our help."

"Oh? Is it sickness? Is she also ill?" Agnes asked, now wondering if they should have not engaged in conversation lest they should become ill themselves.

"Not illness, no."

"Then, I don't understand— " Edward realized he did not know the man's name and paused to introduce himself.

"Sorry, I am Edward and this is my cousin Agnes and you are?"

"Frederick. The answer about Clara is that she has been detained."

"Detained?" Agnes said.

"She's..." he paused, visibly shaken by what he said next, "She's being held for their murder."

CHAPTER TWENTY-TWO

"Do you know her?" Edward asked Martin, as they sat together with Agnes now. He sat back in his chair and the sun whispered through his hair. Agnes sat forward, poised to hear him answer.

"You are intrigued," Martin said to Agnes, "but alas sitting forward will not help me remember any quicker."

"Why—how did you know I had sat forward? It was not even a conscious thing that I was doing," Agnes said, in amazement.

"May I?" Edward said, his appetite whet to provide an answer when so many questions encumbered their progress.

"Go on," Martin said, a smile occupying his face.

"Did her voice become suddenly louder, so that you knew she was closer?"

"Ah, you are becoming good at this!" Martin said, pleased with Edward's deduction.

"And I know what else, my chair must have squeaked, because yours has just done so now," Agnes said, clapping her hands together in delight, like a young girl playing a game.

"Correct," Martin said, sitting back in his own chair now.

"Well, I did not hear the squeak and so I was not at liberty to know that," Edward said, in playful jest to his cousin. His face was awash in the merriment of the gathered company, but something ignited in Edward at the mention of the squeak. How had he been able to hear the tiny bird's chirp from two stories below when he could not, half a year later with his hearing improving rather than deteriorating, hear the squeak of a chair within reaching distance? A shiver trembled over Edward. Was he going crazy? He asked himself the question that plagued his mind once again. But if he were truly crazy, wouldn't he think he were sane? But then, what of the moments like those this morning spent in solitude with the painted lady when he felt such uncharacteristic and unexpected fondness for her?

"I don't think I know her, to answer your question. I only saw her through your eyes the once, Edward."

So enraptured was Edward in his thoughts of the painted lady that, for a moment, fear gripped his heart as he heard Martin's answer.

How do you even know about her?

He was on the verge of saying it aloud, until Agnes cut across his thoughts and returned him to reality.

"Frederick, the man who was digging the grave, said her name was Clara and that she needed our help. I'm terribly confused, though. If none of us know her, how are we to help?" Consumed in their thoughts, silence settled over them.

"Perhaps, he was just distraught. He did seem rather shaken," Agnes said. Martin sat forward suddenly.

"What is it?" Agnes asked.

"I know who she is! Clara is that girl who was in the Silvertown explosion and got amnesia."

"Who?" Edward said, rejoining the conversation.

"You know, the girl who lost her memory."

Edward looked at Agnes inquisitively, but her face looked just as blank as his own felt.

"I don't think we know about her," Agnes said now.

"No? I was sure I told you. Well, no matter. As I said, she was in the explosion in Silvertown and lost her memory. The way I hear it, she's utterly alone in the world with no living relations."

"How very sad," Agnes said, her face clouding; she too was separated from those dear to her.

"So, how do you know all this?"

"Harold, the man who brought her into the country from the hospital, knew her grandfather. He stops by occasionally to talk with me."

"Well, then we must get word to this Harold. He would

want to know," Agnes said, the teacher in her taking control and devising a solution.

"Quite right!" Martin said, "I have his address here." He paused momentarily to retrieve it from his pocket. "He left it for me, if ever I should need him. Perhaps—"

"Yes, yes. We'll go at once," Agnes said, before he had time to make his suggestion. Though she was considerably shorter than her cousin, her presence and strength resulted in indulging her whims and she pulled Edward by the arm to his feet.

"Goodbye, Martin," Edward called over his shoulder, a moment later. He had barely had time to stand and somehow Agnes had already pocketed the address and was hurrying away from the house.

Must be a family trait, running headlong into problems we know nothing about.

"What do you make of it?" Agnes asked now, not slowing her brisk pace.

"What do I what?" he asked, losing some of her words in their haste.

She slowed her pace, though only by a fraction. They were still walking fast enough that, when they neared the ground the birds were walking on they scattered into a great swell of a black cloud. Their wings gathered now, as they soared above Agnes and Edward, leading them on like a steady arrow on their path.

"What do you make of it? What do you think happened?" Agnes repeated, being sure to turn her head toward Edward as she spoke, though her feet continued to carry her swiftly along the path.

"I don't know, but she lost her memory Martin said. We don't know how lucid she is, perhaps she did something without realizing."

A heaviness lodged itself in his heart at the thought of the girl in the sunshine being whipped into an undertow of darkness. Why were the women of his life perpetually drawn from the shadows, harbored in secrets, and lost to all others?

"Here, let's stop beside the brook for a moment," Agnes said, tossing herself onto a fallen log and leaning against a branching oak for support. Edward, ducking his head to avoid the low overhang of the branches, sat beside her. Here, so close to the earth with the grasses and shrubbery enclosing them in a herbaceous fence, his mind wandered to the forests of home. He had stood beneath the mighty redwoods with their massive trunks, wider than the span of his parents' arms and his own spread wide touching fingertip to fingertip to encircle the tree. Awestruck Edward raised his eyes higher and higher, first tens then hundreds of feet into the air to observe such magnificence.

"We have places like this at home," his mother had said.

"You have trees this big in England?" Edward asked, his five-year-old mind not quite sure how to picture the land of his mother's birth.

"Not so tall, but just as beautiful."

"Well, I think these trees are nicer. They must be the biggest trees in all the world and that makes them the best!" he said with childhood logic.

"*When I was a child, I thought as a child—* " The verse ran through the adult Edward's mind now. In that moment of declaring his trees as best he had been blissfully unaware of the tears that would follow so shortly after.

"Come and look at this fern," his mother said, holding out her hand to Edward and beckoning for him to crouch low and see.

"I don't want to see any tiny fern. I want to be as big and mighty as those trees!" he said, his eyes still high in the heavens.

His father joined Edward's mother beneath the canopy of fern as Edward twirled through the trees, content only in finding a larger and therefore better tree than the last.

"Crunch!" a loud crack bellowed under Edward's foot. Ignoring the noise he took another step forward but his foot became ensnared in a tree root and tripped him, landing him in a thud hard on his stomach. His twirling had caused him to fall in the direction he had just come from and he came face-to-face with the cause of the loud noise.

Horrified Edward saw a tiny frog, unable to move because its leg was crushed. Forgetting his own fall, he scooped up the frog that in its fear wildly tried to break free of Edward's grasp but was restrained by the injury that he caused.

"Fix him! Fix him!" he cried in anguish, running toward his parents.

"Edward, whatever is the matter?" his mother asked alarmed, rushing to her feet to come to her son's aid.

"Fix it! Fix him!" Edward said again in desperation, as he thrust the crippled frog toward his father.

"What have we here?" he said, looking closely at the specimen Edward had deposited into his much larger hands.

"I'm afraid I can't fix him," he said, bending to the ground and placing the frog under the cool shelter of the fern. Edward let out a whimper at the diagnosis. His mother put a protective arm around him and he buried his face against the folds of her skirt. He could picture it still, a navy dotted with tiny flowers. As his man-sized tears rolled down his boy-sized face he had felt as if he were watering the flowers of her dress.

"I'm sorry, Edward about the frog. I am glad that you stopped looking up long enough to see some of the treasures of the ground as well." What she had meant as words of comfort only intensified his tears. Their saltiness clung to his cheeks, burning their filthy imprint into him.

"But, I didn't stop," he said between his sobs.

Gently, she pulled him away from her skirt so that she could hear him better. She bent down, so that she was eye level with him.

"Now, suppose you tell me what happened."

"I was running through the...the...forest," his words were muffled through his tears, "and I—I—trr...tripped and then I saw that..." Edward's sobs were making it near impossible for him to speak now.

"What did you see?" his father said, sternly. His mother looked at his father harshly, one of the very few times he could remember her doing so.

"We both know what happened," she said, over Edward's head.

"I want Edward to say it. I want him to face up to what he's done."

Mustering all the bravery he could, Edward turned away from his mother's embrace. He stood as tall as he could, not wanting his father to be cross with him any longer.

"I was running too fast and I wasn't watching. I hurt the frog." His voice wavered ever so slightly, as he said it.

"Good. Now, I don't want you to allow this poor creature to suffer any longer."

"Oh Henry, he's just a boy," his mother protested, at what she knew was coming next.

"Alice, it's the lessons we learn as children that make us into good citizens. Children not as privileged must hunt and fish for their own food in many places. Edward has never had to see such realities. He needs to learn to fix things and to pay attention to all around him, even when he thinks it's not interesting or important."

"Fine," Alice said, "but, I'm not watching. I don't agree, but it's clear I won't change your mind." With that she departed the two persons whom she loved most, to avoid becoming a witness.

"Edward, I am not doing this to be mean. I want you to be concerned about those less fortunate than you. Do you know what I mean by less fortunate?"

Edward looked up at the man towering over him who always held the answers, but was asking him for them now.

"No," Edward said, shaking his head and hoping he had not disappointed his father.

"It means that some don't have life as easy or as nice as we do."

"Like the frog?" he asked trying to understand, his nose scrunching in the sunlight to aid his thoughts.

"Yes," Henry said and, for a moment, he saw such innocence in Edward's face that he hesitated at what he had intended doing. Resolved in his decision, despite knowing that Edward's innocence would shatter like a broken dish, he said now,

"Edward, if you were older, I'd have you shoot the frog, but you are too small to hold the gun." He stooped low beneath the fern.

"Come," he said, without any of the welcome in his voice that Alice had when she had spoken the words before. This time Edward did not turn away, but turned toward his father. Helpless, the frog sat beneath the fern where Henry had placed him. He lifted a stone, larger than the frog but not too big for Edward's hands.

"I want you to put this over him, so he won't suffer anymore." Edward looked at his father, shocked by what he had heard but feeling the weight of the stone in his hands now and having no choice but to do as his father said.

"Look Edward," Agnes said now, breaking into his thoughts. He followed her finger to the grassy area beneath the shadow of the log they sat on. Unsure of why he said what he did, she heard Edward whisper,

"I'll fix it," to the frog she pointed at.

CHAPTER TWENTY-THREE
Virginia
1781

Rains pelted against the window, as Sarah sat beside the fire. Her fingers cramped from her sewing in the cold and she stretched them to the fire's warmth. Oh how Jeremiah must have suffered in that terrible winter spent at Valley Forge with General Washington! His letter had been penned in bravery, but even trying to spare his mother's concern did not allow him to conceal all from her. Enough grit had leaked from the words to give her some indication of the harsh environment he had faced. Though he had not told her, she had heard rumors that not only the excessive snow threatened lives but also dwindling supplies and vast shortages of food. It had seemed that their plight was hopeless. How could the mighty British army, a domineering force in the world, be defeated by a fledgling democracy of backwoodsmen, planters, and merchants? Yet, the impossible was seemingly, somehow, coming true. The British had a strong military history, but this legacy locked them into the regimental battle practices that severely limited them. The colonial militias, which now were assembled as the American army, moved freer, stealthier, certainly smarter in Sarah's opinion, by not adhering to the practice of standing in formation and waiting to be picked off. Rather, they often caught the British by surprise or the Hessians, as they had done on Christmas day. And while the British had the Hessian mercenaries, the American colonists were aided by the French and Prussians. Lafayette and von Steuben stood upon American soil, offering the training that was so vitally needed and providing power. This was especially true at sea.

A cold chill swept through Sarah. As infrequent as word was from Jeremiah, she had heard nothing from Jacob since Thomas's letter. She lived only in the knowledge of rumors.

Some prisoners had been taken as far away as Scotland, to dwell in the prisons of the imposing Edinburgh castle. Though she did not know where he was, she did know that he was regarded as a pirate because the American navy and army were not recognized as being legitimate.

"Come home to me," she said, her voice giving sound to her thoughts. Sarah fell asleep beside the fire and dreamed of a time that seemed so far removed, when Jacob and Jeremiah bounded through the door each day for dinner and when Adam was still within her reach.

"A flower for the loveliest woman in all of America," he said now and bent to kiss her cheek. She awoke with the feeling of her hand pressed against her skin, in place of her husband's touch.

"Silly dream, really," she told herself, to dissuade the looming sadness from gaining ground.

"You never were that sentimental. But I love you Adam, and aye, I shall see you again," she said, in the early morning shadows. She stretched her limbs, which burned in stiffness from the night spent in the chair. Her stomach grumbled, declaring it was ready to begin the day even if Sarah were not.

The cold of the floor pressed against her feet, as she stood to light the fire in the hearth.

"Good morning," she greeted the painted lady, looking to her portrait that she had moved to be within her view near the fire. Alone in a house for the first time in her life, she sought companionship in her lifelong friend of pigment and brush stroke.

Perhaps, I should never have told Jeremiah about you. The fire crackled as it came to life, flickering warmly and erasing the last traces of night from the corners of the room.

"No, I don't suppose it would have mattered. He'd have left anyway, wouldn't he?" she said aloud now.

Ordinarily, Sarah ate from the simple and practical clay

dishes fashioned from the rich earth her sons struggled for now. She reached for the bowl, but her hand hesitated as she remembered something.

"Can it be?" she said. Her head tilted to the side as she thought and her hair, which had loosened in her sleep, tumbled softly over her shoulder.

"Today, we will use the silver because it is your birthday," her mother said from the annuls of memory now. Having remembered that today was indeed her birthday, she left the pottery bowl on the shelf and took down the silver plate instead.

"Well, happy birthday to me," she said, looking to the painted lady, with the silver plate of bread upon her lap.

"I am coming home."

Sarah jumped, knowing full well what had happened, but momentarily having forgot that it could.

"But, what can this mean?"

"I am coming home. I will be with you soon."

A strange sense of uncertainty overcame her. What could this mean? Wasn't she already home? The painted lady had always faithfully conveyed the contents of her heart to her, but for the first time she was utterly confused at the meaning. Was the Revolution doomed and she would be returning to England? But, England was the home of her grandfather and not her own. She had lived in Virginia all of her life and so had her parents before her.

No, there must be some mistake. She had only thought it and, in her muddled confusion of still being tired and having awoken from her strange dream, she imagined it all. Hadn't she? Surely, yes, that must be it. She began eating, the crusty bread crunching as she bit into it and her teeth sinking into the soft center. Caroline had always admired her bread and had even told her it was the best bread in Virginia. The woman who had frequented her home and shared a meal so many times with Sarah could not understand why Sarah would not offer her a cup of tea in those days of tension in 1774.

"But Sarah, you have always served me tea."

"I'm sorry Caroline, but tea is no longer served in my house. May I offer you a nice cup of coffee, perhaps?"

"We are English citizens. How could we distance ourselves from our customs?"

Sarah had not wanted to cause offense, but she believed in the future of her country.

"Do you not think, Caroline, that we ought to have a say?"

"A say in what?" she asked, her eyes scrunching in confusion.

"In how we are governed, in our rights."

"I think, Sarah, that you are the one without rights. I know, because we have been friends for so long, that you love tea. Neither England nor the king nor Parliament are denying your right to tea. The only one who is doing that is you."

It was the last conversation the two had shared. Sarah was willing to overlook their differences, but Caroline's husband was an ardent Loyalist and discouraged his wife in socializing with a "dangerous revolutionary". She had heard that Caroline's mother had died and Sarah sought a way to reach out to her friend, but her correspondence had been unanswered.

Poised to take another bite of bread, which she had been steadily eating while her stream of thoughts washed over her, Sarah's heart seized in sudden fear. Her eyes grew wide, as the thought confronted her. What if the painted lady had meant that Sarah would soon depart her earthly life? She had said that she was on her way home. She stood abruptly, setting the plate on the chair she stood up from. Racing to the mirror to examine her reflection, she wondered if she had aged more than she realized. Seldom did she take the time to gaze upon her appearance, but now she studied each crease and each hair intently. There were traces of gray and lines near her eyes, but no, an old woman did not face her. She was still young—young enough to live at least.

She spent the remainder of the day, which was intended to celebrate her birth, wrapped in the uneasiness of uncertain mortality. Sarah jumped, as the wind slammed the shutter against the wall of the house. The rains, which had appeared suddenly on a wind from the east, railed against the now exposed pane.

She pulled her woolen shawl around her shoulders and over her head and ducked out into the inclement weather, to secure the flapping shutter. Already, the rains had saturated the ground and the mud sloshed noisily beneath her shoes. The drops pelted her with unrelenting determination and hissed against her skin, as stinging tongues lapping against her.

"Stay," she commanded the troublesome wood, as she reattempted to fasten it to the wall. Paying her no heed, it whipped from its resting place and hurled itself open.

"Stay!" she commanded with more vigor this time.

"I think, perhaps, you had better stay," a voice sounded from behind her. Sarah's body went awash in chilling fright, as she turned at the voice. Filling the lands before her home stood an amassed troop of red-coated soldiers.

"Who are you?" one of the soldiers asked, stepping forward to address her now.

"Sarah, Sarah Andrews."

The men surrounded the house, ensuring that anyone inside would not escape through the back door.

Bypassing Sarah, two of the soldiers rushed forward into the house with their bayonets at the ready. With no choice but to stand and wait, Sarah's knees wobbled beneath her skirts. Her premonition had not been unfounded after all. Her demise was imminent. But, wait. These were English men, not savages. Her spirit rivaled her sons' for who was the greater patriot, but her spirit was housed in the body of a woman and not that of a soldier. What was more, the body she dwelt within had accumulated more years than the age she felt. As she looked at the men now, she realized they were the contemporaries of Jacob and Jeremiah. Had her grandfather not come from England, any one of them might have been her son. The knowledge thawed the icy hand of dread that had seized her heart and a sense of serenity, from some wellspring deep within her, surged to life. She had almost forgot entirely the fear that filled her. Almost. Her hands, to her annoyance, still quivered in uncertainty.

The trees, which played witness to the escapade, also seemed calmer now. Their leaves no longer shook with the ferocity of the gale that the rains had demanded. Though the winds abated, the rains continued to fall in their steady rhythm. They drummed their repetitious beat against Sarah's skin and echoed the resonance of her own heart. Her shawl, intended as her shield against the weather for a moment or two at most, clung heavily around her shoulders and was weighed down by the rains soaking through onto her thinner clothes beneath.

The men, who had been left outside, clumped together like young schoolboys. Suddenly she was struck with the reality that her struggle was not only against the elderly wig-covered heads of Parliament, but against young boys who had no more rights to determine taxes than she did. Whatever pity or commonality she felt with them lasted a mere moment. From her home, the two soldiers burst with their arms overflowing.

"What are you doing?" Sarah said to the man, spotting her beautiful silver, crafted lovingly by her grandfather and the subsequent men of her family, in the arms of this stranger.

"Taking back what belongs to England," the soldier said.

But, those things were made in America, here in Virginia. Her lips knew better than to betray her safety and she remained silent. Her intention was successfully carried out until, she eyed something that changed everything. Under the arm of the second soldier, wrapped haphazardly in a cloth with an exposed corner, was the painting that was always so much more than canvas and paint.

"Sir, that is only a worthless painting, something of my family. Surely, you do not wish to take that. Allow me to indulge my sentimentalism and keep the painting, please."

"Let's go," he said, ignoring her request. They hurried away with only a glance of apology over the shoulder of one soldier, when he was already halfway down the lane. Standing alone, she watched the last member of her family who had not left slip away from her vision and life.

For a long while she stood planted, unable to lift her feet from the place that claimed her lifelong companion. Slowly she turned now toward her home, entering the place of welcome and finding it decidedly less inviting.

"I'm going home." The words echoed in her mind, from earlier in the day.

"You were thinking of yourself and not speaking of me," she said aloud, to her absent friend.

She was both comforted and confounded by the thought. Her life was not in danger after all. For surely, more even than this realization, was the probable threat that her encounter with the soldiers threatened her safety more than any forthcoming event would and she had emerged from it, soaked, but in one piece. But, how could a painting prophesy its own future? For that matter, how could a painting speak at all? Yet, that improbability she had accepted readily. Perhaps, this was a new facet. With a sense of sadness, she knew she would be unable to further investigate the matter since the painting was long gone. She peeled the soaked shawl, which smelled of wet wool, away from her hair and skin. It had plastered itself to her and clung with the dedication of moss on the walls of a house. She dried herself before the fire and prepared her house for the night, too consumed by the day's events to discourage the relief of sleep any longer.

What was that? Sarah awoke with a start. She gripped the blanket tightly, straining her ears to hear anything more.

Perhaps, it was just the wind drumming its rapacious fingers against the walls. A thudding pounded against the doorstep. No, it was outside, lingering beside her house. She stood from the bed, the frame creaking beneath her. She shot it a look of scorn, imploring it to quiet itself. Behind the door was the musket she retained for safety. Living on the fringes of civilization all of her life equipped her with the knowledge of the frontier. As a young girl, her mother taught her to make the famous bread and her father taught her to handle a weapon. She slipped its reassuring weight of safety into her hand and crept silently from the room.

The footsteps grew louder. She risked stumbling in the dark, so as not to give herself away to whomever was outside. How many were there? She pushed her ears to hear more. It sounded like a solitary set of footsteps. But—they were approaching. Flustered and shaken from the events earlier in the day, Sarah swallowed hard. The door rattled. Someone was trying to get in! She drew herself behind the door with musket poised.

The door swung open, ushering in a chilling sweep of wind with the person who entered. Sarah studied the sounds made by the intruder to deduce all she could to have an advantage. The person was not walking evenly and seemed to heavily favor the left side. Perhaps, someone was merely wounded and had spotted her home and hoped to use it as refuge. But even if that were true, the dark concealed the color of his coat from her eyes. Like a fiery blaze, the red coats of this afternoon had seared themselves into her mind and inclined her to believe she was now faced with one. The moonlight played softly through the shutters, casting the faintest glimmer of light onto the room. She would have to act now. Stepping from behind the door, she raised the musket and planted it into the shadowy back. She allowed the muzzle to be her voice and waited for her captive to speak, so as not to give away that she was a woman.

"Ma?"

All of the tension that surged through her body collapsed in a heavy sigh of relief.

"Jeremiah," she said, lowering the gun and hugging her son in the dark.

"Not going to shoot me, are you?" he said and though it was dark, she heard the smile in his voice.

"My goodness, no! I cannot believe that you are here. So often I have dreamed of this."

She knew that she should light the lantern, but she was unwilling to relinquish her hold on her son.

"It's almost over, Ma. I was injured and so I was told to come home. The troops are gathering near Yorktown, so it wasn't so far really."

"Will your leg heal?"

"How did you know—"

"You shuffled when you walk. My goodness, it's good to have you home."

She let go of him, but only for a moment and soon he found himself emerged in her embrace once again.

"I kept telling you in my head that I was coming, that I would be here soon."

The words of the painted lady echoed in her mind now, as he continued,

"I thought of you so often and of the painting, hoping that somehow you would hear my message."

She said nothing but hugged him tighter, knowing that somehow she had.

CHAPTER TWENTY-FOUR

Clara sat on the edge of the cot, imprisoned by far more now than the hindrance of amnesia.

"What are we going to do with her?" a guard said, nudging another.

"We just have to wait for now."

"I still think she doesn't look like a murderer."

"You never can tell, though. Remember that one—"

Clara shut her ears to their conversation, which was only succeeding in tying her stomach into knots. She laid down on the bed and covered her head with the pillow to hide from the world.

Why is this happening to me?

Hot angry tears pooled in her eyes and dragged their wretched fingers down her cheeks, streaking them with salty residue and anguished moisture.

She could remember only traces of the night in question that had locked her behind these bars. She had told Emma goodnight. Then, she had gone to bed like any other night. Screams had awoken her and she knew that this was a somewhat regular occurrence. Lady Pemblebrooke suffered from nightmares. Wasn't that what Frederick had said? And then, she had fallen back asleep and had been woken again. No. Wait. That didn't seem right. In the beginning, she had thought she had risen from bed and seen the others immediately following the scream. But, now she wasn't so sure. The more she tried to remember, the more muddled her recollection became. Still though, she was now nearly certain that she'd been awakened twice in the night.

"But, I didn't do it, Emma. I promise I didn't," she had protested, when the police had been called.

"Maybe, something happened that you don't remember," Emma had said, not wanting to doubt her young friend, but shaken over the crime.

"Emma, I didn't do it! I didn't do it!"

Frederick, who had been talking with the police, had joined her.

"Clara, try to calm down. It will be all right. I'm sure that you did not mean to do it."

"But, I didn't. I would remember even if some awful accident did occur, don't you think?"

"Well— " Frederick had said, a thoughtfulness setting in around his eyes.

"Well, *what*?" Clara demanded, becoming desperate and trying to remind herself that hysterics would hinder rather than help her case.

"I think Frederick means that sometimes the most traumatic events are the very ones that suppress our memories most," Emma said looking to Frederick to see if she had conveyed the message accurately. He nodded that she had.

"But, I *would* remember!" Clara said, in a feeble attempt to alter their minds. She already realized it sounded wobbly at best, given the circumstances.

"Clara, I don't like to admit it but, sometimes you cannot remember much more than your name," Emma said, with all the usual joviality wiped from her face.

"Sometimes, our conversations are repeated nearly verbatim day after day," Frederick had said.

A wash of sadness, embittered in fervent frustration, overtook Clara now. How could she remember such a hurtful conversation as this and yet her traitorous memory inhibit her from arguing her innocence?

"Time to eat," the guard said, as he opened the door and set down a tray with bread and a bit of thin broth before her.

"Thank you," Clara said, acknowledging his presence and hoping to at least preserve her dignity, especially if she had nothing else. The thought spread a cloak of darkness over her. She took a bite of the soup, which was only tepid in temperature and water-logged in taste. A lump of bread, dark and hard, sat unappealingly beside it. She lifted the bread and took a bite, but her teeth did not sink into it. Instead, they pushed against it uncomfortably and Clara felt as if she were eating a stone.

"If I can get any good bread, I will give it to you," a voice said, from the recesses of her mind. No doubt, it had been Emma. But no, that didn't seem to make sense. She stopped eating and stared hard at the floor, as if the name of the person who had spoken the words might be inscribed there. No, she couldn't place it on the face of anyone she remembered. It was definitely a female voice, but not Emma's. Was she remembering something from before? The thought seemed too tantalizingly delicious to be true and was assuredly more tasteful than the food she was attempting to eat.

She paused in her thoughts, as she heard the footsteps in the corridor. Was the guard back so soon for the tray? She had nearly eaten a quarter of it.

"I'm not yet finished," Clara said, without looking up. But, rather than hear the guard's reply, she heard someone say,

"Hello, Clara."

This voice, unlike the one who had commented on the bread, she could place.

"Harold!" she said, looking up now.

"Ah, so you remember me. I am glad to see that."

"Yes, Harold, I do." She stood and crossed to him now.

"They think I did it, Harold, but I didn't. I didn't!" she said, her eyes widening in expression as her emphasis heightened.

"Yes, Clara. It will be all right," he said, trying to reassure her. Through the bar, he pat her hand that she had not noticed she had gripped the bar so tightly with when professing her innocence.

Noticing that her grip had loosened and she seemed generally calmer, he spoke again now,

"Clara, I have some friends who would like to help you."

"Friends?" she repeated.

"Yes, they are young and your age. They have all been affected by the war also and they would like to try to help. Is that all right with you?"

"Yes, I—I guess so," Clara said. Moments before she had felt deserted by all, including herself, and now strangers wanted to help her. As if on cue, three sets of footsteps filled the corridor and waited just beyond her line of vision. Harold motioned to them and three persons, in the form of two men and a woman, accompanied the footsteps.

"This is Martin," Harold said, gesturing to the first man, who Clara noted did not look at her at the introduction. She soon realized that he was not being elusive or averting his glance, but that he was blind.

"Hello," he said cheerily, "Harold and I know each other and I thought I might be of some help. I'm a bit of a mystery fan," he said and then a slight look of regret touched his cheeks, as if he had perhaps said too much.

"And these are Martin's friends," Harold said, sweeping away the embarrassment with his words.

"Yes, I'm Agnes and this is my cousin, Edward," the woman said, stepping forward.

"Yes, hello," Edward said. His voice fell on her ears as an oddity. The others' accents largely resembled each other, but his seemed out of place and foreign to her.

"Now that you know everyone, we would like to be able to help you," Harold said.

Clara nodded and he took it as a sign to continue,

"Can you tell us what you re—about that night." He seemed to change his mind on the word "remember", lest it be too painful for her.

"It was an ordinary night. I said goodnight to Emma and went to bed."

"Emma is my sister," Harold added for benefit of the

others. Clara continued, recalling the story that she had just relived by herself.

"I awoke from screams, but thought little of them."

Agnes's eyebrows darted up in question. Taking note of her response, Edward said,

"Was it not odd to hear screams?" He spoke the words delicately, allowing them to softly descend over her, the way that the sunshine had on that afternoon when he had first seen her.

"Lady Pemblebrooke had nightmares and often awoke in a fit of screams," she explained. Her face paled at the mention of the woman who caused her to be locked behind bars.

"And then what happened?" Harold coaxed, gently.

"I arose and Frederick told me the awful news."

"Frederick, right, we met him the other day and he is your fiancé. Is that right?" Agnes said.

"Yes, yes, that's right. He was here yesterday, assuring me that all would be well. I have only just remembered that. The visit had slipped my mind."

Seeing the look of pity that covered their faces, when she had forgot what had happened the day before and they were intending to prove she remembered the previous week, she wondered if perhaps she had said too much. Feeling suddenly very exposed in front of so many strangers, she surely would have declined to speak further had it not been for the reassuring look on Harold's face that had remained so constant throughout her testimony.

"Who was present when you heard the news?" Martin asked now.

"Just Frederick and Emma and me. We all gathered after the second scream."

"The second scream?" Agnes asked now in confusion. Either not hearing her or choosing not to address her, Clara continued,

"Yes, and I remember thinking how much colder it was

than when I was upstairs last."

"Well, it was night then," Edward tried to offer helpfully.

"Yes, the night seemed warmer the first time."

"Night? Do you mean that you had been upstairs that night already?" Martin asked, hinging on her words for the information he could gather. Their expressions of realization at what he had just suggested, he could not see, but he felt the heaviness descend over them and move Agnes. She was standing just beside him and she slightly swayed at what he said. Clara seemed the last to deduce the implication, but when she did, a horror transformed her face.

"But...I...I didn't do it!" she stuttered between gasps of trying to take in enough air to breathe. She began to cough, choking on the very air she had hungrily inhaled.

"Shh, Clara my girl. Calm down, dear Clara. It will all be all right," Harold said, in a reassuring gesture. Martin, whose comments had induced the anguish, felt a deep sense of remorse. He shuffled his feet awkwardly and Agnes took hold of his arm, as if to say it was all right.

"I think, perhaps, we best go," Agnes said, taking charge of the situation, as she was so accustomed to doing in the classroom.

"Yes, I think you are right," Edward said and the two, along with Martin, departed after bidding Clara and Harold goodbye. The words failed to reach Clara's comprehension. The horror-inducing shock of Martin's words had cast an eerie numbness over her. It was too dreadful to think what it could mean.

"Clara," Harold said, now that they were alone, "I know this is extremely painful, but do you have any idea why you went upstairs—for the first time?"

"I—I don't know."

She looked at him, so broken and empty but without any of the vacancy in her eyes that one would expect in such a situation.

"That's all right. If you remember, you tell me, yes?"

She nodded, though her eyes no longer met his as they spoke.

"Clara, I am going now but, I will find a way to return soon. All right?"

"Yes, Harold. That will be fine," she said flatly, succumbed to too heavy a burden for anyone to bear, especially one who is already internally distraught.

"Is everything all right for you here?" Harold asked, as he prepared to leave.

"Yes, the guards are nice to me. Not so bad for a prison, really."

"I'll be back, Clara." He bid her farewell, walking away with an unbearable sadness in his heart.

Martin, who had excellent hearing, had heard Harold's conversation with Clara from the spot he waited in with Agnes and Edward down the corridor.

"Prison?" he said, surprised.

"What was that?" Edward asked, thinking he must have missed half of what Martin said. To merely say "prison" made little sense.

"I'm afraid I don't follow either," Agnes said, knowing that she had heard what Martin said but, not being able to make any sense of it either.

"Clara just said something about being in prison," Martin explained. Edward and Agnes looked at each other, still confused. Harold approached them now.

"Why did Clara say that about prison?" Martin asked, not waiting to first hear the voice confirmation that yes, it was Harold and choosing instead to identify him by the sound of his gait.

"You could hear that?" Harold said in surprise but then, saddened still by Clara, continued,

"I fear it's worse even than I thought. Emma was

concerned about how she would face being here, but Clara doesn't even seem to realize where she is. She thinks she is in prison, rather than here in the asylum."

CHAPTER TWENTY-FIVE

"What do you make of it all?" Agnes asked Edward, as she pushed open her front door.

"I have to agree with what Martin said, when we dropped him off on the way home. There's more to this."

Agnes nodded and held the door open for Edward to enter.

"It just doesn't seem like she's guilty, does it? She's just so utterly confused that it's difficult to know what she thinks at all, let alone what really happened."

"Harold took the news hard, didn't he?" Edward said, sitting down at the table now. She had insisted that he stay for supper.

"I think he was friends with her grandfather and feels responsible toward her."

"She's all alone, then? I couldn't quite hear everything that was said."

"I think so, yes. Mystery seems to follow us, doesn't it?"

She looked to Edward for a response, but his gaze was fixed on some faraway thought and she knew he was not really present.

"I do wish I knew what sweeps you away from me so completely," she said, with no real intention of him hearing.

The metronome of Edward's mind clicked rapidly through his thoughts. He began to tap his hand against the table in rhythmic accompaniment, as the series of thoughts reeled faster through his mind. His tapping stopped abruptly and he looked at her.

"Do we know how long she was in employment at Rosebrim Manor?"

"Hmm?" Agnes said, now swept away in her own thoughts. In an uncharacteristic reversal of action, he repeated his statement for her to hear.

"Do you know how long Clara was at Rosebrim Manor?"

"Oh, I don't know exactly—I imagine it was a few months ago when she first came. Why do you ask?"

"A few months are long enough to convince someone of a person's character, aren't they? I mean, shouldn't someone be able to say something to shed some light and clear her name?" She crossed the floor and came to sit across from him now. Looking at his intently set features, she was certain that Clara's case was yet another cause he had taken up to champion. She realized now, for the first time, that his plight was perhaps not only that of a good Samaritan. His dedication to others could stem from some self-serving reason of proving himself, in addition to his altruistic undertaking. He was staring at her, waiting for her reply that she realized she had not yet provided.

"It seems so, yes. I think they are all so shocked by what has happened that they don't know what to think. At least some time has been bought for her, since they insisted on sending her to the asylum rather than prison."

"Yes, how did they manage that?"

"Oh, then you didn't hear what Harold said. Well, I suppose he was speaking rather low at the time. Anyway, it seems that Emma has a friend who is a policeman and explained the situation about her amnesia. Frederick, completely distraught over his fiancée's predicament, suggested that they send her to the asylum until she could regain her memory and then properly stand trial."

"Then, they think she did it?" Edward asked, sitting forward. The clock ticked methodically from the wall above their heads, reminding them that every moment mattered in such an instance.

Agnes lifted her eyes to Edward's face. She shrugged, as she said,

"I don't know, but I think we all know she did it. It's just that everyone is hoping to prove it was an accident."

"Why do you suppose that is?" he asked, shifting uncomfortably in his chair. The cold and rains had pounded their way into his bones during those long years on the front and, even in the balmy days of summer, they could grasp his joints without warning and stiffen his body into regimental submission.

"I think we are all surprised at even the thought of someone like Clara being accused of something so terrible. The war is our horror, but at home in England nothing so black is supposed to exist."

She had captured his thoughts so eloquently from the day they had seen Frederick digging the graves that he stopped and looked at her, feeling as though he was looking into a hazed mirror. Perhaps, the painted lady was not the only woman who could read him.

Her mystery, which he had wrapped himself in so entirely, felt somehow less important next to Clara's case. And yet, from the beginning it had never really been about the painting. It had been about him. In finding her story he could, perhaps, have the courage to write his own. He knew that now. And just maybe, it could also be about Clara and discovering the events of her story.

"Are you all right?" Agnes asked, as they ate their meal largely in silence.

"Hmm? Oh, just thinking."

Believing that she knew the reason for his contemplation, she didn't press the matter further.

"Another cuppa?" she asked when their plates, bolstered by the summer vegetables, were cleared.

"If you don't mind, I think I'll be headed home now."

"Oh yes, of course. I am tired from the day as well."

He made no attempt to correct her, but he wasn't tired. On the contrary, he was enlivened by the prospect of delving into Clara's case through the painting.

Abandoning his fear of the painted lady, which had abated during his intimate portrayal of her, he marched into his house with steely determination. Lifting a glass of water to her, he stared into her unmoving face and waited for her words, which had the power to alter so much.

"What happened with Clara?" he said, with stoic strength.

"Fix it, must fix it," the painting replied.

"Yes, let's fix it," he repeated.

"Remember, remember, remember," the painting said. The hairs at the back of Edward's neck stood on edge.

"How can I remember that which I don't know?" he said in annoyance, to the unobliging painting. As he spoke, his hand involuntary lowered, taking with it any chance of hearing her.

"No, you're right. I mustn't be cross with you. How can I expect answers, if I am not concentrating hard enough? Yes, that's it. I'll concentrate more." He spoke the words as if in reply to some objection from her, but really the remark had come of his own logic. He lifted the glass before his companion to entice her to speak.

"Lady Pemblebrooke." This time he was certain that it was not his own thought, but hers.

"Yes, yes, what about Lady Pemblebrooke?" he asked, becoming excited at the promise of a lead.

"I was only trying to help."

"Trying to help? What? Who were you trying to help?" he asked.

"Father."

"Yes, yes?!"

"Agnes and James."

He turned his back to her in anger.

"You weren't supposed to be talking about me! You were supposed to explain about Clara! You weren't supposed to cross that boundary. You betrayed my trust."

He sat down heavily in the chair, causing it to scrape across the wooden floor as it inched backward. His knees jutted up, as he bent his tall frame into the confines of the chair. He was reminded of the desk in Agnes's classroom and how he seemed never able to comfortably fit here in England. He never remembered having this problem before. Was furniture larger in America to accommodate him easier or had his discomfort morphed him in a physical sense as well?

"Ah! I'm losing my mind," he said, sitting forward. His head hung down, as his shoulders slumped. His arm extended toward the floor and the glass hung limply in his hand. It teetered on the verge of spilling, the way his threatening soul did.

"A man could lose his mind in a place like this," James said, from some faraway memory. The distance was soon bridged, transporting Edward once again to those murky mountains of hunkered bodies and cesspools of discarded bullet cartridges, fluids, and dreams.

"You scared?" a man younger than him, whose name he could never remember, asked. The young soldier's eyes bulged in that frantic mix of fear and grit. Edward hadn't answered the question. He felt the thin shoulder, not yet old enough to carry the developed muscle of men Edward's own age, through the coarse fabric of the material.

"We'll beat them," Edward said, as he pat the man's arm, before turning away. Bile churned with its vitriolic grind in his stomach, offering its own reply. Yes, he was scared all right.

"Let's move out," the voice to his left said. Edward nodded, slamming the weighty security of the metal helmet down against his head. He had been careless and his skull throbbed with a dull ache, disgruntled from his rough treatment. Edward's thoughts blurred, as bayonets clicked into place and bullets were loaded in preparation to tear into flesh and shred it into oblivion.

"How did we get here?"

"What did you say, Edward?" James said, from the spot beside his elbow, where he had hunkered down.

"Oh nothing," Edward said, not intending to have spoken aloud. Preoccupied with his own preparations, James accepted the dismissal of words without a second thought. But, Edward gave it a second thought and even a third.

Isn't man beyond this yet? Aren't we in the twentieth century?

He had, from those early childhood days of examining the toy train, always delighted himself in the progress of man. But, progress was supposed to eradicate war. This was, the politicians were saying, "the war to end all wars". But how could something be ending, which seemed to be growing daily in more ferocity? Progress was supposed to be about finding a better way, not about new ways to mangle and kill with ever increasing destruction and consequence.

"Edward—Edward, are you all right?" James asked, staring at him now.

"Just remembering our training," he said, emerging from the philosophic aura that had bound him captive.

Orders hurried along the length of the trenches.

"Remember me, all right?" James said to Edward.

"Remember you?" Edward said aloud now, breaking the spell and transporting him once again to his house in England. The water sloshed over the side of the glass. His hand, unnoticed by him, had shaken at James's words. Had James ever really spoken those words? Edward thought they sounded misplaced and inaccurate in his memory. Plunging into battle was hardly the time to utter such a request. But, there was much that had blurred about that day and it was difficult to remember that which he had suppressed for so long. No, he must have altered the memory, because of the painted lady's words. She seemed always to admonish him to remember, when for so long all he had wanted was to forget. That day was too painful, too—

A rapping at the door interrupted his thoughts. Who could it be at so late an hour? Edward stood and turned to answer his door. The knocking pounded heavier.

"Yes, I am coming. I hear you," he said to the impatient knocker. The stone walls, heavyset and staunch, concealed his voice from the outside world. He found himself locking his door more habitually lately, not that anyone really came anyway—until tonight.

Edward opened the door to the blackness of the night. Clouds clustered around the moon and blocked its radiance. Only the faintest shade of dim played across the figure before him.

"Agnes?" he said, surprised.

Her face, paler than the retreating moon, looked into his own now. Her eyes remained fixed, as she reached into her pocket and pressed a telegram into his hands.

Fear gripped his stomach with a powerful punch. He dreaded what the telegram would hold, but knew he must read the words. The war had taught him, and the painted lady had reminded him, that there was no escaping that which came to him. A shudder convulsed in his body, but he swallowed it and began to read. Before he could finish, Agnes spoke the awful words aloud,

"John is missing."

Having spoken them, she quivered at their sound and collapsed against Edward, no longer able to bear the weight of them alone.

CHAPTER TWENTY-SIX

Clara stared at the concrete wall, so austere and unwelcoming. The confines of a person's home ought to radiate with the serenity and warmth expressed in the interaction the inhabitants share with each other. Clara's surrounds lacked all the familiarity and cheerfulness of such a situation. Instead, the sparse and clinically sterile room embodied the sentiment of Clara's mind and she was perpetually taunted by their reminder of her absent memory.

She struggled against the tyrannical reign of her amnesia, by finding whatever means she could to remember. Her pale finger lifted to trace the place on the wall that captured her so intently now. A host of tiny marks, where the tines of her fork during meals had peeled and chipped away the topcoat of paint, stood as soldiers summoned to attention before her.

Had she really been here so long? She had vowed to herself that if memory failed her, she would find her own way to mark the passage of time. Though alarmed that so many days had passed, she was comforted that the tedium of the days had been erased in her lapsed mind. Clara began counting the marks on the wall, resolved to know just how many days had passed. With a cursory glance she had already realized that months must have passed in the confines.

"One, two, three," she counted. No sound escaped but her lips moved in silent accompaniment, as her finger moved from one mark to the next.

Steps echoed from somewhere down the hall, momentarily distracting Clara. Had she counted twenty-four or was it thirty-four?

Think. Think. Maybe, it was twenty-four. A flush of heat rolled across her body from the deep confines of her stomach. The steps grew louder. Clara's hand shook at their sound and she lost not only the number in her head, but her finger also slipped from the mark she had last counted.

"No, don't come for me," she whispered, toward the corridor. She turned her back on the bars and refocused her attention on the microcosm of her world. She lifted her trembling finger and let it slide into the groove of the first day. It shook violently, as the steps neared her. Clara lifted her left hand to steady her right hand. She clamped it against the right wrist to guide her movement. As the footsteps neared, they pounded against her head threatening to undo her composure of herself. Despite trying to steady her hand, it shook again as she realized now that there were two sets of footsteps drawing close to her. The wave of heat that swept through her body now prickled against her with an icy needling of her nerves.

The marks on the wall, which had been intended for comfort, now felt like an overturned hourglass. The passage of time meant the inevitable consequences for what had happened would surely come soon. She had no real rationale for why she remained in captivity but unpunished. As if someone had punched her stomach hard, all the air within her dissipated and a monstrous fear gripped her body. What if the trial had already happened? What if like so much else, having no recollection of it having taken place did not mean, as she had supposed, that it had not occurred but simply that it had become yet another casualty in her inability to remember.

"Miss Banks," a voice broke into her thoughts. Such horror convulsed through her body that the words felt as though they were clawing through her. She kept her back turned, intent upon counting the days to wrestle back any control she could have in the situation.

"Miss Banks," the voice repeated.

"My time isn't over yet," she said, through gritted teeth, in more of a whisper than anything else.

The feet hesitated in front of the cell. Hanging on the possibility provided in the moments, Clara counted the days from the first marks again. Purgatory had never really occurred to her, but in the midst of war with so many dying daily there very well may be a waiting list to get into heaven. Clara had been consigned to waiting for so many months, first for her memory to return and then in confinement. Now, she felt she could wait no longer.

"Ten, eleven, twelve," she continued counting the days, needing to know how many had passed that she could exchange for her waiting time to enter heaven when— when the punishment came. Perspiration glistened on her brow and trickled into the creases formed in her concentration and desperation.

"Thirteen, fourteen."

Clara's finger, which had been steadily moving along the marks, wavered over the fifteenth mark. She wanted to hasten her arrival in heaven, to no longer prolong the torturous waiting, but—the thought struck her like lightning—what if she really had killed them? What would become of her?

The tremor in her hand spread like wildfire and her body convulsed. From the disturbed clutter, whooshing foggily through her mind, appeared the taunting sound of silence.

"No, not yet, I'm not ready," she whispered to the wall.

"Miss Banks," the voice said again but she refused to acknowledge its presence, certain that it could only lead to the gallows. Already, she could feel the abrasive rub of the rope on her delicate porcelain skin. The air would suddenly abandon her, as it had that night. A flash of a person, small in stature and dark in hair, struggling to breathe confronted her now. Her eyes opened wide at the jolt to her memory.

Who was he? I went upstairs and—

"Clara," a second voice spoke now and cut through her thoughts with the clarity and certainty that only his voice could hold. She spun abruptly, the rope on her neck slipped to her wrist and strung her to him.

"Frederick," she said, as he stepped forward.

"I see she remembers you, even if she won't answer me," the guard said, "I'll leave you be to talk."

"Thank you, yes," Frederick said, turning momentarily from Clara to face the guard, before turning back to her. She stared at him with such surprise that he wondered if she had suddenly forgot who he was. Her eyes remained fixed on him, following his every move. If the two had not been here and instead strolling in the park, certainly anyone who observed her would be sure that she was utterly devoted to him and hopelessly in love. Frederick knew better, though, and that it was her ability to remember the constancy of him in a fleeting sea that she was enamored with, rather than him. She only confirmed it, as she said,

"You came back."

Such wonder and innocence filled her face that anyone would immediately have questioned the sanity of the accusations. Frederick's eyes flickered in sadness, their chestnut brown deepening to mahogany.

"What is it?" Clara said, always able to observe the smallest change in Frederick when she could ignore whole conversations of someone else entirely.

"Nothing really," he said, attempting to brush it off.

"Oh Frederick, please tell me," Clara said, stepping even closer to him to intimate that he should disclose whatever it was.

"It's safe. They can't hear us here," she whispered. She meant it as comfort, but the words only more strongly drew forth his sadness. It clustered in his eyes and dug its trenches into his forehead.

"My poor Clara," he whispered back to her. She reached through the bar and gripped his hand, as her eyes went wide in horror.

"You have heard something! I have little time left." Her words shook him from the melancholy that had descended over him.

"Oh no, it isn't that," he said to assure her, "it's just that we all hoped that your memory might return, so that you can clear your name by stating whatever really happened. Surely, they will take mercy on you when they see it was an accident. Lady Lu— Pemblebrooke was beloved, but so too are you, Clara."

"But, you are here now and so I can remember. I remember that you are my fiancé. I didn't forget that. I told you I would not," she said, holding his hand and nearly pleading her case.

"That is true, but Clara, I do come often. I fear my presence is not helping you remember, as much as I hoped it would."

His hand went limp beneath hers, as he coughed. It was the deep throaty cough of one much older who had been worn thin and to the bone. Clara tightened her grip on his hand, determined not to allow him to give up on her. He was all she had, wasn't he? Well, there were Harold and his friends but cordial as they had been, what could they do that Frederick, her fiancé, could not? Such lucid rational thinking only served to frustrate her more that she could not remember the details of the night. How could someone so logical have done such a thing? But no, that wasn't the right thing to think. If she said that they would be certain that she had been calculating enough to carry out such a deed.

Frederick looked to her face and how could she be denied with such intent streaming from her eyes?

"All right, I will help you remember."

"Good. Now, how shall we do this?" she asked, eagerly. His presence had shifted her mood and a glimmer of optimism whispered from just beyond her reach.

"I will tell you what I remember," he said, wearily.

"Yes, yes, I'm sure that will work." The doubt in his eyes

prompted her to ask,

"You are not so sure?"

"It's only that we've done this before." He coughed again and it bent his body into an arch, forcing him to drop her hand that had been clutching his own.

"Are you all right?"

"Fine, fine," he said, his voice hoarse and raspy.

"If you're able to go on, then I am ready," she said.

He cleared his throat, which only sent him into another fit of coughing.

"Right," he said, when the coughing had subsided, "I heard a scream in the middle of the night. This was not out of the ordinary, but then the screaming continued." Clara stared at him, hanging on his words.

"It got louder and louder." His face paled at the remembrance of the night.

"I can hear it!" Clara said, having successfully summoned the memory.

"Her screaming was worse than usual, like some wild, savage beast," he said, his eyes gone wide at the horror.

"Yes, yes," Clara said becoming wrapped in the memory like a blanket, a blanket that—

Clara's eyes widened and remained fixed, as though she were staring at something too gruesome to speak of.

"Albert was calling out in the night. It must have been his voice, small though as he was, it did not sound wholly feminine," he said, taking note of her reaction, but knowing he must continue to talk to help her remember.

"Shh, don't worry. I'll help you get warm," Clara said, now wrapped in a daze, as she relived the night.

"So, you gave Albert a blanket to keep warm," Frederick said in conjecture, to help her fill in the missing pieces.

"Here, it's all right. I'll tuck you in," Clara said, oblivious to Frederick and her surroundings.

"You tucked Albert in," Frederick said, his voice no longer as steady as it had been, much like a horse slowing to a canter from a gallop.

Clara said nothing further.

"And then?" Frederick said, to prompt her to remember.

Clara said nothing, but crossed to her bed where she pulled up the blanket to tuck in the absent Albert.

"There, now you won't cry anymore," she said. Her words would have raised no alarm, had she not been pressing her weight against the bed. She was reenacting not an act of compassion, but as Frederick whispered it now,

"Suffocation."

CHAPTER TWENTY-SEVEN
Paris
September 1783

Daniel observed the high-arching flying buttresses of the carved stone of Notre Dame Cathedral, as he bustled along the streets of Paris. The soaring spires and high walls of the buildings, lining the banks of the Seine, rose toward the billowy clouds as the tall trees in the seemingly endless forests of the American colonies had.

No, that wasn't right. They weren't colonies anymore. They had asserted independence, fought against the crown, and somehow emerged as a nation of their own. They never would have been able to either, if it hadn't been for those meddling French!

"English," a passerby whispered, gawking at Daniel openly. He paid them no heed and hurried on his way. He crossed the Seine and was assaulted by the smells of all that occupied the river and all who dwelt beside it, carrying out their business, bartering for goods. If these peasants should suddenly revolt against Louis, would they be as fortunate in their traitorous uprising? Ah, but then there would be no mighty French navy to come to their aid, or any gallant Lafayette to befriend them. The thoughts hinged on the caustic disapproval of sarcasm that bellowed from the depths of his stomach.

The stiffness, felt on the breeze at the earliest sign of autumn, encompassed him now as he continued along the other side of the Seine. The weather reminded him of the changing seasons, but it was the altering nature of the world that more heavily lay upon his mind. The future, though always changing and approaching, seemed especially keen to morph itself into some new dimension of reality as of late. Upheaval of all that Daniel had grown up to believe was permanent eroded under the heat of the American sun, as he marched proudly in his red woolen uniform prepared to die for king and country. But Daniel hadn't died or even suffered injury. But, England had. Like the hundreds of arms and legs no longer attached to the bodies of his comrades, the colonies had been amputated from King George.

In his haste, he stumbled against a stone in the street and steadied himself. Everything from rocks to ideas seemed out of place. But no, perhaps he hadn't really been prepared to die for the nation. What good did dying do, when being alive provided a means of seeing all that lay ahead? As irate and incredulous as he was about the colonists' disloyalty and subsequent victory, his interest was piqued at what would unfold—or would it unravel, instead? Well, that's what they were here for anyway, to take a step into the future, to settle the terms of victory. England must recognize the sovereignty of its former possession. The words still raked across his mind with acidic tines. Accounts must be settled and for more than the land.

His feet turned onto Rue Jacob, but his memory transported him to Virginia. It was the last weeks of war, also in autumn, but two years ago now. King George hadn't yet released his *Proclamation of Cessation of Hostilities,* which was issued barely half a year ago, but it was the end of the real war. The final battle at the coastal town of Yorktown, where General Cornwallis had surrendered—Daniel still could scarcely believe it, had happened days later. But Daniel's memory carried him farther inland to a family's property that would not be restored, unlike the Loyalists whose property and rights were provided for in the signing of this Paris Peace Treaty they were all gathering for.

He had been on patrol, when those hostile rains of the eastern seaboard had begun to fall. In a clearing, a cottage with a woman outside came into view. Daniel was sure they must have appeared pompous to her. They were, more than anything else, tired and hungry and searching for food. Never did they expect to find such beautiful silver and fabrics inside. There had also been a painting, Renaissance in origin if he were a correct judge of it. The woman had pleaded that they not take it and while the other men had reacted callously toward her, he had felt regret at the dealing. What good was it to protect the English way of life, if an English solider was not a man of his word? At least, he was certain that's how his God-fearing, morally upright mother would have felt. The men, who had no intention of returning the painting to her, did not even seem to want it for themselves. They eagerly divided the silver, pawning it off for profit, only a meager portion of which they spent on food despite having told Daniel it was necessary so they would be fed.

"No one wants the painting?" Daniel had asked, seeing it strewn carelessly onto a pile of clothing needing to be washed.

"You can have it," one had said.

Another, drunk and speaking as a mad man, slurred something about it being haunted and that there was witchcraft in this cursed land after all. Daniel dismissed the claims, but gathered the painting and prepared to return it to the woman. He had every good intention of doing exactly that but as he rounded the bend that brought her house into view, he caught sight of three gathered in the alcove rather than one. Two men, dressed in the garb of the colonial army and navy, flanked her sides like the cannons of a ship. That potential for bombast was precisely what daunted him in his errand. He had come upon the house from the back and, taking a leaf from the tactics of the colonial army, hid behind a bush as he crouched low to the ground.

"Jacob, oh Jacob! You are home!" she repeated over and over.

"Where did they have you? We were worried something fierce," the man, he guessed to be Jacob's brother, said now.

"I was in Scotland, held in the dungeon of Edinburgh Castle, as a lousy pirate," he said, with more fatigue than bitterness.

"Well, you are home now. Praise be! Both of my boys are safe and the war will soon be over," she said, ushering the two inside the house.

As Daniel watched them, he thought of his own homecoming. His mother's arms would soon be around him as well, welcoming him home as a hero even if England were not victorious. He had hoped to return the painting as an act of charity to assuage his own guilt. It would no longer be the centerpiece of her day as he had envisioned, but it would nonetheless complete the homecoming.

What was that? A rattling, or perhaps a scampering, through low brush was not ten or twenty paces away and distracted him from his plan. He had decided to leave the painting on the doorstep when all were tucked safely inside, but now his immediate preoccupation dwelt in determining what had made the noise. He concentrated his efforts on the bush, while attempting to conceal himself. As he spotted who it was, he stepped from the clearing. Another scarlet coated solider stood before him, well intending to walk in the direction of the cottage.

"There's nothing there worth looking at. We might as well head back," Daniel heard himself speak the words, before he had time to make his decision. Apparently, it had been made for him. For whatever reason, he had taken it upon himself to protect the family from discovery. He had been unable to prevent the plunder of the woman's home, but he was now able to protect the removal of the woman's more valuable sons. With his decision, the chance to return the painting had disappeared; he didn't much think the woman would mind.

Perhaps indulging his sentimental side too heavily, though Daniel preferred to think of it as holding onto a souvenir of war, the painting had remained in Daniel's possession and traveled across the blood-spoiled waters of the Atlantic.

Three Americans had journeyed abroad to this conference, as well. As he approached the British embassy at number forty-four, he saw a cluster of men talking together on the street. He squinted to see if he might be able to see the wiry glasses of Benjamin Franklin. He could see no glasses, but perhaps it was merely because of the distance. Or perhaps, it was David Hartley he was spying. He was certain that Mr. Hartley, with his disregard for the slave trade and as a fellow British citizen, would have acknowledged his need for gentlemanly civility.

"Daniel, Daniel!" a voice called out to him, rushing forward. He turned to see another young soldier, assisting on this momentous occasion of the signing of the peace treaty.

"Yes, what is it?" Daniel said.

"With all these signings of treaties, with the French and the Dutch and the Spanish— "

"And the Americans," Daniel added.

"Yes, yes, the Americans. All this trouble is about them, after all. Anyway, with all these making amends with our enemies, we are not to forget the loyal Hessians and I have been called upon to supply a gift."

Daniel stared at the prattling man, waiting for him to reach his point. When he had come to the end of the explanation, the essence was still nowhere in sight and so Daniel asked,

"And, you want me to do what?"

"Well, I cannot simply buy something here. Everything is so... so..."

"French?"

"Yes, exactly and we cannot give our ally something French to commemorate our battle against the French."

"No, I don't suppose we can," Daniel said, wanting to be rid of the conversation and inside the building for the signing. Despite not wanting to accept the final act of divorce, he had hoped to be present at the occasion.

"Daniel, do you think I could have it, to give them as the present then?"

"Have what?"

"Well, it doesn't look especially American or French or anything insulting. I don't think so anyway. I think it's rather ordinary looking, but in a nice way."

"Have what?" Daniel repeated, hoping this time to have his question answered.

"The painting, that portrait of the woman dressed in the silks that you showed me. Would you mind?"

Daniel looked at the man before him. It seemed like a simple enough request. What he couldn't reconcile was the growing lump in his stomach.

"I'll fetch the painting from my quarters, as soon as the treaty is signed."

And with that, he distanced himself from his piece of America while England formally acknowledged the disappearance of her colonies.

CHAPTER TWENTY-EIGHT

The winds of autumn rustled the leaves of England, as Edward walked through the grounds of his estate. Their bronze beauty graced the trees and, for a moment, he was swept once again to France. It had been much like this when he had left the trenches to return with bread, such an ordinary necessity on a commonplace day. How quickly it all had changed so shortly after, when the bullets had rained down in the tempest that waylaid him on his journey. Or perhaps, he thought, with a touch of philosophic musing, it had really set him forth upon the sea of discovery he found himself sailing on now. Had a year really passed since that deafening blast?

Limited as his hearing still was at times, there was an abundance that he did hear. The sound of the rains on the window panes still sent his body quivering in remembrance of the soaked trenches and brought to mind the smell of the mold, forcing it into his nostrils and he sent it away with the expulsion of his cough. So too could he hear the tears of Agnes, hidden away, disguised among the dark solitude of night as his own tormented cries had been so many times in the months he'd spent in her home. John's disappearance only became worse and more unbearable in the daily reminders of her home. Edward's house, despite its drafty corridors and mysterious framed inhabitant, had offered the serenity his wearied soul sought so fervently. Agnes's home had stolen all solace from her, chaining her to the tormented pain of memory. In every chair, John's smiling face had sat. In every room, his melodious whistle scattered the stillness. Her heart broke at the thought of those lips never parting again. She could not bear the possibility of him not returning.

"Edward, I can't handle it. He is everywhere I turn, now more so than ever before. I find myself remembering the smallest gesture, a faint snippet of conversation, some tiny mannerism or expression. Rather than comfort, they torment me. What an awful sister I have become!" she had said to him, broken in those first days after the telegram's arrival.

He had wanted to say that he understood. James and the faces of so many others, which he had regrettably paid less attention to at the time, haunted his own mind as well. But, Edward could admit no such thing. Instead, he had said to her,

"Agnes, come and stay with me. I offered before and you were unready. Come now."

He held out his hand to her with all the kindness in his heart. He knew the kindness could only thrive because of her own compassion she had not merely shown him, but heaped upon him, this past year. She looked at him with a look he had felt within himself so many times before. Agnes's grief had hardened her in determination. Realizing it was futile to pretend she could withstand the circumstances alone, she gave in to Edward's suggestion and stopped trying to protect everyone alone.

There was also the sound of the names of Ypres and Passchendaele, which crossed the lips of hundreds, which months before had spoken of Verdun and the Somme. New weapons, new troops, even new countries with the arrival of the USA this past summer found themselves in new places to fight, but the war was the same, unrelenting and unyielding.

The painted lady, rather out of character, had yielded little to Edward either as of late. With the great cacophony of sound enveloping him, she had been unnaturally quiet. It was almost as though she were a person, contemplative on the matters as the rest of them were and so reserving her speech. Such a thought was lunacy though, because any right-minded person knew that she had no knowledge of what was occurring in the war. For that matter, she had no knowledge at all. No, it must be something else. Perhaps, Edward was simply not allowing her enough time to speak. Their conversations were reduced to the status of a clandestine affair of stolen moments with Agnes present. He had been certain that was the case anyway, until Agnes had returned to the rooms of the school and the words of the other woman in his life still had remained absent.

Well, absent was a bit of an overstatement, but the woman who had before seemed unable to do anything other than lob a barrage of questions at him, was now refrained in her words. The bold and brazen woman of accusation had become the shy temptress of contemplation. Maybe her coy nature was a personality trait he had bestowed upon her himself since she no longer adorned the spot above his mantel, prominent and center-stage, but now was tucked into the wardrobe safely stowed away from Agnes's eyes.

He told himself that concealing the painting was an act of benevolence. Were he to expose Agnes to so severe an examination of herself, what resolve she had mercifully managed to maintain may very well crumble. It was a compassionate solution to prevent Agnes from seeing the painted lady. Logical as his rationale was, Edward knew full well that it was not the complete truth. No, to be honest, Edward knew that it was not even what constituted half of his reason. It was rather, only a pleasant and convenient side effect. The impetus behind his stealthy stowaway was not even entirely to prevent Agnes from thinking he was crazy, as he had imagined the reason to be at the beginning. Edward realized now that he desired to keep the painting hidden, because she was his. The statement seemed rather ill-fitting to his reality, as he walked through the wide open grounds of his house now. He was not a pauper clinging desperately to his only possession. Despite the war, Edward was a gentleman of means and had managed to acquire a house full of costly possessions. Edward stopped in his tracks, his head suddenly reeling in confusion. What was he doing? How could he have proven that he was more than just a man of wealth, dressed in John's clothes, insisted upon enlisting and being a soldier, no better off than any other soldier who had been a farmer or a blacksmith or a factory worker rather than the son of a factory owner and land holder, to return unchanged?

It was far from true. The air whistled harshly against his left ear, stinging it with a pulsing burn of cold. He was changed. His hearing would probably never fully be restored and his memories hounded him wherever he turned. Somehow though, the arduous task of remaking himself had not happened. Edward sat down hard, allowing the dirt to push against his trousers and leave its muddy handprint on him. Is that what he had set about to do? Had he become so disillusioned with wealth in the face of suffering that he had subconsciously decided to abandon it? Is that why he had decided not to return home to California? If it were true, then he had failed. Almost immediately upon returning to England, he had immersed himself in the hunt for the owner of the largest house in town and then proceeded to buy it! He had devoted himself to the mystery of a painting, when surely Agnes could have needed him more. Had he seemed ungracious to her? He'd torn from her home, as one caught on the tail of the wind, on so many occasions to sneak away and spend time with another woman. Worse, she did not even need him and was pigment rather than flesh and blood.

There was, of course, another woman who was in desperate need of help. As Edward's eyes surveyed his now harvested fields— perhaps there was some good in wealth after all— he became lost in a vision of Clara in the gardens of Rosebrim Manor. So little of her case made sense. How could she have done it? Her disposition was nothing of a murderer—but, then neither was his and surely bullets he had fired must have ripped into the bodies of men he'd shot at across the trenches. His stomach lurched forward, as nausea swept across him in its body-gripping intensity. How many had he killed, anyway? The nausea sent chills of discomfort with sickening speed throughout his body.

But, with Clara it had been different. She had known these people. They were not the nameless strangers blindly fired at across the fences of wire and from the turrets of the towers of sandbags. As poorly as he could comprehend her ability to commit such an act, he had even more difficulty in fathoming how she was physically able to complete the task. She was not an especially tall woman, though she was an inch or two taller than Agnes. She had easily hoisted the laundry basket in the afternoon sun but within the mental hospital, at closer range, her muscles had seemed normal in size. He had heard that suffocation was involved but if one of the three had succumbed to so tragic an end then, surely, the other two would have noticed and prevented falling victim to the same crime. Wouldn't they have? Well, wouldn't they have? The words echoed in his mind, sounding much like the stream of commentary hurled at him by the painted lady on her more gregarious days. His thoughts spun, dizzying his senses and heightening his nausea.

Acid crept from the base of his throat and he spat it out against the deep brown of the soil. He pushed himself up with his hands and continued in his walk. The trees had already begun to shed their summer coats. Their stark bareness, disrobed of the luscious greens of spring and summer and then the crackling fiery colors of autumn, had always before appeared lonely to him, stripped, and exposed. Now, for the first time, he began to envy their lithe nature that would be forthcoming in the subsequent months. They would be unencumbered, their load would be removed and they would be truly free.

A haziness arose from the shifting light, flitting between cloud and sun, as a witness to the alteration of the seasons. The traces of light filtered lazily through the leaves above, sending a mosaic onto the ground at his feet and speckling his memory. The light lulled him into a fogginess. It was far more pleasant than, but not so different from, that haze that had rolled over those vast expanses of open spaces in France. Tiredness seemed to come upon him instantaneously, leaping upon him as though he were its prey. The predatory confusion of torn affliction and deepening mystery pressed upon him in the form of an unnaturally heavy burden.

"Edward," James called to him from beneath the shadow of the tree he approached.

"Edward, don't forget to wear your mask."

CHAPTER TWENTY-NINE

Martin stretched his legs, as he arched his back against the wicker back of the rocking chair on the porch. A slight wind brushed against his cheeks, not abrasively but in the gentle playfulness of nature's blush he had relished as a young boy. Woodsmoke, heavier and more frequent lately as the weather cooled and the villages heaped their hearths more plentifully, wafted tantalizingly toward him and settled in his nostrils. His favorite season was erupting around him in glorious color. He was unable to see the foliage that hung above his roof, but he drifted easily on the sea of remembrance to the mighty oak aglow in crimson, scarlet, burnt umber and sienna. He breathed in his memory, bending beneath the sweeping boughs of the tree toward the mossy ground. He lifted a delicate leaf and proceeded to examine it. His fingers moved across the arm of the chair, tracing the scalloped edges of the recollected leaf. His finger stopped abruptly in its movement. What did the veins look like? How did they branch?

"Open your eyes," he whispered, in the memory, "Just look at them. What do you see?" The leaf, which he tried so resolutely to focus clearly on, blurred beyond recognition.

"No, no, come back! Come back!" Martin cried out in desperation.

"I can do it! I can see," he said, with gritted teeth, "Just open your eyes! Open! Open!" He urged his eyelids to lift, as a curtain does at the opening of a theatrical performance to allow all to see the splendor, but they were unrelenting. Locked firmly shut, they would not consent to his plea to see. Sitting back, exhausted at the mental exertion, he focused his ears, forcing them to observe all for him. A flock of birds twittered above in a stream of winged camaraderie. Martin had once been part of a group, as well. Some men had isolated themselves, keeping separate from the others in the trenches. Martin had long suspected that Edward, surrounded in his cloak of somberness, was one of these men. But Martin had endeared himself to the other soldiers, befriending all, talking of home with whomever would listen.

Constantly attuning his ears to the most sensitive of sounds caused Martin to hear things he didn't even realize he was listening to. This happened now, as footsteps weighed heavily on his front walkway.

"Hello, Harold," Martin said, as though he'd been expecting to see him all along.

"Martin, you do amaze me, my boy with your ability to hear all," Harold said, breaking into a smile that reddened the pronounced apples of his cheeks, giving substance to their name. He had spoken his greeting before realizing that Harold, or anyone for that matter, was in front of him and was slightly surprised at hearing Harold speak.

"It's just become habit, I suppose," Martin said with a trace of a smile and then, realizing that Harold must have come for a reason, continued,

"What brings you here today?"

"I just thought I might come for a visit," Harold said, his voice becoming louder as he neared Martin. There was a hint of something in his voice that he could not conceal that said there was another reason entirely why he had come, but Martin was too polite to question what Harold had said.

"Well, your company is always welcomed." Martin said, though his aura of cheerfulness was somewhat dimmed from his melancholic thoughts before Harold's arrival.

"And how have you been?" Harold said, plopping himself into the chair beside Martin. For the slightest moment, Martin considered answering with the truth, but no, he couldn't do that. If the facade slipped for even a second, a crack could form and begin the impending shattering.

"Oh fine, yes. It's a beautiful autumn day. I think a slice

of Agnes's cake would make it even better and I have some just inside. Would you care for some?" Martin said, the smile he had forced at the beginning of his answer now shone through with the genuineness elicited from the prospect of Agnes's cooking. Harold sat back and his hand moved across his stomach, as if determining whether he should risk its expanse.

"Ah come on, Harold. It's just a little cake," Martin said, his spirit of joviality returning. The subject naturally turned to the supplier of their happiness as the two sat together with their, larger than modest but smaller than greedy, slices of cake.

"And how are Agnes and that cousin of hers, what was his name—Edwin?"

"Edward. Agnes feigns bravery, but her brother John is missing. I can hear her voice taut with worry."

Harold paused, mid-bite. It didn't seem right to be indulging his appreciation for finery, when being told of the baker's misfortune.

Harold made no sound and Martin realized he must be nodding. Edward, Martin had noticed, on occasion did the same. He would pause and then awkwardly mumble his agreement, having realized that Martin could not see. Harold made no such utterance of affirmation and Martin realized that he must not have noticed what he'd done. Rather than return to the cake, Harold sat back and said,

"It seems to me that I recall something of her having a fiancé in France, as well. Has there been any word from him?"

"That's right. George is his name. It's infrequent, but she hears from him. It's even longer in between now than before."

"Hmm, I see, yes," Harold said. His appetite seemed on the verge of returning, as he picked up his fork and pushed around the morsels of cake remaining on his plate.

"And what of Clara?" Has she remembered anything?" Martin asked.

"Her fiancé, Frederick, came to see her. It seems Lady

Pemblebrooke and her children were suffocated and Clara has admitted to it, though she does not yet remember," Harold said, with the heavy tones of sadness and all hopes of returning to the cake abandoned at the mention of dear Clara. Martin sat forward.

"Pardon? How can that be?"

"You see, she didn't admit to it with words. Rather, as Frederick explained it to me, she reenacted the events of that night and it confirmed the cause that he'd long suspected based on the condition of the bodies when he found them. The only bright spot in all of this is that the authorities have decided she had no cruel intention, but acted in compassion."

"Compassion?" Martin asked, sitting up once again, his interest piqued like that of a dog's ears twitching forward in joyful concentration.

"She was, apparently, calming them of their anxieties."

Martin shifted from one side of his chair to the other, as his mind shuffled what he'd been told. He searched for any clues, as his favorite fictional detective was so apt at doing.

"Clara suffers from memory loss. This we all know to be true. But, she seemed quite lucid when we went to visit her. The act you described seems to be something that would be done by one who has gone mad."

Harold said nothing for a moment and in the peace of a quiet part of a tormented day, full of frustration and question, Martin was comforted by the mournful cry of some overhead bird. Harold sat forward now and ran his hand over his chin, as he prepared to speak. Martin sensed Harold's hesitation and braced himself, preparing himself to hear what Harold would say.

"I am not sure how to say this really."

"Go on, Harold. I'm not glass and I will not break," Martin said, with a smile.

"It's just that it's about the fighting."

Martin shifted, mentally preparing himself for whatever was ahead.

"Neither you or I like to talk on difficult matters. It's far nicer simply not to but, in order to help Clara, we must. Were you exposed to any gas in the trenches?"

Martin's face wrinkled in thought, trying to make sense of what Harold had asked him.

"No, I mean—gas didn't do this to me," he paused, moving his hand in front of his eyes to illustrate that he meant his blindness and then continued, "shrapnel did this." Martin sat more stiffly now, as though the shrapnel were still lodged inside of him and any movement could cause excruciating pain. Harold bent forward and pat Martin's arm.

"I'm sorry, Martin to make you relive that. I cannot imagine how difficult it must be."

No, you can't.

Martin's thought was devoid of any biting sarcasm or bitter remorse that most would have felt. Martin, like a mighty fortress, only allowed certain ideas and feelings and dispositions to dwell within him. It was not that he was any better or stronger than any of the others who had been ravaged by war; he was, rather, at the root of everything grounded in fear that the fragile shell of humor he'd told Edward he had wrapped himself in was cracking. Were it to do so, he would be undone. All the anger and sadness he had banished from his soul would converge upon him, in one hellish banquet. Martin would become chained to the abyss of desperation, which he had already seen the smallest glimmer of this afternoon. He knew it would be a thousand times worse and would plague him, as the gases had hunted the men he had seen affected.

"I wasn't gassed, but I saw the effects on some of the men," he said, at last. Harold sat forward, speaking gently so as not to tread too heavily on Martin's exposed wounds.

"Did you, my boy? I had meant that in my question, if

you had witnessed the effects. I believe I asked rather poorly the first time." Martin swallowed. He had to be careful. His facade was slipping dangerously away. His wits were poised precariously close to the edge of the cliff that haunted his nightmares. They were what he had dismissed so easily, trying to absolve himself of them, when speaking with Edward. Why was Harold undoing them and he had been able to remain calm with Edward who should have provoked the stronger reaction?

Because, Edward needs you. You were able to hold it together for you and for him. You were still part of that line in the trench, like the flock of birds earlier. Your body was ripped from that place when your eyes gave up, but your heart hasn't stopped fighting. That's why you shroud yourself in laughter. You began easing your comrades and yourself with your jokes and you haven't stopped yet. But in Harold's presence, you are reminded of your youth and you see that it's been tarnished and it's too murky for the laughter to appear.

A fog lifted from Martin's mind at the thoughts. They had poured into his life as suddenly and steadily as a summer afternoon rainstorm. But like the cooling effects of the aftermath of the rains, he'd been refreshed. Seldom did such clarity grip him, but as of late, with more time devoted to thought there was the occasional dissolving of confusion as had just happened. No longer distracted, he turned his attention toward Harold. He'd been quietly waiting and hoping young Martin, whom he was so fond of, was not being too greatly burdened by his memory.

With his strength returned, Martin's body relaxed into the chair as he spoke,

"I didn't know anyone personally, thankfully, but I saw what it could do to a man. It could send him into a state of utter confusion and fright, setting mischief alight in his mind."

Harold, forgetting himself, nodded slowly.

"And, could it cause someone to do something very out of character?"

Martin's hand lifted to scratch the back of his head, as he answered,

"Oh yes, certainly. A chap could seem normal one moment and then act in an altogether foreign matter as though his mind was suddenly crippled by the fumes."

Harold said nothing and Martin realized some revelation of his own must be sinking in.

"Harold, why do you ask?"

Harold took a deep breath before answering.

"I was in London."

"Oh?"

"Yes, you see I went there in hopes of finding anyone or anything that could clear dear Clara's name."

"I thought they decided it was an accident and that she didn't know what she was doing, so she is safe."

"For now, yes. But, I fear that could be overturned. Were it someone from a small village that had fallen victim to such unfortunate events, I feel there would be no cause for alarm. But, we mustn't forget of Lady Pemblebrooke's influence. Her grandmother was a childhood friend of Queen Victoria. Did you know that?"

"No, no. I didn't know that at all," Martin said, taking a sudden new level of interest in the case. Hitherto, he had examined it as a wish to help a friend of a friend. But now, it took on a whole new dimension.

"Sorry, what does this have to do with gas?" Martin asked, mentally analyzing the clues he had.

"You see, I went to the hospital where I had first met Clara. Her doctor was not on duty but I spoke with another doctor who, upon hearing where I was from, said that he remembered there had been a patient who was treated for gas before traveling on here."

"But, Clara was in the factory, not the trenches."

"Yes, that is precisely the thought that I'd had as well.

Until—"

"Yes?"

"As I was walking out, down the corridor, I overheard a girl talking to a nurse. She had come in because she'd not been feeling well. I noticed that her hands were coated in traces of yellow and then I remembered that when I had first seen Clara her hands were also yellow, from her work in the factory. I slowed my steps to hear what I could and the nurse began asking her about the fumes in the factory."

Martin sat forward suddenly.

"You think Clara was affected by gas the way some of the soldiers have been?"

"That's right. I fear the worst damage to her happened long before that blast ever went off."

CHAPTER THIRTY

James haunted Edward wherever he looked. He would turn-up when least expected, beside the brook or standing starved as a skeleton in the now vacant fields of grain.

"Why are you following me?" he said to James now.

"Don't forget your gas mask, old chap," James said, becoming more quintessentially English as a figment of Edward's imagination than he ever had been in real life. James had now been absent from his life as long as he'd been a part of it and began to take on the quirks of Edward's new life. He would look at him with that impatient smile of Agnes's or laugh away his troubles as Martin did to hide from the pain.

Though he hated the reason, he knew why James followed him more persistently of late. October was washing over Edward in all its shades of red and orange. Leaves fell earthbound now, but the bullets rained more ferociously in his memory. Confronted everywhere by his memory of James, to the point of seeing him materialize before him and addressing the empty space, Edward was left in desperate need of someone to speak with. It would have made sense to turn to Agnes or Martin. Both would willingly have listened, but Edward had not yet emerged from within his inner turmoil enough to be able to seek solace in another. And so he turned to the one who had offered him pittance in the way of comfort, but in whom he had lost himself entirely: the painted lady.

Edward sat on the floor of his bedroom with the cold of the wooden boards pressing against his skin through his trousers. His hand brushed against a blanket, as he reached under the bed. Dust gathered beneath his fingertips and felt like dissolving balls of softness. Like a kitten batting away a ball of yarn, he pushed the dust aside as his fingers crept toward the frame. Taking her out to view now, he propped her against the wall and remained seated on the floor facing her.

She looked at him with eyes unmoving. Every line of his companion had dried centuries before. In a world of continuous change—soldiers felled like trees, revolutions rocking Ireland and Russia, now with the Communist party and a man named Lenin in power this month—she peered out at Edward. She taunted him but, once before, she had seemed able to calm the storm. But, there was also the chance that she would churn the waters and like the disciples on the Sea of Galilee, Edward faced the possibility of losing his faith and becoming petrified leaving him huddled at the bottom of the boat.

"Well, let us begin," he said, taking a deep breath and holding a silver picture frame to her. He had forgot to bring a glass with him from downstairs, but perhaps this would be better. This was the date he'd been shaken. This could be the day of revealing the truth, framing it neatly and boxing it in safely.

"Just do it for James," Edward told himself, gathering his courage. He stared hard at her and, for a moment, nothing happened. Edward readjusted the mirror, ensuring it was correctly positioned to cast a reflection on her silent face. Still, nothing happened. Edward leaned in, bridging the distance between the two. He fixed his eyes level with hers, but only pools of brown and black paint returned his gaze.

"You can't leave me," he whispered to the canvas, "It isn't fair. I'm not finished with you. I need more answers."

James's face flickered across his memory.

"Please someone help me," the shadow of James said, from the back of his mind. Edward shut his eyes tight and reopened them to find his answers in the painting.

"Why? Why?" Edward said to her, as she had said to him so many times in those previous months.

"I need my answers. Don't abandon me."

"Didn't mean to," the painting said at last, her voice barely a whisper within Edward.

"No, not that. Please not that," Edward whispered back,

nearly regretting that she had spoken at all.

"Someone help! Edward? Edward! Edward where are you?" James cried to him from the darkness of the memory. A shroud of hazy mist descended over the dreamlike vision of Edward. Where was James? Edward felt himself scrambling against the harsh earth. Dirt filled his hands in dampened clumps as he scratched his way through it, searching with his hands for James. Soil and debris rained down upon him, displaced and upturned from the blasts surrounding him. Perfect hearing still in his mind, if not in his ears, heard the mournful shrill of the siren cranked to warn of the incoming gas. And then, even stranger than having his world flipped upside down and the dirt becoming not only Edward's walls but his ceiling, scents familiar to those he'd smelled in the kitchen at home wafted around him. He couldn't quite place the ingredient, but it was a favorite of their Italian cook. Garlic. That's what it was. Edward's blood ran cold, as he reached for his gas mask.

"Edward, where are you?" James called again.

"James? James, I can't see you," Edward said through the mask, his voice becoming muffled. A hand reached out and pulled Edward back by the collar.

"I have to go for James," Edward protested, trying to break free of the hold.

"If you go out there, you won't be able to save James or anyone else. You'll need saving yourself."

The gas poured in more heavily. Edward felt a sting on his leg. If was only after the battle that he noticed a hole in the fabric of his trousers. Beneath it lay the exposed flesh, raw and blistered from the mustard gas. The fabric was not the only part of Edward that was missing. James too had slipped away in the gas, too hurt to move, too hidden to be helped.

The memories, which Edward had hoped to be healed of, had become too powerful to bear. He buckled under their weight and collapsed there on the floor beside the painted lady. The frame slipped from his hand and, with it, his chance for absolution.

⟶•⟵

"Edward, what are you doing?" Agnes asked, later that afternoon. She had found Edward dragging crates and boxes across his front room.

"It's time to open the shop. I've been saying I would like to for nearly a year now and the tide of war is changing for us. It will soon be over, anyway. It's bound to be," he said, brushing aside his true feelings as he had seen Martin do so many times before. The most peculiar look filled Agnes's eyes, as she looked at her cousin and tried to discern if this were an act of insanity or clarity.

"Yes, I suppose that is true. I hope so, anyway. Can I help you?"

He looked up at her, attempting to see if she knew his awful secret. For over a year she'd spoken with him, eaten with him, and lived with him both in her house and then his own. She was perceptive and intelligent. She had to know. Didn't she?

Can you help me dear Agnes, can you help me? Can anyone? I am a coward and there is no cure for that.
Instead though, he said,

"Yes, would you like to help arrange the displays?" She agreed and devoted herself more wholeheartedly to the task than he was able to do himself. She needed busyness, though. He had learned that she thrived on activity, on helping others, and making a difference.

"The children have asked if we can take up knitting again, now that the garden is finished for the year," she said, as she unfolded a box of fabrics and refolded them, making them uniform in size with all their corners neatly tucked in on themselves.

Edward had been reading over his inventory list and

looked up from it, tucking the pencil behind his right ear as he did.

"Knitting? Oh yes, that's good."

"Edward, what were the reactions to the things on the front? I mean, did you get as much out of everything, as we did in sending them?" she asked. He had noticed lately that she took more liberty in asking him about life in the trenches. What had once been an unspoken agreement to not trespass upon, now was brought up frequently in conversation. Perhaps, Edward was simply getting better at masking his inner turmoil and so she thought it safe to have those conversations. Or maybe, John's disappearance had rejuvenated her need to know every detail of that life that she felt so acutely bonded to, but knew so little of.

"Believe me, we got more out of them. They are treasures in the trenches."

"Good," she said, a look of pleasure and contentment at making a difference now passing over her face. But, Edward didn't see her expression. He had been whisked away on the winds of recollection, which were so often armed with discord biting at his soul.

"New gloves?" Edward asked James, eying the knitted skeins of green yarn wrapped around his fingers.

"That's right. Genuine English knitting by the award-winning Mrs. Beatrice Grant," he said, proudly.

"And just who is Beatrice Grant?"

"My neighbor and every birthday, since I was six years old, she knitted me a new pair of mittens. You see my ma, as much as I love her, can't knit worth a darn. Worth a darn!" he said, breaking into laughter.

"It isn't right," Edward said.

"What isn't right?" Agnes asked.

"What?" he said, surprised at her question because he'd not intended to speak aloud.

"I asked what isn't right," she repeated.

That men filled with laughter should be ripped from the earth.

"The numbers here were added wrong," he said to her. They continued in transforming his parlor into the shop. As they did, a nagging thought mounted in his mind, gaining momentum. By the time Agnes left for the evening, it was all he could think of. Edward returned to his bedroom and sat on the floor beside the bed again. Muskiness emanated from the aged walls. He reached under the bed and pulled out the painting.

"You've outlived your stay. It's time for you to go," he said to her. Downstairs, he placed her against the wall, with the other paintings he had assembled to sell.

CHAPTER THIRTY-ONE

The Journal of Nathaniel Lenton on his Tour of Europe

March 26, 1826
After an uneventful crossing from Dover, I am landed on the continent. French, which I have only ever spoken with my tutors, now surrounds me on the streets. I must stop my record now, as the candle is waning.

March 27
I have had the most glorious day. Hutchinson, my guide, insisted upon showing me the smallest shop I have ever seen filled with more works of art than I am sure all of Ireland holds! The green hills are of a different shade than at home and the paintings seem more vibrant. The real jewel of the day came, not in the form of scenery or a framed canvas but, as Miss Eloise Hampton. She is traveling with her father and Hutchinson has offered, after consulting me, to be their guide as well and so they are to travel with us. I am overjoyed and this trip is bound to be even better than I had imagined.

April 10
We have been traveling with relative speed across the countryside and I fear I have neglected my travel journal for far too long. I cannot be blamed, though, for I have been spending my evenings in the company of Miss Hampton. She is a sheer delight to be around, but is cloaked in a shyness. I shall have to endeavor to get her to speak more. As for the journey, we are to be in Paris tomorrow. My days are bound to become even busier with music and dancing lessons in the city.

April 13
J'adore Paris!

April 30
We are to leave tomorrow. I have bought a settee and two landscape paintings to fill the rooms when my house is completed. Regrettably, I have rarely seen Miss Hampton but Hutchinson has informed me that our little group will spend more time together as we journey east as, he informs me that the absence of the Hamptons is owed to Mr. Hampton's business dealings. I do not know precisely what he does, only that it is something in London.

May 20
The Germanic countryside is exquisite. If I could carve myself a portion to carry home and add to my estate, I would. Miss Hampton's shyness seems to be dissipating. She has even, on occasion, asked me to tell her of Dublin and my plans for my estate.

May 23
We are well into Hesse now and have been following the path of the Rhine River. It is so much wider than the Liffey at home and, in several places, castles dot the hillsides. I have spent the afternoon drawing the views, as it is my hope of acquiring some of my own sketches. Later, I will paint them to add to those of the true artists who will adorn the walls of my house. Hutchinson is taking me to meet with an old friend of his tomorrow, an old Hessian soldier who fought in the American Revolution. I should like to journey to America someday and explore as Lewis and Clark did. Though, perhaps, I shall wait until the cities are better established. I am so devoted to art and culture!

May 24
The Hessian, whose name I am unable to accurately spell so I

shall not attempt to do so, made a wonderful host. The stories that he told have made me even more determined to travel to America eventually, to see its beauty. He had the most beautiful home and I found myself examining the works in his house as a study for how I ought to design the interior of my own. Hutchinson has told me that this was his intention from the beginning. By a rather fortunate turn of fate, I have acquired a lovely portrait. The Hessian, who noticed I was staring at the painting while we ate our lunch, very kindly offered that I take the painting with me. I was completely astounded at his generosity, even more so because he refused to allow me to pay him for it. He said that it was a gift from a British soldier and so it should return to an Englishman. He didn't understand that I am Irish! But the painting is beautiful, a truly wonderful addition to what I have gathered so far and now that I think of it, she bears a striking resemblance to Miss Hampton. I shall have to show it to her, as she was not at lunch today.

May 25
We are traveling south toward Switzerland. My heart leaps at the thought of soon seeing the Alps. I am certain that they shall be even grander and larger than I imagine them.

May 30
Grand cannot begin to explain the beauty and that is not even of the mountains but rather my painting, the one that the Hessian gave to me. The painting—I fear I will be seen as a lunatic for writing this—but, it speaks! I will write more, when I have figured out how this has happened.

June 4
Much of the past few days has been spent in the mountains. I persuaded Hutchinson to take me wandering to view the

waterfalls and flowers. Their majesty is breathtaking. How short the peaks of Wicklow at home now seem—though it is with fondness that I think of them. My heart wilts a little at the thought of the distance now between me and them. I have tried to breathe the fresh air into my thoughts to create some sort of structure for them. I shall relate the story of what happened with the portrait now—or at least try my best to make some sense of it. Miss Hampton and I were speaking together after dinner on the evening of May 30th. Both her father and Hutchinson had retired for the night and we were thus alone. I took out the painting to show her, thinking she would like to see it. We have spoken on art on occasion together and it always seems to delight her. I do not know how it happened— and no logical reason is forthcoming—so I shall simply say that as Miss Hampton gazed upon the painted face of the portrait, and I in turn gazed upon her, I saw wonder transfix her face entirely.

"What is it?" said I.

"You shall think me silly," said she. I assured her that such a thing was impossible, as I hold her in the very highest esteem.

"Look at her," she said at last and so I willing obliged and set to work examining the portrait, searching for some small detail of importance I had previously missed. She watched me expectantly. I am certain that I would have blushed, from so thorough an observation she cast upon me, had it not been for my sincere desire to comply with her bidding that I find what she implored I search for. When I failed to produce the expected reaction, she studied me and then the painting alternatively with a steady intensity. She did this for a few moments, until her eyes came to rest fully on me.

"Why did you not tell me?" she asked, with sudden tenderness in place of her scientific scrutiny.

"Tell you? Tell you what?" asked I.

"How you feel for me, that your heart quickens at my

presence, that you wish to marry me," she replied. At hearing her words I was so utterly astounded that I am certain I made a complete fool of myself, stumbling over my words as I scrambled to make some sort of reply.

"How could you know that?" asked I, when my words finally regained my senses. A soft smile spread across her face in the dimming light of the evening and she took on a loveliness that nearly stopped my breathing. Before she offered explanation, more clumsy sentences and rambling questions spilled from my lips.

"I don't understand. Perhaps a look in my eye or some small mannerism that I did not notice betrayed my heart, but how could you know? That is to say, how could you know in such detail my very thoughts?" And then, she said the strangest thing, which I am certain anyone would think me a crazed fool for writing. Gesturing toward the painting, Miss Hampton said,

"She told me."

"What? I don't understand," said I.

"I do not really understand it either," said she, "but I felt her words in me, as surely as if I were hearing them." Amazed, I looked down at Miss Hampton. I saw my face reflected back at me from the silver pendant she wears around her neck. I am certain that more would have been spoken had Mr. Hampton and Hutchinson not suddenly burst from the room they had been sipping brandy in to join us. Regrettably, Miss Hampton and I have not had a moment alone these past few days in which to speak of the painting again. It seems, we have taken a kind of silent oath about it when in the company of others.

June 7

Finally, a quiet moment arrived this evening for Miss Hampton and I to sit together alone with the portrait. An idea had been building in me the past few days and, when we were alone, I immediately presented it to Miss Hampton.

"Might I put on your pendant?" said I, as I began to unwrap the portrait.

"Whatever for?" said she and then suddenly seeming to realize, "you want to read my thoughts! Why, Mr. Lenton, that hardly seems gentlemanly," said she and, for a moment, I lost my courage at her rebuff, gently spoken as it had been.

"I assure you, Miss Hampton, I made the suggestion of no other impetus than that we might undertake a scientific endeavor to examine the strange predicament surrounding the painting."

"Well, all right then," said she. After a moment's hesitation, her fingers moved to the clasp at the back of her neck and she unhooked it to loosen the chain holding the pendant. She passed it to me and for a moment I held her hand in mine, before I placed the pendant around my own neck. With excitement building in my stomach, I looked into the portrait and, sure enough just as Miss Hampton had described, a voice ringing in clarity spoke from somewhere deep within me in a voice other than my own. I was certain that the painted lady was speaking to me. And though I was amazed by this discovery, my thoughts soon turned cloudy as I realized I was not hearing the thoughts of the painting but of Miss Hampton.

"How can I tell him that Father will not approve? I love him. We are leaving soon to return to London."

"What's this about not understanding and leaving and all?" asked I, unable to decide whether to celebrate that she felt the same as I do for her or to be concerned that we might not be together any longer. And then, realizing what had happened with a look of surprise said I, "Oh! It works." I shall have to stop my pen, as the candle is dwindling.

June 10
Sure enough, as Miss Hampton feared and I learned in the painting the night I wore her pendant, Hutchinson and I are to

journey south into Italy alone while Mr. Hampton and Miss Hampton (ah, my heart sighs to even write it) are to turn north and return to London. I had fancied myself walking the halls of the *Uffizi* gallery in Florence with her at my side or even, if I am so bold to admit, entertained the notion of stealing a kiss beside the canals of Venice.

It seems my dreams are not to be though and I really should stop my pen, as my intention has been from the outset to keep a diligent record of what I have seen, done, and acquired for my home and it has rather of late become a musing of what is not to be. Allow me to say only that I had every intention of speaking to Mr. Hampton about my desire to marry Miss Hampton, but she forbid me to do so, saying the time was not right. I assured her that, when my journey is complete and I have returned home with my estate completed, I will seek her out in London. She was good enough to give me her address, which I shall place here for safekeeping. With sadness in her eyes, but a brave smile, she bid me adieu this evening. At least I have the assurance that she will not forget me, for I have left the portrait that held our secret love with her as a souvenir of our friendship and in hopes of it blooming into a full romance. Well, that is all to say on the matter and I shall speak no longer of Miss Hampton or the portrait. Tomorrow we leave for Italy, but my heart has already departed, rushing on ahead to some future time when I might gaze across the beauteous Irish hills with the lovely Miss Hampton at my side.

CHAPTER THIRTY-TWO

Martin insisted upon accompanying Harold to visit Clara. They were decided that they would observe her behavior to determine if their theory on her exposure to the gases seemed accurate. Relying solely on his ears, Martin did what he could to compare Clara's mannerisms to those he'd witnessed firsthand.

"Mr. Emerson, may I speak with you?" one of the nurses asked, as they rounded the bend in the corridor when their visit with Clara was concluded.

"Oh yes, yes, of course. Martin, I shall just be a moment," Harold said, turning to follow the nurse. Though Harold had departed, Martin sensed that he was not alone and his suspicion was confirmed as a voice beside him spoke now,

"Your name is Martin, isn't it?"

"Yes, that's right. And you are?"

"Oh, I'm Florence," she replied, sounding surprised that he had asked her name because she had become so accustomed to namelessly providing the service others so desperately needed.

"Florence, like Florence Nightingale," he said, with a smile.

"Yes, I suppose that's right. Is Miss Banks a relation of yours? I've seen you visit her from time to time," she said.

"Clara? Oh no, she's not related to me," he answered.

"Oh, is she your sweetheart?" she asked, her voice dropping slightly as she did.

Martin let out a soft chuckle,

"Oh no, she's just a friend." Though he could not see it, he was sure a smile now lighted her face.

"Would you care for some sunshine, Martin? I think it will feel just glorious on our faces. We should take advantage of it, before the cold of winter grips us too tightly."

"Yes, that'd be fine," he said and allowed her to take him by the hand to lead him outside, though really he would have been capable of doing so without her guidance.

"Here, there's a nice seat for us," she said, sitting beside him on a bench in the hospital's garden.

"Describe it for me, would you?" he said, turning his face to the welcoming sun that offered the radiance Florence had promised.

She looked at him, amazed by the lack of bitterness in his words at the request.

"Well, the sky is nearly empty of clouds but, the trees are full of leaves that almost seem to be dancing in their painted coats."

"That's how I think of them too," Martin said, smiling. Perhaps because she had already held his hand to guide him, perhaps because the grandness of the autumn day awakened the boldness in her, or perhaps for some other reason entirely, she reached out now to take his hand in hers. In her touch, Martin felt the looks that the shy eyes of the girls had cast upon him in his school days. It had been so long since he'd felt that sort of a touch. Agnes's hand always lingered with a pitying sadness, but none was present here. Her skin reminded him of Rebecca, when she had—

"Florence? Oh there you are. Dr. Markinson needs your help," a nurse called to her from the door.

"Sorry, Martin. Harold should be out soon though," Florence said, as she stood from the bench to return to the hospital.

"Florence?"

"Yes, Martin?"

"I was just wondering why you showed me such kindness," he said, needing to know the origin of her action that extended beyond a nurse's mercy.

"Because, you've made me smile. I've heard your wit and humor and admired you for them. I wanted to try to bring a smile to your face in return," she said.

"Thank you," he said, moved by her words and unable to say anything further, which for Martin was rare indeed.

"Goodbye, Martin. I hope to see you soon," Florence said, her voice fading as she moved toward the door.

"Yes, me too," he called after her. Left alone with his thoughts, Martin's mind alternated between the giddy joy Florence had imparted to him and a curiosity of what had detained Harold. His hearing seemed always on high alert, like a rabbit with his ears sticking straight up. Inside the hospital, someone laughed. Behind him, some small animal, probably a squirrel, scampered across the ground. And then, a voice found its way into his hearing. The words were inaudible and the person was no doubt too far away to make out anything. The inability to discern the words suited Martin just fine, as he had no intention of eavesdropping. The voice became louder, but oddly there was no voice that replied to the first. Martin could now distinguish the voice to be male. For a moment, he wondered at this one-sided conversation until he remembered that he was in a hospital for the insane and troubled. Dozens of the patients inside might readily talk to themselves. The matter would have been dropped entirely had Martin not heard what he did next. From a sea of indistinguishable words came the insertion of "Clara" that rang with certain clarity.

Well, just another patient that knows her.

He sat back to further enjoy the warmth of the sun's rays. Steps neared and the chatter of the man continued. Although he now sounded quite close, he seemed to remain oblivious to Martin's presence and he began to wonder if Florence had led him to some concealed location. Perhaps, one of the trees she spoke of was blocking the man's view of Martin.

That's not English.

The words became louder.

Why, that's German!

His senses heightened and his concern piqued, Martin stood

preparing to enter the hospital alone to inform someone of what happened before it was too late. The door to the hospital creaked open alleviating Martin of a portion of his worry. Whoever had exited would also soon hear the man speaking and be able to identify who the threat was.

The stride of the steps that sprang from the hospital bellowed with familiarity.

"Ah, hello," Harold said.

Martin opened his mouth to speak, but shut it again quickly when he realized Harold had not addressed him, but rather a voice that sounded like someone he knew that he couldn't quite identify.

"Oh yes, good to see you," the voice of the man replied, sounding somewhat flustered at the beginning and then relaxing into a comfortable ease.

"I'm sure Clara will be glad to see you," Harold said.

"Yes, yes, I will see you later, Harold."

"Goodbye, Frederick."

Martin's heart seized. He stepped forward toward Harold's voice. There was no greeting and so he decided he must be hidden behind trees. He took another step in Harold's direction. His walking cane sank into the ground, missing the path he was walking on.

"Oh Martin, there you are. I didn't see you from behind the tree there," Harold said, his voice sounding more serious than it usually did. Then, taking note of Martin's expression, he continued,

"Martin, why do you look so grim? Surely, you have not yet heard what I have."

"Oh? What have you heard?"

"Just as we feared, trouble is being stirred for Clara. It seems a Mr. Charlton wants to press charges against her. Now, please tell me what it is that troubles you."

Martin took a step forward and spoke slowly as he said,

"Just before you came out I heard someone speaking German and then you addressed Frederick immediately after. I am quite certain that it was the same voice."

"Oh goodness! Good heavens, good heavens," Harold said, becoming flustered, "do you realize what this could mean? Something is certainly amiss here and I fear this is even larger than we thought."

"Emma! We should go to Emma and enlist her help," Martin said.

"Right. Oh dear Clara, I pray it is not too late."

⁂

"What is it that we're looking for?" Emma asked, looking up from the pile of Frederick's clothes she was rifling through.

"We don't know really," Harold said, as he shifted the contents of Frederick's belongings from one pile to another.

"Have you ever heard him say anything suspicious?" Martin said, as he sat at the edge of Frederick's bed and the other two conducted the search.

Her face ruddy, from the haste of the search coupled with the concern of Frederick returning at any moment, Emma looked up to answer Martin. Her hair tumbled disobediently out of her cap as she cocked her head to the side, trying to remember. So confounded was she that the entire search had been carried out without so much as a hint of a whistle.

"I don't know. I just always had this odd sort of feeling about him. Of course being Clara's beau and me being so fond of Clara, I tried to give him the benefit of the doubt," she said and then continued in her search for a moment, before pausing again and turning toward the men once again.

"Come to think of it, there was this one night when I overheard Frederick tell Clara the most peculiar thing. I was certain at the time that I had simply misheard him and so I dismissed it, thinking no more of it."

"Yes? What was it?" Martin asked, feeling very like the detective of Baker Street once again.

"He said something about Lady Pemblebrooke being in mourning for Lord Pemblebrooke, but of course that's not the case. We all know that he is alive, though abroad at the moment."

"Did Lady Pemblebrooke seem as though she were mourning? Certainly Clara would have been suspicious of her behavior, if what Frederick said seemed out of the ordinary," Martin said.

"Oh Lady Pemblebrooke, bless her soul, was a delicate creature. We all fussed over her so as not to upset her any. Her nerves were shattered when the Zeppelins began falling over the countryside. She was certain, though I assured her many times that it would not be the case, that she would not survive the war," Emma said. A look of sadness swept across her face, as she said,

"I don't rightly know why she was so morbid but she was right in the end, wasn't she?" Her voice wavered at the end of her question. Harold crossed the small room and draped his arm around his sister.

"I don't see anything here. We better clean this up so he doesn't suspect anything," Harold said.

"Right, well, I'll continue to try to find something out. I'll pay careful attention to him," Emma said. Harold began refolding the clothes, now strewn about the room. In his haste, he leaned too heavily on the chest of drawers and it moved backward creaking against the floor.

"What was that?" Martin asked.

"Oh, nothing. I just pushed against the chest," Harold said, but Emma, who had turned at the noise, was pointing to the now exposed space that the chest had sat above.

"What's this?" she said, swooping down upon a slip of paper, the way a hawk does to its prey. She unfolded the page, which was well-worn as though it had been folded and refolded many times.

"Harold, come here," she said, as she saw its contents. He took the paper from her and his breath drew in.

"Emma? Harold? What is it?" Martin asked.

"A newspaper clipping, written in German with markings made on it. Pemblebrooke is written on it," Emma said.

"And look here. It says 'Clara' next to the underlined passage," Harold said, his eyes gone wide.

"And what of the article? Can either of you make anything out?" Martin asked.

"Well, I can't read German," Harold said.

"Neither can I," Emma interjected.

"But," he continued, "underlined beside Pemblebrooke it says s-t-e-r-b-e-n. I wonder what that could mean."

Martin's face paled.

"Martin? Martin, what is it?"

"It means died."

CHAPTER THIRTY-THREE

"Can you read it?" Harold asked, pressing the page into Edward's hand. Harold and Martin had set off immediately from Rosebrim Manor after their discovery. Edward lifted the page, his eyes widening at the manic scribbles around its borders, but he shook his head no.

"If it were in French, I could but I'm afraid I know only one or two words, same as Martin."

"That's what I was afraid of. Where are we going to get anyone that can read the language of the enemy in war or even admit to it? You know how paranoid everyone has become," Martin said.

"If only I could speak with our washerwoman in San Francisco for a moment. Her family was German," Edward said, a look of chagrin tinting his eyes.

Harold clapped his hands together.

"Wait, I've got it. There was a woman who married an Englishman and settled somewhere around here. Well, it was so long ago, she might not even be around anymore," Harold said, the excitement in his voice turning into sadness at the end.

"Well, we must try to find her. She speaks German, you say?" Edward said, enlivened at the prospect.

"Oh yes, the woman I'm speaking of is German," Harold said.

"That would work, yes, that would work just fine," Martin said, "and where does she live?"

Harold's hand flew to his head, as he tried to remember. His fingers worked across his temple, as he said,

"It's been so long. That's the difficulty you see, but I seem to remember it had something to do with water. I don't think the name of the place was in English either."

"Was it in German?" Martin asked.

"No, I seem to recall it was in French, named during the

time of the Huguenots."

"Ah!" Edward exclaimed, spilling over in excitement.

"Edward, what is it?" Martin said eagerly.

"Yes, Edward, do tell us," Harold pressed him for information.

With a smile, as though revealing a winning hand of cards, Edward said,

"Harold, was the name perhaps 'The fountain'—*La font*?"

"Yes, yes, that's it! But, how did you know that?"

"I have been there."

"You know the woman?" Martin asked.

"Well, I know of her at least. She wasn't too welcoming when Agnes and I went to her home before, but we've got to try. It's the only way we might learn the truth," Edward said, refueled with purpose. His heart sagged, as he thought of his last visit. He had been so occupied with that silly painting that had stolen so much of his time and sanity. He realized now that he had been far too involved in the painting. The last time he had visited the woman, he had attributed her frosty reception to wanting to guard the secret of the painting. How much more sense it made now that fear of being discovered as German, when her adopted country was at war with her homeland, was the root of her absence of cordiality.

"Well, shall we go now?" Harold said, meaning it more of an instruction than a question. He was already standing from Edward's table, prepared to leave.

"Yes, as soon as possible is best. But, I think perhaps Agnes and I ought to go to her alone."

Disappointment crept into the corners of Harold's eyes, but then he realized the sensibleness of Edward's nature and said,

"Yes, I suppose you are right. We don't want to overwhelm or frighten the poor woman."

"Yes, and because she seems rather reclusive, hidden away

in her home in the meadow I don't want her to think that others know where she is. I think she will feel more secure," he explained.

"Yes," Martin added, "we must have her feeling secure, if she is to offer the assistance we need."

"Right, then it is decided. Martin and I will return to his house and wait until you and Agnes have delivered the information to us and then, God willing, we will put this matter to rest," Harold said.

"Agreed," Martin said, reaching out to shake Edward's hand in a show of well wishes.

"You were right, Edward," Agnes said, as their steps carried them toward the house in the meadow.

"How's that?" he asked. It was always more difficult to catch every word that was spoken when walking, especially when the pace was quick as it was for them now.

"I said you were right. When I was upset at how she treated us, you said it was probably because of the war."

He had said that. But, he hadn't been right. He had said it only as cover, more fully believing she was protecting the painted lady.

Oh, how you mocked me with your torturous words maintaining that coy smile all the while!

"*Edward,*" his mother said, from some faraway memory, "*Bitterness does not become you.*" Realizing he had not yet replied to Agnes, he said,

"Let's just hope she is able to help us and will not turn us away again."

Agnes raised her hand, poised to knock at the door.

"*Déjà vu,*" she said. Edward nodded and watched as Agnes's hand fell against the door, rapping on it. The door creaked open.

"You again?" the raspy voice said, in surprise. She coughed and what little they could see of her shook in frailness as she did.

"We do not wish to bother you," Agnes said, with her sweetest smile.

"Then, you would not have come," the woman interrupted her.

"It's just that we need your help," Agnes said, not deterred by the interjection.

"My help?" she said, her look shifting to surprise. Edward took the change as a sign that he should continue, while her guard was lowered.

"Yes, you see we have a friend and her name is written on an article. We think we might be able to help her, only we can't read what it says."

Confusion dotted her face.

"You can't read what it says? But, I thought you were a teacher, you said," she said, gesturing toward Agnes.

"Yes, that's right. I am," Agnes said, finding hope in the knowledge that the woman had indeed been listening to them the last time, despite seeming as if she were not.

"You see," Edward said gently, knowing this could be the moment when they would lose her if he did not tread carefully, "the article is in German." A look of panic crossed the woman's face.

"Why should you think that I would be able to read German?"

"Because," Agnes said softly, almost too quietly for Edward to hear, "we know that you are German."

Her face paled.

"I love this country. It has been good to me. I don't want any trouble."

"Of course not," Edward said, attempting to reach out to put a reassuring hand on her arm in a sign of friendship.

"We promise that we don't want to cause you any harm. We won't even tell anyone else that you live here. Just please, help us. All that we ask is that you tell us what the newspaper article says, so we can try to help our friend," Agnes said. Seeing past her fear and into the sincerity of Agnes's heart, she opened the door wider to them.

"Come in."

"Oh thank you!" Agnes said, scurrying into the house with Edward at her heels. They followed her to a small table beside the fireplace. An aromatic stew bubbled happily above the lapping waves of the fire.

"Please sit," she said, gesturing to the chairs. When seated, Edward reached into his pocket and set the clipping down on the table in front of her. She picked it up, but shook her head.

"I'm afraid I can't read it either."

"Oh," Edward said, his face falling, "it's not in German? We were so certain that it was."

"Oh it is," she said, "it's just that I need my spectacles." She stood quickly and turned away from the two to retrieve them. Agnes took hold of Edward's arm and pointed to the painting above the mantel. A woman reclining in the meadow surrounded by flowers smiled out at them from the frame.

She is pleasant, but not near as beautiful as my painted lady. No. Stop. She's not yours anymore.

"Yes?" he said.

"You were right again."

"Pardon?"

"The painting I remembered as a child is here as we thought."

"She's lovely," Edward said, but his heart was sinking. Someone was trying to tell him to abandon the painting entirely. She had no meaning anymore.

Agnes seemed not to notice and a smile, which so rarely crossed her face now, settled comfortably over her. Well, at least that was something.

The woman sat down beside them again. Close to her, she did not appear nearly as old as Edward had presumed her to be. Her hands still looked youthful, as she unfolded the spectacles and placed them neatly on her nose. It was Edward's natural inclination to ask what her name was, but he resisted. It would be better to allow her to supply the information, if she felt safe enough to do so. The last thing Edward wanted was to spook her, when they'd come so close to the answers.

Her eyes moved rapidly over the column. Agnes watched her expectantly, hoping she would offer some translated fragments to them. Instead, she seemed to be waiting to deliver all the news at once. As she silently read the article, her face became grim. Agnes reached for Edward's hand, not wanting any further bad news. He squeezed it reassuringly and she was reminded that this, whatever it was, was in the past. Whatever happened was already completed.

When she reached the end of the page, she looked up to meet their expectant eyes.

"This paper is from Vienna. It says that in a small town there was a noble woman who was kidnapped by her servant. Sometime later, an anonymous witness told the police that she witnessed what had happened."

"I see," Edward said, "and is there any other information? No matter how small it may seem, it could be of use."

"Well," she said, trying to think of anything else, "It says the man reported was a stable boy and engaged to a woman, who disappeared shortly after an execution. That is all I can find that may be of help."

"Thank you," Edward said and the look he exchanged with Agnes confirmed that she too felt the growing lump from the pit of the stomach.

CHAPTER THIRTY-FOUR

Agnes had departed to tell Martin and Harold of their discovery. Edward had told her he needed time to think and hurried home to bury his thoughts in the encompassing walls of his accommodating friend.

"Think about this," he said aloud, hoping to clarify the whirlpool of racing thoughts in his mind. He sank into the rough leather of the wobbly armchair placed beside the window of the front room. His weight pushed the chair back across the floor, scattering dust and screeching against the floorboards.

His eyes flitted to the space above the mantel. For a moment, he expected the painted lady to fill his vision. But no, she wasn't there. She'd been banished.

"Maybe, I ought to consult her," he thought and then batted away the idea, feeling the flush of shame on his cheeks from the foolishness.

"No, that's not what I need," he said, speaking to her from the chair, as he had so many times before, though now she was absent.

"Stop distracting me," Edward said, shaking his finger at the empty expanse on the wall. He shifted in the chair, diverting his eyes from where they strayed. He sat forward, his weight balanced on his knees as his forearms rested against them.

The woman's words echoed in his mind.

Engaged to, engaged to, engaged to.

Clara's guilt had been deeply suspicious to him, since first he had heard of the crime. Her innocence, shining in the light of the sun, had remained his vision of her. The thought of her behind bars had never seemed an accurate portrayal of her. His hand clenched.

"How can I free you?" A low whistle swept across the floor. Edward's eyes lifted at the sound of it. A huddled ball of fluttering wings and feathers rested in the doorway.

"How did you get in here?" he said, hoping his voice was not louder than he intended. Edward sat forward in his chair, watching as it happily chirped, moving from one foot to another. The bird hopped toward Edward and the whistle turned into a song.

"You sound very much like," Edward thought, not wanting to speak aloud and interrupt the song, "but no, that couldn't be." A bird's song, especially to muffled ears must sound very familiar. It is not so different as the voices of people are. Yet, there was something in the song, some persistence that Edward was certain he had heard before. The bird, which had been moving steadily toward him, now turned abruptly and fluttered skyward. Edward was compelled to follow it, as it flew down the hall and into another room. Not wanting to startle it, lest it should become frightened and fly headlong into a wall, Edward crept behind it keeping his distance. From the open spot on the floor where it had stopped to rest, the bird spread its wings and took to flight. The room was smaller than the main living area where he had been sitting before the escapade. Edward was forced to duck as the bird flew over him, grazing the air above his head and narrowly missing him. He decided to leave the bird shut in the room, where the window was open, so that it might escape when ready. Edward turned to leave but the bird, flying wildly, crashed against the wall and fell to the ground. Fearing the worst, Edward knelt behind the box where the bird had landed. It was not the lifeless form, which he was certain he would find, that met his eyes but rather a struggling mass of feathers seemingly attempting to right itself as a person tries to stand after a fall.

Edward unrolled the cuff of his sleeve, so that it covered his hand. He slowly crept on bended knee toward the bird. Preparing to scoop the bird up, to assist it in escaping out the window, the flutter of feathers became more frantic. The little bird had misunderstood his intentions and feared for its life, desperately trying to get away from Edward.

"Wait—I'm just trying to help," Edward said softly to the bird. So much had slipped from Edward's grasp already. He had been unable to help the others. The bird had to stay; Edward needed, for his own sake, to help it.

Engaged to, engaged to, engaged to.

The words of the woman repeated in his head again. Mounting pressure coursed through his chest, causing his muscles to tense. Spurred on by the words, the frantic nature of the bird spread over Edward infecting him with desperation. The bird wobbled unsteadily and then took to flight, ascending from the area between the boxes and rising toward the sky. The bird soared past Edward, unbalancing him and sending him toppling backward against the crates. Edward caught his balance, as the bird escaped through the window, but not without kicking the box the bird had nestled beside.

A crashing thud, from something falling against the floor, startled Edward and made him jump. He edged his way between the crates to see what had fallen. The paintings he had propped against the crates scattered themselves in an unstable arch from the crate to the floor. He bent to pick them up and lean each back against the crate. When he reached the bottom of the pile, he knew he would be faced with the painted lady since she was the last he'd placed there. Sure enough, the familiar frame pressed against his fingertips as he lifted the painting. He was determined not to turn her toward him, lest her bewitching ways should cast their magic on him. He placed her, face down, at the top of the stack leaning against the crate, when his eyes noticed something. The corner of the frame had come ajar in the fall and a sheet of paper had pushed its way through the now exposed crack. Tentatively, Edward reached for the paper and carefully tugged it loose. Rather than a single page though, it seemed to be some sort of tab that was attached to something much larger. Edward peered down the gaping hole, trying to pry apart the now visible notebook from the back of the painted canvas.

Edward's heart thudded unnaturally in his chest and his fingertips quivered, as he pulled the notebook loose. Despite his best intentions, the painting had drawn him to herself again as if saying that although he had decided he was finished with her, she was not yet finished with him. The pages felt hefty beneath his fingers and they had the look of age to them with yellowed corners. He would wager, though, that they were infantile compared to the accumulated years of their painted guardian.

"I can't believe this was here all along," he said, incredulously, as he turned the notebook over so that the spine slid into his left hand and the book was righted. What had seemed thick while wedged behind the painting was dwarfed by the size of Edward's strong hand. Edward's breath drew in sharply, as his eyes moved over the page that was the cover.

"Lefront," he said. He turned the page, not trusting his hand to be gentle enough and fearing that the paper might tear. On the first page was a sketch of the painted lady, like the one he had seen those many months before in Lefront's drawing notebook.

"Marie Régine Lefront," he read, seeing the signature tucked into the bottom left corner of the painting.

"That was my mistake. I was looking for Mr. Lefront. I should have been looking for M.R. Lefront," he said, in realization. An uneasiness enveloped him.

"Edward," he said cautiously to himself, "your mind was fooled before. Don't do it. Don't go back." His words of warning were too late. Already, the shadowy figure of James was calling to him,

"Edward? Edward?"

Gripped too tightly by the tangled web of the mysterious painting, Edward turned the page out of compulsion, rather than decision. In the scrawling penmanship, which perfectly matched the signature on the sketch of the painting, Edward read,

I, Marie Régine Lefront, place this notebook detailing my experiences behind the canvas of that which had consumed my being these past few months. I place this here to be read, knowing that anyone who finds it will have embarked upon the same journey as I have.

Edward paused. What was that word? He had not realized that he was reading in French, until the word became unclear. He concentrated on the word for a few seconds, but was unable to remember the meaning and skipped it. He continued to read,

It comes at a time when most needed and I do not wish to linger too long, but only to write my intention of recording the truth. The eyes hold the truth and so too do the portrait's. She is the guardian of all that is most right and real, if only we should allow her to disclose it to us. The following pages outline my story. I have recorded them for myself, not so that I will remember for I would be unable ever to forget, but so that my sanity will not be questioned. And I have recorded them for you, friend, whoever you are.

Marie Régine Lefront
17th of June, 1888

Edward, sitting on the hard floor with the solid truth before him, turned the page to the notebook. Before reading it though, his hand lingered on the edge and he shut the book. He reached for the portrait of the painted lady and spun her around to face him. He had to know his own truth, before discovering that of this stranger's. He wasn't crazy after all. He knew that much. For the moment, it was all he needed to know. M.R. Lefront's words had been the armor required to step into battle. The painting was not the arbiter of what was real. She merely reflected it. In running from her, he had turned his back on the truth. Whether or not she spoke the story within him, it was still his truth and it was still his reality he had to live with.

He turned the painting fully toward him. Lifting his silver

pen from his pocket, he held it to her.

"Who?" she said, speaking more clearly than he had heard her since those first conversations.

"It is me, Edward," he answered.

"Who is Katrine?" she said.

"I don't know who Katrine is," he said.

"Voices in the forest," she said, slowly.

"What voices?" he asked.

"Voices in the forest. Don't be frightened," she said.

Edward stared hard at the painting. His eyes grew wide and then he fell backward, as if confronted by a strong jolt to the stomach.

"I know what happened," he said, trying to sit back up. A weight pressed against him, though nothing was there. His eyes blurred.

"Why are you dancing?" he said, to the painted lady. She wavered unsteadily before his eyes. Heat rose from Edward's back and prickled his skin. A wave of nausea clawed at Edward's intestines, igniting the bile of his stomach in a roaring fire.

"Edward? Edward?" James called to him, through the blurriness.

"I know what happened," he said again, trying to see the painting. Blackness, like heavy dark curtains, fell over him as Edward collapsed against the floor.

CHAPTER THIRTY-FIVE
Pagny-sur-Moselle, France
April 21, 1887

Marie Régine sat beneath the Mirabelle tree that hung heavily with the sweet yellow plums in the summer months, but was now sprinkled with the white petals of the spring blossoms. The breeze ruffled the pages of Jules Verne's *Around the World in Eighty Days* that rested in her lap.

"You always have your nose in a book," her mother so often remarked.

"I think I should like to write one sometime," she had recently replied, "but, I wouldn't know what to write about."

"It seems to me," her mother had said, shielding her eyes against the sun and her face crinkling in the sunlight and looking much as the apples did when dried in winter, "that if you have a mind to write a book you ought to begin with what you know."

Then, my book would be of sadness.

At fifteen, Marie Régine was the youngest and while for some that might mean they are lavished in attention, for Marie Régine it meant she was always being left behind. By the time she was old enough to join the others in an activity, they were gone. Henrie, the eldest, had married when Marie Régine was ten and left for their father's native lands deep in the Alps to seek his fortune. And now Genvieve was to leave for the shores of Brittany, as soon as she was married to Pierre.

If only travel were as easy as Mr. Verne portrays.

Her eyes moved above the tree's branches to the billowing clouds and, for a moment, she sailed above them in the basket with the silk balloon attached. As she drifted along the housetops with Phileas Fogg as her only companion, her troubles shrank beneath her into tiny dots on the horizon in a blur of sand and space.

The dream burst against the call of her mother's voice,

sending her catapulting to the ground from her lofty dreams.

"Marie Régine?"

"Yes, Mother?"

"Come inside and help. We are having a guest for tea."

"Yes, Mother," she said, standing from her place beneath the tree. Her legs were unsteady, as she tried to walk. A cramp in her sleeping foot, from sitting too long in the same position, slowed her progress toward the door. Her foot felt disconnected, until the tingling of awaking swept its fiery fingers over her. She reached the door and pushed it open. The sweet aroma of apples, mingled with sugar and floating above a buttery pastry, drifted into her nostrils.

"Set the table, please," her mother said, from the kitchen.

Marie Régine unfolded the tablecloth and unfurled it across the shining wood of the table. She had spent hours polishing the wood and thought it a pity to cover it where no one would see it. Still, her mother insisted upon the best for company.

"Mother?" she asked, as she placed the porcelain plates around the table.

"Yes?" she said, between the rhythmic beating of the wooden spoon against the ceramic bowl.

"Who is our company that is coming?"

"Mr. Monclare."

"Who?" she said, not recognizing the name. Before her mother could answer, a knock at the front door from the other side of the house sounded.

"Oh goodness! He's early. Marie Régine get the door, please. I look a fright." She moved to the door, smoothing her wrinkled dress as she did. Opening the door, a smile was instantly summoned to her face. A man, relatively tall, tipped his hat to her with a twinkle in his eye.

"Hello, *Madamoiselle.* Are you by chance Marie Régine, whom your mother has spoken of so much in her correspondence?"

"I am," she said.

"Well, I am Patrice Monclare," he said. She opened the door wider for him to enter.

"Please come in." She ushered him into the room and by that time her mother had appeared, looking more suited to entertaining company than to working in the kitchen.

"Ah, Patrice, hello," Mother said, clasping him into a welcoming hug. Marie Régine lingered in the doorway, unsure if she were invited to be present for this meeting of friends.

"Here, you sit here," Mother instructed, pointing to the nicest armchair beside the window.

"And Marie Régine, you come sit beside me." A smile lighted her face at the instruction. She was to be included!

"How was your journey?" Mother asked, turning to Patrice.

"Altogether uneventful until I arrived in town."

"Oh?" Mother asked.

He looked at Marie Régine, gauging whether to say anything further on the matter.

"I don't know whether I had... " he trailed off.

"Oh please, Mr. Monclare, do not hold back on account of me," Marie Régine said.

Seeing her earnest, Mother nodded her consent and he continued,

"Well, everyone was talking about a man named Guillaume Shader, no Schnaebele, that was it. It seems the German police have arrested him as a spy. He was on his way to Metz and they were unhappy he crossed the border."

"A spy?" Marie Régine said, sitting forward. Though she felt sorry for the man, a shiver of excitement spread across her skin. Perhaps, interesting things could reside beyond the pages of a book.

"Goodness, well, let us hope the matter is settled

quickly," Mother said, deterring Marie Régine's hope of hearing more. The matter was fully dismissed, as Patrice reached into his bag and pulled out a notebook.

"I thought you would want to see these," he said with a smile to Mother. Marie Régine perched on the chair, leaned into Mother as Patrice passed the retrieved notebook to her now so that she could see what was inside. Mother opened the notebook and a beautiful scene of boats on the water met Marie Régine.

"Did you draw this?" she asked in awe, admiring the curve of the wave that seemed real enough to splash off of the page onto her.

"That's right," he said.

"Patrice, these are wonderful," Mother said, as she turned through the pages.

"You are an artist, Mr. Monclare?" Marie Régine asked, looking at him excitedly.

"That's right," he said again, as he had before.

"Mr. Monclare is from Normandy," Mother said.

"Normandy? Do you know Monet?" Marie Régine asked, nearly unable to contain herself.

"I have met him. He was in England as I was," he said.

Her eyes grew wide.

"You were in England with Monet?"

"Well, not with Monet, my dear. We were both there—well, artists are better at holding paintbrushes than guns," he said, simply.

"Oh—oh yes," Marie Régine said, picking up on his allusion to the war two years before her birth that France had fought against Prussia.

"I think you are a better artist than Monet," Mother said, moving their conversation away from any discomfort, as she admired his work.

He laughed,

"Well, I am not so sure about that. But, thank you." A

look of reminiscing passed across his face.

"We both know who the best artist was." Mother looked at him, needing no time for the memories to return. The years were dissolved instantaneously and for a moment Marie Régine was forgot and they were whisked into some shared recollection. Marie Régine suddenly felt as though she were trespassing.

"I wonder where she is now," Mother said, breaking the silence.

His eyes softened into a smile, deepening the creases beside his blue gray eyes and betraying his age. Patrice pat the bag beside him. Mother's eyebrows rose in surprise.

"I thought that she was lost," she said, unable to comprehend the presence of this mysterious girl.

"I found her recently. I thought—" he said and nodded toward Marie Régine. Mother looked from Patrice to Marie Régine and then nodded.

"Marie Régine, are you prepared for a tale better than any Jules Verne could write?" Mother asked, including her once again in the conversation.

"Oh yes, Mother," she said, hoping her earnestness did not negate the solemnity she was trying so hard to attribute to the occasion.

"Your mother is my oldest friend," Patrice began, "And, in the spirit of full disclosure, I shall tell you, young lady, that I would have married her had my means as an artist been more stable than they are."

He paused for a moment, a touch of melancholy touching his lips and causing the corner to twitch. Ignoring it, he pressed on with the story.

"As you have already learned, I was in England during the war. Your mother and I had discovered something that allowed us to speak with each other despite the distance. Well, perhaps I am getting ahead of myself. We were—"

"Your age," her mother interjected. Patrice's eyes

widened.

"Can you really be as old as fifteen now?"

"I am," she said, anxious for him to continue the story.

"Well, then, when we were your age we found a painting in my grandmother's attic. My grandfather was given it by a business associate from London. We knew nothing of it at the time but when we pulled it from the attic, my grandmother dismissed it as some old rag rather than the beautiful painting it is. I never have been able to figure out why that was."

"Maybe," Mother said, "she was afraid of it."

"Afraid of a painting? Why would someone be afraid of a painting?" Marie Régine asked, her face clouding in confusion.

Her mother took her hand.

"Marie Régine, you trust me, don't you?"

"Yes, Mother," she said, wondering what could merit such a question.

"The painting is special. You see, this is going to be hard to believe, but the painting is a sort of message system."

"There are symbols hidden in it?" Marie Régine asked, trying to understand.

"Not quite," Patrice said, "you see, the painting is able to deliver messages."

"She can speak," Mother said. They both turned toward Marie Régine, watching to see her reaction.

"I don't understand. How is that possible?" she asked.

"I don't know. I just know it works," Mother said.

"You see, things we were thinking of when we thought of the painting seemed to be carried to the other as we looked at the painting."

"You could read each other's mind through the painting?" Marie Régine asked, trying to make some sense of what she had been told.

"I suppose," Patrice said, "you could think of it like that, only it wasn't random chaos but rather focused messages."

"It's possible, though," her Mother said, "that if someone were not aware of what was happening, disorder could appear in place of the orderly message system we had."

"I see," Marie Régine said, though really she did not.

"I have been searching for the painting since it became lost on my return from England and I have only just found it."

"You've been searching for it for over seventeen years?" Marie Régine said, looking rather amazed at the thought of a treasure hunt lasting longer than her life.

Patrice exchanged glances with his lifelong friend over her daughter's head before saying,

"She's more than a painting. Once you've met her, she has an intoxicating presence since she is able to connect you to those you hold most dear."

His hand moved to Marie Régine's mother's and lingered for a moment, before he continued,

"And I am certain that she will be a loyal companion to you."

He looked directly at Marie Régine, as he spoke the words.

"To me?"

"I know, my dear," Mother said, "that you often feel you are alone, left behind because you are younger."

"I would like," Patrice said, "to give the painting to you, so that you might speak to Genvieve."

"Speak to her? Through the painting you mean?" Marie Régine said, both excited and fearful at the prospect.

"But, I don't understand, Mr. Monclare. If you have been searching for her all these years and have only just found her, why would you give her away so quickly?" Marie Régine said. Now it was Marie Régine's hand that he took in his own.

"Because it is time. You need her and I want you to have her." Patrice bent to lift his drawing book from the place on the floor he had set it down.

"And I would like for you to have these."

"Your drawings?" she said in surprise.

"The notebook is full. I can always draw more," he said with a smile, "but, you must do one thing for me."

"Yes?"

"When the painted lady has touched your life, as she has mine and your mother's, draw her portrait on the last page."

CHAPTER THIRTY-SIX

Agnes squeezed the water from the cloth, letting the excess drip into the basin. She pressed the back of her hand against his forehead, feeling the feverish burn push back at her.

"Edward," she said as sternly as she could, though her concern was dampening the effect, "you are not allowed to be sick. Do you hear me? You get well."

She laid the cool cloth on his forehead and sat back in the chair. She picked up his hand and cradled it in hers.

"I wish I knew how long you'd been lying there when I found you. I just am glad I did."

His body, which she had seen strengthened since his return from the trenches, now lay pale and feeble looking. She had propped him between two chairs, making a bed of them. It had taken considerable effort to move him in his half lucid state. The only beds were upstairs and there was no hope of being able to move him so far. She could only hope that in his semiconscious state, he was unaware enough to not be too uncomfortable.

Edward shivered, causing the blanket to slip from his shoulder. She reached for the corner and pulled it back across him.

Edward tossed, restless in his sleep. Coughing convulsed through his body. Agnes rested her hand on the cloth, testing the temperature. Already, the cloth had turned warm at its application to his scorching skin. Agnes's hand trembled in worry. She dipped the cloth into the water, returning it to its cooler temperature. When cool she pressed it to his head once again, then sat back and clasped her hands in prayer.

"Please, God," she prayed. They were the only words she spoke, but they were enough. How many times had she prayed those simple words, pouring into them the whole weight of her heart? So often the words were prayed for John, for George.

"Edward," she said, fearing his temperature was too strong and if she spoke too loudly he would break,

"You have become more of a brother to me than a cousin and I won't bear losing you too." Despite trying to hold them back, a single stubborn tear fell across her cheek, burning it with the same fiery intensity of Edward's fever.

Gripping his hand, she willed her strength into him. Agnes sat back, her eyes heavy with the pull of sleep.

"Agnes? Agnes, don't be cross. I didn't mean to," George said, in the land of dreams. The ribbon from her dress, pulled off from his stepping on it, hung tattered in his hand.

"I'm not cross," she said, pretending to sound stern but unable to conceal the smile rapidly spreading across her face.

"Here, let me see that. I'll sew it back on," she said, holding out her hand for him to place the ribbon on it. He laid it down but the silken length transformed into a dirtied piece of bandage, muddied and bloodied. She looked to George, but his freshly laundered suit was hanging in shreds making him look like a frightened scarecrow in the fields. Agnes tried to drop the bandage, but in doing so she only succeeded in unwrapping tremendous bolts of used blood-stained gauze. They trailed out from George's body, flapping wildly in the winds. Picking up speed, they churned as one monstrous cyclone engulfing him.

"George," she cried to him, but he could not hear her. Blood-soaked bandages plastered themselves against his ears.

"Where are you? Are you there?" he cried, desperately. It was then that she saw those same bandages covering his eyes. He shrieked and turned, his body morphing with the tempestuous winds.

"No, no, no!" she yelled, unwinding the bandages with all of her efforts proving fruitless.

"Agnes! Agnes!" George screamed. Violently, she shook awake.

"Agnes," Edward murmured, in barely a whisper. She

shook herself free from the gripping hands of unsettling dread.

"Edward, I'm here. What is it?" she asked, leaning close to him and uncertain whether he was dreaming.

"Agnes, Agnes, Frederick did it," he said. His words, spoken in the hoarse voice of his raspy cough, set him into another set of body-shaking coughing.

"Shh, Edward, save your voice. It's all right. I know Frederick did it. The woman told us when she read the clipping."

He said nothing further and lay very still. She was quite certain that he had fallen back asleep and so spoke in confidence that her words would not disturb him.

"I have been trying to figure out how we might help Clara. We know that she did not do it. The great difficulty rests in her inability to remember. If only she could, her case would be so greatly helped. Oh Clara, come on remember."

Edward stirred and Agnes feared she had spoken too loudly.

"Remember me. Remember. I remember, James, I remember," Edward said, weakly.

"Shh, Edward, sleep," she said, smoothing his hair back with a soothing hand. He had never spoken of James, but it was a name that was well familiar. He had awoken with those terrifying night tremors, screaming for James on so many occasions.

He mumbled something that she could not make out. Crouching beside him and pressing her ear nearly to his lips, his hot breath exhaled as she heard him say,

"Dead."

"No, Edward! You are alive. You are going to live," she said emphatically.

"Not dead," he said, hoarsely.

"That's right dear cousin, not dead."

Exhausted from his speaking, he collapsed deeper into the cushioning embrace of the chair. A quiet settled over the house, with only Edward's strained breathing marking any passage of time in the labored inhalation followed by the raspy exhales. In the dimming light of the evening, as the shadows lengthened and having slept little, Agnes began to doze. The dreams, which had spiraled so vividly around her, mercifully remained absent. An uneasy calm washed over the room, sweeping its rejuvenating rest across the wearied inhabitants.

Agnes awoke to the strong grip of Edward's hand squeezing her own.

"Lady Pem—" he said.

Agnes blinked back the heavy tide of sleep, trying to make sense of Edward's words.

"The painting... told me... Pem..." his words came as raspy interjections on a sea of wheezing.

Agnes reached for the cool cup of water on the floor beside her and raised it to Edward's lips.

"Try to drink this," she said softly, allowing the water to trickle into his mouth. He began to cough and it sputtered over his cheeks. Agnes mopped up the spilled water. A knock at the door made her jump.

"Now, who could that be?" she said, standing to cross to the door.

Agnes smoothed back her hair and straightened her cotton dress that had crinkled from her hours of sitting at Edward's side. She switched on the lights, as she approached the door. Opening it, she was met by the face of a stranger. It was a very rare occurrence for a town as small as theirs.

"Hello," the woman said, a rosy smile spreading from her lips to her cheeks. Though she spoke in English, her words were marked with a heavy accent.

"Hello," Agnes said.

"I have come, because I was told the owner of this house plans to open an antique shop. Are you the owner?" she asked, stepping into the light.

"No, my cousin Edward is," she said.

"Oh, is he in? You see, I've traveled some distance, though I know it is late. Perhaps, he will make an exception to allowing a visitor in so late?"

"I'm sorry, but that isn't possible. He's very ill and in no condition to receive visitors."

Concern clouded the woman's face and Agnes was moved by her visible empathy for a stranger.

"Yes, of course. I understand. I'm sorry to hear of the illness."

She spoke the words as though preparing to leave, though she lingered in the doorway.

"Is there something else?" Agnes asked, hoping her exhaustion did not make her sound curt.

"Would you mind terribly, I know it must be an imposition, but might I just take a look? You see, I'm searching for a painting. It's for sentimental reasons, really."

Agnes looked at her, feeling as though Edward were speaking to her though he lay asleep and sick in the room behind her. There was a determination in her eyes that she had seen so many times before in Edward's face. There was little she could do for him now except to wait, but perhaps in helping someone who showed so much of his same spirit, she would be able to accomplish some good. Edward would open the doors wide for her to enter and assist her in this search that was so important to her. Agnes was certain of it.

She leaned back on the door, causing it to open more as she spoke.

"If you are willing to risk exposure and if it is as important as you say, please come in."

"Oh, thank you," the woman said, and stepped inside.

"You said you're looking for a painting. I think Edward has gathered them here," Agnes said, pointing to the room piled high with crates that adjoined the room Edward lay sleeping in.

"Thank you," she said. Her eyes filled with hunger for the pursuit of the painting. Agnes watched as she knelt beside a crate on the floor and began sifting through the paintings, as she turned away to return to Edward's side.

The cloth on his head had risen in temperature from the tepid water she had left with him. She raised the cup of water to his lips once again.

"Drink it slowly," she warned. As he awoke to feel the coolness of the water descend his scratchy and aching throat, he struggled to speak again.

"Frederick... Lady Pem... not dead..."

"What Edward? You must be having a bad dream."

"The painting spoke."

"You poor man. You are sicker than I realized," she said, refreshing the cloth and laying it back against his forehead.

From the room where she had left the woman, she heard the scrape of boxes moving across the floor. Edward sat up suddenly, staring straight ahead,

"In the forest... hiding...alive...cottage beside the creek." A fit of coughing overtook him.

"Edward, please, lie down," Agnes said in worry, as she gently pushed him back against the chair. His body did not resist her guidance and soon the heaviness of breathing while sleeping coursed through his body, raising and lowering his chest.

Steps approached from the hallway. Agnes turned to see the woman standing there. She clutched a painting to her chest and a look of satisfaction filled her face, though she held back the smile that consumed her eyes out of respect for the sickness that dwelt within this man.

Setting down Edward's hand, Agnes stood and crossed the room to speak with the woman in the hall.

"How is he?" the woman asked.

"Feverish, but he seems to be resting better at least," Agnes said.

"Would you like me to tend to him? Tiredness is flowing out of you," she said.

"Thank you," Agnes said, "but, it's something I have to do."

"I understand," the woman said, patting the painting beneath her arm.

"You found it then?" Agnes said.

"I did. Give him this for it when he recovers, would you? It can be his first sale," she said, as she took a pouch of money from her pocket.

"Oh thank you, yes," Agnes said, surprised at the weight of the pouch as the woman deposited it into her hand.

"I think it's a fair price," the woman said.

"Please, what is your name so that I can tell Edward who made the first purchase from his shop? I am Agnes."

"My name," she said musically, like a bird's song, "is Marie Régine."

CHAPTER THIRTY-SEVEN

Agnes watched over Edward, willing herself to stay awake deep into the hours of blackest darkness. The claws of uneasiness dug into her mind. Drifting in sleep, she was engulfed in a deep black canyon.

"Is there anyone... anyone there... anyone there?" her voice echoed against the stone walls. Winds whistled through the canyon, pushing her to her knees. A loneliness, deeper than the sea, filled her as the chilling wind whipped around her. The faces of her parents, George, and John whooshed past her, abandoning her to the emptiness. Edward walked into the canyon and bent beside her. She grasped his hand, but he turned away from her.

"Edward, don't leave, don't leave me!" she urged, but the wind caught him, pushing him farther away from her.

"Goodbye, Agnes," he said, fading into the black.

"Agnes? Agnes?" she awoke to her name being called. The vision before her convinced her she was still dreaming. She stared, unable to speak.

"Agnes? Don't you know me?" he said, taking her arm.

"Are you... real?" she said.

"Yes, my love," he said.

"George," she said, breathing him in and lifting her hand to trace his features.

"You are home, oh George, you are home," she said, a sigh of contentment washing over her.

"I went to your home and no one was there, so I began asking for you. I met a woman, she was French, on the road. She said you were here with Edward and that he is ill."

"When did you get here? Are you hurt?" she asked, moving her hands across him, searching for some wound. Her hand moved down his arm and came to rest at his hand. There was not skin beneath her fingers, but rather the rough cloth of a bandage. The memory of her dream, with his bandages swirling around him flooded her mind.

"What happened?" she said.

"Agnes, we don't have to speak about that now," he said, softly.

"George, you don't have to fight your battles alone anymore. I am here. Tell me," she said.

He looked at her. Gone were the curls of the school girl who had turned school mistress. Before him was a battle-hardened veteran who had never been to war. She had, he realized now, her own scars to bear as a result of all that had happened.

"All right," he said, looking into her eyes, "I was in the gun turret, loading the powder shells. It was dark and I hadn't slept a full night in days. I guess my hand must have slipped. It's all foggy in my mind now, but the gun powder sparked and I was knocked back. I was certain, Agnes, that all was lost, that it was too late for me. I saw your face. You were in a meadow, surrounded by flowers. I tried to call to you, but you couldn't answer."

"I had that dream. So many times I tried to call to you, George, but you couldn't answer. I thought I wouldn't see you again."

Before he could reply, a groan escaped Edward's lips. Agnes knelt beside him, clasping his hand in her own.

"How long has he been this way?" George asked.

"I've been beside him for two days now. I can only hope that he was not passed out for too long on the floor when I found him, though it couldn't have been too long since we had been with the woman at the cottage discussing the article earlier that day," she said, taking the cloth from his head and dipping it into the basin for what must have been the hundredth time that day.

"Woman in the cottage? Article?" George asked, lifting the cup of water to Edward's lips.

"I forgot you could not know of everything that has happened. I carry you with me at all times and even when I felt very alone, your presence in my mind made it seem as though you would know. Does that make any sense?"

He nodded.

"It does. I was half surprised to hear you ask what had happened to my hand, until I remembered that of course you could not know."

"We have met so many people this year. Martin is a blinded veteran and Clara is accused of murdering Lady Pemblebrooke and her children."

"Lady Pemblebrooke is dead?" George said, looking up from Edward to Agnes.

"Yes, well—she is, only Edward seems to think she is not. I fear his fever has made him delirious. He has been sitting up and saying Lady Pemblebrooke is not dead and that a painting spoke to him."

"I saw men like this," George said. The look of pain of harsh memories, which she had witnessed so many times in Edward's face, played across him.

"The trenches made them lose their minds from the strain of it all and from the gases."

Agnes looked up from Edward to study her fiancé. She moved her hand to clasp his that was not bandaged.

"I hate what happened to you, to both of you," she paused and nodded toward Edward as she said it, "to all of you."

The way she said it triggered something in him.

"You have heard from John?"

"He's..." she swallowed, "missing."

"We'll find him, Agnes. I promise."

"George, how can you promise me such a thing?" Her face was taut at the conversation.

"Because, John never belonged in the war. He was too young. It wasn't right." He said the words to appeal to her logic.

But Agnes had seen too much, lived too much to be naive.

"No," she said, "there is no justice or fairness in war. There is no bargaining or settling of accounts. There simply is. We have no guarantees but—" she looked at him, "we have each other. You came home to me and I pray that John will as well."

"Clara," Edward mumbled, "Stop Frederick."

Agnes's face wrinkled, a look that George had observed so often when she was trying to make sense of something.

"What is it?"

"A talking painting and a woman who is dead being alive makes no sense. That I know. But, he remembers that Frederick had something suspicious surrounding him. After the woman in the cottage read us—I should say, translated for us, an article from Vienna, we learned of a murder that seemed very much like Lady Pemblebrooke's. In this case though the woman was hidden in the forest, kidnapped first."

Agnes's eyes grew wide, as she realized what Edward had been saying.

"George, he might be talking nonsense, but somehow I think he figured out or at least thinks that Lady Pemblebrooke is in the cottage by the forest. I think we have to go there. We have to see if Lady Pemblebrooke is still alive."

"I will go," George said, "Edward can't be left alone."

"I think I had better go. You have never seen Frederick before. If he is anywhere near the cottage, we will have to stay away so as not to spook him."

George nodded. They stood and he embraced her. She pressed her lips to his and then, with them hovering above his, she whispered,

"I love you. Don't you ever leave me again, George Hamilton."

"I won't. I wouldn't dare. I love you too much." It was torturous to tear herself away from him. It was like ripping a bandage. But, he was here. He'd returned. She could breathe again. Live again. And part of living was rescuing Clara, and possibly—if they were lucky, the not dead Lady Pemblebrooke and her children. She stepped from the embrace and slipped from the house.

Her muscles ached from being confined in the cramped position of nurse for so many hours. She stretched her legs with her longer than usual strides. Her calves burned, slowing her steps more than she would have liked. Edward had not been very descriptive in his feverish ramblings and a fair amount of deduction was required to make any sense of what he had said. There were scores of cottages in the meadow. Narrowing her search to only the cottages along the creek eliminated some, but there would still be far too many to determine which was the right cottage. Did Edward even know? Was he even making sense?

The path sloshed beneath her feet. Popping crunches, reminiscent of the sound of wadding paper, punctuated the slush of the mud. Her steps carried her toward Rosebrim Manor. It made sense to her that if a kidnapping had taken taken place they would not have been transported too far, especially if a single person were the perpetrator.

There. In a grassy knoll, sheltered beneath the sweeping arms of the willow, nestled into the banks of the creek with the cattails and piles of brown leaves surrounding it, stood a dilapidated cottage. Its thatched roof had gaps of missing straw, causing it to look like an old beggar with missing teeth. As she rushed toward the cottage, a nagging fear tugged at her heart. Suppose, Frederick was inside. He would be none too happy to hear her accusations. She had no weapon with her, because she had no reason for one in daily living. Agnes had never held a shining blade or a metal gun in her hand before, but now her fingers twitched molding themselves around the absent weapon. Creeping quietly toward the cottage, with the first rays of morning sunlight dancing delicately across the sky, she spotted a pile of stones through the clouds of white smoke that passed from her lips. Slipping them into her woolen coat pocket, she gathered her courage with the stones.

Standing as tall as she could, to draw upon every inch of strength she contained, she rapped on the door. Nothing happened. Perhaps, no one was even inside and the cottage was only the derelict abandoned relic it appeared. But, if Edward were somehow right, this location would make the most sense. Palming a stone in her hand and finding comfort in its smooth river-washed surface and weighty bulk, she pressed against the door. It was unmoving. Agnes gathered her skirt into her hand and waded across the mud to the back of the cottage.

Something moved to her left, rustling the brambles. Her heart seized. Uneasily she waited for the sound of Frederick's voice to cut through the morning air, piercing her life like a knife. No voice came, but the branches rattled again. Perhaps, he was sneaking up on her. Without hesitating, she spun, hurling a stone toward the noise. A bushy tailed squirrel scampered from the bush, frightened but unharmed. A breath of relief filled her lungs, tightening in her chest and then slumping her shoulders forward in release of the fear.

November rains saturated the grounds behind the cottage, causing her to sink into the soil as she neared the door. She paused just outside the cottage, listening intently, lest there should be some real interloper other than the squirrel. Agnes was not prepared to march in as liberator only to become part of some macabre scene.

The house appeared still and if anyone were inside the cottage, Agnes wagered they were asleep. Convinced that it was time to act, she pushed against the splintered wood of the door. A crackle of paint fell off into her hand in so doing, but sure enough the door edged open.

The early morning light filtered through the opened door, illuminating the dark and cramped cottage. Agnes's eyes took a moment to adjust to the heavily shadowed room. Seeing the far corner of the room, Agnes rushed forward. Huddled against the ground were three bodies, a woman and two children. The forms appeared pale and lifeless in the soft blue light of the morning. She crouched beside them and laid a hand on the woman's chest. There was movement!

"Lady Pemblebrooke?" she asked, hoping she was the woman, but never having seen her before.

The woman's eyes widened in fear. She jumped backward, her bones highlighted by the frail cheap material of the dress she wore.

"I'm sorry. I didn't mean to frighten you," Agnes said, offering a reassuring smile.

The woman stared at her, too fearful to speak.

"I'm Agnes and you are?" she said, hoping the woman would confirm her identity. She made no reply, but Agnes's voice startled awake the sleeping children. Dirt smeared their faces and their eyes harbored the look of hunger she had seen in those of her poorer students, when the harvest had been disappointing.

"Please, I mean you no harm. Are you Lady Pemblebrooke?"

She stared at Agnes, appearing to judge her trustworthiness.

"If you are not, I would still like to help you, but are you Lady Pemblebrooke?"

The woman shook her head.

"She's dead," she said, barely audible.

Agnes's heart sank. Edward had only been delirious after all. Trying not to let the disappointment show on her face, she held out her hand to help the woman to her feet. Seeing her hesitation, Agnes said,

"I have food." This removed the doubt and the woman took hold of Agnes's hand. Though her hand was dirtied, it lacked the roughness she expected to find. There were no callouses or signs of a life of toil, which would accompany one as impoverished as this. She helped the woman to her feet, as the children clung to her skirt. The sunlight flowed more readily into the cottage and it caught a glimmer of something. Agnes followed the light to the woman's other hand. A ring, grander than any dream so poor a peasant could have, shone from her finger.

Agnes felt a prickle of excitement tingle along her spine. Her questions having failed on the mother, she turned to the children.

"I know this must be frightening, but I only want to help you. What are your names?"

The little girl looked at Agnes with skittish eyes, but found in her smile a reassuring presence.

"Mary," she said.

"Well, Mary, it is very nice to meet you," she said, with a smile. Encouraged by his sister's example, the boy stepped forward,

"I am Albert."

Agnes turned her attention to him now, and said, in her most charming voice,

"Albert Pemblebrooke?" The children looked to their mother, unsure of what to say, but it was enough. Agnes had her answer.

"Please, Lady Pemblebrooke, I can help you. We can leave and you will be safe," Agnes said, feeling as though she were attempting to persuade a student rather than talking to someone of the aristocracy.

She shook her head.

"I cannot. He will come back."

"Please, I can help you. We can get your life back for you."

Lady Pemblebrooke studied her. Her eyes moved from the place beside the fireplace where Agnes had found them huddled together to the opened door, beckoning for them to reemerge in a world that had considered them lost.

"Are they terrible?"

"Is who terrible, Lady Pemblebrooke?"

"The invaders... the enemy," she said, her eyes darting from corner to corner, to see if any might be hiding among the shadows.

"I'm not sure what you mean," Agnes said, patiently and puzzled.

"It's over. The war turned against us. There is no more... England," she said.

A look of pain, as though someone were driving a spike through her heart at the sound of the words, covered her face.

"Did he tell you that?" Agnes said.

She nodded, sadly.

"It isn't true. England is still England. The war continues, but our hope is not lost. The Americans have joined the fight. There have been advancements," Agnes said.

A look of surprise painted her face.

"Is this true? We are still free? That is— "

"Shh, listen," Agnes whispered, cutting her off. The front door began to rattle.

"We have to go, now!" Agnes said, pulling Lady Pemblebrooke by the arm with her. Mary tripped from her legs being cramped in her sleep. Agnes reached down and restored her to her feet. The doorknob was turning. They scampered from the cottage, but the front door had already swung open.

"You! Stop!" Frederick yelled.

"Go! Run!" Agnes said, pushing them forward.

She reached into her pocket and retrieved a stone that she threw at Frederick. He dodged it and it fell harmlessly to the floor.

"Run!" Agnes said, obtaining another rock. She lobbed it at Frederick and it pegged him in the shoulder, causing him to stumble. Taking her chance, she threw another. It missed her target but hit him squarely in the knee, forcing him down. Confident that he was delayed, if only for a moment, she ran with all of her might. Lady Pemblebrooke and the children had retreated into the forest. She was on the edge of the treeline. Frederick had not yet managed to stand. Agnes ran forward and, with a mighty leap, tumbled to the earth.

CHAPTER THIRTY-EIGHT

The Outskirts of Vienna, Austria-Hungry
June 1914

"Johann Schrader, you are under arrest for the murder of Lady Ludstein."

Johann blinked his eyes in disbelief, struggling to see the face of the policeman in the dark shadows of the night.

"I don't understand. There must be some sort of mistake."

The policeman, tall and robust, stepped nearer, clapping handcuffs around his wrist.

"You are Johann Schrader?"

"Yes, but I didn't do it," he stammered, struggling to make eye contact with the policeman towering above him.

"You've been identified, Mr. Schrader. I'm afraid it's up to the judge now to decide your fate."

"Katrine?" Fritz asked, hearing the sound of the door creak open. The cottage was filled with darkness, offering no cheerful glow of sanctuary from the impending black of the surrounding forest. Katrine was reminded of the stories she had heard as a child of forests such as these written by the Grimm brothers.

"Yes, Fritz," she said, ducking through the low door erected by some cottager shorter than either of them.

"Were you followed?" he asked, worriedly.

She shook her head no and then, realizing he could not see her, struck a match and lit the lantern beside the door, as she said,

"No, but—"

"Katrine! What are you doing? Put out that lantern!"

"No, Fritz. We're safe now. That's what I'm trying to tell

you."

His face bore the fret of a man hounded by nightmares in day, destined for insomnia by night.

"What do you mean?"

"I... arranged things."

"Arranged things?" His left eyebrow arched, puzzled by her words.

"My father arranged my future, attempted to I should say, and I made the most of the arrangement," she said, her lips remaining even as she spoke, betraying no hint of emotion.

"Johann?" Fritz said, his eyebrows darting together, meeting in the meridian of his forehead, before a slow smile spread over his face.

"Johann," he repeated, the choice sounding perfectly logical on his tongue, "so, that so called fiancé of yours has some purpose after all."

⟡

"Johann Schrader, you are hereby sentenced to death for the poisoning of Lady Ludstein."

The words punched Frederick hard in the stomach, leaving him gasping for air.

"No," he said, barely audible, his voice miniaturized by the weight of the news.

The crowds in the courtroom erupted into multiple conversations.

"Good. Serves him right for the terrible crime against Lady Ludstein," a man said, to another half his junior.

"He has a guilty face," another said. Frederick pushed his way through the crowd, determined to reach Johann.

"Johann!" he called across two men. He turned to face Frederick.

"Come along," the guard said, trying to move Johann out of the courtroom.

"Please! Let me speak to my brother," Frederick said, in desperation. His eyes filled with fright and the guard took pity on the not-still-a-boy, not-quite-a-man before him.

The guard nodded, but remained at Johann's side as Frederick stepped closer. Johann, dressed impeccably, looked at Frederick with a leveled gaze. For a man condemned he seemed calm, almost serene.

"Johann!" Frederick said, bearing all the frustration, outrage, and fear that his brother lacked.

"Frederick, do not fear for me. I am an innocent man. Men have condemned me, but God will not." The guards on either side of Johann exchanged glances over each other's heads. He didn't seem to be a ruthless criminal, but how could anyone tell in this modern age?

"But Johann, we must find who did this!" Frederick said, grabbing his brother's arm, "Why are you giving in?"

"Frederick, little brother, there is nothing that can be done. I have given my testimony. I have assured them of my standing. You have spoken on my behalf. It wasn't enough. Their anonymous witness holds more sway for whatever reason."

"I did not testify well enough! I did this to you. I failed you," Frederick said, his dark eyes clouding in self-acceptance of guilt.

Johann shook his head.

"No, you are my loyal brother. That means you cannot fail me."

A third guard, a thick mustache twitching impatiently below his protruding nose, stepped forward,

"Let's go. Move the prisoner along."

Their order issued, the guards began to walk, forcing Johann with them.

"Johann! Don't leave me," Frederick pleaded, feeling like the small child who had unsuccessfully admonished his fever-stricken parents to remain with him.

"I am always with you, Frederick," Johann said over his shoulder, as the guards escorted him from the room.

Johann disappeared through the doors and, despite Frederick's pleas, he was not permitted to follow. A loneliness cloaked in grave injustice inhabited his being, as he was left utterly alone. He stayed unmoving until the crowds thinned and the last remnants scattered. As he turned to leave, two women, wearing aprons and armed with brooms entered the room and began sweeping away the courthouse dust and airing the undigested morsels of the case.

Frederick's footsteps slowed at their words.

"With a witness like that, no wonder he was convicted," the older of the two, with a bun of coiled blond braid pinned to the top of her head, said.

"Imagine your own fiancée accusing you in the crime," the younger said, stopping to lean against the broom for a moment. Frederick's stomach churned.

Katrine? Had she been the witness? He strained his ears, lingering at the doorway.

"Shh, someone might hear," the first warned, "We weren't supposed to hear that or know that she came to see him. We can't tell anyone what we heard."

Heeding the warning, she turned the conversation to a new topic.

"Did you see the gentleman standing by the door? Wasn't he the most handsome man you ever—"

Frederick turned from the door, accepting that he would hear nothing further of use. His thoughts whirled.

I have to speak with the judge. I have to find out what happened.

"Enter," the judge called, through the closed door.

Frederick pushed it open and was absorbed into the judge's chambers.

"Excuse me, sir but I need to speak with you," Frederick said, to the man before him.

"Yes, what is it?" He was not unkind, just busy.

"My name is Frederick Schrader." The judge's eyebrows rose at the name.

"And my brother—"

"Is the man I've sentenced," the judge continued for him.

"Yes, only he didn't do it."

"Young man," he said, sitting back in his chair and then rocking forward, "It is an unhappy side effect that in my administration of justice and ensuring the laws are upheld and the people protected, that family members of violent criminals become unfortunate hostages to the turmoil of the situation."

"But, sir," Frederick said, crossing the room to stand before the mighty, polished oak desk now.

"There has been some mistake. I have heard that Katrine Windger has testified. How can this be? She is my brother's fiancée. Surely she would not condemn him. She has been tricked, set up."

The judge snapped to attention at the mention of Katrine. He sat forward, studying Frederick carefully.

"How do you know about that? No one is supposed to know. She is an anonymous witness to protect her delicate place in society."

"I overheard someone say it," Frederick said.

A look of worry creased the judge's face.

"Young man, that anyone knows the identity of Miss Windger is of serious concern. You must repeat this to no one."

"I won't sir, but my concern rests in my brother's conviction."

"Yes," the judge said, "it is difficult for the families, but you must understand that Miss Windger's testimony closed the case. If Mr. Schrader—err, your brother, was condemned by his own fiancée, his guilt was proven certain. If a stranger had identified him, it's possible a mistake could have been made but Miss Windger, distraught as she was, coming to bravely speak the truth sealed his fate. Well, I'm sorry, Mr. Schrader but there is nothing that can be done. The truth has prevailed, as unfortunate as you find it."

"Sir, I must repeat," Frederick said, his face stoic, "Johann is innocent. Surely you do not wish to send a guilty man to his death?"

Frederick's fist clenched as he spoke, harnessing all his anger into his tightened fingers.

"Mr. Schrader, my mind is made up, the decision is set. I am confident, but in the unlikely chance that I am somehow miraculously wrong, your brother still has a chance to stand before another judge, one who makes no mistakes."

The words spoken, Frederick departed.

A heaviness, more unbearable than Frederick could have ever imagined, became his only companion in those dark days following Johann's execution. Being a man of means had never been a source of contention before, but now Frederick found himself longing for a trade to immerse his sorrow in. He had wandered across the countryside, restless, arriving in Vienna. Frederick sat outside on the street, sipping coffee and wishing for something stronger. He pulled his hat over his eyes, shielding them not only from the sun but also the people on the street who bustled by him, oblivious to the pain he bore. He opened the newspaper left behind by some previous customer and scanned the articles, reading the words but too distracted to comprehend their meanings. His mind wandered to his memories of Johann. They had fought as children on so many occasions. Frederick had tagged along, not welcomed by Johann.

"Frederick, stop following me," Johann would say, exasperated by Frederick's persistence.

"But Johann, it isn't fair. I want to go with you," Frederick would protest, his childhood heart breaking at his brother's reluctance to include him.

Johann Schrader— he read in the newspaper. His heart thudded, threatening to beat so quickly that it would cease. Horrified, he read the account of Lady Ludstein's kidnapping and the subsequent discovery of her body. The doctors attributed her death to poisoning.

Frederick stopped mid-sentence. He could read no farther. Two women, seated at the table nearby, showed no scruples in continuing to read the article and quoted large portions of it to each other.

"It says here that an anonymous witness confirmed Mr. Schrader's identity."

"Well, I heard that his fiancée, Miss Windger, disappeared taking along a mere stable boy."

"It's really quite scandalous, isn't it?" the first said, her voice bearing far too much amusement for so austere a conversation.

"You haven't heard the best part yet," the other said tantalizingly.

"Oh?"

"This stable boy was an employee of Lady Ludstein, until quite recently when he left, angered that his family starved when there was not enough money to buy adequate food."

"You don't say? Well, that is the most scandalous thing I've heard all week," she said the words, savoring the information.

"Where did they run off to?" the other said.

"Well, Katrine Windger is half English. Her mother's from some tiny hamlet outside of London. I'd say there is a good chance they ran off there together, since Mr. Windger was certain to arrange another marriage for her if she had remained here."

"And how did you find out all this delicious gossip?"

"My maid's sister works for the Windger house. She knows how I delight in such stories and is always most agreeable to indulge me. She's the—"

Her words were drown out by the sudden commotion in the street.

"—he's been shot."

Frederick stood to hear the words more clearly.

"Franz Ferdinand has been shot!"

CHAPTER THIRTY-NINE

Mud splattered Agnes's face, as she landed hard against the ground. She tried to scramble to her feet, but the fall had not left her unharmed. Falling hard, she had twisted her left ankle and was reduced to hobbling. Frederick had regained his footing and was nearing.

"You! Stop!"

Hearing his captor's voice and seeing his liberator slip farther behind in their retreat, Albert reached down to pick up a stone. Following Agnes's lead, he hurled it toward Frederick.

Agnes wobbled forward, caught between Albert's stones in front of her and Frederick's at her back.

"Agnes, look out!" little Mary cried, rushing past her mother's skirts and gathering up an arsenal of her own stones.

Agnes looked over her shoulder at Mary's warning, dodging the stone Frederick had thrown and watching it land inches from her. Lady Pemblebrooke stood shivering in fear, unable to join in the barrage. Mary picked up a stone, larger than any Agnes or Albert had thrown, and sent it catapulting through the air. Agnes ducked as it soared above her head and hit Frederick, knocking him backward. He fell to the ground, a gash in his forehead, unmoving.

"Children go! Run!" Agnes said. Lady Pemblebrooke stood transfixed, staring at the scene.

"Lady Pemblebrooke, come on!" Agnes said, grabbing her hand and pulling her along.

Agnes's trek through the forest was slowed by her twisted ankle. Lady Pemblebrooke, uninjured physically, bore the internal wounds of her ordeal and moved as though walking in a dream. The children, awakened from the slumber of submission, ran ahead and emerged from the forest to the road. An elderly man, grayed and walking with a limp that was supported by a cane, appeared on the horizon.

The children ran to him, nearly knocking him over, as they skidded to a stop and sent clouds of dust flying from their feet.

"What is this?" he said, as Mary reached up to tug on his coat sleeve.

"We're alive!" she said.

"And we want to go home," Albert said.

"What are you saying child? I see that, of course, you are alive."

Agnes burst from the forest, limping much the same as the bewildered old man, with Lady Pemblebrooke at her side.

"Your Ladyship!" he said, taken aback and attempting to bow to her. Lady Pemblebrooke wavered at the greeting.

"But, how can this be?" he said, and then realizing what the children meant, he turned to them and said,

"You are Albert and you must be Mary."

"That's right," Albert said.

"Yes, I'm Mary." She took his hand as she spoke, finding a kindness in him that instantly removed any remaining shreds of shyness.

"My goodness, your father will be delighted to see you," he said, looking at them and then back to Lady Pemblebrooke.

"But—my husband is—he—was killed at the front," Lady Pemblebrooke said, stepping forward.

The man looked at her peculiarly.

"I don't know what you mean, Ma'am. There's talk all over town today that he is set to return to Rosebrim Manor next week."

Lady Pemblebrooke's face took on a ghostly pallor.

"He's alive?" she said, weakly.

"Yes, as alive as we are," the man said. The children, upon hearing the news, ran into their mother's arms singing joyfully,

"Father is alive! Soon we shall all be home together!"

They burst from their mother's embrace and danced around the old man, making up a song of jubilation.

Children are easily swayed by the changing tide around them, but Lady Pemblebrooke could not as easily cast off the cloak of lies that had taken her stability away from her.

Agnes said softly to her,

"Did he tell you that as well?"

She nodded,

"Long before we ever left the house. I shut myself away in mourning with the children. Oh, I deprived them needlessly of so much."

A forlorn look crossed her face, as she spoke.

"Lady Pemblebrooke, you mustn't worry about that. You can make a difference for the better now. An innocent girl, Clara, is being held for your murder. You must go to the police and explain what has happened."

"Oh," she said, "I don't want any publicity."

"But Lady Pemblebrooke, Clara has done nothing wrong. She too has suffered. She lost her memory in an explosion."

"Was it a Zeppelin?" she said, her eyes wide in fright as though remembering some terrible scare. Agnes, her deductive skills fully engaged, said to her,

"Lady Pemblebrooke, is that what happened to you? Were you in a Zeppelin attack?

Her breathing quickened,

"Yes... we... were... away."

"It's all right, Lady Pemblebrooke. You are safe," Agnes said.

"I was so ashamed," Lady Pemblebrooke said now, her breathing becoming steadier.

She paused and, seeing that the children were still occupied in their celebration, spoke lowly to Agnes.

"I was so afraid of the Zeppelins, that we would be invaded. I had such wicked thoughts, that I would...smother... the children in their sleep and then myself if one should land so that we would not suffer occupation."

Agnes listened to her, trying to provide the comfort needed as a lump grew in her stomach. She had heard of such occurrences as Lady Pemblebrooke spoke of. Hearing the horror, she longed for George's arms to be around her, but she did not let on that she was so deeply affected.

"I thought," Lady Pemblebrooke continued, "that I was being punished for that when we were kidnapped, when he told me we were dead to the world."

Agnes took hold of her arm.

"But, now you are free... shouldn't we do the same for Clara?"

Lady Pemblebrooke looked at Agnes, still frightened but her shell slowly cracking.

"How do you have so much courage?" Agnes was surprised at the question. She looked to the children, who had stopped singing and were listening to a story told by the man of a ship laden with gold.

"I just do what is right," she said.

Lady Pemblebrooke considered her words and looked into her eyes, a clarity returning to them.

"I remember her. She brought me tea once," Lady Pemblebrooke said, "Agnes, I would like to regain my courage and setting her free is what is right."

***

"I am free?" Clara said, the guard's words not making sense in her ears. She feared her lapse in memory now extended to the meaning of words.

"Miss Banks, we cannot hold you for a crime you did not commit, in fact a crime that did not occur. Lady Pemblebrooke and her children are alive and Frederick Schrader has been arrested for their kidnapping. That means Miss, that you no longer have to stay here. If you want to because of your memory, then arrangements can be made."

Clara looked at the guard, her eyes narrowing as she said,

"Those with amnesia may choose to stay in jail?"

The guard shook his head, cradling his cheek in the palm of his hand.

"Miss Banks, you aren't in jail. You never have been."

"I—I'm not," she stammered, "and who is this Mr. Schrader? He shares his first name with that of my fiancé."

His eyes softened into compassion from the confusion that had filled them, as he spoke to her now,

"Miss Banks, Mr. Schrader is your fiancé."

She reeled at his words, sitting back on the bed.

"He set me up?"

"I'm sorry, Miss Banks. It seems that way," he said, crossing to stand beside her.

"Schrader—that doesn't sound like any name from around here," she said.

"No," the guard said, stepping forward to rest his hand on her shoulder, "When they found him in the forest, where Miss Walters said he lay injured, he began speaking of Vienna and saying he had failed Johann, that he was sorry."

"I, I don't understand," Clara said, shaking her head.

The guard turned at the sound of footsteps.

"Hello, Clara," Agnes said.

"Hello," Clara said, looking up, surprised to see another appear as her thoughts spun dizzily around her.

"Perhaps, Miss Banks, it would be better for Miss Walters to speak with you," he said, moving aside for Agnes to enter.

Agnes sat on the edge of the bed beside Clara. The room pressed in around them and Agnes felt a nauseating suffocation crawl from the pit of her stomach.

"Clara, my name is Agnes," she introduced herself, unsure if Clara would remember.

Clara nodded.

"Tell me please what happened," she said looking up into Agnes's eyes.

"My cousin Edward and I discovered in a newspaper article that a woman was kidnapped and murdered near Vienna."

"Frederick did this?" she said, her eyes wide in dismay.

"No, his brother did."

"I don't understand," Clara said, her shoulders slumping forward.

"Neither do I, but we know you didn't do anything wrong. You have suffered long enough, Clara and if you would like, you can come to stay with me."

"Thank you," Clara said. She looked down at her hands, seeing Frederick's hand around her own, feeling she had been guided down some terrible dark path that had made things appear far worse than they were and caused her to doubt even herself.

"Agnes?"

"Yes, Clara?" she said, wishing there was something that she could do to erase the needless pain Clara had suffered in betrayal and isolation.

"I need to speak with Frederick."

"Clara, dear Clara! I've just heard the news," Harold said breathlessly, as he rushed down the hall toward them. Martin followed close behind.

"Harold, Martin, hello," Clara said, becoming slightly overwhelmed as the crowd around her grew.

"Oh Clara, dear Clara, I knew you were innocent," Harold said, stepping forward and taking her hand in his.

"Congratulations, Clara," Martin said, a smile playing over his lips as he spoke the words.

"I—didn't do—uh, thank you," she said. Sensing Clara's discomfort in the midst of so much confusion, Agnes turned the conversation.

"Thank you, for your support. Clara needs some time to get ready to leave now. She's agreed to come home with me," Agnes said. Clara looked at her gratefully.

"Yes, of course," Harold said, "If you need anything, do let me know."

"Thank you, Harold."

"Martin is the one that really deserves the thanks. He's the one that heard..." Harold trailed off, as he realized the pain that must be caused for Clara, knowing she'd been betrayed by a man who had promised his loyalty and love.

"Thank you, all of you," Clara said, "If you don't mind, I'd like to gather my things together to leave." After they had wished her well and departed, a familiar scent appeared at Martin's right side. Violet water mingled with the medicines and freshly mopped floors.

"Florence?"

"Yes, it's me. Hello, Martin. Wonderful news about your friend Clara. There's been such a sadness in her."

"Yes, I'm very happy for her," he said, but the playful smile that so often frequented his face was missing. Florence leaned closer to his ear,

"But, perhaps, a little sad for yourself?"

He lowered his face, ashamed at her insinuation. Though he could fool the others, Florence could see straight through him. She put her hand on his arm.

"It's all right, Martin. I've heard of something that may help you. I'm sorry I can't restore your sight, but I've heard about a new idea where dogs are trained to help those that are blind."

"Trained dogs?"

"Yes, they become your eyes for you. Would you be interested?"

"Yes, Florence, thank you," he said and slid his hand over hers that rested on his arm.

⟡

"Frederick?" Clara said, placing her hand on the bars, now on the other side of a true jail cell. He looked up at her, his eyes holding a foggy haze.

"I knew I would find you in England. Where are you hiding him?"

"What? I don't understand what you mean," she said, consumed with the confusion that so often filled her when in his presence.

"Fritz, where is he?"

"Who is Fritz?" she said, her legs beginning to tremble beneath her dress, feeling as though she were caught in some bad dream.

"You know very well who Fritz is, Katrine. He's the real murderer of Lady Ludstein, your lover, and the reason my brother is dead."

He looked at her, his eyes wild as he moved restlessly through the cell. Clara let her hand slip from the bar and she stepped backward, away from his unpredictable behavior.

"Frederick," she said, trying to soothe his temper, "I think you have mistaken me for someone else. My name is Clara, not Katrine."

"You changed your name. You hid. But, I tracked you down. I found you. And everything was going to be made right. This time you would suffer and endure the consequences of your betrayal. I made you live through what you did to Johann!" His eyes flashed in anger.

"Frederick, I'm sorry for what happened to you, but I can no longer be a pawn for you. I have to leave and put this behind me. I hope you find your peace."

Her words spoken, she turned with the decision made to live under her own control. A doctor, younger than herself, with a pair of spectacles on his nose, stood in the hall.

"I heard what you said to him, Miss Banks."

"Oh?" she said, worried if she had said something the doctor did not approve of.

"I admire you for showing such grace. I understand you have suffered from amnesia and Mr. Schrader told you that you were engaged to him. If it helps to know at all, though, Miss Banks I don't think Mr. Schrader intended to do what he did. At least, I don't think he was thinking clearly. A colleague treated him in London for severe burns. His uniform was so badly damaged in the trenches that it was removed so there was no indication on him to which side he belonged. He told the medics that he was English and so they shipped him to London. It seems the Schraders were quite affluent and Frederick's uncle often traveled to England, taking the boys with him. Surely, that is how he learned English so well, to be able to acquiesce."

Clara's head tilted to one side, processing what had been said.

"But, how did burns affect his thinking?"

"Miss Banks, the burns were caused by mustard gas."

CHAPTER FORTY

"Agnes?"

Edward's eyes struggled to open, after having been held captive by the confines of the heaviness of illness.

"Edward, I'm here," she said, leaning into him and placing her palm against his forehead.

"George! It's gone. His fever is broken!"

"George?" Edward said, his eyes fluttering open and searching for the long- absent man.

George stepped forward for Edward to see him.

"I'm here, Edward."

A smile, slowed by the fatigue, spread across his face in gratitude.

"You are home?"

George nodded.

"Agnes, I'll fetch him some soup," he said, leaving the cousins alone.

"Edward," she said, taking his hand in hers as she had so many times when he was ill, gladdened now that his eyes sparkled full of life, "you were right."

He tilted his head to the side, allowing her words to wash over him and make sense.

"About Lady Pemblebrooke and the children. They were safe when I found them in the cottage. Clara is innocent. She was set up—well, there is plenty of time to tell you everything later. The important thing is that you were right and you're getting better," she said.

⋆

A full two days passed before Edward was recovered enough to convince Agnes to leave him alone for the day. She returned to her students, who kept interrupting their lessons to hear of her heroic tale of rescuing Lady Pemblebrooke and the children. Clara and George rested by the warmth of Agnes's hearth, while Edward focused his attention on the source of another fiery place. When at last he was alone, he wearily walked to the room that beckoned to him. It was early in December, at the dawn of the day. Woodsmoke from the cottages on the surrounding lands wafted through the window, as he propped it open. He breathed in the fresh air, inhaling too deeply and causing a cough to begin in his chest and rumble through his throat. Edward steadied himself against the windowsill, before turning toward the crates.

Edward's body, stiff from the illness, bent awkwardly toward the stack of paintings. Too tired to hold himself up he sat back heavily against the floor, the weight of the boards pushing up on him. He underestimated the amount of energy required to complete the simple task of flipping through the paintings. His hands moved steadily over the oak and maple frames and the raw canvas of those that lacked a wooden perimeter.

Where was she? He had reached the end of the pile with no trace of the painted lady. He began the arduous task of searching through them again. A growing sense of desperation surged through him, as he neared the end of the stash of paintings.

Edward fumbled with hands outstretched, sweeping them across the floor, waiting for the painting to materialize. He had been right about Lady Pemblebrooke and the children, when he allowed the painting to help clarify his thoughts. There was so much still that needed to be examined. His body on the mend, he was ready to be fully healed and to claim the elusive peace that hitherto remained beyond his grasp.

A cough rocked his body, irritated by the draft of cool air that bellowed through the window. Edward shivered and stood to shut it. He squeezed between two crates to make his way to the window, rather than going around the crates as he had when entering the room. The toe of his boot kicked something loose, causing him to stumble. Crouching down, a stream of hope flooded him, as he lifted the thin notebook from the floor.

Forgetting the window, he leaned against the stack of crates and opened the book. Turning the delicate pages, he opened to an entry dated April 23, 1894.

I write this to keep my promise to a dear friend. He entered my life one sunny afternoon, bringing me two gifts. The first was something I have shared openly with those around me and hope to someday present to the world: art. It awakened a passion for color and form to record the world around me. The second is something that must be hidden, but that has consumed my being more than any other earthly thing. The pigments I use in my own art pale in comparison to the vibrancy of the woman who delivers the messages.

Edward paused in his reading, contemplating the meaning of the ascribed name for his painted lady.

Well, she was an artist. Maybe she was speaking metaphorically, alluding to the painting's power to communicate the thoughts buried deepest inside. He continued reading.

Perhaps you, my fellow secret keeper, have given her some name of your own. If you are reading this, then I am certain that she must have touched you as she has me. I made a promise seven years ago that I would draw her portrait in a notebook given to me by the man who gave me my true friend and confidant, the painting. From the moment I swore my allegiance to his promise and he wrote my name at the front of the journal, passing the torch to me as it were, I remembered the words. And though I completed the task assigned many years ago, I was compelled to record her story, for a portrait copied cannot accurately convey the great depths surrounding her. I often think of her history, trying to imagine who else must have gazed into her eyes, who first gave her birth upon the canvas and how her magical ability came to be. I know of no such record and I hope that I am not acting in some way counter to the wishes of those who know her truth as I do, but it is my intention to write my history with her today so that others after me may know where she journeyed before, so that in the future others will at least know part of her story that came before their encounter with her. I want whoever is reading this to know that she has lived in Pagny-Alsace in France and is now traveling to England with me. How ironic that I always felt left alone, until the painting entered my life, because my brother and sister moved to other regions of France, and now I am to move to the homeland of my new husband in England! I hope that—

"Edward? Edward where are you?" Edward jumped at the sound of Agnes's voice. He slid the notebook beneath the crate and scrambled to his feet.

"Edward?"

"I'm in here, Agnes," he said, speaking a bit too loudly for his throat and sending him into a coughing fit.

"Edward? Oh, there you are. My goodness, you're pale. Are you overexerting yourself?" she said, entering the room and seeing her disheveled cousin before her. He couldn't help but smile, as she fussed about him. Since George had returned, she seemed different, enlivened, rejuvenated by his presence.

"What are you smiling about?" she said, a smile of her own seeping from the corner of her mouth, at the sight of Edward's infections grin. The smile disappeared just as quickly though, when she saw the opened window.

"Edward, it's freezing in here! No wonder you are so pale," she said, crossing to the window and closing it. With her back still turned to him, Agnes said,

"Oh Edward! I haven't told you yet. While you were so ill, a woman came and," she paused, pulling on the window hard to free it from its stuck position.

"Yes?"

"You made your first sale," she said cheerily, securing the window shut.

"Tell me," Edward said, his stomach sinking, "Did she by chance buy a painting?"

"Yes, that's right. She said it was for sentimental reasons. I knew that if you were well, you would have helped her find it. She reminded me of you in a way, how you were relentless in your search for the house and then how you were so dedicated to helping me."

"Did she, by tell you her name?"

"Marie Régine. I made sure to ask for you." The window firmly in place, she turned with a smile.

"Edward? What's wrong? You've gone positively ghostly!"

Edward struggled to control his heart, which thudded at a quickening pace.

"Just a little tired, Agnes."

A full week, wrought with worry and immersed in Marie Régine's journal, passed before Edward felt strong enough to begin his search for her. He feared that if he asked for Agnes's help, while he easily could have made up an excuse for wanting to speak with his first customer, he would not have been afforded the privacy needed to meet with Miss Lefront.

When at last he was able to set out to find her, the search proved fruitless. No one had heard of Marie Régine Lefront. Resting on the bridge, looking down at the silver ribbon of water dotted with islands of ice, Edward realized his mistake.

"I've been a fool," he said, his breath turning to smoke in the frostiness of the day. Marie Régine Lefront was an unmarried woman in France. Through reading her words, he had come to think of her as a friend but, he had overlooked her words. She was leaving for England with her new husband. Marie Régine had told Agnes the name that Edward, if he had discovered the secrets of the painting, would know her by. But conveniently, it was a name he could not trace. Certain that if he did find her, she may be unwilling to relinquish the painting that she had paid so handsomely for, Edward carried on, determined to recover the painted lady.

For another week, he searched both the houses of the surrounding land and the pages written by the woman who escaped his search. The familiar pull of desperation, eating away at his insides and leaving him feeling exposed and raw, returned. Something, beyond his ability to comprehend, compelled him to continue his search. His wandering steps, aimless but with the compass of determination, carried him across the sweeping country, desolate and bleak with the hold of winter.

A barking dog bounded down the path, welcoming him.

"Edward?"

"Yes, it's me, Martin and—I'm sorry I don't know your name," he said, to the woman sitting beside Martin.

"I'm Florence," she said, "Edward, I've heard so much about you from Martin."

He stepped forward, joining them on the porch.

"Well, I am delighted to make your acquaintance," Edward said.

"What brings you here, Edward? You are always in search of something when you come to visit it seems."

Edward, looking rather sheepish, said,

"Well, I did hope that you might be able to help me in locating someone. She is a French woman who married an Englishman. She must be in her forties or fifties. Her maiden name was Marie Régine Lefront."

Martin shook his head.

"No, sorry Edward, I don't know anyone by that name."

"I do," Florence said, "At least, I think I may know who she is. There's a woman named Marie Fielder who speaks with a French accent. She comes into the hospital and reads to the patients sometimes."

A growing tide of hope built in Edward, soothing some of the raw desperation.

"Thank you, Florence," he said, nodding to her. He turned to leave, but not before adding,

"Oh, and Martin, she's lovely."

"I know she is, Edward," he said with a smile, lacking all the armor of hiding and as genuine as any Edward had seen, "I can see her spirit."

CHAPTER FORTY-ONE

"Yes?"

The door creaked open and a woman, with graying hair but cheeks rosy still with the blush of youth, greeted him.

"Mrs. Fielder?"

"Yes, that's right."

"And were you by chance Miss Lefront?"

She eyed him curiously.

"Yes, that's right."

An involuntary sigh of relief slipped from his lips.

"My name is Edward."

A smile accompanied her words, as she said,

"Please, come in. I've been expecting you."

He ducked his head to enter her low door.

"You've been expecting me?"

"That's right," she said, gesturing for him to sit in an overstuffed chair beside the fire. Her home was bathed in color and the walls hung heavy with canvas. Marie Régine's many paintings converged into one large mural, a symphony of pigment.

He felt as though he knew her from the many times he had read through her most private thoughts and so entering her house felt as though he were somewhere he had been before. Her comment though had puzzled him and upon seeing this, she said,

"She told me." Her eyes traveled from Edward to the portrait of the painted lady.

"I don't understand."

Her eyes narrowed in puzzlement.

"Oh? I was certain that you came because you know her secrets, as I do."

He hesitated for a moment, as a strange feeling of freedom overcame him. For the first time, he acknowledged to another,

"Yes, she speaks—spoke to me."

"I knew she did," Marie Régine said, with a slow and steady smile.

"You mean, because she spoke to you, you knew that she must have to me as well," he said, trying to clarify.

She looked at him, almost piercingly so.

"I mean," she said, "that you cast yourself into her."

Edward shifted in his chair.

"Cast myself?"

"Is it possible," Marie Régine said, sitting forward and leaning into Edward, "That you do not know about this? Tell me please, what is your experience of being spoken to?"

He shifted, feeling once again the oddity of being able to freely speak about what he had hidden from all.

"If something reflective—glass, metal—was held to her, she would convey my thoughts, my feelings, often that buried deepest which I did not wish to confront."

She nodded, listening intently to his words.

"And did you ever use her to deliver a message to another?"

His look of confusion provided the answer she sought.

"The painting was presented to me, as you know by a friend, but what you do not know is that this man, though not my father, loved my mother. They discovered the painting as children and used it to send messages to each other when they were apart. My sister and I did the same."

He listened carefully, appreciative that she did not speak as softly as many did so that he did not have to ask her to repeat what she said. Understanding now what she meant by "the woman who delivers messages", he sat back and said,

"If she were as important to you as all of this and if you thought so fondly of her, then why did you let her go? In your writing I read of how you were moving to England, but you gave no indication that you were not taking her with you and I found her in my house in England, so what happened to separate you?"

"Some of my goods became lost when we moved to England. I was told later that they were sold to an elderly couple, who unknowingly purchased them from the thief who masqueraded as a salesman. I searched extensively for her but could find nothing until I heard that a young American, you, planned to open an antique shop. I hoped against hope that I might find her and I did."

He nodded at her slowly,

"Do you think," he said, "that it is possible that when a message seemed especially harsh or not to fit with something inside of me that it was a message from you?"

Her interest piqued, she sat forward and grasped his hand,

"You experienced things that felt unnatural for you to know?"

He nodded.

"My goodness, this is quite serious."

"What is it?"

"Edward, when my search produced nothing after a year, I put her out of my mind. I was convinced that her time with me was finished. It was only on a nostalgic whim that I came to you when I heard about you. I see now why I did, though. You had no knowledge of this, but I did and so I had to tell you. Edward, I think someone else is trapped inside the painting."

He sat back heavily from the gravity of what she said.

"You think someone else knows her secrets and is trying to speak through her? But the messages have been so unclear."

"Then Edward, that is the most extreme of all. Someone without a voice, who has been trapped by something, is trying to find himself again through the painting."

She stood and unfastened the painting from the wall. Hugging the frame to her chest, she handed the painting back to Edward.

"I will keep my voice separate and out of the painting. Only you can discern what is your voice and what belongs to the other. Good luck. May God be with you in your work," she said as he stepped away from Marie Régine Lefront, with the painted lady resting safely against his heart.

He returned to his house, carried by the wind of exhilarated purpose.

"Edward! Oh Edward!" Agnes said, racing toward him, waving something in her hand as he approached the house.

He looked up, so absorbed in the world of the painting, that he was startled by her presence.

"Yes? What is it?" he asked, seeing her happiness radiating like rays of sunshine.

"John! He's safe! He's in London! He was wounded but the doctors say he's going to be just fine. George and I are leaving at once to be with him. We should be home within the next week or two."

"Oh Agnes! That's wonderful," he said, putting his arm around her for a hug.

"Goodbye Edward. Take care of yourself. We shall all be together soon," she said. With a kiss on the cheek, she hurried down the lane, nearly skipping.

A burden of sorrow removed at the joyous news of his cousin, he turned his attention fully to the painted lady as he stepped inside. He sat in the room where she had first spoken to him, where he had cursed her existence and where now he hoped to discover the truth. As he looked into her lovingly painted eyes, he greeted her with all the familiarity of a confidant and the fondness of a dear friend. She had been his accomplice, his motivation, his desperation, his frustration and his *raison d'être*. And now, he would set her free from whoever was entrapped inside. He felt he owed it to her, after all they had been through together.

He held a glass to her, as he had done so often before, and his hand trembled at the thought of what he was doing.

"I missed you," he said, sincerely to her.

"Everything will be fine now. Just remember—I know what the truth is," she said.

He struggled to separate his voice from the other, as he was now certain that Marie Régine had been right.

"Remember, remember, in the meadow."

"Lady Pemblebrooke is already free," he said, remembering the last time the meadow had been spoken of.

"You don't have to prove yourself anymore. You've done it." A sense of revelation came to him at the words. They were his deep truth that was at last set free.

"Concentrate," he told himself, feeling the strength of the belief in himself required to complete what he set out to do.

"Remember, remember me," the voice said.

Edward stared harder at her.

"Remember—yes, that's it—remember." Her voice grew fainter, a hushed whisper.

"No, come back," Edward said, "don't leave me."

As he spoke the words, James did not fill his mind haunting his confidence. Edward had been a good friend; he had done what he could. He was free of it. All that grasped him now was the painting and he feared that she would abandon him.

A knock at the door startled Edward. He set down the glass in front of the painting and left to answer it.

"Clara, hello, come in, please," Edward said, opening the door to her.

"I wanted to thank you. Agnes said that somehow you figured out that Lady Pemblebrooke was in the meadow. I don't know how you could have known that, since only Frederick did —well, and I heard him say it, the night they were kidnapped, after I tucked Albert back into bed, when he awoke crying. Unfortunately, my memory failed me and I couldn't remember that night. The doctor says my memory may have suffered more, because of the trauma of being accused. Anyway, thank you for setting me free."

"Clara," he said, suddenly struck by what she had said, "would you mind looking at something for me?"

She shook her head.

"No, of course not. What is it?" He led her into the room where the painting rested. Upon seeing it, she clapped her hands together in delight.

"Edward, my grandparents had a painting just like this in their home when I was young. I have been remembering so much more lately." She knelt, a smile filling her face, beside the painting. He lowered himself to join her. Looking into the painted lady, with the glass in front of him, he heard the painting say,

"I remember."

He looked to Clara who had no reflection before her, but felt a tingle cover his skin, which only heightened as she said,

"I've been trying so hard to remember. Just before the accident, in Silvertown, I was thinking of my grandparents' house and this very painting and now here I am remembering it all. Isn't it marvelous?" Her eyes were so full of purity and joy, without any hint of having heard the words, that he was certain he was the only one who had been in the shadow of reflection.

Edward turned to Clara, took her hand and said,

"It no longer speaks my heart. You do. But, I suppose you always have." She tilted her head to the side, uncertain of his words but warmed by them, and smiled. Despite all they had learned, neither knew that centuries earlier a tear of compassion and love had changed their lives. Now, Edward felt no malice at the thought of being read. The seed of fulfillment, sown in the bleakest soils of war-ravaged land and his discontented soul, had supplanted it and bloomed in perfect completion.

Book Club Questions

1. What did you like most about this story?

2. How does the painting function throughout time and what effects does it have on the different characters?

3. What do you think of the parallel journeys of Edward to his answers and the portrait to Edward, where a new layer of its story is uncovered in each segment?

4. Having suffered the brutality of the trenches, Edward finds it easier to surround himself with things than people. What are the benefits and drawbacks of this, both for him and more broadly?

5. What did Edward hear? Consider all layers to this.

6. What role do Edward's hearing loss and Martin's blindness play?

7. Which characters were most positively affected by the painting? Which were most negatively affected? Did this have more to do with the character or where they were in the chain of the painting's events?

8. What surprised you most?

9. If you could ask any character a question, what would it be?

10. Agnes is a teacher by profession. Who else is a teacher? What lessons are taught? Who learns what and do any lessons remain unlearned?

Acknowledgments

I would like to thank those who have encouraged and supported me, specifically in my writing. That includes family, friends, fellow writers, teachers and especially Stephen. I would also like to thank the readers for their enthusiastic welcome to my debut novel, *Flight Before Dawn*. Thank you for choosing to read this novel. I enjoy hearing from readers and can be reached at Megan@MeganEasleyWalsh.com. To learn about my upcoming releases, visit me at www.MeganEasleyWalsh.com.

About the Author

Megan Easley-Walsh is an author of historical fiction, a researcher, and a writing consultant and editor at Extra Ink Edits. She is an award-winning writer and has taught college writing in the UNESCO literature city of Dublin, Ireland. Her degrees are in history-focused International Relations. She is American and lives in Ireland with her Irish husband. *What Edward Heard* is her second novel and she is also the author of *Flight Before Dawn*.

CPSIA information can be obtained
at www.ICGtesting.com
Printed in the USA
BVOW04s0525240517
484987BV00001B/113/P

9 781366 694195